SWEET SURRENDER

With the unleashed power and grace of a lupine animal he sprang forward from the shadows, catching Abbie Lee completely by surprise.

She had a brief glimpse of a darkly tan, dangerous looking face partially disguised by a bearded stubble as he came at her out of the darkness. He appeared frighteningly tall and muscular, enough to send the hammer forward on the gun and a startled cry to escape her.

"Madre de Dios!" Sonny snarled as the revolver exploded next to his ear. He had knocked Abbie to the ground and now straddled her, a knee on either side of her waist, her hands pinned back over her head. "You almost got me with that goddamned thing!"

Abbie swallowed convulsively. "I meant to!" She glared right back at him. Now's not the time to panic, Abbie, she willed herself. It's dark, he's facing you, his ears are probably still ringing like church bells, and if all else fails, you've still got your legs free. A well placed jab in the right place could turn the tables real fast.

"Now," he breathed. "Suppose you let me explain why I'm here."

As she prepared to make good her escape, she found herself staring into piercing eyes that were an unusual silver-gray and as wily as a fox.

Oh, Abbie Lee, her inner self warned, I hope you haven't underestimated this devil. . . .

ROMANCE
From the Civil War to the Wild West

REBEL PLEASURE (1672, $3.95)
by Mary Martin

Union agent Jason Woods knew Christina was a brazen flirt, but his dangerous mission had no room for a clinging vixen. Then he caressed every luscious contour of her body and realized he could never go too far with this confederate tigress.

SAVAGE TORMENT (1739, $3.95)
by Cassie Edwards

Judith should have been afraid of the red-skinned warrior, but those fears turned to desire as her blue eyes travelled upward to meet his. She had found her destiny—bound by his forbidden kiss.

FORBIDDEN EMBRACE (1639, $3.95)
by Cassie Edwards

She was a Yankee nurse, and he was a Confederate soldier; yet it felt so right to be in each other's arms. Today Wesley would savor Serena's sweetness because tomorrow he had to be gone with only the memory of their FORBIDDEN EMBRACE.

PASSION'S VIXEN (1759, $3.95)
by Carol Finch

When Melissa ran away into the mountains, her father paid the handsome woodsman, Zack Beaugener, to find her. Succumbing to her captor's caresses, she prayed he would not betray her love.

WILDFIRE (1737, $3.95)
by Carol Finch

If it meant following him all the way across the wilderness, Alexa had to satisfy the sensual agony Keane ignited in her soul. He was a devilish rogue who brought her to WILD-FIRE.

Available wherever paperbacks are sold, or order direct from the Publisher. Send cover price plus 50¢ per copy for mailing and handling to Zebra Books, Dept. 1842, 475 Park Avenue South, New York, N.Y. 10016. DO NOT SEND CASH.

CARESS OF SILK

MARY MARTIN

ZEBRA BOOKS
KENSINGTON PUBLISHING CORP.

ZEBRA BOOKS

are published by

Kensington Publishing Corp.
475 Park Avenue South
New York, NY 10016

First printing: July 1986

Printed in the United States of America

For the Irish rogue and his beautiful lady—Jack and Sally O'Neill—you're everything parents should be.

Special thanks to some very dear people:

My son, JAMES MARTIN, my computer whiz who was always there whenever I managed to push the wrong buttons and went into a state of panic.

My eldest son, TOM MARTIN, who runs my errands and enjoys Friday night as much as I do.

BOBBI SMITH, who encourages me and shares my belief that heroes are special, as is friendship.

KARYN WITMER-GOW, my favorite art teacher who was kind enough to share her knowledge with me.

Chapter One

Viva la revolucion

Mejico, 1866

The Juaristas were everywhere. In the north, Porfirio Diaz advanced, and in the south, Juarez left Paso del Norte to claim Chihuahua. The Emperor Maximilian was stunned when strongholds such as Tampico, Monterrey, and Orizaba capitulated to the liberals. All around the French invaders the net was tightening. In Mexico City they had already withdrawn from the fighting and did not intervene when units of the Imperial Army came under fire. Only when directly attacked would they fight back.

With whole provinces falling to Juarista generals, it was no surprise to hear rumors that Napoleon III was growing uneasy. His War and Finance Ministers, frantic over the turn of events, repeatedly urged him to evacuate the French military. Dissension ran rampant. Americans called Maximilian an adventurer. In Mexico, the cry of "Death to Maximilian!" rang louder through the cities. The cause appeared lost.

Day by day the Imperial Army dwindled as the enemy

thrusts became bolder. Determined to rid their homeland of the invaders the armies of *el presidente* continued on their relentless march. Even now, the reported sighting of the *guerillos* on the outer fringes of Chihuahua sent soldiers of the Mexican Loyalist Army packing frantically.

Gen. Ramon Basilo stood in the relentless sun mopping at his brow and shouting orders. *"Pronto!* We must leave at once before it is too late!" He had heard stories of what the Juaristas did to Imperialist troops they captured. Savage, unthinkable atrocities! He shuddered, turning to observe one of his men lead a lumbering ox toward him. A paper appeared attached to the beast's horns.

"The beast was sent here by the liberals, general," the soldier explained.

Basilo reached out and snatched the tattered paper. The contents of the scribbled message caused a red flush of anger to stain his fleshy cheeks.

Here is something for the Imperial Army to eat so that they can be captured alive.

The general, his pride pricked, swung his gaze to a cluster of frightened villagers huddled together against an adobe wall. A printed *pronunciamento* on the peeling plaster glared at Basilo. *Viva la libertad! Death to Maximilian!*

It was like waving a red flag before an enraged bull. The general turned to his soldiers and ordered them to raise their rifles. "Take aim!" he commanded.

Men pleaded for mercy as they gathered their families close. Women wailed and children cried—but to no avail.

"Fire!" Basilo yelled.

When the sharp volley of rifle shots ended, the soft sobbing of the villagers lingered only on the wind.

Without any sign of regret, General Basilo signaled his men to mount up and ride out. He agreed with the decree that Maximilian had set forth. If Juarez could not be run out of Mexico the alternative was to blot out his ardent supporters. There were none left in this village. Now they must move quickly if they were to avoid a confrontation with the *guerillos*. The tide of the war had been turning for weeks. The followers of Juarez were dedicated and stubborn, and since the *Americanos* had begun supplying the rebels with guns, their armies were winning victories at an alarming rate.

He was so intent on these concerns, he paid little heed to the man who rode boldly along the troup-infested roadway and into the war-torn village.

The stranger could easily have passed for an *Americano*. He was dressed all in black, from close-fitting shirt and pants to expensive leather boots. Crisscrossed cartridge belts were slung across his broad chest and pearl-handled Colts rode low on his hips. He wore his ash-brown hair long, curling about his shirt collar, a full moustache enhancing harshly handsome features.

The soldiers, accustomed to seeing *Americano* mercenaries, gave him only a passing glance as they hurried about their tasks.

As he swung off of his horse, Basilo looked over at him, still not alarmed. He assumed he was a *norteamericano* fighting for Maximilian who had become separated from his unit. Until he drew closer and he saw the anguish in the glittering silver-gray eyes. The general grew wary.

"What do you want here?" Basilo demanded in an authoritative tone.

The stranger eyed him coldly, glancing over at the slain bodies lying crumpled and still. "Just doing a bit of stalking, general. Something you seem to know a lot about."

Basilo became frightened and glanced about for his aides. They were busy across the plaza and paid no attention to the two men. The general began to sweat profusely. He knew he should cry for help, but he was ashamed to do so. Stammering, he said, "What—is it you want of me?"

The stranger did not blink. His tone, when he lazily drawled his reply, sent chills racing along Basilo's spine. "Nothing you are prepared to give, I'm certain, but it's

11

something I'm taking anyway—just as you did—with my brother and his family."

The general choked on his terror. He sensed death and his sweaty fingers crept downward toward his service revolver. "If—I—so much as flinch my men will be all over you," he stammered, attempting to draw the man's attention away from his movements.

Silvery eyes squinted mockingly at him as the stranger's gun swiftly cleared leather. "There's a good chance—you won't even flinch."

Basilo's eyes widened disbelievingly just as the bullet tore through him. No one heard the gun's report as it had been muffled against the general's massive stomach.

Basilo felt himself growing dizzy. There was no immediate pain, only a sense of weightlessness as his knees gave way beneath him, and he fell heavily upon the ground. The last thing he heard was the stranger's deep voice.

"My people shall live forever in this land. *Viva la revolucion.*" Santiago Malone y Alvarez stared dispassionately at the still body of the cold-hearted executioner. Only the shouting of the liberals' voices as they swept over the town roused him from his silent vigil.

"Viva Diaz! Viva la revolucion!" they shouted in triumph.

The cry rang somewhat hollow in his ears as he glanced over at the bullet-riddled bodies of his family. He felt dead himself at that moment. He had been scouting ahead for Juarez when he'd come upon peasants fleeing Chihuahua. They'd told him the butcher, Basilo, was in the village—where his brother lived. Fear and desperation clouded his reasoning and he'd continued onward alone, praying he would not be too late. Now moisture formed beneath his eyelids and he blinked it back. He had indeed been too late, and by only minutes.

A hand grasped his elbow and brought him spinning around, gun ready to fire.

"Do not shoot, Santiago, it is Reeno," a familiar voice

12

hurried to explain.

"Damnit, Reeno, I almost blasted your fool head off sneakin' up on me like that." The hammer on the polished black Colt clicked back into place.

"I am sorry about your *hermano* and his family. I prayed we would be able to take this village without losing any of our people. I prayed—but I did not hope."

"The murdering bastard struck again." The silver-gray eyes blazed with hatred. "But no more." His hooded gaze swung to the inert form of Gen. Ramon Basilo. "No longer will *al hambre* prey upon the *inocent.*"

Reeno nodded, his face grim. *"Si,* I understand. But I am afraid Basilo's death will not go without retaliation."

The man called Santiago lifted one dark brow. "I can take care of myself just fine, *compadre.*"

"Si, I know that. But this man was an important officer. He was a friend of the emperor. It could spell disaster for your mother and grandfather in Mexico City. Maximilian is still there. Think, *compadre!"* Reeno persisted. "The war is not over. Your family is not untouchable. We must dispose of Basilo's body before anyone else learns of this and keep his death quiet. You have to lay low until victory is assured."

"Just how in the hell am I supposed to do that?"

Reeno considered this and then said. "Across the border, in Texas. You can work behind the lines with the *Americanos* who supply us with weapons. It is the only way, Santiago, and as your commanding officer, I order you to go." With a heavy heart, Reeno inclined his head in the direction of a black and white pinto. "Viento can make it. He's never failed you yet."

Santiago scowled. "If it weren't for the fact of endangering my grandfather and mother, I would stay to see the French dogs flee with their tails between their legs. But I can see how it must be as you say."

"There is no other way," Reeno sighed.

Santiago nodded curtly.

13

Later, after they'd quickly buried the general's body and Santiago was preparing to leave, Reeno found himself reluctant to say good-bye.

"I am going to miss you very much, *amigo.*"

The tan face of Santiago Malone y Alvarez bore a sly half smile. "Are you so certain of that? With me out of the way pretty *Dona* Carmelita is all yours."

Reeno's grim expression altered slightly, his dark eyes taking on a hopeful gleam. He had momentarily forgotten the fiery Spanish beauty whose favor he'd tried so hard to win, and who only had eyes for the wild, irrepressible Santiago. "She is your woman. Her heart belongs to you," Reeno answered.

The lithe revolutionary vaulted into the saddle, his grin turned reckless. "I give her to you, Reeno. A little going away present to remember me by."

Reeno's gaze flew to his compatriot's face and found it indifferent. "You always were a *bastardo* where your women were concerned," he said with a shake of his head. "But I will make her forget you. *Si.* No longer will she quiver at just the mention of your name. I, Reeno Sanchez, will see to that."

Santiago extended his hand and felt it grasped by Reeno's firm, steely grasp. "Good luck to you *hermano.* I will see you get the best damned guns available. Come for me when the heat dies down."

Reeno replied unhesitantly. "Of that you can be certain. *Vaya con Dios.*"

Santiago nodded and, touching a spur to the prancing stallion, leaned low over his neck and whispered a command. The pinto sprinted forward on powerful legs, carrying them both toward the border and Texas.

San Antonio, Texas, two months later

Abbie Lee Caldwell, a flush of excitement enhancing her

14

delicate features, leaned forward from her horse to stare at the hoof prints along the banks of the gurgling creek.

"I knew it, Romeo, the mare's been here. We've finally managed to catch up with her." Dismounting from the blood-bay stallion, the young woman patted his neck affectionately, then stretched her weary frame. She'd been pushing the big horse all afternoon. Having been in pursuit of the wild mare since early morning, she felt they'd earned a rest. The Texas sun was brutal, and even though she dressed accordingly and kept her tan-colored stetson pulled low over her face, days on the range were draining. She yawned, exhausted, and winced. She felt like a baked clam.

Abbie led her horse to a thick grove of trees shading the gurgling stream. She laid her forehead against Romeo's soft muzzle. "That mare is just as tired as we are. Morning's soon enough to continue. The cowhands and *vaqueros* can manage things without us." She had left them in charge of the wild mustangs they'd captured and took out alone, determined to come back with the spirited filly who had escaped their carefully constructed catch corral. It wasn't anyone's fault. They'd put together a natural looking enclosure in a favorable spot; strung booger wire and camouflaged it with brush. Then they'd meticulously removed all trace of their having been there. It appeared as though that mare could read signs that were all but invisible, and her uncanny sense was costing Abbie plenty. She had a contract with the government to have a hundred head of mustangs in San Antonio within two weeks. She had to meet that deadline for the Bar C was a big spread and it took a great deal of money to operate it. Abbie wanted that mare. She would bring a good price. She had set her mind on it and did not intend to come back empty-handed.

"I don't know about you, fella, but I'm all for calling it a day." Abbie's gaze scanned the far reaching plain of brown and intermittent green broken only by sage brush and mesquite trees. By the deepening purple shadows on the horizon it would soon be dark. Experience told her that it was about time to bed down. Nights on the range, when the clouds promised to haze the moon, were as pitch black and unpredictable as the fleet-footed mare she was chasing.

Abbie's gaze followed her mount's movements as he meandered to the stream's edge and buried his muzzle in the cool water.

She watched him carefully. "Go easy, Romeo, I can't afford having you get sick." When she felt he'd had enough she led him away, removed the saddle, and proceeded to rub him down with the woolen blanket. Tethering him in the shade, she left him contentedly munching a portion of oats and headed back to the stream. Dropping down on one knee, she scooped up some water and splashed it on her parched face. It refreshed her, and she suddenly thought of stripping down and diving in. Why not, she mused with a shrug. It was still as hot as hades, and there wasn't a soul around. She was accustomed to these solitary jaunts and wasn't frightened of being alone.

Five years ago, after her father Walt had been killed in a stampede, she had begun coming out here alone to work through her grief. She knew her mother worried every time her daughter left the ranch area. But the spirited Abbie could not be held back. Even the thought of her mother's disapproval made little difference. She considered it briefly as her slim fingers began undoing the buttons on her shirt—but it didn't divert her from her objective.

Tossing the garment aside, she yanked off her fancy-stitched boots and peeled her tight-fitting pants down her slim legs. When she had divested herself of her clothing she waded out into the stream until the water lapped gently about her bare breasts. Easing onto her back, she floated about, enjoying the sharp sting of the cold water against her parched skin.

"Ah, Romeo," she called to the faithful steed whose ears pricked forward at mention of his name. "This is sheer heaven—beyond comparison." Abbie splashed and swam until she felt refreshed once again. After scrubbing herself clean with a bar of scented soap she kept in her pack, she waded onto the bank and spread out her bedroll. Flopping upon it, she contentedly basked in the waning rays of the sun, reveling in the freedom her nakedness allowed.

Texas may be hard on its women folk—at least that was her mother's favorite phrase—but to an independent woman like Abbie it held no boundaries, no restrictions. It suited her just fine.

Just before her eyelids drooped closed she slid into a blue cotton shirt and curled deeper into the bedroll, one hand protectively grasping a long-barrel six-shooter.

Something woke her, an indeterminate sound, a sixth sense. Opening her eyes, she peered about. It was dark. The sun had long since set behind the thick grove of trees and a campfire blazed cheerily. Abbie smiled, feeling warm and drowsily content. The aroma of freshly brewed coffee wafted to her nostrils, and she remembered thinking how nice it was that some of her men had come looking for her. She sat up to greet them, her eyes searching the area for their familiar faces. There was no one. What was going on, she wondered, still somewhat sleep-dazed.

"I see sleeping beauty has awakened."

The sound of a strange male voice brought Abbie Lee straight up like a cat that had been scalded.

It was an unknown voice, deep and masculine, and sent gooseflesh scurrying along Abbie's spine. The click of a gun hammer was her only reply.

She heard his sharp intake of breath and assumed he'd gotten the message. Until she remembered she was standing in the glow of the fire, in only a long-tailed shirt. Cursing her own stupidity, Abbie held her ground, determined to shoot if he so much as made one wrong move.

"I think you'd better come up with a real good reason for being here, mister. This is Caldwell land, and you're trespassing." She thought she caught a movement, a tall, broad-shouldered form as big as a bear. Her heart hammered against her rib cage.

"And just who am I addressing?" The husky timbre in his voice rattled Abbie Lee clear down to her bare toes.

"The Caldwell that's going to put a bullet in your hide if you don't state your business, and quick!" She knew that infernal shirt was hanging mid-thigh, and she tugged viciously at it in hopes of stretching it down past her knees.

"Now ma'am, that's a downright unneighborly tone you're using. And I don't like being threatened, even by someone who can make an ordinary shirt look like poetry in motion." The words rolled off his tongue as smoothly as freshly churned butter.

Abbie Lee felt hot color flush her cheeks scarlet. "Mister, I'm going to count to three real slow like, and when I'm through, I start shooting."

"Is that the thanks I get for sitting here watching over you? I even made you some coffee—figured you might be a mite grumpy when you woke up."

Abbie's jaw almost fell open. No one wheedled a person who was about to lace them, and their freshly brewed coffee with lead—did they?

"Just one cup," he coaxed softly. "It'll soothe those rattled nerves of yours."

Abbie favored his shadowy image with a narrow-eyed glare. "All right, if you're so all-fired set on me drinking some of your blasted coffee, then you bring me some—over here."

"So you can put a hole in me big enough to drive cattle through?" he snorted. "Huh, uh, sweetheart, no deal."

"Then I'd say we have a standoff," she replied, gun unwavering.

Any other time Sonny Malone would have enjoyed this

little cat and mouse game, loved it as a matter of fact. For just the sight of the sleep-tousled woman, standing there in that unforgettable shirt with those long coltish legs all sleek and golden, was enough to cause all sorts of ideas churning in his brain. Ideas his practical side chose to remind him of. Forget it—you've got other things to consider right now. Like a ruthless killer out there somewhere and convincing this woman that it's dangerous for her to remain here alone.

Sonny had trailed the bandits from Fort Sumner where they'd sold some stolen beef to the army, then down the Pecos on the edge of the Llano, to here, on her land. He couldn't waste time with her and lose them. He'd come too far and searched too long for that. A beautiful woman and a six-shooter stood between him and his objective. At the moment he wasn't certain which was the more deadly.

"I'm through counting, mister."

Sonny heard the underlying steeliness behind those words and decided it was now or never. The lady meant business.

With the unleashed power and grace of a lupine animal he sprang forward from the shadows, catching Abbie Lee completely by surprise.

She had a brief glimpse of a darkly tan, dangerous looking face partially disguised by a bearded stubble as he came at her out of the darkness. He appeared frighteningly tall and muscular, enough to send the hammer forward on the gun and a startled cry to escape her.

"Madre de Dios!" Sonny snarled as the revolver exploded next to his ear. He had knocked Abbie to the ground and now straddled her, a knee on either side of her waist, her hands pinned back over her head. "You almost got me with that goddamned thing!"

Abbie looked up into the cynically hard face glaring down at her and swallowed convulsively. "I—I meant to!"

"Damned if you didn't," he growled, shaking his dark head in an effort to dispel the ringing in his ears. "Thank God you missed."

"I didn't miss!" she snapped back defensively. "You moved!"

He saw her stare longingly at her gun now lying in the sand.

"Don't get any bright ideas, chiquita. Target practice is over for the evening. You've managed to alert everyone that we're here."

Abbie squirmed angrily beneath him. He jerked rudely on her imprisoned wrists. "I'd quit that if I were you, unless you want things to get even more out of hand than they already are."

Her horrified brain registered mortification. She had played right into his hands! Here she was pinned to the ground, and she was afraid to think where that shirttail now lay!

"I can hear you thinking, pretty lady. Don't go doing anything foolish that we're both going to regret."

Abbie stared right back at that narrow-eyed glare. Now's not the time to panic, Abbie, she willed herself. It's dark, he's facing you, his ears are probably still ringing like church bells, and if all else fails, you've still got your legs free. A well placed jab in the right place could turn the tables real fast.

Sonny stared down into aquamarine eyes enhanced by a sweep of thick sooty lashes and almost drowned in their sultry depths. She looked half savage, half bewildered lying beneath him with her long chestnut hair all tangled and entwined about them both. His pulse leaped. Unknowingly, she pressed her slender body closer, and he felt a quiver of desire race through him. A mocking smile curved his sensuous mouth as he felt her struggles cease.

"That's much better," he replied calmly, although his pulse was pounding. "Now," he breathed, "suppose you let me explain why I'm here."

"By the position I find myself in, I'd say that was fairly obvious."

Abbie's wary gaze battled his. Mesmerized, she found herself staring into piercing eyes that were an unusual silver-gray and as wily as a fox. Oh, Abbie Lee, her inner self warned, I hope you haven't underestimated this devil.

As if sensing her thoughts, he chuckled huskily. "I've no intention of harming you. I'm only concerned for your welfare."

Her snicker of sarcasm caused his eyebrows to shoot upward. "Pardon me, but I think you are full of bull!"

His eyes bore into her. "Damnit, you're sure making this a whole helluva lot harder than it was supposed to be."

She almost choked. "Me! Making things difficult!"

"Quit acting like a little bitch," he ordered impatiently. "Before you woke up I sat there thinking about how sweet and innocent you looked; how you needed someone to watch over you." He grinned coldly. "But it seems you're so tough you don't need protecting." He felt her tremble with surpressed rage.

"I don't give a hoot what you think of me," she hissed. "All I care about is getting your big carcass off of me before you squish every part you've so effectively ogled."

"Do you really think that's a good idea—considering your predicament?" A devilish smile lifted the corners of his mouth.

"Yes—I mean—wait!" She grabbed at his hands. "Ummm—perhaps we can talk right here."

"Suit yourself," he mocked, allowing his hands to rest lightly upon her rib cage. He could feel her heart pitter-pattering like a frightened rabbit's beneath his long fingers. He watched her intently, his eyes tracing the finely etched features before him. She was a beauty, with high cheekbones, wide-set eyes, creamy skin, and lips just made for kissing. But it was her chestnut hair that proved her most glorious feature. It was thick and sweet-smelling, and he was tempted to bury his fingers in it until they caressed her skull. His gaze lingered on the beckoning vee of her shirt. So tempting, he cursed inwardly. And so unwilling.

Abbie noticed the discernible change in him with a sinking feeling. She knew she was completely at this outlaw's mercy. And he had to be an outlaw; he certainly looked and acted like one. He was roughly dressed and carried two Colt revolvers tied down on his hips. She sensed the unbridled power within him and felt doomed. The air was thick with repressed emotion. Somewhere a panther screamed. It had cornered its prey and was moving in for the final assault.

Abbie stared wide-eyed at the lithe powerful man towering over her. "If you lay a hand on me—I'll kill you," she whispered through trembling lips.

"Don't flatter yourself," he snarled savagely, and taking her with him in one smooth motion he leapt to his feet. She came up against his hard chest with a gasp of disbelief.

"You—you mean—you don't intend to to—" she stammered.

"You sound almost disappointed, Miss Caldwell."

She glared up at him. "I am. I should have shot you before you even had a chance to move!"

"You are the most bloodthirsty female I have ever had the misfortune to run in to. I'd sooner ask a bad-tempered grizzly to share my bed than the likes of you."

Her chin lifted defensively. "I'm certain the two of you would make the perfect pair."

He favored her with a withering look, snorting effectively. "This is the most ridiculous conversation I've ever had in my life! I'm standing here in the middle of the godforsaken prairie arguing with some ornery gun-toting female over my preference in bed partners!"

Suddenly, a shot rang out in the night, whizzing by them and prompting Sonny to drop to the ground, yanking Abbie with him.

"One of your ex-lovers come to pay her respects?" Abbie hissed.

"No such luck, sweetheart. We've got us some kind of trouble here, and they won't waste their time playing games with you, so stay close."

Abbie sensed that her very life depended on this man at the moment. She lay snug against his lean form and hated herself for feeling grateful for it.

Romeo nickered in terror. She wriggled free and started to scramble toward the grove of trees.

"Get your butt back here, lady!" he commanded. "Unless you don't mind someone taking a potshot at it."

Abbie dropped like a stone, making certain that her shirt-tail remained exactly where it should.

Sonny quickly withdrew his pistols, and an exchange of gunfire exploded in the night. Abbie looked longingly at her revolver lying useless some yards away. She scooted over beside him. "This is all your fault, you know. I could have taken care of myself just fine. Now, look at me!"

"Dear Lord," Sonny moaned, "spare me this crazy female. She's going to end up getting us both killed."

Abbie lay rigid as a board beside him. "Who are those men?"

"I had hoped to discuss that with you earlier, but you never gave me a chance," he said grimly near her ear. "Now you listen, and listen good. If something should happen to me, you get out of here—fast. You don't want them to get hold of you. I'd sooner shoot you myself than have them get you." He glanced over at her. "And get some clothes on!"

Abbie scrambled to do his bidding, pulling on her trousers.

Almost as quickly as it had begun the shooting stopped. An uneasy silence lingered.

Sonny rose cautiously to his feet. "If we're lucky, they've gone. I'm going to check the horses. I hope I'm wrong, but I think they may have taken them." He pointed one long finger at her. "And you stay here."

"What if they're still out there?"

His sarcastic reply was flung over his shoulder, and she winced at his caustic words.

23

"I'll just tell them they'll have to go away—that they're on Caldwell land." He was gone so long that she began to wonder if he was coming back. When her jacket landed unceremoniously in her lap, she jumped as though it were a snake.

"Put it on," he ordered, hunkering down beside her. "No sign of them, and we have one horse left, mine. They got yours."

"Romeo." She half sobbed.

"Better him than you."

"Who took him? Tell me, please."

He favored her with a narrowed-eyed glare. "Please, is it. All of the sudden we've lost our high and mighty Caldwell airs?"

She shrugged into her deerskin jacket. "He is special to me. My father and I trained him together."

His rigid expression softened. "Yeah, well, I can appreciate your feelings. Family and horses are special. I'm sorry about your horse. If it's any consolation to you he'll be well looked after. I expect he'll become some Comanche's pony."

"The Caldwells get on well with the Comanche around here, mister. Those weren't any Comanche."

He considered her silently, then said, "I've been trailing a fella clean across the state of Texas for weeks. It's a personal vendetta. Picked up his trail at Horsehead, on the Pecos. Followed him north to Fort Sumner where he met up with an Indian agent. Seemed they were cooking up some sort of deal between them." Sonny shook his head. "Never did have time to find out what it was when that devil lit out again, disappeared in the Yellow bluffs near New Mexico and came out again with a crew of *bandidos*." He looked at Abbie. "Ever heard of that territory and the men who ride those trails?"

Abbie nodded mutely. "I heard my father repeat stories he'd been told." She shuddered. "Comancheros—the unscrupulous gypsies of the plains. They ride with the

24

scroungers and the renegade Indians, dealing in stolen plunder. The Palo Duro Canyon is their hideaway."

"Yeah, and also the place where they peddle human lives," Sonny finished, reloading his Colt.

Abbie gaped at him. "They might have kidnapped me, you mean! I may have ended up at that other place—the Valle de Las Lagrimas, the Vale of Tears."

His tone was flat as he added, "Where savages tear mothers and children from each other's arms and trade them to different Indian bands."

Frightening pictures formed in Abbie's mind. "And who are you?" she stammered, "and how do you know so much about them?"

"Name's Sonny Malone. About a year ago my father, who was a sheriff in Santa Fe, went after a judge's son there who had murdered a prostitute. Followed him into Mexico where he had no jurisdiction, but he wanted that fella bad. He was a cold-blooded snake, liked to use his knife like a carving tool." Sonny gritted his teeth, remembering. "My father's a Texan and proud. My mother and I knew he wouldn't return until he flushed Lucien Rodriquez out of hiding and back into Texas where he could nab him."

"And did he?" Abbie inquired.

"Return? No. But Rodriquez has."

"And now, you are after this same man?"

"He's back, and my father isn't."

"Did you stop to think your father may be—"

"Dead," he finished for her.

She nodded mutely.

"There's only one way I'm going to find that out for certain."

"Get this Lucien person yourself, right?"

"I almost had him, too." Contempt curled his mouth. "Until you."

"I never asked you to play the white knight," she replied angrily. "And if you wish to leave, go ahead. I'm used to taking care of myself out here."

"Lady, you're tough, but not that tough," he snarled. "Out here alone, without a horse, you wouldn't stand a chance in hell."

She stared up at the hard gleam in his eyes and did not doubt the truth of that statement. "What now, shining knight?" she quipped sardonically.

"I guess I'm stuck hauling you with me," he shot back with a scowl.

All sorts of images raced through Abbie's mind. Spinning on her heel, she tore off in the opposite direction. "Over my dead body!" she screeched as she sprinted away.

"Don't tempt me, sweetheart," he mumbled, taking his time packing up the gear. When he'd finished, he swung up into the saddle and followed in the direction of her hasty departure.

Abbie had no idea how she intended to escape him, or for that matter, how she was going to get there. She only knew she had to get as far away from Sonny Malone as her two legs would take her. Then maybe she would wake up and find that this was nothing more than a bad dream.

Sonny reined his horse in behind her and followed at a leisurely pace. God! she is an exasperating female, he thought once again as he watched her march determinedly over the darkened landscape. He could see her slim back held ramrod straight and found himself grinning as he observed her angry stride. To his surprise, admiration began wedging out his annoyance and mentally, he began making note of her redeeming qualities. True, she was lovely, and he couldn't help visualizing her lying naked and willing beneath him. But there was also something else, something that held him spellbound and brought a smile to his lips as he kept her slim form in sight.

"Miss Caldwell. Oh, Miss Caldwell!"

Abbie heard her name called mockingly soft and cringed. "Go away! I was hoping you were nothing more than a bad dream!" Her stomach fluttered in fear as the horse's hooves came nearer. She broke into a run.

The chase didn't last long. He easily covered the distance between them. As he leaned over in the saddle to sweep her up before him she sensed an unwelcome stirring of desire that brought a soundless cry of denial to her lips.

His warm breath caressed her cheek as he whispered victoriously, "Your white knight is back, my long-limbed beauty." His lean fingers stroked her thick hair soothingly. "And willingly or not, I am going to rescue you." He laughed huskily, as though it were nothing more than a game to be played. But it was not a game, and she struggled in the imprisonment of his arms.

Abbie turned her head to snap at him and their eyes met in a glittering match of wills. "I'll make you pay for this," she vowed. "When we get to civilization I'll have you arrested for kidnapping. By the time I'm through with you, mister, you'll wish you'd stayed with your own kind—the varmints!"

Beneath the dark-bearded stubble a muscle twitched. The teasing smile vanished, and his eyes were suddenly cold, like ice chips.

Abbie grew still, glaring silently at him. It wouldn't do to push him further; to do so might be hazardous to her health. As she felt the horse surge forward she haughtily turned her head and stiffened her spine, determined not to touch any part of him. She would just ignore the brash devil, she vowed firmly.

His arms encircled her waist, hard and sinewy. She bit down on her bottom lip. Just bide your time, Abbie, she mused, play your cards right, and soon you'll have him eating out of your hand.,

She smiled a secretive smile, feeling more self-assured. For Abbie Lee Caldwell was a stubborn filly, and she hadn't met a man yet who could best her.

Chapter Two

As the new day stole gently over the rolling plains, transforming the moon-streaked shadows of night into a pink, dew-soft morning, Abbie fixed her bleary-eyed gaze on the sky where perfectly sculpted clouds appeared to skim the very base of the earth. The land stretched out before her all the way to the horizon. Today, it seemed vast, endless and uncertain.

"Where are you taking me?" she asked stubbornly.

He sighed. "Must I answer that again?"

"Yes!" she snapped.

"I believe you just want to hear the sound of my voice so that you can stay awake and sit in that ridiculous stiff-backed position," he taunted.

"I can stay awake forever, if necessary," she said tersely, "for as soon as you nod off, there's only going to be one of us riding this horse."

"If that's the case, then we're both going over the side together," he drawled, his arm tightening about her middle, forcing her to lean against him.

She resisted, but he was having none of it. She was very aware of his warmth pressed so intimately near. "You're despicable, and I'll make you pay for this, Malone, you can count on it!"

"So tough for so slight a creature," he retorted dryly.

Unrelenting, she tried bribery. "I have some money. I'll pay you to take me back home."

"Just simmer down, pretty lady. I'm not losing this man's trail for love or money. I've come too far and searched too long for that." She felt a quiver of suppressed violence ripple through him and shivered.

Sonny realized her fear and sought to relieve her anxiety, but his words sounded gruff even to his own ears. "If we come to a way station I'll send you back home. Until then, just make the best of it. *Comprende?*"

She nodded miserably, his hated voice becoming a dull buzzing in her ears. Her body was bone tired and her eyelids drooped heavily. He felt her body go limp as exhaustion overtook her.

Abbie was barely aware that he'd shifted his weight in the saddle and that her head was now buried in the curve of his shoulder. Drowsily content, she snuggled closer.

Manly scents: Sun-bronzed skin, tobacco, leather, and a lingering trace of bourbon, stirred almost forgotten memories of another man and time and the trust they'd shared between them. Her father. She knew this rough stranger and Walter Caldwell were like night and day in comparison. This gunman cared nothing about her or her feelings. But then she felt the stranger's arms draw her protectively closer, and she began to have her first doubts.

Sonny bore her slight weight against him without complaint. She was so soft, so vulnerable and, for the moment, so blessedly quiet.

He had been surprised when she'd managed to keep that spine of hers ramrod straight for hours, refusing to touch any part of him. The lady had stamina and a sharp little tongue to go along with it. One slim hand curled against his chest and he sucked in his breath. The intimate contact of their bodies was arousing some elemental feelings and disturbing the hell out of his lower solar plexus. He almost preferred her relentless harping to this new, more effective type of torture.

"The two of us on this one horse is going to be a helluva lot harder on me than on you, little firebrand," he whispered against the silky head tucked beneath his chin.

This time it was the heat that woke her. Hot, scorching rays that made her feel as though she were melting by slow degrees. She came awake feeling nauseous. His voice addressed her in a derisive tone, his breath caressing her ear. She gritted her teeth.

"It's about time. I thought you were going to sleep the whole day through, and my arms are about to fall off."

Abbie pulled away, scrambling out of his arms. His mocking laughter and soft teasing words infuriated her beyond reason.

"I'd be willing to bet that by the time you get back home, Miss Caldwell, you'll undoubtedly have the best damned posture in the entire state of Texas."

"I'm going to give it my best shot, Mr. Malone. Of that you can be certain!"

"I never doubted it for a minute," he replied dryly.

Neither said very much after that, and Abbie was relieved when she felt him rein the horse toward a grove of mesquite trees that would provide a brief reprieve from the grueling sun. He slid off Viento's back and turned to help her, arms outstretched. She ignored him, swinging down with graceful ease. He had expected it, but it rankled him nonetheless.

His eyes shot silver fire. "You're the hard-headest female . . ." he growled. Abbie returned his pointed stare, refusing to cower beneath that chilling look. With the canteen dangling from his shoulder he spun about and stalked toward the trees.

Abbie followed at a distance, her gaze making note of his long legs, his smooth, loose-limbed stride. Her thoughts and

31

emotions, when it came to this ruggedly attractive man, were confusing. It disturbed her, furthering her desire to escape him just as soon as she could find a way. She didn't trust him, and worse yet, she was beginning to wonder if she could trust herself. Pent-up frustration from constantly having his body pressed against hers made her despise him all the more. His voice broke through her thoughts.

"Are you hungry?" They had reached the clustered shelter of trees. He offered her the canteen first.

"A little," she replied sulkily, reaching forward, her fingers accidentally brushing his strong, brown ones. Their eyes met. His gaze flicked over her with careless regard. Slowly, he released the canteen.

"I've some dried beef in my saddlebags."

She nodded curtly, then drank deeply, feeling his hooded gaze upon her. Water trinkled down her chin, along the graceful curve of her throat to disappear tantalizingly between the swell of her breasts. Her shirt clung to her moistened skin and when she glanced up, his eyes had shifted from her face. She cleared her throat, and they slowly returned.

"Would you care for some, Mr. Malone?" she inquired haughtily.

Sonny knew she meant water but couldn't resist the mocking uplift of one dark brow. His silver-gray eyes glittered wickedly, challengingly, as they stared into hers. Silence hung in the air between them.

Abbie's cool composure crumpled. With a vengeance, she flung the canteen at him, not even caring if the precious water spilled out upon the ground. Spinning around, she marched with stiff-backed indignation toward his horse. He managed to catch the canteen upright. Ah, hell, it had been a loaded question.

She sensed his quiet approach, yet she refused to acknowledge him. She deliberately stared across Viento's back while munching on a strip of jerky she'd withdrawn from his pack.

His arms appeared to innocently circle around her as he hooked the canteen on the saddle horn. He didn't hurry his task, and she renewed her vow to hate him forever. She could feel the muscles of his arms ripple with each movement and almost choked on the stringy jerky. She knew this was his way of reminding her just how easy it would be to control her if he so desired.

"Did you bolt down all of the jerky or did you leave me some?" he quipped.

She bristled but, reaching into the saddlebag, she flung a strip over her shoulder. "Here—enjoy!"

"Thanks," he drawled, laughing softly.

When they'd finished eating, she probed deliberately. "How much further today?" She turned to see his dark brows drawn together in annoyance.

"Are you going to start again?" he snarled. Removing his dark stetson, he wiped his brow on the curve of his arm.

"I hope you get sick to death of hearing my voice," she stated with a smirk.

"If I do you can bet I know an effective way to silence it." His eyes strayed to her full, pouting mouth.

She swallowed and looked away, hating herself for letting him brow-beat her.

Without warning he grasped her arm with one hand while the other cupped her bottom and propelled her upward into the saddle. Abbie gasped, her back going rigid with anger. She glared disapprovingly at him. He was so tall that even sitting high on Viento's back she barely had to incline her head to meet his gaze.

A pair of steely-gray eyes challenged her azure ones. Unexpectantly, he grinned crookedly. "Time to hit the trail, Miss Caldwell. Devil's Bend is a good ride from here, and I have a rendezvous with an associate near there."

"Undoubtedly someone I'm going to be just thrilled to meet," she replied sarcastically.

One corner of his ash-colored moustache lifted in amusement. "I reckon not. This fella runs guns for profit. If Rodriquez is trading guns with the Indians, then this man can get me some to use as a lure."

"A gunrunner—and you condone this sort of thing?" she gasped.

"I'll do anything it takes to get near Rodriquez, and sometimes gunrunning can benefit a worthwhile cause," he replied, thinking back to the goodly share he'd bought from Tyrell Jones for his compatriots in Mexico. Pivoting and walking on ahead, he called over his shoulder, "Let's move it. I've wasted enough time as it is."

"Aren't you riding?" she questioned.

"Viento needs a break. And so do I!"

"Suit yourself," she replied with a sly smile. Fixing her gaze on the terrain and away from his lean, predatory stride, she began to plan a hasty escape.

"By the way," he warned, glancing over his shoulder. "While we're together I expect you to stay close to me." His tone was hard as nails. "If you don't, it could cost you your life."

He continued onward, expecting no contest, and this time, she didn't give him one; but her mind panicked as his cold declaration rang in her ears. Abbie considered her situation as she rode along. The thought of his taking her to Devil's Bend weighed heavily on her mind. She knew it was a well-known haven for every sort of riffraff that rode the outlaw trails of Texas. And it was on the very edge of the Llano Estacado. If the outlaws didn't get her, the Indians surely would! She could find a way station on her own. Let him hike all the way to that god-awful place! Praying she could get away fast enough, she jabbed her booted heels in Viento's sides and yanked on the reins. The big pinto danced nervously beneath her. An expert rider, she quickly brought him under control and sent him galloping in the opposite direction. Let the buzzards have Malone; she was going back home!

Sonny spun around and observed her hasty departure with an amused shake of his dark head. Cupping his hands over his mouth, he yelled, "Hey, Viento, *alto, amigo!*"

The stallion came to an obedient halt, propelling Abbie Lee forward and over his head. She hit the ground with a bone-jarring crunch that knocked the air out of her. All thoughts of escape vanished as she fought to regain her breath. Automatically, her knees pulled up to her stomach as she tried to draw air back into her lungs. Panicking, she thrashed about in the sand, gasping, emitting choking noises.

Sonny was immediately beside her, his voice commanding. "Quit fighting it, straighten out your legs! Damnit, listen to me!"

Abbie tried, but she was too frightened. She felt his big hands grasp her beneath the arms and haul her upward against him. Her legs immediately unbuckled. The pain in her chest began to recede as blessed air returned to her lungs.

Sonny stroked the wobbly head on his shoulder with tender concern. "Don't ever try that again," he warned, smoothing back the tangled hair from her face and fighting the desire to cradle her close.

She only sniffled, staring up at him in humiliating defeat. The look in his eyes belied his gruff words, but Abbie failed to notice. Anger quickly returned to fire up her flagging spirits. Chokingly, she sputtered between gulps of air.

"Get your filthy hands off me, Malone. And rest assured that I would sooner walk than ride that mule-headed animal of yours another mile." Her little fists balled up and struck out at his chest. She met the unrelenting silver brilliance of his eyes and gave him one last whack before realizing she may have pushed him too far. Her hands froze in midair to be captured and held by his, mastering her in a way that no one had ever dared. When she attempted to break free of his grasp, his arms closed around her like two steel bands. His mouth hovered inches from hers.

35

"You've been asking for this since the first—" Crushing her to him, his lips fiercely claimed hers.

Abbie whimpered in protest. She tried to remain rigid, not to give in to the thrill racing through her, but in the end, she did. Her lips softened beneath his and she moaned.

His tongue ran across her moist lips, invaded them, and brushed lightly against her pearly teeth. It caused a surge of heat to build within her. Abbie surrendered her mouth to his sensual probing. She had never been kissed this way in her life, and the sensation was unexpectedly thrilling. She didn't protest when he pressed her back against the ground, pinning her arms with his strong hands, his long, hard body sliding over her, moving suggestively against her. She could feel his heart beating wildly and instinctively she arched her hips against his. There was a frantic urgency to her movements.

Sonny desired her more than any other woman he'd ever met. She was all fire, all female, with an air of touch-me-not about her that tantalized a man until he would do anything just to break through that cool exterior to possess her. Even now, with her body pressed tightly against him, eyes ablaze with passion, he knew that she would betray her body's need and scratch his eyes out if he released her wrists. She was a bitch, a hellcat in a long-tailed shirt, and he wanted to make love to her so badly that he was half crazy. He groaned softly, rolling over onto his back, pulling her with him. Her body relaxed in his arms, and he loosened his punishing grip. If she chose to break free, he would let her. He wouldn't take her by force. He was surprised when she only clung tighter.

Viento's nervous whinny broke through their haze of desire and sent them scrambling apart. They both knew that out here, anything could be stalking them. Sonny wasn't about to stick around and find out what it was. Racing to the pinto, he vaulted easily into the saddle. "Quick!" he ordered, holding out his hand. "Let's move!"

Abbie stared at the strong hand reaching out to her for an

eternity, it seemed. It was a powerful hand, lean and viselike in its grip. She longed to turn away, feeling more confused than ever now. He was taunting, hard, and ofttimes seemed cruel. But yet, hadn't she just discovered how caring and concerned he could be, and surprisingly, how very much she had enjoyed their close contact?

She put out her hand, felt his fingers entwine with hers. He pulled her up into the saddle before him, a triumphant smile turning up the corners of his wide, sensual mouth.

As the sun swept across the continuous archway of sky, dark, threatening clouds swept in from the west. Sonny's eyes immediately sought a place of shelter where they could spend the night. The terrain had begun to change. It was rugged, interspersed with scrub oak and cedar. Jagged streaks of lightning charged through the low-hanging clouds, seeming to light up the entire earth as they pierced the dusky gloom.

"Keep watch for a place to camp where we'll stay reasonably dry," he said.

"It looks like it's going to hit any minute," she commented worriedly.

"Yeah, and a mean one, too." He pointed up ahead in the distance. "Over there, seems like a good place to tuck in."

She saw that he was indicating a high bluff with a shelf-like overhang. "As good as any we're going to find."

The wind increased as darkness settled over the land. Sonny and Abbie hurriedly retrieved their gear, hobbled Viento, wrapped blankets about themselves, then sat together to wait out the night.

The fury of the storm hit with a force of cold rain that prompted the two people to huddle closer together. Sonny's big body felt comforting to Abbie, and when he opened the end of his blanket in an unspoken invitation, she quickly accepted.

Sleep that night came in snatches. They managed to keep their upper bodies relatively dry, but their legs and feet became soaked. Abbie began to shiver, her teeth chattering, and nothing Sonny did dispersed the chill that had settled deep in her bones. By early morning he knew she'd come down with pneumonia if the blasted weather didn't let up soon.

Abbie dozed fitfully. She was freezing, growing numb as the icy drizzle seeped through the blanket and down into her boots. She was only dimly aware that Sonny had maneuvered her body against the rocky wall, removed her boots and soaked trousers then lay snug against her back, his own exposed to the windy tempest.

"Don't get sick on me, sweetheart." His voice was husky and familiar, and for once, Abbie welcomed his gruff command.

Stiffly, she nodded her head. It felt on fire. She sniffled miserably, praying for the night to end.

His big hands constantly massaged every part of her bare legs. They were warm and sure in their touch. His voice crooned soothingly and at last, the rain stopped.

Morning came bright and fast. The sun popped up over the rolling hills and the birds sang merrily at its return. Sonny felt like doing the same as he left Abbie to make them some hot coffee. He frowned when she didn't stir. Poor kid, he thought. She doesn't deserve what I've put her through. With resolution, he swore to find a way station before he had more to regret than he already did. Even as helpless as she was last night, just the touch of his hands on her smooth legs had been sheer torture. It had taken iron control not to caress her everywhere, for he wanted her more with each passing second. Abbie woke, feeling his hands turning her body toward the sun. "Sonny?" she groaned through dry lips.

"Yeah, baby, it's me." He was relieved the little hellcat was all right. "Here, drink some of this. It'll warm you up."

She looked at the tin cup he held. Steam drifted enticingly from the contents, and Abbie reached for it.

"Let me help you," he said, his free hand easing behind her neck with a gentleness that surprised her.

She sipped the fiery brew slowly, feeling life begin to flow back into her stiff limbs. Her eyes watched him over the rim of the cup as he sat back on his haunches and smiled at her. It was a sincere gesture, with no hint of sarcasm, or amusement. It pleased her.

"Do you feel any better?"

"A little," she replied, her fingers enjoying the cup's warmth.

"Good." He nodded. "'Cause we're going to have to move on. This is Indian country, and I'm not hanging around any longer than necessary." He stood and began gathering up her wet things. He held up her trousers, "I don't think you should put these back on just yet. You'd do well to let the sun dry out your bones."

Her huffy manner immediately returned. "You'd just love to keep me undressed all of the time, wouldn't you?"

He grinned. Yep, she was definitely feeling better. "Please, Miss Caldwell, can't we at least bury the hatchet until we're out of this?" he offered.

She crossed her arms protectively over her chest. "Where do you want to bury it, in the back of my neck?"

"You are the most ungrateful woman I've ever met!" he roared, angry again.

"Ungrateful!" she hissed. "Just what in hades do I have to be grateful to you for?" She rose to her feet and wobbled toward Viento, clutching the blanket around her. She could feel that cold, hard stare of his piercing her in the back. "Are you ready to leave Mr. Malone?" she snapped heatedly as she glanced back over her shoulder.

"I am over ready," he growled, stomping toward her.

After he tied down their packs, he swung into the saddle, completely ignoring Abbie, who waited expectantly for him to extend his hand.

When he did not, she gritted her teeth and tugged herself up behind him, fingers curling tightly into the waistband of his black trousers.

He issued a short command and Viento sprang forward, almost unseating Abbie from her precarious perch.

Out of the corner of his eye, Sonny noticed the ends of the blanket blowing freely in the breeze, exposing finely shaped limbs to the warmth of the sun. Suddenly, his black mood lightened. There was more than one way to tame a stubborn Caldwell, he thought, smiling once again.

The day sped quickly by, and it wasn't until late afternoon that Sonny looked up to see buzzards circling ominously in the blue sky. An uneasy feeling settled within him.

"It could be just a dead animal." Abbie's gaze followed his. "Couldn't it?" A sense of dread was in her tone.

Sonny's hand covered her bare knee, squeezing gently. She realized he wanted her to hush. For once, Abbie didn't argue.

"Whatever it is, it's just over that next rise. We're going in slow and easy," he said softly.

When they'd almost crested the hill, they dismounted. She shrugged into her dry trousers. Sonny crept steathily forward, dropping to his belly the last few yards. His face, when he turned back to Abbie, registered disbelief as he motioned for her to come to him.

Abbie's body quivered with anxiety as she crawled up the incline and lay next to him. The sight that met her eyes brought her hand over her mouth.

A lovely lake lay in a valley surrounded by towering trees. A peaceful setting, except for the Kiowa Indians who appeared to be everywhere. Their half-naked bodies glistened in the hot sun as they moved about setting up their encampment. They were painted, feathered, and regal. Their faces were distorted by hideous masks of color. One group built huge fires, talking loudly and joking amongst themselves. Longhorn cattle were slaughtered, the half-cooked meat devoured and the fresh blood drunk. The Indians were enjoying themselves. This was their land; they were not afraid. Abbie was, and she tugged frantically at Sonny's shirt sleeve in an effort to pull him away. He brushed her hand aside, turning to glare impatiently at her. She lay still, wishing she were invisible.

Before long, the sun set and once again night was upon them. Many fires now burned below and the laughter had grown louder. Sonny and Abbie continued their vigil. And when the shapes of two-wheeled *carretas,* drawn by lumbering oxen, loomed out of the shadows and into the Indian encampment, Abbie realized why Sonny had insisted on remaining.

Rough-looking men: Mexicans, half-breeds, aimless wretches, rode beside the vehicles which contained barrels, crates—and huddled human forms. Comancheros. The word used to describe gypsies of the plains, once again came to mind. She could well understand now why her father had coined that phrase.

She watched, abhorred, as women and children were dragged sobbing from the carts and paraded before the leering Indians. It was all Abbie could do to keep from crying out in horror.

Whiskey poured freely from the huge casks. Jewelry, trinkets, and bright yard goods were strewn about for the Kiowas to inspect. They looked like over-eager children: grabbing material, draping it about themselves, stringing strands of beads around their necks with gleeful smiles.

They allowed the children some hot food, then they were led away to the carts to sleep. They would begin their new lives tomorrow and would soon forget any other way had existed. The Kiowas would treat them well. They would suffer no harm and be adopted by various members of the tribe.

One tall dark man appeared to be the Comanchero leader.

He was dressed in dark clothes, a wide sombrero pulled low over his features. He walked with a fluid stride, much like a panther. Chihuahua spurs that were silver-inlaid glittered in the firelight as he strode over to one woman who fought everyone who came near. Brutally, he grabbed a fistful of her hair and jerked her to him. She spat in his face. His other hand moved to the *camisa* she wore and ripped downward. Her full breasts were exposed to his leering gaze. He reached forward to cup one in his hand, squeezing cruelly. It was his way of telling her that virtue meant nothing here. She attempted to bite him, and he backhanded her across the mouth, sending her sprawling into the dust, blood trickling from her split lip.

Laughter and obscene gestures circulated among the bloodthirsty group. Abbie started to protest, but Sonny's harsh voice stopped her.

"Damnit, do you want to trade places with her?" he hissed close to her ear.

She shook her head from side to side, her eyes big and terrified. He glared sternly.

"Is he the one you're after?"

"Lucien Rodriquez—yes."

"He's—an animal," she choked.

"Worse. He's *el diablo* himself."

"What do we do now?"

"Not now, Miss Caldwell—no questions, please," he said, clearly irritated.

Abbie's face looked bleak and pitiful as she stared up at him.

Sonny felt a wrenching in his gut when he thought of what would happen to her if they were discovered. She read the unspoken message in his eyes and a quiver raced through her.

"I'm giving you back your gun," he informed her. "If necessary, use it." He withdrew her six-shooter from his waistband and handed it to her.

The handle was warm from his body as Abbie grasped it. She liked the reassuring feel of the solid steel against her palm but was startled that the lingering warmth of him disturbed her in a way she would never have thought possible.

They continued to watch silently as a Comanchero led a sleek black horse before the leader. The animal snorted in fear. It was unmistakable. It was the wild black mare that Abbie had chased for days. And Abbie had no doubt that Romeo was also there somewhere. Wasn't there anything they didn't poison by their touch? She found it all so repulsive and unbelievable.

Appearing like hideous demons, they caroused in the moonlit shadows throughout the night. And still, more came: Covered wagons, buckboards, anything that could haul plunder converged upon the scene.

Trading was vigorous and whiskey flowed freely. The woman who had fought off the leader was traded to a drunken Indian for three ponies and a bale of buffalo robes. Abbie felt pity for her and tears welled up in her eyes. Most of the men had chosen a woman to wile away the hours. It was a sight that Abbie could not bear, and with a sob she ran back to wait beside Viento.

Sonny kept watch on the Comanchero leader. The ruthless *bandolero* sat patiently before one of the fires smoking a long cigarillo and staring into the flames. He hadn't chosen a woman. His manner was solemn and aloof, as though he held himself above the bedlam around him and only tolerated it out of necessity. Behind him, men were dragging crates of rifles from wagons with false bottoms. The Indians showed great interest, and bartering was vigorous. Sonny knew then what sort of deal Rodriquez and the agent from Fort Sumner had concluded. Guns, stolen from the government and traded to the Indians. Gunrunning was a profitable business no matter what sort of war it was. Sonny had been involved in a bit of it himself to insure his Juarista compatriots guns. The government of the

United States had Spencer carbines. Sonny had seen to it that a goodly share made it across the border into Mexico. But this was different. Innocent people would be slaughtered with those guns. He would get Lucien Rodriquez. His plan would work, he had no doubt. But first, he had to get rid of the girl.

An eery silence settled upon the area just before dawn. Everyone had either left or lay passed out drunk upon the ground.

Still, Lucien Rodriquez waited. It wasn't long before a dun horse came out of the west, a dark-haired woman upon its back. Sonny couldn't make out her features, but she appeared very happy to see Rodriquez still there. It seemed he had been waiting just for her. She smiled, her white teeth flashing in the dim light as he rose to his feet and watched her approach. Her slim body swayed with the dun's motion, alluringly, seductively, and when she reached him, he pulled her roughly from the saddle into his arms.

Sonny glanced back at Abbie and for the first time noticed that she had retreated from the scene. He knew it had been a horrid thing to witness. One that she would not soon forget. Feeling guilty, he rose and went down the hill to stand beside her.

"I'll get you back home safely, Miss Caldwell," he promised as he peered down at her with serious regard.

"Abbie Lee," she offered. "Miss Caldwell is too formal out here where one doesn't know from one minute to the next what is going to happen to them."

"All right." He smiled. "Abbie, it is." He took her arm. The electricity was still there, stronger than ever. "Mount up, we're getting out of here."

Her face bore a look of surprise. "I thought you wanted to get this man."

"I do, and I will. But certainly not here, and not with you around. Devil's Bend is soon enough."

Mounted, with Abbie within the circle of his arms, they rode swiftly away from the Comancheros.

With startling clarity, Abbie Caldwell realized more than ever just how much her survival depended on this enigmatic man, Sonny Malone. Death did not particularly terrify her—but the other did.

Chapter Three

Dust was slowly gathering the last vestige of blue from the cloudless sky. A thin mist swept over the land, a slight breeze eddying the vapor, swirling it about the weary travelers.

Tired but alert, Abbie glanced around her at the difference in the terrain. Where once the land had stretched endlessly for miles, now there were flat, high bluffs, ridged with outcroppings of rock along their crests. Masses of red-flowered yuccas, prickly pear topped by bright yellow blossoms and acacia thickets, fragrant with blooms, dotted the landscape.

Abbie stared longingly at the beautiful scenery wishing she had her watercolors and painting equipment with her. She would have loved to capture the still-life scene on paper. She could almost feel the brush in her hand, the smell of paint in her nostrils. The young woman had inherited her considerable talent from her mother. Several of Martha Caldwell's watercolors and charcoal sketches could be seen hanging in her neighbor's homes. Generous to a fault, she gave them away, refusing compensation.

An overwhelming longing for everything she held most dear prompted Abbie to exclaim, voice trembling, "I can't wait to come to the end of this quest of yours, I've just about had enough, Malone."

Sonny felt uneasy with the moment. "You've been real good, today, Ab, don't go getting testy on me now."

Abbie scowled. "You haven't even seen my bad side yet, but you will if you don't send me back home soon."

"Be still. I don't need this now," he said impatiently.

She clamped her lips together, vowing yet again to make him pay dearly for all that he'd put her through.

Despite her best efforts to keep her chin elevated obstinately, Abbie began to yawn sleepily. It wasn't long before her chin rested upon her chest. She wasn't aware that she'd dozed off until they crossed a dry wash, startling a flock of geese, sending them overhead in flight. The unexpected sound brought her head up sharply, her fingers grasping the butt of her gun.

Sonny immediately grabbed her arm. "It's only geese, Ab. Take it easy, I know you're tired and jumpy. We'll be there soon."

"You talk as if you know exactly where you're going!" she snapped, leaning forward, her keen eyes making note of a vine-covered trail they appeared headed toward. "I hope you know what you're doing for both our sakes," she grumbled. "Following that cliff ledge looks mighty risky."

"I know a little bit about this area, so just let me handle things, okay?"

She drew herself up. "I hope it's better than you have shown up to now."

Sonny snorted, realizing the barb. "Just you keep remembering whose arms you'd be in right now if not for me."

Abbie sat forward, her face hot. Damn, if he didn't throw in that threat whenever he felt she was getting the best of him. Her smoldering eyes concentrated on their precarious descent, watching wide-eyed as the pinto carefully picked his way down the steep incline. Observing the boulder-strewn path with a great deal of trepidation, she held tightly to the saddle horn, her knees clasping the stallion's sides.

She felt Sonny's hands firmly grasp her about the waist,

giving the pinto free rein. The heat from his fingers scorched her through her clothes, making her heart beat wildly.

Shortly they passed beneath a rocky ledge to enter an enclosed canyon. She twisted in the saddle to look up at him accusingly.

"You knew this was here all along, didn't you?"

"Let's just say I've been here before, on several occasions," Sonny drawled, offering no further explanation.

"Looking for the elusive Rodriquez?" she probed.

"No," he replied blandly. "Riding with the Comanche."

A tendril of chestnut hair whipped about Abbie's astonished face, and she brushed at it absentmindedly. "With—the—redskins?" Her gaze left his to scan the passages of purple and yellow limestone and far-reaching surfaces of pale gray dust. Weird-shaped rocks shielded swaying willow trees and a clear, inviting stream. High in the twilight sky a hawk circled, searching for a glint of silver in the blue-green water below. It appeared such a quiet, peaceful place.

"I know what must be going through your head," he said, sensing her unease. "But you're safe with me." He handed her something. She looked down at the small beaded pouch. "This is a medicine bag, isn't it?"

"Yes, a Kwahadi pouch. My blood brother's family gave it to me."

"The antelope eaters—so, it is true. You were one of them," she murmured, clutching the bag.

"Yes, it's true."

"You never cease to amaze me, Malone," she said, her face appearing whiter beneath the golden tan.

"That works both ways." He grinned suddenly. "It's nothing all that mysterious. I saved a Comanche brave's life in this canyon." Releasing his hold on her waist when they reached flat ground he continued. "Our meeting was purely coincidental, believe me. He'd been hunting and I came upon him unexpectedly. Thinking I was going to attack him, he came at me with a knife. We were going at it pretty good when he rolled to one side to escape my lunge and was bitten by a rattler. I stayed with him, nursed him back to health, and on his insistence, went back to his village with him to meet his family."

"You actually stayed with those people?" She stared up into his eyes, close enough to see the fine lines that winged out from their corners, evidence of days spent outdoors squinting against the bright sun.

"I couldn't offend them, and besides, it can be a satisfying life for a man. Only the Indian's rules exist out here. The People are as free as the wind and the rain. They did not start this war. They believe the white man has no right to cut their land in little squares and to encroach on their hunting grounds. They're only asking for what's rightfully theirs." He halted the stallion and they dismounted.

Abbie recalled his prowess with weapons and his ability to move stealthily without detection. She had sensed something untamed and savage in this man; perhaps now she knew why. There was still much about him that was a mystery. She was surprised to realize that at that moment she was more in awe of him than anyone she'd ever met before. He was like a beckoning flame burning hot and bright, tempting the fluttering moth ever nearer. Abbie realized how imperative it was for her to avoid that luring flame. She instinctively knew her emotional survival depended on her continued indifference.

Walking behind him, her fatigue suddenly caused her to lose her footing on the rocky terrain. Immediately, his arm snaked out to steady her.

"Are you all right?" He regarded her with those compelling eyes of his.

"Yes, at least I will be as soon as I can sit and rest for a while," she stammered.

"Not quite yet," he said offhandedly, turning to Viento to remove their gear. Casually, he tossed the saddle packs in

Abbie's direction. "There's work to be done first. The sooner we set up camp the sooner we get to rest."

Determined that he would not see her weaken, she grabbed for the bags only to fumble with one and have it land painfully against her chest. Her turquoise eyes shot fire, and she flung the cumbersome packs to the ground with a vengeance.

Sonny glanced pointedly at her, one brow cocked, ignoring her glowering expression. "Don't just stand there—get moving. I'm going to catch us some fish for our supper. You can start the fire." He pointed to a hollowed-out section along the rocky wall. "And while you're at it, put our bedrolls over there. It'll give us some shelter."

He paused as her eyes widened with indignant fury. "I suppose you'd like me to rub down your horse and make you some coffee while I'm standing around doing nothing!"

Sonny removed the cartridge bandoliers from his chest, dropping them to the ground. He grinned tolerantly, the deep grooves on either side of his mouth evident beneath the bearded stubble. "I'll take care of my own horse—but the coffee's not a bad idea."

Leaving Abbie muttering angrily, he unsaddled Viento. Talking soothingly, he praised the valiant steed as he removed the saddle with Spanish style pommel and briskly rubbed down the horse with the blanket; then he slipped off the silver-mounted bridle and wiped it clean. His actions were quick, precise, and as Abbie sliced him a hard-eyed glance she did a quick appraisal of the rigging he used on his mount.

She was aware that this particular saddle and bridle were popular with the Spanish; quite different from her split-ear headstall and Texas iron-horn saddle.

His rigging revealed he'd spent time in Mexico; perhaps even lived there. He'd never mentioned his home or background, but then, he never talked much about anything. All he ever did was order her around.

51

She stared at the saddle that was of hand-carved leather, the headstall, richly silver mounted, and then at the copper visage of Malone. His father may have been Texan, but his son did not follow in his footsteps. She would swear he was from Mexico, perhaps even a fugitive from the war there. Yet, Mestizos couldn't afford gear this grand.

A shocking thought suddenly occurred to her. Could this man somehow be a Criolla: a pure-blooded Spaniard born in Mexico? Could he have come from some sprawling hacienda, well accustomed to a life of grandeur?

But if he had money, why didn't he just hire someone to find out what had happened to his father? Why wasn't he fighting with his countrymen—protecting his family? Intently, she studied his dark, chiseled features: his high-bridged, aquiline nose, the sensual, well-formed lips, the silver shells on his vest; and she was momentarily stunned by her summation. But then just as quickly her gaze was drawn to the breed clothes, the tied-down guns, the hard gleam lurking in his eyes, and she declared the notion ludicrous.

Forcing all thoughts of him from her mind, she turned to the task at hand: finding firewood.

She searched the surrounding terrain until she'd managed to collect an armful of firewood. Trudging over to the area she'd cleared, she dropped it on the ground. Using a stick, she dug a small hole in the earth and placed brush and pieces of wood inside. She touched a match to it and studied the flickering flame.

Before long the smell of freshly brewed coffee wafted through the air to tantalize her nostrils. She was just about to pour herself a cup when she happened to glance up just as Sonny finished rubbing down Viento and was unbuttoning his shirt.

Abbie could not tear her eyes away as Malone casually shrugged out of his shirt and, as if he sensed her observations, he favored her with a keen, hard look that made her insides quiver with longing.

He was all sinewy muscle, bronzed perfection; and she found herself mesmerized by the play of those muscles beneath his taut skin.

Abruptly, he turned away to break off a branch from a nearby tree. Withdrawing his knife from a sheath on his belt, he began to whittle the end of the branch to a sharp point.

From beneath a sweep of dark sooty lashes her eyes flicked over the wide breadth of his shoulders, across his hair-roughened chest only to pause when they reached the tip of his belt buckle.

Dressed only in tight-fitting trousers with "breed" leggings, which were rawhide strips protecting his lower legs from thorny brush laced about his calves, he appeared, she thought, to be every bit a part of a savage land.

His voice startled her from her thoughts. "I'll be back with our dinner shortly, so keep that fire hot."

Another command. She glowered, saying nothing in return, watching him stride to the stream's edge.

She stared curiously as he poised motionless beside the water, slowly raising the crudely fashioned lance over his dark head to sling it powerfully into the water.

"Got one," he yelled back to her.

Abbie gasped in surprise when he withdrew the lance with a fish speared on the end. Leave it to Malone, she snorted.

He waved it at her. "Nothing to this sort of thing. Why don't you come give it a try!" The corded muscles on his chest rippled with each movement of his arms, and she tried not to recall how hard and secure they'd felt wrapped about her as they'd ridden together all those endless miles.

"Come on, Ab," he encouraged, his husky voice sending a heady warmth racing along her veins.

Desire coiled within her, aching so sweetly. "That's all right. You're doing just fine without me!" Furious with her unpredictable woman's body, she pivoted toward the fire, her nerves badly shaken.

"Stop it, Abbie," she ordered herself. "Just keep your wits

53

about you and you'll be fine. He is not the first man you've found attractive."

She recalled blond-haired Brett Whitman from a neighboring ranch who courted her before going off to fight for the Confederacy in the Civil War. She'd handled him very effectively. But this man is not Brett, her inner self warned. Brett was just a gangling boy compared to Malone.

The coffee boiled over on the campfire, breaking through her heated reverie. Not thinking, she grasped the handle of the pot and, with a gasp of pain, quickly set it down.

"Darn, darn." She blew on her stinging palms. "Serves you right for not paying attention," she chastised herself.

She glanced up just as Sonny approached her with several nice-sized fish.

He handed her the rawhide stringer he'd managed to fashion. "Looks like you get to cook them," he said with a teasing glint in his eyes.

"Now, how did I know you were going to say that?" she retorted dryly. Hands still smarting from her mishap, she gingerly accepted the fish and tossed him a towel and her precious bar of soap. "You first, and make it quick. I'd like a bath, myself."

He noticed the reddened tips of her fingers. "Something wrong with your hands, Ab?" he inquired knowingly.

She whirled on him. "No! Now go take your bath so I'll be able to have mine before dinner."

"I'm not opposed to sharing," he countered smoothly.

"No doubt in the same manner that we've shared your horse," she said cuttingly. "With you leering over my shoulder the entire time."

He laughed good-naturedly and left. By the time he'd finished bathing, she had the fish grilling nicely over the fire and was patiently awaiting his return. Night had fallen. Abbie faced the fire, suddenly sitting up straight, sensing his presence even before her ears picked up his light step. Her pulse leaped when he leaned over her shoulder and whispered near her ear.

"Your turn, Ab, and I'll be glad to help you with your back."

Abbie had begun to recognize that familiar sensual note in his voice, and she grabbed the bathing articles away from him. "You could get yourself in a lot of trouble coming up on me like that," she stated huffily. Rising to her feet, she moved away from him. "And I can manage my own back just fine!" Retrieving clean clothes from her pack, she fled hastily into the concealing shadows, his soft laughter ringing in her ears.

Upon reaching the stream, she waited almost expectantly for a moment before stripping down to her chemise and snug bloomers. She would have loved to bathe nude, however, she felt it in her best interest to remain partially clothed.

She managed to wash herself until she was refreshingly clean, her skin glowing pink from her scrubbing. After she'd soaped and rinsed her hair she dried off with the towel and put on clean clothes.

Abbie always brought along a change of silk undergarments, for she loved the sensual feel of it next to her skin. She had her personal items made in San Antonio. It was one of the few luxuries that she allowed herself.

Assuming he was out scouting the canyon, she withdrew a tortoiseshell comb from her pack and sat cross-legged before the fire. Leisurely she began to work the comb through her tangled hair.

Sonny prowled the area, checking every obscure place that could harbor an intruder. When he was satisfied that there were no lurking predators, he strolled unhurriedly back to camp.

She was there before the fire, the sight of her taking his breath away. Her thick tresses tumbled in lustrous waves about her shoulders, the flickering light from the flames bringing out the reddish-gold highlights he'd admired so often as they'd ridden together beneath the burning Texas sun.

One of his mother's favorite phrases suddenly rang true. "A woman's crowning glory is her hair," he murmured.

He'd always thought his mother had lovely hair. But this infuriating woman had the most beautiful hair he'd ever seen. He tried to calm his racing thoughts as he walked into the lighted circle of the campfire. He had no doubt that this was going to be the longest night of his life. "Abbie," he called huskily.

Abbie glanced up at him, her color high, her turquoise eyes wide and bright. She glimpsed a bit of his soul within that silver gaze, and the revelation sent a delicious shiver along her spine.

He handed her his bundled neckerchief. "Here," he said, "I thought you might like these."

She was surprised to find it filled with wild berries. She smiled at him, confused, yet appreciative of his kind gesture. "They look delicious. We can have them with the meal," she said softly, wondering if perhaps she'd misjudged him after all. His next words quickly dispelled any further notions she might have had.

"Listen, Ab," he said offhandedly. "After dinner, while you're not doing anything, I'd like for you to wash up some of the dirty laundry. I'm down to my last clean shirt."

Abbie almost threw the berries back in his face! "Oh, you would, would you," she hissed in his startled face.

"Yeah, I would," he shot back defensively, surprised by her hostile reply. "After all, isn't it a woman's place to do those kind of things? Or am I supposed to take care of everything, as well as protect you and put food in your belly!"

"I'm sick to death of hearing you dictate what my place in life is supposed to be. Nobody asked you to do anything for me, Malone!" she cried in exasperation. "You took all that upon yourself, remember!" She gave him a measured look. "So, do your own damned laundry and from now on, I'll find my own food to eat!"

They faced each other like two sparring partners ready to

slug it out. Sonny was the first to turn away. Tight-lipped, he helped himself to the cooked food, dishing out only one plateful.

Abbie bit back a stinging retort and silently served herself.

Not surprisingly, dinner was a quiet affair, and just as soon as the meal was finished, Abbie sullenly gathered up her soiled clothing and dirty dishes and started toward the stream.

His hunger appeased, Sonny leaned back on one elbow and yawned contentedly. "Couldn't have done better myself," he said, grinning when he caught the slight stiffening of her back.

"Don't get too used to it," she snapped. "Just remember, I don't intend to cook for you again."

Sonny gritted his teeth in frustration. God, how he would love to turn her over his knee and whack her good a time or two! She was a selfish, self-centered brat. He sighed. But it was his fault, not hers, that he found himself stuck with her. The words were out before he realized. "Ab, do you need any help?"

There was no hint of sarcasm in his tone, and she turned to search his gaze, then nodded slowly. He smiled, gathered up his laundry and dishes to join her.

His sincere gesture declared a truce, at least for the remainder of the evening. After settling before the campfire, they conversed quietly while watching the blood-red moon rise full and hauntingly beautiful over the canyon.

"A Comanche moon," Sonny commented, pouring himself some coffee. "They'll be out raiding the countryside. That's why I thought it best to tuck in here for the night. No sense looking for trouble." He blew on the steaming contents of his cup and observed the beautiful woman at his side through narrowed eyes.

"You can't live in Texas and not know a moment of fear each time you see the moon rise full and red."

"The Comanche do have another theory about that moon,

57

you know?" he said huskily. "I like it. They call it a night to 'make something' together." There was a strained silence. Abbie cleared her throat.

"Well, we've been doing that all right," she replied wryly. "We've been making life one living hell, together."

Sonny could not help laughing good-naturedly at the truthfulness of that statement. "No argument there, Miss Caldwell. We have at that."

"You really enjoyed the time you were one of them, didn't you?" she inquired.

"They treated me well," he replied.

"And I think you respect them in many ways for standing up to the white man."

"I respect anyone who fights for what they believe in." His somber face was transformed by a wide, meaningful smile. "Even little wildcats in long-tailed shirts."

Abbie laughed delightedly. Sonny became immediately entranced by the melodious sound. This was the first time they'd shared something honest and pleasant together. He felt powerless to break the spell of the moment. She was a lovely woman, and he was damned tired of fighting his desire for her.

Abbie watched the conflicting emotions on his face. The amused expression in his eyes had changed, becoming heated and sultry. He was watching her with that hard, piercing way of his that made her wonder what it would be like to make love with him.

His fingers gently pried the cup from her clenched fingers, lingering over hers, causing the breath to catch in her throat.

"No," she breathed as his head dipped forward.

"Yes," he whispered, just before he lowered his lips to the throbbing hollow of her throat. Desiring the womanly taste of her, he tongued the area lightly. "I've been wanting to do that forever, it seems."

Abbie did not possess the inner strength to resist the teasing, circular motions against that pulse point that sent a

58

wild yearning racing through her. It started as a burning ache deep within her, quickly spreading in a blaze of desire as his hands found their way to the base of her spine, urging her against him.

He tasted the warm saltiness of her skin, inhaled the clean, soapy scent that clung to her, and gently caressed every part of her slender back. Before she could protest, his hands moved up under her shirt, hesitating briefly at the lace hem of her camisole. He was somewhat surprised at the silk that lay beneath the severe clothing. It pleased him, was easy to the touch.

The contact of his long fingers on her bare flesh was electrifying to Abbie as he stroked her quivering stomach. His open lips wooed her slowly, working their way up the slender column of her neck to the shell of one tiny ear. He tantalized the sensitive area just behind her lobe with agonizing slowness. His hard length pressed demandingly against her slim form, lowering her back onto the bedroll. Abbie's body yielded even as her mind rebelled. With a groan of need his body slid up and over her, his warm mouth capturing hers, seeking hungrily what he knew she had within her to give.

Abbie hesitated only momentarily, then parted her lips, surrendering the soft inner recesses of her mouth. The tip of her tongue unhesitantly met his, caressing, exploring, tasting of the heady passion that she found there.

Her boldness increased his desire. He had to touch her breasts, caress the small, hard nipples pressed against his chest, feel them naked against his bare skin. He pushed the ends of the long-tailed shirt and camisole upward, slipping his hands beneath the material. They moved over the length of her, traced the fine bones of her rib cage, tantalized and cupped the fullness of her breasts.

Abbie moaned softly. The sound excited him further, and he explored the gently curved mounds with lean, sure fingers, caressing them, massaging them, and when she pushed upward, he gently squeezed the throbbing buds until the hot ache of desire threatened to overwhelm him. Still, he knew she was yet untouched, and if he didn't go slowly he would frighten her away.

Certain that she was a virgin, he resolved to leave her untouched. He'd intruded on her life enough, and soon they were destined to go their separate ways, for they were from worlds apart.

However, there were ways of sampling, without despoiling, and as he tore open his shirt and pulled her tightly against him, he decided he would show her just a few.

Abbie gasped as his hair-roughened chest made contact with her sensitive nipples, but she didn't pull away. Instead, she slid her arms around his neck and threaded her fingers in his thick hair. Her hips moved against him. She felt his desire, hot and hard, return her thrust and the world spun away. She wanted all of him, needed all of him. Every nerve in Abbie's body screamed for release. Nothing with the gangling Brett Whitman had prepared her for this. She was afire, consumed by the flame of desire that this man had ignited. Her legs opened of their own volition, permitting his hips to nestle against that warm place he longed to possess. His hips tantalized and promised as he taught her the motion.

She boldly followed with an enthusiasm that made his body long for complete possession of her.

He wanted so to strip her of her clothes and bury himself deep within her. His mouth seared its way to her nipples, suckling each, nipping gently. She sighed from the unfamiliar onslaught on her senses, barely hearing him whisper.

"You can let yourself go, Ab. Just follow my lead and let yourself soar." She peered deeply into his eyes. His gaze, so clouded with desire, held no trace of mockery.

"I don't know what it is I'm seeking," she stammered.

His fingers smoothed the wayward strands of damp hair from her face. "Let me show you. I promise I won't hurt you in any way. I'll not take anything from you, baby. I'll give you exquisite pleasure."

She wanted what he so tantalizingly offered, but she was bewildered and unsure. Her body's quick surrender to this man, little more than a stranger, disturbed her. This was an emotion without control, a complete loss of will. Abbie Lee Caldwell always kept her life and her feelings under strict control. She oversaw the running of the Caldwell empire. Her sense of propriety was a source of pride with her. Until now—until him. She shivered with passion and uncertainty, but she nodded.

"Abbie," he murmured huskily, his mouth closing over hers.

His lips drugged her sense of reason, and when they moved downward along the slender column of her throat, she felt her mouth go dry and her stiff propriety melt away in the security of his embrace.

Gently, his hips pinned hers beneath him. She felt the hardness of him between her legs and urged him closer with her movements.

His kiss probed deeper, hungrier, and she surrendered her remaining will into his keeping. She could feel his throbbing maleness upon her most sensitive place. His hips continued their circular motion, and between her legs the smooth silk moved and clung, and desire raged out of control. Abbie writhed against him, straining, seeking a release from this burning heat in her loins.

"Let yourself enjoy, sweet Abbie," he murmured softly. "It can feel so good—so incredibly good."

The sound of his deep voice excited her unbearably. "It feels wonderful," she heard herself saying.

His lips moved downward, placed moist kisses upon her bare stomach as his fingers effortlessly undid her trousers, tugged them down to her knees. She started, her eyes flying open as he placed his warm lips upon the vee of wispy silk protecting her womanly charms. He tongued the area, felt the dainty bud throb beneath his lips. He nipped gently,

61

insistently, sending her senses reeling.

She was drowning in a sea of desire, drifting aimlessly on waves of ecstasy. Somehow, she knew she must halt his shocking actions. Forcing reason and will to return, she gasped. "No—Sonny—please stop." She attempted to twist away from him as she struggled to pull her trousers back together.

He glanced up at her stunned face and sighed. "All right, Ab, perhaps it's too soon for that." He pulled her back into his arms, molded his long frame over hers, kissed away her further protests, and without removing a single piece of her clothing he brought her slowly to the edge and over with just the sensual movement of his hips.

Abbie was swept into a whirlwind of pleasure, crying out his name when she reached the very peak. It was so sweet, so good, that she wanted to stay in the glorious limbo forever. With a groan, she plummeted back to reality.

She opened her eyes to see him watching her closely. She felt her face flush in humiliation. She didn't realize how much he'd given of himself, how carefully he'd guarded her purity. He had shared feelings with this woman that left him totally stunned.

Cold, hard reality returned, and Abbie could not face it honestly.

God! she cried inwardly. Why did I let him take advantage of me like that? Scrambling from beneath him, she pulled her shirt down, further mortified by the realization that he hadn't removed even one article of her clothing! He'd taken control of her swiftly and effectively, and she was numbed by it. When he reached out to draw her near, she cried out, "No—no more!"

The sense of wonderment left him. His face was once again a cold, hard mask. He sat up with a smothered curse, his breathing heavy and labored. He knew she was frightened by what she'd just experienced. But at the moment, he was encountering feelings that were confusing to him also. He wasn't familiar with this kind of emotion, and he wasn't sure what he was supposed to do or say.

He'd allowed her to spin her silken web completely around him, until he could think of little else but her. But never again! Snorting in disgust, he reached inside his shirt, withdrawing a cigar. Lighting it and inhaling deeply, he let the pungent taste of the tobacco wipe out the lingering trace of her in his mouth. But it was not that easy with the visions of her imprinted in his mind.

He realized the sooner he was away from her the better off he would be. He heard the thoughts inside his head and groaned. You're falling for her, Malone. You're falling hard and fast and sure.

Abbie lay there trying to calm her pounding heart and quell her runaway emotions. She viewed him through downcast lashes moistened by unshed tears. She was certain by the look of disgust on his face that he surely must despise her now. She did not understand why she had lost control. She considered herself a woman of principles, of iron control. The idea that someone had managed to shatter that safe illusion now threw her into a panic. At the moment, she couldn't think of anyone but herself and how he had deliberately manipulated her.

Sonny watched her as he leaned back on one elbow, smoking his cigar. Her staunch, erect carriage returned, her chin once again thrust forward in haughty repose. Bitterly, he congratulated himself for the fool. She was selfish, self-centered and above anything else, she was using him because she knew she needed him to get out of this alive. With a snort of disgust, he tossed the cigar aside and rose to his feet. Then, without so much as another glance in her direction, he stalked to the other side of the campfire. Spreading out his bedroll, he lay down and turned his back to her.

Abbie Lee stared after him in a dazed stupor. Still bewildered, she stretched out on her own bedroll.

But sleep did not come easy for either one. They were both

completely confused by emotions that neither wished to confront.

At last they slept. But it was a troubled slumber, and in the early morning, when they rose simultaneously and stared across the embers of the fire at each other, their eyes were wary, their emotions carefully guarded. Throughout the day it remained the same. They continued onward, but this time Sonny walked more than he rode but, when they did ride together, he made certain a bedroll was wedged firmly between them.

Chapter Four

For two days Sonny had scouted the crest of each swell before allowing Abbie to ride beyond. Because of the rougher country and the slower pace they were once again riding double. They rode in silence along a high, flat butte through a mist of low scudding clouds, prompting Abbie to feel that she could reach and touch them.

Sonny stopped the horse and slung the rifle over his shoulder. "Stay here until you see my signal." He dismounted and began walking toward the edge of the bluff.

She couldn't resist snapping, "You are sorely straining my patience, Malone. I'm sick to death of all of this!" As she observed his narrow-eyed glare, her chin jutted upward. "When are you going to let me go, or am I to suffer longer because of what happened between us in the canyon?"

He faced her, standing aloofly distant, resting the long barrel of his rifle casually on his shoulder. "You mean because of what didn't happen, don't you?" he drawled sarcastically.

Abbie clenched her fists. She was bone tired and fed up with his humiliating treatment. "You bastard," she hissed. "I should tell you to go to hell and find my own way. And if I really wanted to, I probably could." Her rage strangled any reason and, quickly dismounting, she strode determinedly toward the flat, open terrain to the west.

"Hey—little wildcat!" he called after her. "Don't even consider such a loco stunt!"

Turquoise eyes flaring with hostility she spun around challengingly, her hand resting confidently upon the butt of her six-gun. She knew she was a lightning draw; her pa had made certain of it. "Don't patronize me, Sonny. I'm not in the mood!"

Sonny noted her look, her stance, and raised a mocking brow, a gesture Abbie was learning to despise. "You've done some foolish things but that would be the stupidest by far," he warned softly. He assessed her cool, unruffled composure and found himself tensely expectant. The eyes were always a dead giveaway, and hers were now narrowed dangerously.

Abbie advanced a few, taunting steps toward him. "Always giving advice, aren't you?" She took a deep breath. "Well I'm sick of it—and you. Let's have it out right here, *caballero*. Whoever walks away has it all. The horse, gear— and freedom." She crouched low, deadly purpose in her stance.

Sonny didn't so much as blink an eye as devilish lights lit up their silvery depths. "I really don't think this is the time or place to shoot it out with you, Ab, although, believe me, at the moment I'm almost fed up enough to do so."

"I can't think of a better time or place," she ground out angrily. "Unless you're just afraid of losing the draw to a woman."

He grinned unconcerned. "Not exactly, sweetheart, but that smoke we've been seeing in the sky for the last few miles are Indian signals. They'd just love to hear the sound of our guns. It would alert them to our exact location." He shrugged. "And, if by slim chance, I'm lying wounded— what then?"

He saw her mentally considering his words and breathed a relieved sigh when she turned away to perch on a flat rock and glare hatefully.

66

"There will be a time yet, Malone. You can count on it!"

His mouth curved into a sardonic smile. "Very good, Ab. For once you thought of the consequences before reacting. Lesson number one, complete. Now, for lesson number two. Remember, from now on I'm calling the shots, all of them. And if you don't move quick like a fox into the shelter of those pines over yonder, I swear by all that's holy, I'll drag you there myself and tie you to a damned tree."

Abbie was visibly stung but wasted not one second in scrambling down the boulder-strewn hill into the covering of pines. She stood and leaned one shoulder against a tree trunk where she could watch his every move.

Sonny climbed to the top of the jutting cliff, stood atop a high boulder, eyes scanning the pinkish-gray horizon. He grunted to himself upon seeing the faint wisp of spiraling smoke in the distant rock-strewn hills. Indian signs. They had been everywhere for miles. These smoke signals were Apache. It appeared there was something about to take place; something of great importance. He squinted his eyes against the glaring sun. From what he could gather those signals didn't have anything to do with him or with Abbie, but still, he wasn't taking any chances. They were moving on.

He trotted down the rocky incline toward Abbie. "They're still out there. There's smoke in the distance."

"Comanche?" she queried.

"No, Apache," he replied solemnly.

Abbie stood motionless. "Is that supposed to scare me?"

He considered his next words carefully. Perhaps it would do well to keep her somewhat fearful. She was too damned cocky for her own good, and the last thing he wanted to do was crease that creamy skin of hers with a bullet just because she forced him into a draw. That, and fight off a war party of screaming Apache. "I was hoping to make you see how important it is for us to stick together."

A stiff breeze blew steadily at her back, but it was not the wind that made her shiver. "Do you think they know we're out here?"

Her mercurial moods were so unpredictable that Sonny could only guess at what was going through her head. "Yes, they know." He watched her, caught the slight trembling of her hands. His searching gaze held hers. "I don't think we're in any immediate danger, but that could change in the blink of an eye." He inclined his head toward the gun strapped to her hip. "I know you can use that gun, and I have no doubt how good you are with it. But try hard to exercise good judgement. Shoot only if we should come under attack and don't miss when you do." His eyes shifted to the terrain below them. "Let's mount up. I noticed a lot of dust stirred up in the distance. I think it's worth investigating."

"Perhaps it's a wagon train?" she said feeling hopeful.

"You'll be free to join them if it is," he replied solemnly. Pivoting sharply, he strode to the pinto, picked up the reins and mounted up. Looking over at Abbie, he watched her silently trying to absorb his statement offering her her freedom. "Isn't that what you've been waiting to hear, Ab?"

There was silence, and then she walked over to him. His hand reached out to her. She allowed him to grasp her fingers and draw her upward into his arms.

"Well—isn't it?" he persisted.

She met his hard stare. "Yes," she replied finally and felt the muscles tighten in his arm that now rested around her waist. He held her loosely, not possessively as before, but still her heart thumped continually at his nearness. God, she was weary of fighting her emotions! She swept her long hair up beneath her stetson and immediately felt his warm breath stir the fine wispy tendrils of hair on her neck. It filled her with a burning need to feel his lips there as they'd been the other night. Without masking her feelings, Abbie turned her head to look up at him. "Considering last night, it's time for us to part."

"I don't see where the serious problem is, Abbie," he said offhandedly. "You've just got yourself so worked up over these puritan standards of yours that you're making more of it than it is."

"All women are playthings to you, Sonny. You wouldn't know an honest relationship if it bit you."

"Got me all figured out, don't you?"

"Men like you aren't hard to read," she snapped. "And you're not going to change any of my beliefs—not one."

"Believe me, honey, I have no intention of trying to change you," he said with a sneer. "There are too many women around who are soft, all female. Not tough as boot leather and cantankerous as a mule."

"You mean weak and submissive—whores," she said snarling. "For that's the only kind that would put up with you; the ones you pay with cold cash!"

"At least they know how to take care of a man, sweetheart," he replied curtly, kneeing Viento forward.

Abbie found herself recalling their encounter in the canyon and felt her face flame. She had been clumsy and inept, but what had he expected? She was all confused inside. She knew she hated him. That was fact. But yet, why did she constantly desire him? Why? She blinked back salty tears, recognizing one area of certain defeat. The feel of him, the scent of him, the overpowering allure of him was in her blood. She would never be completely free of him, never. He was still a rough, unpredictable stranger in so many ways. All save one. Physically. She knew every hard, muscled contour of his body. She wished she was able to read the thoughts behind that stormy gaze he fixed upon her of late. But she couldn't. As they drew near the swirling clouds of dust, the sound of jangling harness and lumbering wagons drifted to them on the breeze.

"It's wagons, all right, just ahead a ways," Sonny announced.

"Look," she said, forgetting her anger temporarily and pointing one finger. "Do you see riders coming this way?"

"Yeah, I do." He saw two Union outriders moving toward

them ahead of a small wagon train, their rifles withdrawn from their scabbards. The canvas-topped wagons moved at a snail's pace, a team of six horses straining in their harnesses against the heavy loads.

The soldiers approached cautiously, well aware of the *bandidos* and renegade Indians who were known to roam these passages and windswept hills.

As they drew nearer Sonny raised his hand in the air and waved in greeting. He saw that one was a Union soldier. The other, an Apache scout, was dressed in army blues, a colorful headband tied about his head to keep his flowing black hair from his eyes.

After the soldiers had reined in beside the pinto, Sonny briefly explained Abbie's predicament and how she wished to return to their fort and send a message to the military base in San Antonio to notify her family of her whereabouts. The young corporal agreed to escort them back to meet their commanding officer.

They were introduced to Commander George Wilkes who told them he was on his way to a parley with the Apache who'd been relentlessly raiding ranches and forts in the area.

"I'm rather new out here," he admitted as they sat relaxing around a campfire while his soldiers made camp with the frugal and unchanging order of army housekeeping. "However I'm hoping we can come to some sort of a compromise with the savages. I know how they love trinkets. I've brought gifts in exchange for a list of things I have here to be recovered." He patted his shirt front.

"So that explains the smoke signals," Sonny exclaimed. "And you honestly believe the Apache are going to accept your offering and return all of the livestock and children they've stolen?"

"They did agree to this parley, Mr. Malone," the major retorted coolly. "And I have an Apache interpreter to converse with their spokesman, so I don't see any reason why things shouldn't go quite well. I have even drawn up a pledge of peace for the old boy to put his X on."

"I'm afraid their chief is not going to tell them to stop raiding in this area just because you have him scratch a mark on some piece of paper he doesn't even understand."

Commander Wilkes puffed up indignantly. "I believe we can accomplish some semblance of peace here. It's been done before on several occasions."

Sonny snorted, pushing his black stetson back on his head, a wavy lock of ash-brown hair falling forward over his upraised brow. "That's the most astounding thing I've ever heard. Those Apache will sit and talk rings around you, Commander. They'll take your trinkets, sign your paper and come back later for your scalp." He rose to his feet. "I'll just stick around until your little parley is concluded. I want to make certain the lady rides off with the right party."

Commander Wilke's face flushed angrily, but his voice remained carefully controlled. "I'll have my men place a tent at the lady's disposal." He turned his back pointedly on Sonny and addressed Abbie. "I would be honored if you would share dinner with me this evening, Miss Caldwell." He took her hand in his gloved one. "A lovely lady like yourself should only dine with gentlemen."

Abbie smiled gratefully. "I would be delighted to have dinner with a gentleman, Commander," she replied sweetly. "Now, if you will excuse me, I should like to freshen up first. And thank you for your kindness."

The corporal was immediately summoned and led the way to Abbie's private quarters. He even carried her saddle packs for her. What a nice change that was as opposed to having them hurled at her. Politely thanking the soldier, she entered the tent, pulling the flap down behind her. Some thoughtful recruit had placed a pitcher of water and a bowl on a nightstand for her. She joyfully anticipated a refreshing sponge bath as she began to remove her clothes.

Supper later was a casual meal of fried jackrabbit, greens, and coffee. While the fare was simple, Abbie found the commander a stimulating conversationalist. He appeared to have sound ideas on handling the explosive Indian issues.

Sonny, whom the major had reluctantly invited, however, thought him a fool, and as soon as the meal was over, he excused himself to join the circle of soldiers playing poker around the campfire.

All through the meal he'd ignored Abbie, and even now walked away without so much as a backward glance.

Her bright turquoise eyes flashing with resentment, Abbie amazingly found herself flirting outrageously with some of the young recruits who'd eagerly gathered around. She didn't realize her fresh beauty, viewed by men who hadn't seen a woman for weeks, was like an intoxicant upon their senses. Night had fallen, the soft flickering glow from the lighted lamps casting wavering beams of gold across her honey-bronze complexion as she smiled charmingly at her attendants.

Gentle, teasing laughter drifted across the sultry breezes to tantalize the somber-faced man sitting before the campfire drinking bourbon. The card game had broken up, the soldiers deciding to turn in early in preparation for the long day ahead. Sonny's long fingers caressed the bottle of bourbon as his thoughts brooded. Damn the woman! What was she thinking of, encouraging those hot-blooded young bucks with coy smiles and promising words. If she wasn't careful she was going to find one of them showing up in her tent later tonight. Then, perhaps that's what she wanted, he mused. Light laughter brought him to his feet, his eyes glaring heatedly in her direction.

Abbie happened to glance over at Sonny and caught the hard glint of anger in the gaze directed at her.

Cursing himself for suddenly remembering the way she felt curled in the closeness of his arms, he took a long pull from the bottle clenched tightly in his fist. "To hell with you, Abbie Caldwell. Let them all have you for all I care. It would serve you right!" he growled.

But even as he said the words his insides tightened at the thought of anyone else possessing her. Stalking toward the darkened riverbank, he wondered why he hadn't taken her when he'd had the opportunity? He sneered, recalling those seemingly innocent blue eyes of hers. By her performance tonight, it was clear she knew how to handle the male species. By the looks of it, it appeared she didn't intend to sleep alone tonight.

Abbie had quickly grown weary of the cluster of fawning young men, and soon after Sonny had disappeared into the night, she'd pleaded exhaustion and retired to her tent.

Now as she lay upon the narrow cot staring up at the play of moonbeams on the tent, she tried to dispel the visions that danced upon her mind's eye for they made her weak with wanting.

Sonny's sun-bronzed body, his savage, rugged handsomeness, the feel of his body pressed intimately to hers.

"Oooh, God, I hate him," she moaned, flopping over on her stomach and pulling the blanket over her head. She didn't know how long she lay like that, dozing fitfully to be awakened by the lone cry of a wolf penetrating her misty dreams. The primitive, mournful sound came once again and suddenly Abbie turned over expectantly. Somehow, she knew he was out there—and that he would come to her. An expectant thrill raced through her body as she lay in the hushed darkness and heard the soft sound of those unmistakable footsteps pause outside her tent.

A refreshing late-night breeze stirred the wealth of chestnut hair about her flushed face as the tent flap parted and a shadowy figure stepped inside.

Her eyes were like twin beacons of blue fire as they fixed upon that familiar broad-shouldered form. "Who's there?" she posed breathlessly, recognizing that graceful, catlike stalk even as she posed the question.

73

"Who were you expecting, Ab?" he returned almost cynically. He was standing but a handsbreadth away, his gray wolf's eyes shimmering with sensuality and purpose.

"Not you, Sonny," she fibbed. "I assumed you'd be sleeping soundly by now, thoughts of me far from your head."

His six-foot-four frame loomed over her, one hand reaching forward to gently caress a silken cheek. "Knights never sleep, Ab. I thought you knew that. They're too busy watching over milady." His eyes followed every delicate line of her face, at last settling upon her slightly parted lips. He sat down next to her on the cot.

For a moment Abbie stared incredulously up at him, her pulse racing madly at his nearness and the message she read in the depths of his heated gaze. "What brings you here?"

His compelling hard stare held her transfixed. "I think you know," he murmured just before his lips lowered to hers in a kiss that took her breath away.

A low moan escaped her as he pulled her into his arms and cradled her against his chest. The lingering taste of bourbon was warm upon his tongue, and Abbie found herself wondering briefly if that was what prompted him to seek her out. But even as her mind pondered the thought, her body swept her onward toward a point where she desired no answer. She felt the blanket slip downward, exposing her slim body to his persuasive touch. His mouth moved from her lips to tease the satiny-soft skin along her neck.

"You want me just as much as I want you don't you, Ab?" he breathed against her throat.

She nodded slowly. "Yes."

He raised his head slightly, looked deeply into the wide blue of her eyes that now glistened with unshed tears. She almost looked frightened. "The other night, what happened in the canyon. It was good for you, wasn't it?"

"Yes," she whispered.

"You weren't really afraid then, were you?" he queried

gently, one hand moving to her quivering breast, his palm caressing the hardened nipple beneath it.

Her breathing grew labored, desire kindling to a fever pitch. "Not after I found out how wonderful it was, but I know tonight you want much more."

"Yes, I do," came his low voice as he buried his face in her cloud of rose-scented hair.

She found her fingers undoing the pearl buttons on his shirt, pulling it open so that the feel of those hard muscles was pressed against her aching breasts.

"I want all of you tonight, silken beauty," he said almost fiercely as he molded his hard body over hers. His arms tightened powerfully around her, viselike, allowing no resistance. His mouth this time when it claimed hers was almost brutal, almost frightening. He was not like the same man. She froze.

"Please," she gasped, twisting her mouth away from his. "Not like this."

His fingers caught her small chin in a firm grip as his eyes searched the depth of her soul. "Like what then, Abbie?" he cajoled, even as his hands continued to caress her full breasts. "Isn't this what you wanted when you were holding court out there earlier?" His eyes turned heated. "Weren't you looking for some stud to service you exactly like this?" He laughed harshly. "Oh, excuse me. You want a gentleman, right?"

"You're drunk," she gasped. "You don't mean what you're saying, you can't honestly believe that!"

His voice was low and husky. "I didn't, until I witnessed your little display." He sneered. "Perhaps you don't want me—just yet—because you've already had what you were seeking. Was your gentleman already here earlier?"

Tears welled in her eyes at his callous statement. She trembled with the turbulent emotions at war within her. One part of her wanted to scratch his eyes out, while the other longed to have him make love to her and prove to him there

75

was no one else that made her feel this way. But he had treated her too horridly for her to succumb to her innermost desires. Instead, Abbie forced icy resolve to take control and lashed out at him with one clenched fist across his face.

He was stunned by her stinging wallop, surprise stripping the mask of cool disdain from his features. Abbie froze at his grunt of pain. His eyes traveled down the length of her body, openly admiring everything he saw.

Her glorious hair lay in wild disarray about her shoulders, and her cheeks were flushed pink from suppressed emotion. A tear trickled from the corner of her eye. It was a bitter tear.

"I'll always hate you if you do this thing," she said with quiet fury.

Sonny felt his senses clear. He reached forward to gently brush the tear away; drew her close to rub his jaw against her temple. "Damnit, Abbie, you have a way of making me crazy," he snarled. "You're like a fire in my blood that's threatening to destroy me." He bent his dark head to kiss her gently. "I want you more than any woman I've ever known."

"Is that all that it is for you, Sonny? Just a desire to possess me?"

He didn't know what he could say. At that moment he hated himself for what he wanted to do and for not being able to say what it was she wanted to hear, so he let silence answer for him.

She didn't pull away, and he kissed her once more, breathing into her mouth. "There is much I want to say. But right now all I want to do is love you."

Abbie knew if she let him touch her intimately again that she would never be free of him. "I can't—I can't," she whispered brokenly. "Not when I know that you'll leave me come morning—just another conquest." She pulled out of his arms. "Go, get out of here. And forget we ever met—as I intend to."

Insolently, those silver-gray eyes roamed over her before

shoving her roughly aside while silently he cursed himself for the fool. Damnit! Why had he sought her out? And why did she fight him when he knew her body longed for his touch? He experienced a fleeting stab of regret as he stood and looked down at the pained expression on her face. Uneasy with the emotions churning inside him, he snarled harshly. "Always happy to accommodate a lady, Miss Caldwell. But if you should find you've changed your mind, my bedroll's just over there—by the rest of your admirers."

Abbie gasped in shock. Sonny spun around and stalked from the tent.

Drained of all emotion, Abbie lay woodenly staring into the darkness. Sonny had come streaking into her life like a bolt of lightning, blazing a burning path across her heart and turning her very existence upside down. And now he was leaving it in the same manner. And she was through deluding herself about him. He was a fever in her blood, a fire in her soul. The faster they parted company the better off she would be.

Abbie stretched as the morning sun brightened the confines of the tent. For just a moment, she thought she'd dreamed the events still fresh in her mind. But then his last words returned to taunt her, and she realized that it had not been a dream; it had happened. Rising and hurriedly dressing, she pushed back the tent flap and saw everyone moving about, making ready to leave. She couldn't resist calling to a soldier who was passing by her tent.

"Mr. Malone, is he still here?"

"No, ma'am," the soldier replied, stopping to explain further. "The parley at daybreak went exactly as planned. He left right after. Anything you need, ma'am, I'd be happy to get it for you."

"No—I'm fine, thank you," she mumbled, unprepared for the feeling of desolation that washed over her. He was gone. Out of her life for good. She turned to reenter the tent and begin gathering up her belongings.

By the time the small wagon train rolled onward toward Camp Lancaster on the Pecos River, Abbie had sought relief by banishing all thoughts of Sonny from her mind. She refused to think of him by using the old firm resolve she prided herself upon.

She was settled upon the high seat of the covered wagon beside the company's big sergeant, a kindly red-haired giant who told her to call him Sergeant Phil. She liked him at once. Throughout the stifling day the detail of two dozen men and a few wagons followed an almost dry tributary of the Pecos River that wound like a snake across the Indian-infested plains.

Occasionally, someone's eyes would scan the wild brush for any signs of suspicious movement. The scouts kept ahead in the distance, searching the area thoroughly before having the wagon train move onward.

Abbie silently watched the sergeant work the reins with effortless ease. The persistent jangling of the harness and the clomping hooves of the horses made conversation a bit difficult, but they talked nonetheless about everyday things to help break the monotony.

Quite unexpectedly, Abbie had turned to say something to the sergeant and noticed him cock his head, his ears attempting to pick up some slight sound. "Is there anything the matter?" she asked.

He pushed hesitantly. "I don't think so."

But even as he said the words, she saw him glance apprehensively toward the outer rim of the riverbed.

Abbie, following the direction of his gaze, tried vainly to see over the edge of the sloped bank. The fine hair on the back of her neck stood on end as she noticed the other soldiers draw their rifles. There was something out there!

"Sergeant, I think—" The words died in her throat as she saw the first hideously painted Apache appear over the rocky bank. Suddenly, the entire rim along the dry bed was filled with grossly painted savages. A barrage of arrows whistled downward through the air. Abbie quickly drew her gun and took aim at the leering savages.

Gunfire exploded around them as well as the screams of dying men. Abbie wasted no shots but made certain she aimed carefully. The feel and smell of death was everywhere, and it terrified her.

"Get ready to jump when I say so, young lady!" the sergeant yelled over the noise around them. "It's the only way I can think to save you!" He directed the galloping team toward a narrow path that led up onto the bank.

War cries echoed behind the lunging team. Abbie wasn't aware that the sergeant had guided the horses next to some thick, scraggly brush. Her head jerked up as he hollered. "Jump—now!"

"I can't leave you!" she cried.

"Don't argue! And don't come out, no matter what!"

She felt his big hand in the small of her spine as he pushed her forward through the air. Arms and legs flailing, she landed with a heavy thud in the brush, her head hitting the hard ground. She lay there barely conscious, hardly aware of the continued massacre around her.

The Apaches charged by her hiding place without notice. They hadn't seen her jump into the underbrush and continued onward after the sergeant. He was felled by an arrow straight to his heart.

Abbie didn't remember when she first sat up to part the bushes, her eyes searching the sandy area. She observed the lifeless forms of the men lying scattered and broken; the awful sight of their scalped, mutilated bodies, the stench of blood that hung heavy in the air, making her stomach heave its contents. Her breath came in great, heaving gasps as she attempted to gather her wits about her. The ambush had been swift and brutal; the aftermath savage and mind-numbing. She lay down, pressing her face against her folded palms and wept.

When at last Abbie found the strength to move it was

dusk. There were no more screams of death. Only the sounds of living things pervaded the scene of the massacre. Her ears heard the familiar whistle of the whippoorwill, the buzzing song of the crickets, and the plaintive howl of a coyote, and it soothed her, kept her sane. Slowly, cautiously, she parted the brush and peered out. The Apaches had not returned, so she crawled from her hiding place and stood up on wobbly legs. Scanning the outer ridges of the draw, she breathed a tremendous sigh when she observed no movement. The savages were gone! She was alive!

Spying her gun lying some yards away, she stumbled numbly over to pick it up, then staggered toward a lone horse grazing contentedly on the wild grass growing inter-mittently along the creek bed.

"Easy, boy," she crooned as she gathered the trailing reins in one hand. With an effort, she pulled her bruised body into the saddle. Nudging the animal with her knees she directed him toward a towering wall of cliffs which appeared to rise from the prairie beyond the horizon. She knew what lay atop that escarpment and stretched for hundreds of miles across the divide. No man's land; the place where the Comanche reigned supreme.

Abbie was dimly aware that Devil's Bend lay very near those cliffs along the Pecos River. She had nowhere else to go. It was either Devil's Bend or the savages. Without hesi-tating she headed toward the notorious town.

Bitter gall rose in her throat when she thought of who she might meet there. "You're the reason I find myself in this awful situation, Malone. And I'll make you pay yet. I swear I will," she vowed.

Sonny Malone had just finished his supper and was relaxing next to a campfire, cup of coffee in hand. He was alone, waiting, listening for a certain distinct sound. A man was going to seek him out tonight. He found himself anxious for the confrontation.

Earlier that day, after making certain the parley had gone well and that Abbie was safely in the care of Commander Wilkes, Sonny had ridden hard and fast to put distance between himself and the blue-eyed temptress.

A woman had never affected him in this manner before. Abbie Caldwell had shaken his self-assurance, made him feel things he didn't want to feel, refused to acknowledge. At least a dozen times that day he'd shaken his dark head in an effort to dispel the memories of her that appeared in his thoughts whenever he least expected it. "I can put a hundred miles between us, sweet Abbie, and I still won't be completely free of you," he murmured under his breath. He closed his eyes, trying to rid his thoughts of her, but it was useless. Her silken beauty stood out vividly in his mind. He saw her glorious chestnut hair, her moist lips, and her willowy body in that cotton shirt that came only to the top of her knees, and knew he was obsessed with her. With a smothered curse, he forced himself to concentrate on the task at hand.

Tomorrow he had only a few miles to cover before reaching Devil's Bend. He was close to Lucien Rodriquez. He just knew it; could sense it. Soon he would learn what had become of his father, Culley Malone. Sonny wondered what he would find. He lay back with a sigh, waiting, knowing he would have a visitor yet that night, one who was to set his carefully constructed scheme into motion.

Sometime later, alerted by the sound of a twig snapping beyond in the darkened shadows, Sonny sprang lithely to his feet. His smooth, quick action was ingrained, and the slightly stooped figure standing across the fire from him gave pause, knowing if he made one wrong move that he would be a dead man.

With lightning speed Sonny whipped the Colt from his holster, a metallic click echoing in the night. "You're going to live a lot longer if you quit sneaking up on a man like that,

Tyrell," he said softly, relaxing his stance.

"Wasn't sure it was you, Sonny," the man was quick to explain. "I saw the light from your fire and thought I'd come over and take me a peek 'fore I made myself a target for some *bandido*." He cast Sonny a smile that revealed several chipped front teeth. "Thought you was going to get here last night. Wouldn't have known for sure it was you, 'cept I saw that big pinto."

Sonny viewed him carefully, then motioned with his pistol for the man to sit by the fire. "Yeah, I got somewhat detained. No offense, Tyrell. I just don't like anyone coming up on me unannounced."

Tyrell Jones spread his hands innocently. "You can just put away that pea-shooter, Malone. I come bearing goods, jist like you asked."

Sonny reholstered the Colt, then casually jackknifed his legs to sit before the fire. Pouring two cups of whiskey, he handed one to his visitor. "All of them Spencers?"

"Yep, jist nigh under eighty-four, crated and ready for ya."

Sonny nodded, pleased. "Good, you always come through for me."

The gunrunner removed his wide black hat to reveal a scalp devoid of hair and hideously scarred. Sonny had seen it before but still found the sight a bit unnerving.

Tyrell Jones had been scalped by Indians some years back and left for dead. The only hair he had left was at the base of his skull, and that hung down his back in a single long braid. Trading on the high plains was a deadly business, one that sometimes carried a heavy price. No one was more aware of that than Tyrell.

"When do you want me to set things up with Rodriquez for you?" Tyrell inquired before sipping from his cup.

"I'd like you to head back to Devil's Bend in the morning and make certain Rodriquez hears I've got guns. We're going to give him such a good deal he'll be chomping at the bit for them repeaters."

Tyrell scratched his scalp with one ragged fingernail. "Still haven't figured out why you would be wanting to sell guns to someone like Rodriquez. I never took you for the sort who was in this for the money."

"If I was in this for the money I sure as hell wouldn't be taking a loss with the Comancheros. I'd go straight to the Comanche who would pay me five times what Rodriquez will."

"This isn't the same as supplying your Juarista friends with guns."

"The Comanche are my friends also."

"Yeah, I heard all about you and that big buck, Night Walker."

"He feels the same about their fight as the Juaristas," Sonny said. "And I have to admire anyone who fights for what they believe in, even if I don't always approve of their methods."

Tyrell sighed. "I know how you sympathize with the underdog, Malone, but these Indians are considered renegade killers. So far, the American government has looked the other way when you run guns into Mexico." He looked pointedly at Sonny. "But they know who you are, Sonny, and whose side you're on. Hell, they want the French out of Mexico just as badly as you do. But these Comanches have every ranger in Texas on their trail. Could mean big trouble for you if them boys catch up with you." Tyrell reached into his coat and withdrew a tobacco pouch and some papers. He proceeded to roll himself a smoke. "You start messing around with this Comanchero, Rodriquez, and you're going to set them to wondering if you ain't in cahoots with him."

"They've got bigger fish to catch than me," Sonny replied, accepting a cigarette from Tyrell. "Rodriquez has two partners, a major in Texas and an Indian agent at Fort Sumner. Both crooks."

Tyrell shook his head. "Everyone's trying to make money off the Injuns, even the ones claiming to help 'em."

"The Indian agent in Mexico is starving the Indians while the major in Texas is sealing their doom by supplying them with stolen rifles." Sonny snorted disgustedly. "Everyone comes out ahead but the Indians. It's no wonder they're staging an all out war on the *tejanos.*" He leaned back on one elbow and flicked an ash from his rolled smoke.

"Yeah, it's a mess," Tyrell replied.

"I remember the first time I discovered Rodriquez's whereabouts. I was in a little town near El Paso," Sonny recalled, "relaxing in a cantina when a cowpoke was found lying shot-up just outside the door. I was friendly with one of the girls there who volunteered to take care of him." Sonny inhaled deeply on the cigarette, staring into the fire. "She told me the cowboy mumbled something about a contract to supply beef to the army for distribution to the reservations. Apparently he had been ambushed because of that deal. Someone rode to where he was holding the herd and jumped him. Left him for dead and took his longhorns. It really hit me then how deeply Rodriquez was involved, and how big of an operation this was."

"Yeah, it's a money-maker all right," Tyrell replied solemnly.

"For the white man, you mean."

"That agent and major must be making a tidy sum on beef and guns."

"Oh, they are," Sonny replied bitterly. "The Comancheros ambush the trail drivers while the agent, with the major's full knowledge, carries out the pen and ink robbery." He glanced at Tyrell. "Neat operation, isn't it?"

Tyrell rubbed his grizzled chin. "So the agent writes up a higher beef tally for beef that isn't delivered and charges the government. The major okays it, and they split three ways."

Sonny nodded. "If I offer Rodriquez the guns for a flat cash payoff, he'll jump at the chance to make some money without having to split it."

"And then you figure on getting next to him and learning what he done with your pa?"

"Exactly," Sonny replied quietly.

"Well, I've got you the best possible lure in them repeaters. A rifle that fires thirteen times without having to reload will have him eating out of your hand."

"And that's just where I want him."

Tyrell stretched his lanky frame and yawned. "Guess I'd best get some shut-eye then. It appears like we've got our work cut out for us." He settled back upon the hard ground, pulling his hat over his eyes. "See you in the morning."

"Yeah. Sleep well, Tyrell," Sonny replied, draining the last of the whiskey from the cup. He didn't bother trying to sleep. He knew it would be impossible with everything that was running through his head. He poured himself a refill and settled back onto his bedroll to wait out the long night.

Devil's Bend was even worse than Abbie had imagined. It sat in the middle of the sun-scorched prairie, a rundown wreck of a town with a single row of clapboard buildings sitting side by side and inhabitants who all appeared of questionable character. A flock of scraggly chickens pecking at garbage in the middle of the street scattered noisily as she rode down the dust-thick street with her long hair tucked beneath the stetson, its brim pulled low over her face.

Drawing her jacket tighter about her, Abbie hunched forward in the saddle, praying no one would pay her any attention.

If Sonny could have seen her now, with her usual erect posture given way to a dejected figure, it would be doubtful if he'd even recognize her.

Abbie's eyes searched furtively for a place that resembled a hotel. Her mouth was parched, her skin sunburned, and her mind numb from all that she'd been through. With an inward sigh of relief she noticed a ramshackle hotel and directed her weary horse in that direction. A couple of drunken *peones* glanced her way as she stopped the foam-lathered animal in front of a dilapidated two-story frame building. She held her breath, but they soon moved onward in merry revelry. She looked up at a peeling sign over the hotel door that read, Rooms, Whiskey and Entertainment. The thought of a bed and four walls of privacy almost made her feel giddy.

With a last comforting pat to her mount's drooping neck, Abbie stepped up on the wooden sidewalk and opened the front door.

Stepping into the lobby, she glanced about. Through a dense haze of blue smoke that swirled about the room, she saw a thin desk clerk leaning with his elbows on the counter, casually observing her from head to toe. Abbie walked over to him.

"I need a room," she said in a voice she hoped would pass for a man's. "And someone to take care of my horse."

"Just happen to have both," the clerk replied in a bored way. "Got any funds to pay for all this, mister?"

Abbie dug into her trouser pockets, tossed down some silver. "I also need food and hot water sent to my room. And is there a telegraph office nearby?"

The clerk handed her a key. "Number seven's empty. Upstairs and to your right." He pointed to the saloon beyond the lobby. "If you're looking for something a bit more exciting later on, that's where you can find it. And the telegraph's down the block a ways."

"Fine, thanks, mister," Abbie returned, grateful that her charade had worked. She felt certain he wasn't accustomed to seeing a woman on her own here. That's why he'd easily accepted her disguise. She strode toward the staircase, her pack slung over her shoulder. The clink of coins and the low rumble of male voices coming from the other room warned her to lower her head as she passed by the opened doorway. She didn't wish to confront any of the hardened men in there.

*　　　*　　　*

Lucien Rodriquez, sitting at a table with Tyrell Jones, glanced up just as the slim stranger strode across the lobby toward the stairs. He caught a glimpse of a dusty, travel-weary figure with the brim of a hat shielding much of his face. But even though he saw only the lower half of the youth's face and caught only a side view of his figure, it stirred something within him and rattled his cool composure.

"Madre Dios," he murmured.

"Something the matter?"

Lucien looked over at the gunrunner, a perplexed expression on his coppery features. "No—nothing. I thought perhaps I saw something—uh—strange." He considered the vision a moment longer before turning toward Tyrell. Lucien smiled, his even white teeth flashing in his dark-bronzed face. "Now, what were you saying to me about those guns? And when can I expect to meet this man who has them?"

"Tonight. Be waiting here in the saloon come sundown. He'll find you."

"I will be waiting." Lucien raised a glass of mescal to his lips, his black onyx eyes observing Tyrell closely. "You have done well for me. I will not forget this."

Tyrell didn't so much as blink an eyelash. "I expect you won't."

Lucien grinned coolly. "Tell this man, *amigo,* not to let me down. I have been doing a profitable business with another party up to this point. It will not be easy convincing him I no longer need his services." He shrugged suddenly. "But then, he has always been dangerous and unpredictable. He has a sadistic streak, that one. I especially like the idea of paying this Sonny straight out upon delivery." He nudged Tyrell with his elbow, grinning. "That means there's more in it for me—eh, *amigo?"*

"Yeah, I figured that would warm your innards." Tyrell slid back his chair and rose to his feet just as a lovely, raven-haired woman walked up to their table. She smiled at Tyrell, a strangely cold smile. "Well, I'll be leaving now that we've worked out our deal. And one other thing that you'll like about this *hombre,*" Tyrell added. "The devil himself can't track him if he doesn't want to be found. He's just your man. Make no mistake about that." Tyrell glanced over at the beauty standing next to him, openly admiring the sultry depths of her wide blue-green eyes.

Being rawboned and ugly as a horned toad, Tyrell wasn't at all surprised when the temptress turned her charms upon Rodriquez, sliding into his lap and wrapping her slim arms about his neck.

As he exited the room he felt the penetrating stare of Lucien Rodriquez follow his movements out the door. He hoped Malone knew what he was doing with this man, for he was like a lobo wolf: He killed for the pure pleasure of it. Even money would not buy Sonny his life if Rodriquez should decide to take it.

The woman in Lucien's bed rolled over to face him and curled one bare leg possessively around his. She wiggled her painted toes against his muscular calf, smiling when she felt him stir.

His black eyes opened with immediate awareness to observe her face closely.

"You are in a playful mood this evening, Sonya *mia,*" he murmured huskily, reaching out to twist a lock of her long black hair around his finger.

Sonya smiled confidently, her hand moving down his flat belly to caress him intimately. "So you wish me to entertain this new gunrunner for you until you are finished talking with the major?" Her fingers tantalized while her eyes promised.

"*Si,* you should enjoy this man. He is not old and vicious like the major." Lucien kissed her lightly. "But young— maybe even handsome—hmmm?"

As his lips closed around a rosy-tipped nipple, Sonya breathed throatily. "You know it's never good with anyone but you, *mi amor.*" She spread her legs invitingly, sighing when he quickly slipped between them to thrust roughly inside her. "You are my *garanon.*" She drew her knees to her shoulders, quivering as his movements increased.

Lucien fixed his dark gaze upon her moistened lips that were inches from his own. "Even though I am aware you do this sort of thing every night for money, it never ceases to amaze me how you succeed in making a man feel as though he is the only one."

She nestled against him, jutting nipples pressing against his dark-matted chest. *"Mi amante,"* she breathed seductively, "you are my only one."

Lucien kissed her passionately. She was something, he thought. And she damned well knew it. Raising his head, he smiled knowingly. "You are a *bruja;* one who loves the sense of power that lovely body of yours gives you." He wound his fingers in the wealth of black hair that fell about her face, twisting purposefully, cruelly. "But not over me, *vida mia.* It does not work with me." He withdrew himself from within her hot flesh, poised the throbbing tip of his manhood inches from her. It drove her wild, and he loved it.

The passion-crazed vixen beneath him shook her head repeatedly, her eyes glazed with desire. "No, Lucien, never. Please—love me, love me," she moaned, grinding her hips upward into his.

"I have every intention of doing just that, but it does not hurt to remind you now and then just who is the master in this relationship." His lips slanted demandingly over hers as he thrust forward and into her.

Sonya strained upward to meet him, reveling in the feel of his hot length pulsating inside her. The heat was increasing, searing flames licking at her loins, melding their bodies in an inferno of desire until she felt she would be consumed by it if she did not reach her peak. She sobbed her need and heard him laugh down deep in his throat. She raked his back with her nails, moaning excitedly. He nipped the column of her neck in response, loving the soft moaning sounds that came from her lips. Their release was simultaneous and explosive. His hands gripped her buttocks, head thrown back, a strangled cry of pleasure bursting from within him. Sobbing, Sonya clung to him as waves of ecstasy washed over her.

Within moments, he was sprinting catlike from the bed, grinning down at her as he patted her bare rump. "And now that I have you sufficiently primed, get up and head off this Sonny. I need to get the major out of here before he suspects we're cutting him out."

Sonya lay sprawled amidst the rumpled sheets, watching Lucien pull on his clothes. "That old windbag major can wait a few minutes longer," she said, pouting languorously. "I want you to hold me."

His sharp retort brought her scrambling from the bed, her lips quivering in fear. "I don't like it when you don't obey me, Sonya *mia*. Now get up or next time I shall pick another of the women to share my bed, one who does what she is told without complaint."

"No, oh, please, Lucien," she gasped white-faced, racing from the bed to throw her arms about his neck. "I will go downstairs and wait for Sonny like you wish and you go and get rid of the major. I will bring this Sonny here and idle his time until you've seen the old man off. Give me an hour with this gunrunner. He will be ready to talk business and to give you a very good price on those guns. Will that please you?"

Lucien walked away, then turned, legs braced apart, hands splayed on lean hips. His swarthy face bore a pleased expression. "That is the way I like to hear you talk, *mujer*. It pleases me very much. And I have been thinking. When I leave here this time I shall take you with me. You shall be *mi mujer* and I your *patron*—for as long as I decree."

Sonya stared at his face, her own softening, becoming less intense. This man meant more to her than anything, and she found that she did not want to leave him, ever. "Yes, Lucien," she replied softly, eyes shining brightly. "For as long as you decree."

When Sonny Malone entered the shabby hotel lobby just after sundown for his meeting with Lucien Rodriquez, the last person he expected to see in a place such as this was the beautiful woman who greeted him as he walked boldly into the noisy saloon. She was sitting alone at a corner table, attired in a deep blue gown, appearing as a sparkling jewel in the tawdry setting. She rose from her seat and smiled at him.

Sonny observed the amusement in her blue-green eyes as she came toward him. They glittered coyly, a measure of provocativeness revealed in their depths. Her ebony hair, fashioned in loose ringlets atop her head, was artfully entwined with blue velvet ribbon. Her figure was slim but lush. She was breathtakingly beautiful with an all-knowing air about her that made a man want to carry her off somewhere private and accept the offer he saw in her eyes.

"Sonny," she purred in a voice as soft as a kitten's. "My name is Sonya. Lucien sent me to keep you company until he takes care of some unfinished business." Her fascinated gaze roamed brazenly over Sonny's face, approving, coming to rest upon the chiseled mouth with the reckless slant that gave him such a ruthless air. She liked that.

"Just how long is that going to take?" Sonny queried, something about the woman's face disturbing him, causing the breath to catch in his throat.

Sonya moved to take his arm. "He did not say. But do not worry. I will keep you from growing restless. We can have dinner together." She cast him a sideways glance. "I just hate eating alone, don't you?"

Sonny followed her lead, his mind racing even as he observed the seductive sway of her hips beneath the satin gown. "A beautiful woman like you should never have to eat alone," he said mildly, "but I never eat anything until after I've concluded business." He couldn't believe he was comparing Sonya's features with Abbie's. He mentally shook himself. What he was thinking was impossible. It was just because his mind was still filled with visions of Abbie. The hair was not the same color; the eyes more green with just a trace of blue; the cheekbones not quite as slanted. But nevertheless, the uncanny resemblance had shaken him down to his soul.

Sonya tilted her head, shaking her mane of glossy curls. "We can have drinks then—in my room. It's private, and we can talk without being disturbed. Lucien will join us there shortly."

Sonny viewed her through narrowed eyes. He hadn't counted on the woman. He knew she was a deliberate diversion, one he'd just have to go along with if he intended to meet Rodriquez.

Appearing outwardly relaxed, he followed Sonya up the stairs, willing to play her little game just as long as she eventually led him to the Comanchero.

When they reached room number eight, she opened the door and entered first. Sonny's eyes did a quick sweep of the dingy room before following behind her. It was sparsely furnished with a bed, dresser, and a table and chairs sitting before a half-opened window.

He immediately walked over to the window and looked out, his eyes taking note of a sloping roof, one that would make for an easy escape if necessary.

"Sit down, please," Sonya stated cordially, taking a chair herself at the table. "I know it doesn't look like much, but Lucien and I will have something really nice one day soon." She picked up a coffeepot, poured two cups, then reached for a bottle of tequila and laced both cups liberally. "Here, this will make you feel right at home in no time."

Sonny sat across from her. He couldn't help grinning slightly when her fingers deliberately brushed his as she

92

handed him his cup.

Sonya smiled back, believing soon she would have him right where she wanted him. It had always worked perfectly with the major. And even though this one was ruggedly handsome and appeared nobody's fool, he did not seem altogether immune to her charms. But then, that was to be expected. Confidently, she slid her knee closer to his.

"I find a man like you so exciting, Sonny. The life you lead is so dangerous, so stimulating." She shivered exaggeratedly, her milk-white breasts quivering above the low neckline of her gown.

Sonny amusedly observed the bright gleam in her eyes and raised a mocking brow. "If you call dodging rangers, bullets, and the hangman's noose an exciting life, then I guess it is."

"Tell me," she inquired huskily, long lashes lowered seductively, "is there a lady tucked away in some bandit's lair, anxiously awaiting your return?"

He felt the brush of her knee against his beneath the table and felt a sharp stab of desire race through him. "And just why would you want to know a thing like that?" he countered smoothly, returning the teasing pressure with his leg. He thought she had the most unusual eyes he'd ever seen. When she turned on her sensual charms they fairly shimmered with blue lights.

Her eyes narrowed, becoming heavy-lidded. "I thought perhaps I could offer you something else besides dinner—since you don't seem to have any desire for food." Brazenly, she leaned across the table toward him, deliberately displaying the soft swell of her breasts for him to admire. She gazed up at him with wide, seemingly innocent eyes.

Sonny stared as if hypnotized by her hauntingly familiar face. Stunned, he found he wanted to reach out and caress every feature, taste the warm velvet of her lips, hear her moan softly as he took her in his arms. But yet, was it truly Sonya he wanted to make love to, or was it Abbie? Did he think by making love to Sonya it would at last banish Abbie from his thoughts?

Sonya touched his arm that relaxed upon the table, smiling assuredly when she felt the muscles tremble beneath her fingers. "It doesn't seem like you've lost your appetite for other things," she crooned with a note of satisfaction in her voice.

Sonny slowly drained the last of the coffee from his cup, the thought of bedding her intriguing; the fact of the danger involved adding to the allure. "Come on over here, baby, and I'll show you firsthand just how much my appetite's improved."

Sonya stood and walked around the table toward him, an expectant smile on her lips. But as Sonny rose to his feet and eagerly drew her into his arms, the silvery light of the moon, beaming through the open window, caught the flecks of aquamarine in her eyes, and he found the memory of Abbie suddenly so overwhelming that he barely felt Sonya's lips moving beneath his own.

Chapter Five

Sonya eagerly raked her tapered nails along his back, clinging to him, giving pain as easily as she gave pleasure.

A shiver of excitement raced along his spine, the pressure of his mouth on hers increasing as she moaned softly. Sexual desire took over his reasoning, and for one blinding instant everything within him longed to surrender. He found himself imagining she was Abbie; his wild, passionate, promising little hellcat. God, she'd been all of that and more. Hungrily he accepted Sonya's thrusting tongue, her seeking hands, and yet, he found her wanting. Just any woman would not do any longer, not after holding Abbie.

Sonya felt she had played him magnificently and experienced an inward sense of triumph when he broke the kiss to breathe huskily. "You're a mighty tempting piece, *chica,* and I'd like to take you up on your offer."

"Then do," Sonya quickly urged.

He was amazed at his own restraint as he unwound her arms from around his neck. "I make it a practice to get business out of the way before pleasure."

"Don't go, sugar," she pleaded softly, knowing how angry Lucien would be if things didn't go as she'd promised. "You've never had anyone quite like me before. You won't be disappointed."

Intrigued by the perverse promise he glimpsed in her glittering eyes, Sonny allowed her to lead him toward a large cheval mirror in the corner of the room.

Her gaze, reflected in the mirror, was confident. "You just watch, honey, then we'll see if you're still in an all-fired hurry to leave me." Slowly, her long fingers began to unhook the front of her gown, pausing enticingly on the last fastening. She laughed throatily as she slid the dress down her shoulders.

Sonny could not help grinning appreciatively when she stepped out of her rustling petticoats and stood sassily displayed in black satin underclothes. She was, indeed, a tempting sight to behold.

Boldly, she bent forward to adjust one crooked lace garter, her delectable, partially clothed derriere temptingly displayed to his sweeping gaze. Snapping the garter tantalizingly, she smiled at the sudden intense expression on his face.

Sonny's full attention was riveted on the alluring scenario before him. His eyes were blank of any perceivable emotion, but inwardly, his pulse was racing like wildfire. At that point, he had to concentrate real hard on those guns.

Sonya's hands caressed the long slim contours of each silky leg, a sound, much like a feline's purr, coming from deep within her. Body writhing beneath seeking fingers, she explored the lush roundness of her breast. "Come closer, sugar," she whispered huskily.

He moved with careless regard to stand behind her. Sonya viewed the reckless lights revealed in his eyes for an instant and had a moment when she wondered just who was playing whom.

"Touch me," she murmured.

He laughed softly, lowering his head to trail tiny, heated kisses along the curve of her neck. His thickly muscled arms encircled her, his hands quickly pushing the chemise down her shoulders, baring her milk-white breasts to his seeking fingers. He rolled the rosy crests of her nipples between forefinger and thumb with practiced ease.

She gasped with pleasure. "I knew you were the kind of man to treat a lady right."

His caresses grew bolder, handling her with a rough expertise that enflamed her. Arching her back, Sonya twisted wantonly beneath his touch.

"Take me sugar—right here where we can watch," she said, panting throatily.

"But there's no rush, temptress," he countered huskily, nibbling the tip of one creamy shoulder. "Let's go slowly. You've got my full attention now." His long fingers moved downward, caressing the flat silkiness of her stomach, teasing her beyond reason as he slid his hands inside the waistline of her pantalets.

Sonya watched fascinated, passion raging. Panting gasps of ecstasy escaped her as his palm flattened against her belly, caressing the velvety texture with a leisurely, circular motion. His firm hand controlled the movement of her hips, keeping her pressed tightly against him.

"Lord, I want all of you," she muttered, "now, right here."

The woman in Sonny's arms taunted the corners of his memory. He observed her assessingly. True, her hair was jet black, her eyes less blue, but still, the unnerving resemblance to Abbie was there stronger than ever. Everything about her spelled serious trouble. He longed to ask her many things about her past but knew that was impossible. That would have to come later. He had more important things to consider right now.

Grinning mirthlessly, he swept her up into his arms and carried her toward the bed.

"Oh, baby, hurry," she muttered thickly, eagerly anticipating their joining. Suddenly, her eyes widened disbelievingly as he extended his arms, holding her away from him over the mattress. She wiggled impatiently, glancing up disbelievingly when she felt the security of his arms give way and her body fall downward, landing unceremoniously in the center of the bed. Her mouth fell open in outrage. "Why you lousy—no good—" She ranted in indignant fury.

His silvery gaze mocked hers as he quipped ruefully, "I'm passing on your generous offer, ma'am. I don't think it would be in my best interest to accept."

Vanity prompted anger to flare up in her eyes, and in that moment Sonny saw something that astounded him. Her blue-green eyes smoldered with suppressed fury, glittering bright flecks of turquoise shimmering in their depths. His body went rigid with shock. Damn, if his mind wasn't determined to compare this woman to Abbie! He grabbed up a red satin wrapper and threw it at Sonya.

"Put it on," he ordered. With a snarl, he dragged her along behind him as he strode from her room out into the hallway. "I'm generally not one to turn down a roll in the hay, however, I came here to talk to Rodriquez. And somehow, I get the feeling that you're deliberately keeping me from him. I don't like that." He swung her forward by the wrist, her back coming up against the wall with a force that made her gasp. "Now take me to him." He stared into her pale, wide-eyed face, his jaw tightening menacingly.

The sound of a gun hammer clicking behind his ear brought him whirling around, his hand clearing leather so fast that it stunned the tall man at his back.

Sonny faced his attacker with a fierce look of death glittering in his eyes.

"So, *amigo,*" Lucien Rodriquez said with forced calmness as he caught the expression in the young gunrunner's eyes and involuntarily stepped backward. "You do not like the little welcome I planned for you?"

Sonny stood tense and guarded, the Colt pointed at Lucien's chest. "What the hell is going on, Rodriquez? I came here to offer you a deal on some Spencers, and I'd like to talk business—now—if we're through playing games."

Lucien grinned. "Put away your piece, gunrunner. It was nothing more than a test." His black eyes danced wickedly.

"I could not have a man who is easily persuaded by a woman's touch, doing business with the notorious Comanchero. If you managed to resist that hot little chili pepper," he said, inclining his dark head toward a pouting Sonya who was standing between Sonny and the wall, "then you can hold up under any sort of pressure."

Sonny was still edgy but forced himself to grin easily. *"Que diablos,* if the games are *finito,* then let's talk money."

Lucien spun his pistol easily into the leather holster at his hip. "Let's go to the bar, *amigo.* We can talk at my private table and enjoy a glass of tequila."

Sonny nodded, reholstering his gun. "That suits me just fine."

Lucien dismissed Sonya with a curt flick of his hand. *"Vamos, mujer."*

Hidden behind Sonny's muscular form, Sonya moved quickly along the wall, keeping well to the shadows until she'd reached the safety of her room. She closed the door, collapsing against it, her heart racing like a rabbit who'd just been released from the wolf's jaws. For now she was safe, but later, she knew she could expect Lucien to seek her out. She shivered. He would be furious. She was frightened but resigned to her fate. After all, she had failed, and only Lucien's smooth intervention and quick thinking had prevented an ugly scene.

The trio had been so involved in the explosive confrontation that they'd failed to notice the woman across the hall observing them silently through the partially cracked door of room number seven.

Abbie clicked the door closed, her heart beating a tattoo against her chest. "Malone—it was you!"

She hadn't seen the identity of the woman who had been with him, for he'd kept her protectively behind his back. But the other man had been Lucien Rodriquez, and it appeared they were arguing over the woman and who was to share her favor for the night.

"You bastard," she fumed, kicking a nearby chair. "You drag me away from my home, abandon me on the damned prairie, leaving me at the mercy of the savages, and all for what!" Her hands clenched into fists at her sides. "To find Rodriquez and squabble over some tramp! I should have known that a woman would fit into this somewhere," she said hotly. "Your father, indeed, and I fell for it." She flopped into a chair, suddenly feeling more betrayed than she ever had in her life. "I hate you, Malone. I hate you." She began to sob with bitter, futile anger and promised herself revenge.

Lucien and Sonny sat at a secluded table in a darkened corner of the dingy hotel saloon sipping tequila and discussing the terms of sale regarding the rifles. The room reeked with the mingled odors of cheap liquor and sweat. A musician strummed a guitar in a rousing tune while a dark-eyed senorita swayed and clicked her castanets to the lively rhythm. Though Sonny sat at a table with Rodriquez, experience reminded him to keep his back to the wall and his gun ready. Outwardly, he appeared relaxed, yet his mind was occupied every minute, observing every move of the men standing along the bar. He knew his survival might very well depend on a split-second move, for they were men of questionable character who wore the unmistakable uniform of the desperado. Wide-brimmed sombreros obscured the top portion of their bearded, scruffy faces while weapons of various length and size hung like ornaments from their belts. And through it all he knew Lucien's hooded black eyes never left his face.

"The Spencers, *muchacho,* how many do you have for sale?" Lucien queried.

"Eighty-five. Enough to turn you a nice profit," Sonny

replied softly, his gaze shifting to the waitress who had brought them steaming plates of *puerco con rajas* and tortillas. She was a pretty girl, with plump, round breasts and wide, shapely hips. She smiled invitingly. He absently returned the gesture.

Lucien scooped up the spicy meat with a rolled tortilla before stating, "I will give you a hundred dollars in gold for every gun you have."

"I hear the Comanche pay five times that much," Sonny stated bluntly. "So maybe I should sell direct to them?"

"No, senor." Lucien grinned coldly. "You are dealing with the only man in the entire territory who meets directly with the Indians. There is only one place where they deal. No white man goes in there and comes back out." He favored Sonny with a probing look. "Do I make myself clear? Do you understand that I am your only contact with the Comanche?"

Sonny faced him squarely. "I'll tell you one thing I do know, Rodriquez." As he spoke he allowed his gaze to swing to the sour-faced half-breeds lounging against the crowded bar. "I know there ain't no honor among thieves, and so that's why before I came here I buried the firing pins to the repeaters." He faced Lucien coolly. "Do I now make myself clear, *amigo?*" He pushed his plate of food to one side and leaned back to stretch his long legs and light a cheroot.

Lucien's drooping black moustache twitched momentarily before he replied smoothly, "It seems you have my undivided attention, senor. Just what sort of deal do you propose?" He refilled their empty glasses with tequila.

"A simple one," Sonny replied, lifting his glass. "I want to be the only gun supplier in this area."

For the first time suspicion flitted across the Comanchero's dark features. "And why should I agree to this?"

"Dineros," Sonny replied. "I can get the best guns for less. And absolutely no one, not even you, can track me if I don't want them to. I have no past, no ties." Smoke spiraled up-

ward around his dark head. "Unlike the major."

Lucien laughed mirthlessly. "You are a man to be reckoned with." He leaned back in his chair. "Your proposition bears some thought. I am growing concerned with the major of late. I'll tell you what. I'm leaving at dawn with some mescal and horses for a meeting with the new Comanche chief, Night Walker. I will tell him I have guns that fire thirteen times without reloading. I know he'll want them. I'll promise him the firing pins upon payment. When I return I expect you'll have them here for me. Then, we'll discuss your proposal further." He signaled the waitress who hurried forward to thump another bottle of tequila on the table. She refilled their glasses.

"Salud," Lucien said.

Sonny nodded as he silently lifted his glass to his lips. He was thinking of Night Walker and the fact that he was now the Kwahadi chief. The old chief had been a good man, Sonny reflected. In *Seyan,* another great warrior joins the others who have gone before him.

An abrupt commotion in the lobby prompted Sonny to glance up and see a man in blue uniform being escorted by two of Lucien's hombres toward the front door. Sonny listened closely to the heated words exchanged between the trio. Lucien frowned and was on his feet instantly.

"I must leave you for a *momento.* Please, join some of my men who are playing poker. I shall return shortly." He hurriedly left the room to approach the scuffle in the lobby.

Sonny meandered in the direction of the card players, silently observing the exchange in the lobby.

The major cursed loudly upon seeing Lucien. "You bastard! I won't let you get by with this. I'm not going to allow you to cut me out of the gun profit just so you can have it all for yourself."

"Silencio!" Lucien growled, grabbing the man by the front of his uniform. "You are a foolish man!"

The major did not back down. "I knew you were up to

something, Rodriquez, when you tried getting me out of the hotel earlier. It didn't work. I'm back. And you're going to have big trouble if you try anything like that again."

Sonny could see Lucien was seriously considering the major's words. Slowly he released his angry grip on the man. "*Si,* you are right, of course." He grinned easily. "We are both just a bit upset. Come." He began to lead the major back toward the stairs. "I changed my mind. We need to talk more—tomorrow. Why don't you go on upstairs and spend the night with Sonya, eh?" He grinned, jabbing the major with his elbow. "We are both just a bit edgy. In the morning we will straighten matters out."

Like hell, Lucien thought. Come morning he'd have his men escort the old man back to the fort and convince him along the way to keep his mouth shut.

The major realized his error immediately but followed Lucien's advice without further complaint. Sighing, he climbed the stairs, then brightened somewhat when he anticipated the night yet to come with Lucien's best whore.

It was well after midnight when Sonny entered his hotel room. He won most of the poker hands throughout the evening, and the men had, one by one, dropped out of the game. Pocketing his winnings and downing a last glass of tequila, he finally headed for his room. The fiery liquor raced through his veins, heated his blood, but strangely, left him sober.

The small room was stuffy, only a pale yellow shaft of moonlight cascading through the window lighting his way toward the bed.

Damn, what a long day, he mused silently as he unbuckled his gunbelt and laid it on a side table. He unbuttoned his shirt and pulled the tails from his trousers. Stripping it off, he tossed it aside, then stretched his broad-shouldered frame, big hands reaching upward. Golden moonbeams caressed the rippling, corded muscles on his lean body, and the woman sitting in a chair behind him felt her pulse quicken in response. Still, she waited, patient as a cat, until she heard the creak of bedsprings as he lay down upon the bed. She sat perfectly still, barely breathing, waiting for him to fall into a sound sleep.

Sonny lay there, sleep impossible as the woman, Sonya, and her uncanny likeness to Abbie whirled around in his thoughts. He'd lost his head earlier with her, but in the morning he intended to seek her out and talk with her in-depth. There was more to this woman than her uncanny resemblance to Abbie. He placed his hands beneath his head, staring up at the peeling plaster on the ceiling. For now, he felt satisfied that Rodriquez had bought his story and the guns. Soon, he'd be exactly where he wanted him. Then, he'd make his move.

Not surprisingly, he found himself thinking, once again, of beautiful, silken Abbie. He even imagined her delicate rose-scented perfume in the room. Recalling how he had left her, he was surprised when concern for her nagged at him incessantly. He hadn't really wanted to part with her, but he knew now he wouldn't have left at all if he'd been near her one more time. In all truthfulness, he was relieved that nothing had happened between them. Most of the women he was used to taking were experienced in matters of the heart. They were just as satisfied as he with a brief, meaningless fling. He'd bedded them eagerly and left them in the same manner. It wouldn't have been that way with Abbie. He knew now he wanted more than that from her.

"Abbie," he whispered, just saying her name enflaming him with desire.

It was then the woman sitting in the shadows made some imperceivable sound; just a slight gasp at the name he'd murmured so tenderly.

The woman's soft sigh triggered an instant reaction in him that brought him leaping from the bed, his silver-gray eyes piercing the gloom of the small room. The adrenaline pounded through his veins as silently and swiftly he withdrew a knife from within his boot and stealthily crossed the room. He felt certain he knew the identity of the female sitting in the shadows. It was Sonya. And with a woman like her it paid to be cautious.

Before she had time to make a move, his arm lashed out and caught her to him. She began to struggle in earnest. He chuckled huskily. "Don't rush off, *chica*" he drawled, lazily pulling her toward him. "You and I have some unfinished business." He decided now was just as good a time as any to get some answers from her. He yanked roughly, and her slender body came up against his. Her delicate perfume wafted to his nostrils. With startling clarity, he realized, without a doubt, the identity of the woman in his arms. Confused, stunned, he stood there refusing to believe it. It couldn't be! Abbie was on her way to Fort Lancaster; he'd seen to that himself.

He grunted when the barrel of a gun jammed his rib cage. "You're right, we do."

His mind raced furiously. Why was she here? By the gun in his ribs he could only assume she'd followed him seeking revenge. "Put the gun away," he urged softly, "before you make me do something I'm going to regret."

Her only reply was a rebellious jab with the barrel. "Move toward the bed—slow and easy."

"All right, whatever you say." He appeared to agree easily. He moved across the floor until he felt his knees bump the edge of the mattress and he knew there was only one way out of this when he heard the hammer click back on the gun. Without hesitation Sonny reached around grabbed her gun hand and flipped her over his shoulder onto the mattress.

The old bed springs creaked beneath the sudden impact of her slight body, and when Sonny landed unexpectantly beside her, they protested louder.

She cried out softly, distressfully.

"Don't ever threaten a man with a gun unless you've got guts enough to pull the trigger," he growled.

"Let me up and I'll show you what I'll do," she hissed.

They tussled upon the bed, each trying to gain control of the gun. She held it in a death grip, refusing to release it, even when she saw the brief glimmer of a sharp blade flash in the shadowy light.

"Drop the gun, little she-cat," he whispered silkily. "We both know you won't pull that trigger, but I don't plan on getting shot even accidentally." His free hand cupped one heaving breast, as the other held the knife poised in the fastening of her shirt. He made a taunting move with the blade as though to rip the material in two.

She went absolutely wild on him then. Clawing, kicking, making threats to fill him full of lead; until growing weary of toying with her, he simply twisted the gun from her hand and grabbed her wrists in a steel-like grip.

"Damn you," she rasped, out of breath. "You knew you meant to do that all along! You enjoyed it!" She thought she saw him grin; a flash of white teeth in the dim light just before his mouth swooped down upon hers in a kiss so fierce it took her breath away. Desperate, she bit down on his bottom lip and felt immense satisfaction when she tasted blood.

He drew back with a snarl of pain. "So you want to play rough, eh?"

Before she had time to react, he'd pinned her arms back over her head with one powerful hand while the other lingered on the top button of her shirt. A tense silence followed, the only sound, the quickening of her breath when she realized his intentions. A gasp escaped her. "Please."

"Please, what?" he whispered back.

"Let me go before you make me hate you more than I already do."

He slid one leg over hers. "I think you've got love and hate all mixed up inside you," he stated thickly. He began unfastening the shirt, stripped it down her shoulders so quickly that she didn't have time to react. He moved over

106

her, and she felt his hair-roughened chest sear her intimately through her wispy silken undergarments. "And I think it's about time I sorted them out for you."

Her legs felt like watery objects beneath the solid muscle of his. Lips as soft and gentle as a summer's breeze pressed against the throbbing pulse in her throat, and she almost sobbed from the intensity of the emotions he had aroused. Fearing he would see how much she desired him, she turned her face away, bit down painfully on her bottom lip.

"Love me, Abbie," he ordered softly. "Love me completely this time."

She sucked in her breath. "How is it you knew me immediately?"

He lifted his head, traced the outline of her lips with one finger. "Beautiful, I would know the feel of you, the scent of you." He kissed her parted lips. "The taste of you, anywhere."

She groaned, senses swimming. "Let me up before it's too late."

"It was too late from the first moment I laid eyes on you." He pressed light kisses upon her closed eyelids. "You know that just as well as I."

"I didn't seek you out to make love with you. I sought out your room number to make you pay for lying to me."

Sonny poised above her, his silvery gaze demanding her to look up at him. She did and knew a moment of self-doubt when she saw the depth of feeling revealed there. "I don't know what you're talking about—lies—but we can talk later." His head bent downward, his lips tasting the velvet texture of her graceful neck, her earlobe, her breasts. Lips and teeth drove her mad with wanting, but still she denied the yearnings of her young body.

Filled with a sense of panic she managed to wiggle one slim wrist free and reached up to claw at his face.

Anticipating such an action, he easily held her hand within his.

"No—I do not want this!" she cried.

He leaned his weight on one elbow, staring down at her, a muscle pulsing in his jaw. "Your body tells me differently. We've been bound to this, Ab, admit it." His lips were tender on hers, belying the indifference in his tone.

She felt one of his hands loosen its grip on her wrists, slide the length of her arms to grab the scarf from his neck. Before she had time to react, he had quickly bound her wrists together, tying one end of the silk scarf to the iron bed-frame.

"I intend to cure you of this hate you say you have for me, *Querida,*" he whispered as he unlaced the ribbons of the chemise and kissed the exposed, creamy flesh. "One way or the other." Her body quivered when the warm wetness of his tongue found one jutting coral-tipped nipple. "They're so round and hard," he murmured thickly, "and they taste so sweet." Lost in a haze of passion she was not aware that he'd removed all of her clothes and that she lay completely naked to his admiring gaze.

His lips and tongue worked magic upon her senses, touching, kissing, tasting of her satiny splendor.

He left her for as long as it took him to remove his own clothing. "I want you so," he told her in a choked voice.

Her resistance completely faded as his fingers stole downward through the downy nest of curls between her thighs to part the gently curving folds and enter her. Instinctively, her hips followed the motion of his fingers as he plied her with a gentle, knowing touch.

She was warm inside, like satiny velvet, and Sonny knew he could restrain himself no longer.

Abbie moaned at the urgent ache within her that demanded to be relieved.

With one deft movement his hand slid her legs further apart, while the other unloosened the silken knot that secured her wrists to the bed.

Without hesitation, her arms went around him, the scarf

fluttering forgotten to the floor. She traced a path with her fingers along the corded muscles of his back, feeling them ripple and quiver beneath her seeking touch. She felt the rough stubble of his chin against one sensitive nipple as he moved it in a gentle circular motion, making her arch upward, cry out his name.

"God—Sonny—what are you doing to me?" she choked, her voice shaky.

"Loving you, Ab, the way you were meant to be loved." His lips slanted in an ardent kiss over hers, taking the breath from her lungs and reason from her mind.

Roughly, tenderly, he wooed the beautiful woman beneath him until he felt the right moment had come. Wrapping one arm about her slim waist, he pulled her against his hot, pulsating length. Gazing deeply into her eyes, he pressed forward, tearing the delicate maidenhead and claiming her for his alone.

A shudder went through her body, a small cry of pain escaping from her lips to die upon his. He kissed her until she ceased to think of anything else but how good it felt to hold him inside her.

He began to move, slowly at first, then powerfully, until sweat glistened on every muscle of his body.

Abbie was lost in a wild vortex of passion from where she wished there was no return Dizzily, she climbed the heights of ecstasy with him, soaring, seeking, until a rapture like nothing she'd ever experienced before gripped her, catapulted her soul, then sent her drifting back into the secureness of his embrace.

She opened her eyes to see his peering softly down at her. "Do you still hate me, Ab?"

There was no trace of mockery in his words or his expression. She found herself whispering as she stretched contentedly. "Mmm—a little less than before."

He grinned, making no move to withdraw from her as he kissed the graceful curve of her neck. "Your kind of hate could be very addictive."

Surprisingly, she found he was ready for her once again. Rolling over onto his back, he pulled her over him. Instinct led her as she rose up, straddling him, sensuously moving her hips in a way she sensed would please them both.

The crooked smile on his harsh features dissolved beneath her heated stare. His large hands encircled her slim waist, held her firm atop him as he thrust into her. "Abbie," he whispered hoarsely, "my silken lady. Never stop hating me."

Abbie moaned softly in her sleep. Turning on her side, she arched her gently rounded hips nearer to Sonny's body resting beside hers.

Sonny lay there, wide awake, a million thoughts racing madly through his brain.

Naturally, as if they shared a bed together every night, he nestled against her, wrapping one arm snugly about her waist. She was his lover, his woman; and like the other half of a missing puzzle piece, he mused contentedly, it appeared she was made just for him.

He wondered just what he was going to tell her when she awakened. There were many things they needed to discuss, explain.

The first, faint rays of dawn crept like misty pink fingers over the window ledge, drawing his solemn gaze to the dawning of a new day. He had a feeling that this one was going to prove quite different from any other. Reluctantly, he shook his lady gently. "Abbie, wake up, sleepy head."

She turned her head drowsily toward him but did not make any move to leave the security of his embrace. "What time is it?"

"Time for you to go back to your own room." He patted her rump affectionately. "There are some people who shouldn't see us together."

Her heart squeezed painfully. Was this how it was going to

be between them? "That—other woman—the one I saw you with last night. Does she have any claim on you, Sonny?"

His eyes moved over her face, then he placed a kiss upon her pert chin. "I don't think that bears answering after what we shared throughout the night."

"I didn't think you were going to toss me out just as soon as you'd had what you've been after since the beginning."

"Damnit, Ab, that's not fair," he replied, scowling. "I can't risk having you seen with me. It just might endanger your life." He stroked the tousled, chestnut head tucked in the crook of his arm. "You mean very much to me, too much. I want you to send a telegram home today and have someone come get you."

"I did that earlier," she replied. "Some of my men will come for me."

"Good, that's one worry off my mind."

"And then you can dismiss any thoughts of ever seeing me again, right?" She twisted in his embrace, one hand resting on his dark-furred chest. Her voice sounded desperate even to her own ears. God, how she hated herself for asking. "Can you do that, Sonny? Will it be that easy for you to forget me?"

"What do you think, Abbie?" he murmured huskily, his fingers entwining in her thick hair to urge her mouth closer. "But you can't stay with me. There's no place for you in my life at the moment. Least of all here in this hellhole."

"I would keep to my own room, have my meals sent up. I don't think I'm in any more danger here than I was on the plains. I've managed to stay alive up to now, and against some pretty slim odds."

With a groan he crushed her to his chest. "Christ, Abbie, don't remind me of any of that," he said, long fingers massaging the smoothness of her upper arms. "I tried to warn that fool commander he was playing with fire bargaining with those Apache. I only left because he repeatedly assured me of your safety."

"You didn't know they'd lay in ambush for us," Abbie replied. "And now it's over. I'm a survivor, Sonny. I always land on my feet. I'm confident I can ride and shoot as good as any man here."

Sonny grinned at the intense gleam in her eyes. "And if I tell you no, you'll undoubtedly pull that damned six-shooter on me again, won't you?"

"Maybe." She grinned.

He kissed her lightly. Propping himself on one elbow he stared down at her. "I think you're too sassy for your own good, pretty lady." His words died abruptly when a faint cry for help came suddenly from the room situated directly next to his. He knew it was Sonya and wondered what entertainment she was into this early in the morning. It came again. "Damn," he swore. "Don't question, Ab, just do what I tell you," he ordered sternly. "Get your clothes and take the adjoining door back to your room. It sounds like trouble."

Already he was on his feet, trousers hastily yanked on, gunbelt buckled even before he tugged on his boots. "Stay in your room until I come for you, is that clear?"

Abbie nodded mutely, inwardly seething in angry indignation. She knew he was going to help that woman. Pulling on her clothes, she left his room for her adjoining one, shutting the door quietly behind her. She ran forward to crack the door leading out into the hall. She saw Sonny standing outside that harlot's door and heard a muffled feminine voice replying in hushed tones. Abbie tried, but she couldn't hear their exchange of words. She watched with a heavy heart as Sonny entered the other woman's room.

Sonya stood wringing her hands nervously as she glanced over at the man sprawled nude upon the rumpled bedclothes. "I didn't mean to do it, Sonny, but the old geezer was meaner than ever tonight," she breathed shakily. "One minute we were having us a wild time and the next he yanked

112

up his belt and started beating me with it." She raised a shaking hand to her white face. "I can't stand that kind of pain," she blubbered. "Oh God, it was awful."

Sonny strode over to the bed and looked down with disbelief at the inert form of the major. The man's fleshy back was marred by angry red furrows.

Sonny snorted in disgust. "It looks like you did your share. What did you do, tigress, claw him to death?" He rolled the heavy body over and saw a knife protruding from the man's throat. "Christ, Sonya! You stuck a knife in him!"

She trembled, then reached for a slender cigarillo lying on the bedside table and placed it between her lips, appearing to suddenly grow calmer. "I couldn't stand the filthy lecher touching me for another second." She paused to light the cigar and pick up a hatpin lying on the bed. "He liked to use this on me slowly and effectively. It was one of the ways he liked to do it. By watching me squirm beneath his hand holding the pin. Tonight, even I couldn't control him." She blew a spiral of smoke into the air. "It was because of you this happened, you know. Everything was fine until Lucien made that new deal with you. The major was furious." She suddenly stomped her foot in a childish pout. "Oooh, Lucien will never take me with him now. You've ruined everything for me!"

"It appears you did that all by yourself," Sonny reminded her. He saw her mind working furiously. "Forget it. You can't cover up this murder. The army will swarm all over this place in search of the major."

Sonya grabbed up a sash and tied it around her black wrapper as she faced Sonny with a malicious, upward look. "They won't have to look too hard, for I intend to give them their major—and his killer."

"They just might go easier on you if you tell them how it all happened."

Sonya smiled benignly. "You tell them—sweetheart," she drawled.

113

"You're crazy, woman. I'm not getting involved in your mistake."

"Oh, but you are." She grinned maliciously just before her shrill screams pierced the early morning stillness. "Help! Murder!"

Footsteps sounded on the wooden floorboards outside in the hall. Realizing his predicament, Sonny's hands automatically fell to the guns on his hips.

Sonya raced for the door, threw it open and ran screaming down the hallway, her gauzy wrapper swirling about her. "There's a killer in my room! He's just murdered the major!"

Two of Lucien's guards drew their pistols and tore headlong into Sonya's room to confront the lithely poised form of Sonny Malone.

Terrified for Sonny, Abbie quickly grabbed up her holster and six-gun and flung open the door. It was then the thin walls reverberated from the explosion of guns that split the air. She barely noticed the woman who tore madly past her, black hair streaming around her pale shoulders, her eyes wide with fright.

Abbie had no idea what she was going to find when she entered that room. Behind her she could hear voices babbling excitedly. Something about that woman's voice appeared achingly familiar, but she didn't have the time to consider it now. She had to reach Sonny.

Sonya threw herself at the sheriff's burly form as he came puffing down the hallway. "Sheriff. Oh thank God you've come! This horrid man whom I met earlier, and turned away, burst into my room in a jealous rage and stabbed the poor major. He's a mad man!"

Abbie ran into the room, the sight of the bullet-riddled bodies on the floor bringing a cry to her lips. "No—oh, Sonny, no."

His voice was grimly demanding. "Abbie, get the hell out of here before you're dragged into this mess!" He grabbed her wrist and dragged her to the open window. "Go out the

114

window and down the roof. It slopes out onto a back alley."

"I can't leave you!" she cried.

"Yes—you must," he ground out between clenched teeth. "And you're not to look back." He swept her up and placed her bodily through the window. "Keep on going and don't stop, no matter what. I'll get out of this somehow." He shoved her forward. "Now get! And don't come back!" He was amazed when she obeyed for once without question.

Spinning about, his mind raced furiously. Damn! They had him! He knew if he went through that window behind Abbie they'd mark her as an accomplice. She might even get hurt. This way, at least she would be safe. He knew he owed her that much. As he stood calmly awaiting his fate, Sonny smiled contemptuously upon remembering the firing pins he'd buried on the plains. Rodriquez was meeting with the Comanches at this very moment to tell them he had Spencers. He had the rifles with him, for all the good they were going to do him without the firing mechanism. Night Walker would not be pleased to buy guns that did not shoot.

Sonny tensed as the sheriff entered the room, his hands automatically whipping out his pistols. But he did not fire. Grimly, he handed over the twin Colts as Sonya smirked triumphantly in the background. She pointed an accusing finger toward Sonny.

"He's the one who forced himself in here and killed the major."

"You're under arrest, mister," the sheriff stated, relieved he had someone to turn over to those army men for trial. If the killer had escaped, those government men would have swarmed all over his town and taken it out from under him, looking for the major's murderer.

Sonny ground out angrily, "I didn't kill the major. I had no reason to!"

The sheriff cleared his throat. "This little lady says differently."

"She's lying!"

"Don't think so. She had no reason to kill the major. He was a good customer." He tied Sonny's hands behind his back and prodded him onward with the barrel of the rifle. "But, you on the other hand, had plenty of reason. You finished him off so's you'd have the gun territory all to yourself. Sonya told me." He jerked on Sonny's arm. "And those army men aren't gonna look too kindly on you. No sir."

As Sonny was led from the room his eyes darkened as they met Sonya's. He couldn't imagine why he'd ever thought to compare her with Abbie. She was a lying, deceitful jade. "Be certain you tell Rodriquez those guns he's selling to Night Walker are worthless. He'll know what I mean." He smiled cockily when her face lost its smug look.

Mind racing furiously, Sonya followed behind the two men, pausing at the front door of the hotel to watch them march toward the jail. She was unaware of Abbie's observing her with a look of disbelief from the alleyway across the street.

For one breathless moment Abbie considered pulling her gun and trying to hold them all at bay until Sonny had time to make a getaway. She considered the matter seriously, and then, her searching gaze fell upon Sonya's pouting features. She knew now why she'd recognized the voice of that sordid tramp.

But now, she had her means to help Sonny. It was a bit risky, but if anyone could manage to pull it off, she knew, without a doubt, that she could.

Later, Abbie lingered before the cheval mirror, her eyes doing a thorough, observant sweep of the image revealed there. She'd managed to put together a passable outfit by selling off her horse at the livery stable and purchasing some extras at the dry goods store.

"I think you'll do just fine," she murmured to her reflection in the mirror. Becomingly attired in a bright yellow day

116

gown, she picked up a sweeping straw bonnet with moss green ribbons streaming down the back and placed it over her upsweep of burnished curls. She tucked every errant strand securely beneath the headpiece. With her rouged cheeks, pouting red lips, and a gauzy veil draped about the bonnet's wide brim, Abbie was convinced more than ever that her plan would succeed. Stepping out into the dimly lit hallway she almost swooned when Lucien Rodriquez came sauntering toward her. He hadn't noticed her as yet, and she hoped by keeping her face lowered, and with the concealing veil, he wouldn't pay too close attention. He strode on by, but just as she passed him, Abbie felt steely fingers grip her elbow and a deep voice speak a name she'd never thought to hear again.

"Sonya *mia,* were you trying to slip by me without even letting me see your new outfit?" He spun her around into his powerful arms, one long brown finger reaching forward to tilt her chin upward.

Abbie gulped, unable to avert her gaze from his black, obsidian eyes. She could feel their piercing heat as they bore into her.

"Very becoming." He fingered the gauzy veil. "I like that. It gives you an air of innocent sensuality. Something you lost along the way, eh?" His hard, sensuous lips tasted hers. She let him probe the honeyed warmth of her mouth without flinching. His kiss was nothing like Sonny's. It was heartless, almost brutal, and when he suddenly released her she almost stumbled backward in her haste to get away.

He gripped her chin cruelly. "Ah, *chica,* never have you fired my blood in such a way as you have just now. I like that. It pleases me very much."

Abbie froze when those seeking fingers began lifting the veil. Quickly, she pulled away from him.

"No, no, darling," she cooed. "You're going to spoil the rest of the surprise I have planned for you if you don't let me go on my way." She placed a finger to his lips. "You go to

117

your room and I will be back shortly. And I promise—I have the surprise of your life in store for you."

He smiled indulgently. "Very well. I don't see as how I can spoil your little game." Lucien ran his strong fingers along the curve of Abbie's cheek. "Hurry back, *bella mia*. I'll be waiting."

Abbie tried not to panic as she casually strolled away from him and down the stairway. Reaching the door with a sigh of relief, she turned the knob and stepped outside onto the wooden walkway.

Just as the sun set over the sordid, dusty town of Devil's Bend, Abbie Lee Caldwell sashayed in the direction of the jail with only one thought on her mind: to rescue Sonny Malone.

The sheriff was preoccupied wolfing down his supper when Abbie brazenly entered the musty jail. She didn't hesitate but walked toward him with a flashy, come-on smile that suddenly put all thoughts of food right out of his head.

"Why, hello there, Miss Sonya," the sheriff crooned. "Just what brings you over here? business or pleasure?"

Abbie cringed inside as she forced herself to flirt coyly. "I just feel so badly about my dreadful mistake, Sheriff, that I wanted to come over here myself and confess." She bowed her head, appearing ever so ashamed.

"Why, honey, what could you have done that was so awful?" He reached out and ran his stubby hands along her arm.

Abbie's skin crawled. She swallowed. "That fellow I identified as the major's killer?"

The sheriff sat up straighter. "What about him?"

She gulped. "I was so confused. I'm just not certain if he's the killer. There was another one with him—and—"

118

"Missy! You'd better be kidding me!"

She shook her head, her expression forlorn. "I'm sorry, Sheriff, but it all happened so fast. And I was on the bottom you see. But I remember now. One of them came through my window and attacked the major while we was—"

"I know what you was doing!" the sheriff roared. "Get to the other man's description!"

She appeared to give his request considerable thought before replying softly, "I think he was a Mexican."

"Damn, woman!" the sheriff declared. "Half everyone in this town is Mexican! Do you realize the United States Government is gonna track that dead major right to our doorstep and we'd better have a murderer to give them or they'll tear this town apart looking for one." He stared pointedly at her. "And how many of us can afford to have them snooping into our personal affairs? And that goes double for Lucien."

"Maybe they won't have to know about the murder. Maybe we could manage to cover it up somehow."

"No, we can't cover up something like this." He raked his fingers through his wiry hair. "That would be worse. If they found out we covered up this killing they'd throw the key away on the lot of us." He wiped the sweat from his brow with the back of his hand. "I knew that sadistic sonofabitch was going to get hisself killed one of these days. But I had hoped it would be by the Injuns and not here, in my town."

Abbie placed one slim finger to her lips indecisively, appearing thoughtful. "Perhaps if I just had another look at this man, out here beneath the lamp. Maybe he is the one—you know—I'd be almost willing to swear to those army men that he is the murderer—almost." She chewed pensively on her bottom lip.

The sheriff rose to his feet, grumbling beneath his breath. "Almost ain't good enough! Don't know why you just can't say he done it—don't matter—just so long as we give them army boys a man to hang."

"I may be a lot of things, Sheriff, but I'm not one to send an innocent man to the gallows," she huffed indignantly.

The hulking sheriff scooped up the cell keys from his desk and ambled toward the back room. "Oh, for God's sake, I'll go get the poor bastard and bring him out here. And I want a positive identification from you. Is that clear?" Just before he disappeared to the back room he turned and observed her closely. "New outfit, hmm? That's what's different about you. Knew there was something."

Abbie's heart lurched. She forced herself to smile. "Yes. Lucien bought it for me."

He nodded. "Looks right nice." Then remembering once again why she was here, he grumbled. "Wait here while I fetch that fella right out."

It seemed like forever until Abbie heard the sound of heavy footsteps returning down the dimly lit corridor. She felt a strange exhilarating feeling race through her at the thought of what she was about to do. She would be on the run with Sonny; he couldn't leave her behind now. Her heart beat excitedly.

Sonny stepped into the light ahead of the sheriff, eyes blinking from the unaccustomed brightness. His hands were shackled, a thin chain running from the cuffs to the sheriff's belt keeping him from going any place.

Abbie almost screamed in frustration. Now what! She hadn't thought about this! She managed to keep calm as she turned to observe the prisoner.

"Well, here he is. Have yourself a good look this time," the sheriff said.

Abbie cocked her head to one side, appearing to study the accused closely.

Sonny glared at her with bitter contempt. He would have loved to have that slender neck of hers between his fingers.

"I—still don't know." Abbie said, sounding uncertain.

"Damnit woman, you are sorely trying my patience," the sheriff fumed. He yanked on Sonny's wrist chain until he'd

120

pulled him directly in front of Abbie. "How's this suit you?"

It was then Sonny looked directly into Abbie's face and saw the truth there to behold. Bright, turquoise eyes, fringed by thick, smoke-colored lashes, held a look of triumph as they stared into his own. He almost grinned. Damn, if he didn't have himself one hell of a woman! She never did a damned thing she was told to do, but this time, he was glad she hadn't.

"It suits me just fine, Sheriff," Abbie replied, just before she reached beneath her voluminous skirts and produced her six-shooter. She placed the barrel inches from the sheriff's bulbous nose. "How's this suit you?"

"Jeee-sssus!" he howled.

"He can't help you now, Sheriff," she said with a smile. "No one can. So just drop your gun real slow like, and then unlock his cuffs."

"Better do as the lady says," Sonny drawled. "I believe she just might blow that handsome nose of yours clean off of your face if you don't."

"Just take it easy there, little lady," the sheriff blubbered. Hands shaking, he quickly fumbled for the key and unlocked the cuffs. He thought Sonya had gone completely loco to pull this.

Freed, Sonny hurried across the room to grab his guns from a peg on the wall. Turning to Abbie he said. "Nice going. You almost had me fooled."

The sheriff's face bore such a look of astonishment and disbelief that Abbie could not help but laugh. She unwound the yards of gauzy material from the bonnet's brim and yanked the chapeau from her head.

Long, chestnut hair, the golden red of a sun-dappled glen in autumn, spilled down about her slender shoulders.

The duped man glowered at the two people. "I don't understand any of this, but you can bet I'll find you two no matter how far you run." He continued to rage as Sonny handcuffed him to his desk. "I'll get you both for this. I swear

I will!"

Sonny's gaze riveted upon Abbie's countenance. "Where did you leave the horses?"

"I sold mine for these geegaws I'm wearing. All we have is Viento. I left him a few doors down tied to a tree behind the dry goods store. I didn't want anyone getting suspicious seeing your horse tied up back of the jail so I rode him over when I bought my things."

"We'll just borrow the sheriff's horse. I saw him from my cell window hitched to a post out back."

"They hang horse thieves in this state, Sonny," she said, chuckling wryly.

"I don't think for this horse they will." His eyes twinkled at Abbie.

The sheriff was gnashing his teeth. "I just bought that horse from Rodriquez! I have a bill of sale to prove it."

Sonny took Abbie's arm. "When I first saw him I figured you must have got him from Lucien." He directed Abbie toward the rear entrance. "I've got a surprise for you," he told her.

Hurrying outside behind him, Abbie's eyes rounded at the animal at the hitching post.

"Romeo. It's my horse!" she cried.

Sonny looked down at her gown. "How are you going to ride like that?"

"I have clothes in our saddle packs. I managed to slip into your room and get hold of yours, too. I'll change as soon as we get far enough away from here." She rubbed the horse's velvet nose affectionately. "I bet you thought I'd never see you again."

"We both did," Sonny replied softly. Grasping her arm, he helped her into the saddle. She glanced down at him. "Did you really believe for a minute that I'd do what you told me, Malone?"

Sonny grabbed the horn, swinging lithely up behind her.

"What do you think?" He reined Romeo toward his waiting mount, kissing the delicate curve of her one bare shoulder.

Lucien Rodriquez had entered his room almost tingling in expectation. Sonya had never been able to make him feel this way before; for that matter no woman had. But suddenly he felt like a stallion who'd just discovered a frisky new filly in his territory. His lusty thoughts brought about an immediate arousal, one that he looked forward to sharing with his enticing, sexy beauty. Glancing over at the bed he did a double take when he saw Sonya sprawled upon it.

"Sonya! What in the hell are you doing in here?" He crossed the floor in two angry strides, yanking her off of the bed before him. She fell to her knees, stunned.

"What's the matter, honey?" she wailed pitifully, cowering before him.

He grabbed a fistful of her blue-black hair and drew her up to face him. "What kind of game is this?" he growled. "How can you be here when I just left you out in the hall?"

She blinked up at him uncomprehendingly. "That's—not possible, Lucien. I've been here the past few hours."

"*Perdicion!* That other one—she looked just like you!"

"What—what other one?" Sonya queried hesitantly, her eyes widening.

"Out in the hallway just a few minutes ago, there was a woman who I swore was you. She even acted like you."

"Oh sweet Jesus," Sonya moaned. "It cannot be—it cannot be, Abbie!"

"Who in the hell is Abbie?" Lucien roared, perturbed. "What has happened around here since I was gone?"

"My twin sister," Sonya replied stunned, vaguely recalling the features of the woman she'd passed in the dim hallway during the shootout. She hurriedly dressed before an astounded Lucien and rushed from the room, already sensing what her sister had been planning and knowing she would be too late to stop her.

Lucien ran after her, demanding an explanation for her actions. Sonya never halted her steps until she reached the jail and heard the sheriff's startled expletive.

"Holy shit! There are two of you!" He pointed toward the alley. "The other gal broke him out posing as you!"

Sonya knew beyond any doubt that she had to stop them. If she didn't, her carefully constructed plan would come tumbling down around her—and she'd hang.

"You have a lot of explaining to do!" Lucien roared, following behind her.

Running to the open door, they saw the fugitives riding eastward toward a horse behind the dry goods store. With Lucien still in fast pursuit, Sonya raced after them, withdrawing a derringer from the garter on her leg.

She aimed quickly for Sonny's back, but the bullet missed him, for Sonny had vaulted from one horse to the other, unknowingly leaving Abbie exposed as the target. Her body jerked forward from the impact of the bullet.

Instantly, Sonny's Colt cleared leather, and an exchange of gunfire took place between himself and the pursuers. Helplessly he watched as Abbie slumped over Romeo's neck, blood streaming from a wound on her temple. He felt as if his heart had just been torn from him.

Still firing, he leaped from Viento's back, hitting the ground in a fast forward roll. He could see Rodriquez coming toward them with several men bringing up the rear. Sonny rolled toward Abbie's horse, grabbing the trailing reins, hearing bullets slash into the dirt within inches of his face.

Something ripped through the flesh of his side, painless at first, then bursting in white-hot fire, racking his entire body. He knew he had to keep returning the gunfire and somehow get in the saddle behind Abbie before she toppled from her horse to certain death. Gritting his teeth, he fired both Colts.

Lucien wasn't certain what had brought this all about. He only knew he had to prevent Sonny's escape in order to learn where those firing pins were buried or Night Walker, the Comanche chief, would find a way to make him pay dearly.

Sonny gritted his teeth, snarling with frustrated rage. Realizing the odds were too great, he managed to pull himself in the saddle behind Abbie. He cradled her against his chest.

"Don't die, my silken lady—don't die," he breathed in her ear, willing her to live for him as he jammed his heels into the snorting horse's sides.

The valiant stallion responded at a full gallop, carrying both wounded people away from the town of Devil's Bend and out onto the open range with Viento following closely behind.

Chapter Six

Abbie's head throbbed agonizingly. Dimly, she was aware of Sonny's holding her protectively in the shelter of his arms. He felt very solid and familiar pressed close to her chilled body. Never had she thought this man would come to mean so much to her. No matter that they fought, scratched and threatened one another at every turn—she knew he would give his life to defend hers.

She lay still, listening. All was quiet save the sighing of the wind through the trees. Abbie was filled with relief. They had managed to escape their pursuers. Her hand sought Sonny's. It was cool and clammy beneath her fingers. Something was wrong—terribly wrong. Her heart pounded, nostrils quivering with the stench of blood and sweat. Forgetting her own injury, she rolled over to look at him and was immediately assailed by dizziness and nausea.

"Ahhh." She couldn't help crying out from the physical pain. Tears came to her eyes. "I've never felt so helpless in my life," she breathed chokingly. Grasping her forehead, she felt something warm and sticky on her fingers. Peering around her, she was stunned to find that they were lying at the fork of a shallow creek where stood a thick grove of cottonwoods. Gritty sand clung to her damp skin and beneath her fingernails. She brushed it from her cheek as she tried to orient herself. Her vision cleared, and she saw him clearly then, lying beside her, still as death.

"Sonny!" she cried, reaching out a trembling hand to caress his white face. His flesh felt clammy to the touch, and she saw that blood soaked his shirt. Shivers of fear tingled along her spine and for a moment reason fled, and all she could do was sit back on her heels and stare at his inert form in shocked disbelief. "No—it can't be!"

A part of her had secretly thought this big, vital man invincible. He was her strength, her will to keep fighting against insurmountable odds. Suddenly, she was faced with the terrifying inevitability of her own death. She had really never thought about dying before. Were they going to die? Taking a deep breath, Abbie drew on inner strength.

She laid her head on Sonny's chest, and upon hearing the reassuring sound of his heartbeat, she almost cried from pure joy. "Hang on, darling—please," she whispered, tenderness washing over her. She thought frantically then of the posse that would be on their trail. She knew who would be leading them and that they would not waste time trying to take them back alive. Dead or alive, it really didn't make any difference now, just so long as they had a body.

"You've got to help me, Sonny. We can't just stay here and wait for the sheriff to find us." She tried shaking him, but he didn't even blink. Looking down at him, Abbie had no idea how they could keep on running or for that matter, where they could run to. Her mind was filled with frightening thoughts and images. She was trying very hard not to remember the cold, calculating expression on Sonya's face as she'd aimed the gun at them and pulled the trigger.

"It had to be Rodriquez. He forced her," Abbie whispered dazedly. She simply could not believe that Sonya had turned as brutal and heartless as the man she'd lived with for the past six years. Abbie knew she was capable of many things—but never murder. And—her own sister!

An animal scream sounded angrily impatient, breaking

through her thoughts and the quiet stillness. Terrified, she glanced in the direction of the piercing shriek, her gaze meeting a new horror.

Sinister, flesh-eating vultures sat on a fallen cottonwood several yards away, flapping their wings in a ferocious display. The awful sight of them made her shudder in revulsion. "Get away! Leave us alone!" she sobbed.

All of the anger and pain within her surfaced, and with a small, ferocious cry she drew her gun and fired with deadly accuracy into their midst. Two of the huge birds fell dead, the others swarming over the twitching bodies as they toppled to the sand.

"What—the hell—Abbie." She heard his familiar grumble. "Do you want everyone within miles to hear that?"

With a sob of relief she shook her head. "I never thought I'd be so happy to hear that snarl of yours." She smiled weakly. "It sounds mighty good."

He reached out a hand to caress her cheek, saw the dried blood on her temple where it had run in rivulets down her lovely face, and impotent rage overwhelmed him. "My silken lady," he said in a hoarse voice, "what have they done to you?"

"She laid her face next to his. "I'll make it. It's just a graze." Her slim fingers stroked the bronzed angles of his face. "What about you? Are you going to hang on for me?"

"I doubt very much if I'd get by with dying if you've set your mind otherwise." He closed his eyes, gritting his teeth against the waves of pain that assailed him. "I hate myself for—getting you involved."

She held him close. "Sh—sh—don't try and talk. You've been hit badly, Sonny. I've got to get you somewhere to have that wound tended."

"I can't ride another mile. Just let me lie here."

She drew back from him, frightened at how weak he sounded. "Damn you!" she shouted, intending to pump fire into him. "You're the one who started this journey, forcing me to go with you, and there isn't any way you're going to just lie here and die! I—I refuse to let you."

She was relieved to see one eyelid open and his piercing gaze view her disdainfully. "Who said anything about dying? After all, you're the one who kept me up all last night. So the least you can do is let me get some shut-eye now."

"I didn't notice you complaining then," she shot back, relief evident in her voice. She undid the pearl studs on his dark blue shirt and carefully peeled it away from the wound. The sight of his blackened, injured flesh almost made her weep. She had seen gunshots before, but this time it was different. Blood oozed in a slow steady stream from a neat round hole in his side. The flesh around it was swollen and puffy. The sight of his dried blood splattered over his body made her feel both angry and helpless. She took deep breaths to fight back threatening tears.

"I need to tend to this, but I've never removed a bullet before."

He sensed her turbulent emotions. "It went clean through me," he stated matter-of-factly. "Just bind me up to slow down the bleeding."

A sob bubbled in her throat. "We can't stay here long, Sonny. You need help."

"Don't go soft on me now, Abbie," he whispered through tightly clenched teeth as he tried to suppress a groan of pain. "You're all I've got, baby. Be strong for me."

She wiped her eyes on the back of her sleeve, willing herself to remain calm, to be his strength. "I'll get our gear. I have some whiskey in one of our packs."

A grin tugged at the corners of that mouth she loved so well. "Good, I could use a stiff drink."

The horses were nearby, grazing contentedly on greens growing near the creek bed. Dizziness overwhelmed her, but she persisted until she had the packs and returned to his side.

She held his head while he took some water, then gave him a healthy shot of whiskey. He lay back with a blissful sigh.

"My angel of mercy."

Abbie tore up one of her clean shirts. "I've got to pour some whiskey in your wound. It's going to hurt like the devil," she warned him.

"Just do it," he said firmly, bracing himself.

Without hesitation she raised the bottle over the hole in his side, tipping it forward. His only reaction was to suck in his breath as the fiery liquor seeped into the raw injury. Abbie thought she would have been screaming her head off if someone had done that to her. Tough as nails, that was Sonny. She began wrapping torn strips of cloth around him, smacking at his fingers when he insisted on trying to help.

"You're making this more difficult with your interference, you know?"

A ghost of a grin tugged at the corners of his mouth. "Just making sure you do it right, that's all." Even suffering from a gunshot wound, just the touch of her fingers on his bare skin sent all kinds of messages racing to his brain.

"You're in no condition, so forget it," she said sternly, glancing up at him. "You look like hell, Malone."

"And you look bad enough to scare a swamp rat," he teased, tenderly observing her bedraggled appearance.

She found herself laughing, then quickly scolded. "Life is not one big joke. This time you've got yourself in some kind of fix." She tied off the ends of the makeshift bandage, tugging gently.

"Laughing in the face of death has saved me on more than one occasion." He winced. "If you're through cracking every one of my ribs, you'd better let me take care of that head wound of yours."

"I'm giving the orders now," she stated sternly. "And I say I'm fine. Now lie back and rest."

"Not this one," he growled, grabbing her arm with surprising strength. "Quit squirming and hold still."

She glared down at him. "Must you always use brute force to get your point across?"

"With you—yes," he snapped.

She soaked a scrap of clean cloth with whiskey and handed it to him. Her eyes never left his as he placed it against the gash on her temple. Not one whimper escaped her.

Sonny watched her admirably. "You are some kind of a woman, *cabecilla.*"

A lump formed in her throat. "Just you remember that," she said shakily.

"You were a cool one the way you staged that jailbreak. I'd say you can be the ringleader of my *bandidos* anytime," he murmured before slumping back exhausted.

She poured some water from the canteen onto a cloth and wiped his face. "Rest awhile," she said gently. "I'll wake you when it's time to move on."

He nodded. "Wait until nightfall, then take the creek bed out of here to cover our trail. Head due southeast and keep going no matter what happens, Ab, is that clear?" he ordered softly.

She knew he meant for her to go even if he didn't make it. "Where am I going?" She swallowed painfully, watching him.

"I know of a village where we can hide out. There are people there who will take care of us without asking questions." She watched as he removed a heavy gold ring from his finger and placed it in her hand. "Keep this. It will get you safely to my friends if I happen—not to make it."

She glanced at the lovely old ring bearing an engraving of a family crest. It also appeared to contain a Spanish inscription of some sort. "It's very beautiful. But I can't take this. It's obviously a family heirloom."

His fingers folded around hers. "You can and you will," he told her brusquely. "It might be the only thing to save your life."

"What do you mean?" she queried shakily.

"If we should become separated and you meet up with any

132

Comanche, show them the ring. They will know who you belong to." He stared at her, defying her to deny she was his. She only nodded. "The same goes when you reach the Spanish village we're headed toward.

She wanted very much to ask him many things about himself but knew that would have to come later. "All right." She wiped his face with a cool cloth. "Rest for awhile, I'll keep watch."

His eyes fluttered closed immediately. Knowing she had to do everything she could to get them both to their destination before he couldn't ride any longer, Abbie forced her mind to remain alert, even though she was exhausted. She managed to revive herself by freshening up in the creek. After changing into her trousers and shirt, she removed Sonny's Spencer from his saddle scabbard and reloaded her six-gun. Her stomach growled persistently. She realized she'd best eat if she wanted to keep up her strength. She withdrew some cold cornbread she'd saved and munched on that while she kept a close watch on the winged scavengers who lurked in the background. The rifle lay comfortingly across her lap, just in case the other species of vultures decided to show up.

She woke Sonny gently just after sundown. He came awake instantly, but in the light of the moon she could already see his eyes beginning to glaze with fever. "It's time, darling. Can you help me? I can't lift you by myself."

"Abbie—go—without me," he mumbled feverishly. "Leave me."

She knew then, beyond any doubt, that they had to find help or he would die.

After changing his blood-soaked bandage, she half dragged, half carried him to his horse. She would never know how she managed to get him into the saddle, but she did. The effort took the last of his strength and he swayed uncertainly.

"Sonny," she gasped, "how are you going to stay in the saddle?" She grew frantic, remembering his earlier statement about leaving him if he couldn't keep up.

"Tie me in." He saw her hesitate.

"If that ragtag posse should corner us, I'll never get you out of the saddle fast enough to take cover," she protested.

"Just do it—and quit arguing," he insisted gruffly.

Biting her lip, she used his *reata* to secure his body in the saddle. Fear was breathing over her shoulder. She tried vainly to stave it off.

Sonny sensed her terror. "You'll get us both through, Ab." He smiled weakly at her. "Wait until Padre Felipe gets a look at you. I expect I'm really going to have some explaining to do this time."

She touched his cold hand, willing strength from her body into his. "I can't make it without you. Don't give up on me. I need you." She turned toward her horse, swung up into the saddle. Determinedly, she kicked Romeo into a trot, leading Viento by the reins behind her, the ground mist surrounding them as they headed into the creek.

They rode hard for twenty-four hours, stopping periodically to tend to Sonny's wound. Quite suddenly, the world had become a frightening, merciless place. Abbie looked over her shoulder repeatedly, praying each time that she did so.

Once, when they had stopped to rest themselves and the horses, Abbie thought for certain Sonny was lost to her. His body, wracked with fever, began to shake with violent tremors. She knew he wasn't in any condition to do any more riding, and she was damned if she was going to leave him. She halted the horses in the covering of a tree that had been downed by lightning.

"We're going to stop for the night and get some sleep," she explained to him when she began untying him from the saddle. Carefully, she eased him from his mount and wrapped him in a bedroll where he lay. If she was forced into a standoff with the posse, then so be it. She would do what she had to to save both of their lives.

With her usual determined grit, Abbie collected every gun and rifle between them and laid them within arm's reach. Night had settled in once again, and with it came the chill. Knowing she had to keep him warm some how, Abbie did the only reasonable thing. She nestled in the bedroll with him, holding him snug against her while one arm cradled a rifle.

Throughout the long night, Sonny alternated between burning fever and shivering chills. He shivered, tossed and rambled incoherently through it all. He appeared several times to call out a woman's name. It was hard to understand him, but she thought it sounded like Carmelita.

Abbie's lips twisted bitterly as his dark head burrowed deeper into her breasts. "Leave it to you, you unscrupulous rogue, to call another woman's name while your face is buried in my bosom." She sighed dejectedly.

In the early pre-dawn light, Abbie had them on the move again. She didn't think he could make it much farther. He had lost too much blood. She couldn't get him to eat and had to force him to drink water.

Come sunrise, they rode along flat, high bluffs through a maze of twisting trails littered with thick clusters of chaparral and mesquite until Abbie swore they were heading around in circles.

Suddenly, Viento's ears perked forward and his pace quickened. Maybe she didn't know where she was, but Sonny's horse knew exactly where he was going. She gave him free rein, almost sobbing with relief when she saw a quiet little village settled just below the ridge of cliffs. It had been difficult to see until she was right upon them as the adobe structures blended perfectly into the nondescript terrain.

"Sonny! We've made it, we're here!" she called encouragingly to him. "Don't give up. Please!"

Abbie followed closely as the pinto led the way down a

barely discernable trail that had been cleverly camouflaged with brush. They rode into the town amidst the curious stares of dark-eyed peones leaning against a crumbling cantina that Abbie thought had surely seen better days. The entire town consisted of a half-mile stretch of street, the town's cantina appearing to claim the majority of the citizens. The men made no immediate attempt to help Abbie and only watched warily from beneath wide sombreros as the gringa and the wounded man drew nearer.

"Lord in heaven, she pleaded under her breath. "Now, what should I do? Is this the right place or have we wandered into some den of outlaws who will finish what Rodriquez started?" She looked farther down the street and noticed an old church sitting silent and watchful. Where should she go? Whom could she trust?

Before she even had time to make a decision, Viento made the choice for her and sidled confidently up to the cantina's hitching post. Something told Abbie that he would have known his way here blindfolded.

At once, a young Mexican girl came running from inside the building, having apparently recognized Sonny's mount. The woman was yelling for someone called Reeno to fetch the padre.

"Padre Felipe—pronto, Reeno! Tell him it is Santiago and that he is badly injured!" The stockily built *caballero* immediately ran toward the church.

Abbie clutched at the ring now hanging on a thin chain around her neck before dismounting. She walked over to Sonny and began to untie the lariat from around him. She was startled when someone's hands brushed her own aside.

Brusquely, the young woman pushed her away, her voice quite cool. "He is our responsibility now, gringa. Please, step aside so that we can carry him into the cantina."

Abbie knew it would be wrong of her to challenge this woman whose eyes glared daggers into her, with Sonny so near death, but, oh how she longed to protest. After all that

136

she and Sonny had been through together these past couple of weeks she felt she had a right to remain by his side. With difficulty, she swallowed her pride and moved away. It was then she noticed a brown-robed figure, as round as he was tall, puffing toward them as fast as his legs would carry him.

The padre called out an order in crisp Spanish. Several of the peones rushed forward to lift Sonny down from his horse. The Mexican girl was right beside them, worry etched deeply on her face.

"Come, come, senorita," the padre said soothingly to Abbie, wrapping a comforting arm about her as he began leading her away, toward the church. "God has guided you safely here, my child. Your trial is over."

Abbie was so exhausted and weak from her head injury that she could only stare at him in grateful silence. She allowed him to take her to the mission where his housekeeper bathed her, bandaged her wound and promptly put her into bed.

Abbie floated serenely upon the comforting cloud, dozing, waking briefly to see the padre's kind face, then snuggling back down beneath the covers to sleep once again. After running and not sleeping for days, she just couldn't seem to get enough. Sometimes, on awakening, she would imagine she saw her twin standing beside her bed, smiling sweetly. Then, in dreams, she recalled the time when Sonya had been very much a part of her life. With a soft moan that brought the padre rushing to her side, Abbie began reliving the terrible period just after their father's untimely demise.

Abbie Lee and Sonya Marie had been seventeen when Walter Caldwell had been killed while rounding up stray longhorns in a violent thunderstorm that caused the herd to stampede. His death was a personal loss to each of them, but for their mother, it was unbearable.

Martha Caldwell had been pregnant at the time of her husband's death. The trauma she suffered brought the baby three months early. The dark-haired little boy was delivered stillborn. The baby was laid to rest beside his father on a quiet section of Caldwell land. Abbie remembered turning to her mother during the service and seeing her staring vacantly across the freshly dug graves.

"We'll make out all right, Mama," she vowed, wrapping one arm about her mother's frail shoulders. "Sonya and I will never leave you, and I'm going to run the ranch just fine, you'll see."

"Oh, Abbie Lee," Martha sighed deeply. "You have no idea what's in store for you. Running this ranch is too big a task for a girl of your tender years, and heaven knows your sister and I will be of no help to you."

Sonya hurriedly stated, "Mama's right. Let's sell all of the smelly, old cows and the ranch. We can get a perfectly lovely home in the city." Her eyes had brightened. "Someplace where there are people to talk to and places to go in the evening."

"Never!" Abbie hissed. "And they're not all cows, Sonya, they're longhorns."

"They look just like dumb cows to me, don't they you, Mama?"

"Hush, girls," Martha sighed. "This isn't the time nor place to discuss this."

Sonya sniffled. "I hate it here, Mama, I always have! And Abbie Lee is just being hateful to me—like she always is." Her bottom lip quivered and tears began to flow.

"Sonya." Abbie grasped her sister's elbow and whispered threateningly, "Don't you dare go pulling any of your cry-baby acts today or I swear when I get you back to the house I'll make you wish you hadn't."

Sonya Marie slowly turned to look her sister in the eyes and saw the blue fire shooting back at her. Her tears stopped immediately. "I'll make you pay one of these days, sister dear, for all of the mean things you've said to me."

Abbie marveled silently at how excellent an actress her sister was. She had truly missed her calling. "I have no doubt of that," she replied solemnly, turning her attention back to her distraught mother.

It seemed after that day that the relationship between Sonya and Abbie steadily worsened. And to make things even worse for the small family, Martha did not recover from the emotional shock of losing her husband and only son. She retreated into the quiet, peaceful corners of her mind, refusing to acknowledge that a world existed around her.

Abbie did her best to try and reach her mother but to no avail. She needed to feel her mother's comforting arms around her. Martha had always been there for her before in times of need. Even though they differed greatly in character, their love for each other was undeniable.

Abbie never had any desire to run a household. She was far too busy learning how to operate a ranch. But Martha had patiently persisted and never gave up in her attempts to teach Abbie sewing, cooking, and all of the things a lady was supposed to know.

"That stitch is a little straighter than the last one, darling," she'd praise with a smile. "Keep practicing. You'll get it soon enough."

And Abbie would try, just to please Martha, but, instead, in the end, her attention would stray and she'd laugh and kiss her mother on the cheek. "I guess you'll just have to count on Sonya to help you with the mending, Mother. I'm afraid I rip out more than I mend." Then she'd dash from the house to go help her father round up a stray calf.

Walter Caldwell had an eager pupil in his unconventional daughter. He was only too happy to teach her everything he knew about ranching, horses, and guns. By the time of his death, Abbie could run the ranch, shoot a hole clean through a gold piece at fifty paces—and if she really had a mind to, bake a blueberry pie that would just melt in your mouth. But it was ranching and operating the vast Bar C that was the most important thing in her life.

Then, quite suddenly, she had other things to consider as well. Her twin sister, Sonya Marie. The girl began acting strangely, skipping out at nights and to places unknown.

More than once, Abbie had awakened in the middle of the night to look over at her sister's bed and find it unoccupied, pillows bunched under the covers to make it look as though she were there.

"Where in the world could Sonya be going in the middle of the night?" She even convinced herself that maybe her sister was finding it difficult to sleep and had gone out in need of some cool air.

But then, one time, Abbie had been waiting for her just as the sun was coming up.

"Good morning, sister," she greeted the startled girl. "Out rather late, wouldn't you say?"

"Stay out of this, Abbie. It is none of your business what I do," Sonya shot back angrily.

Abbie leaped from the bed and grabbed her sister's shoulders. "Everything around here is my business now, Sonya, and I want to know what you're up to."

Sonya jerked away from her, eyes blazing. "If you must know, I'm having a little fun, sister dear, with a man yet!" She laughed at the astonished look on Abbie's face. "I realize you wouldn't have the faintest idea what I'm talking about so I won't go into details." She slipped out of her riding outfit and went to stand before the oval mirror beside her bed. She openly admired her lush figure in the glass.

"How can you do this, with Father just buried and Mother so distraught?" Abbie demanded heatedly.

Sonya smiled at her in the mirror. She shrugged, running her hands over her slim form as she admired herself. "Life must go on, darling, and I don't intend to miss a minute of it."

"You make me sick," Abbie choked.

Sonya laughed mirthlessly. "You mean jealous, don't you?"

Before Sonya had time to move, Abbie walked over to her and smacked her squarely across the face. "Get to bed!" she hissed. "And remember this. If mother ever hears of your activities, you'll be answering directly to me!" Her eyes were narrowed threateningly and her expression brooked no denial.

Sonya had reeled backward from the unexpected force of the blow and stood silently, grasping her reddened jaw. Tears of pain and humiliation streamed down her face. She had always been the spoiled and pampered one, always demanding her way, spending a fortune on gowns she'd never wear on a ranch. Her parents had always complied with her demands, loving and sweet as they were. She vowed openly to make her twin pay for this assault on her person. "If you ever do that again," she sobbed, "I'll make you pay, Abbie Lee! I swear I will!"

"I'm sick of hearing that idle threat," Abbie had replied. "Now you either live here like a proper lady or get out."

Sonya clamped her lips tightly shut. Things had quieted down for awhile after that, but then, one night, Abbie heard her sister leave and decided that this time she was going to follow her. She was stunned when Sonya rode out across the plains. Abbie quickly swung up bareback on her horse and rode out after her. She followed Sonya to a remote supply shack on the north range.

Abbie waited outside, some inner instinct warning her she was not going to like what this night would yet reveal.

A big blue roan was tethered beside Sonya's chestnut mare. It was a horse Abbie recognized well. She saw it every-day when they worked the ranch together. The animal belonged to their married foreman, Luke Stone.

Her mind raced furiously as she tried to determine her next move. She decided to wait and see for certain if indeed it was Luke who left the cabin with Sonya. God, how the thought of the two of them together sickened her. She'd always known her sister was selfish and cared for no one but herself, but still, Luke's little Mexican wife was a dear friend to Sonya. Abbie groaned. She could not believe what her sister had become. It was just too awful to comprehend.

Just before daybreak, Abbie saw Luke Stone stride out of the shack, playfully tugging a giggling Sonya behind him.

"Come on, baby doll," Luke implored. "The sun's coming up and Margarita's beginning to suspect something's up."

"Oh, pooh on her anyway," Sonya said sulkily. "She can never make you feel as good as I do, so what do you care if she finds out about us."

It was obvious to Abbie what had taken place the past few hours.

Luke coaxed her along toward her horse. "You're truly something, baby, but I gotta get on home now. Breakfast will be ready pretty soon."

"Is that all you can think of after the lovely time we just had? Food?" Sonya gasped.

"No, of course not." He managed to get her to her horse. "There, now, get on Brownie like a good girl and I'll see you again tonight."

Sonya mounted, then leaned over to place a farewell kiss on his lips when the sound of a gunshot suddenly echoed like a cannon through the still morning air.

Abbie jumped as Luke Stone's body was flung forward into Sonya's arms from a single shot to his skull.

She watched, helpless, as Sonya fought to keep her frightened horse under control and claw at Luke's fingers which still held hers in a death grip. Blood from his head trickled down her chest. Gray matter splattered like jelly from a broken clay jar clung to her sister's riding outfit. Sonya began screaming.

"Oh, please, don't kill me! I never wanted to—he forced me—it was him!" she babbled.

Abbie recovered from her stunned state and hurried

forward to help Sonya. Reaching her side, she shouted firmly. "Sonya! Get hold of yourself. Duck down before you're shot next!" She drew her six-gun, preparing to protect her twin with her life if need be.

Margarita, Luke's wife, stepped out from behind a large rock. "Get out of the way, Abbie. This is between your sister and me." She cocked the hammer of the gun she was holding. "She's nothing but a *puta,* that one. My Luke deserved to die for sleeping with the likes of her."

Sonya began to wail louder while Abbie did her best to talk the distraught woman out of shooting her. "I can't let you kill my sister, Margarita. Please, put down the gun." She pointed her gun at her. "Don't make me do it."

The two women faced each other. Sonya, seeing her only opportunity to escape death, spun her horse around and whipped it into a gallop.

Margarita began shooting wildly at the fleeing Sonya. Abbie returned the shots, deliberately aiming wide in an effort to give her sister protective cover. Suddenly, Margarita stepped into the direct line of fire and was felled by a fatal shot to the heart.

Abbie stared in horror at what she'd done. Never had she taken a human life. "No—Margarita—no!" She rushed to Margarita's side just as the woman took her last breath. She fell to her knees, cradling Margarita's head in her arms, rocking back and forth moaning, "Why did you do it? He wasn't worth it. Neither of them were." She turned her face to the heavens and screamed out her sorrow and rage. It was there that the Bar C *vaqueros* had found her several hours later.

Abbie tossed restlessly in her sleep, reliving once again the inquest that had followed in San Antonio.

Sonya, petrified of being implicated, had disappeared on the morning they were to leave for the hearing. Abbie had no one but her fancy attorney present and a few of the Bar C hands.

The judge had been a long-time friend of Abbie's father. He listened kindly to her accounting of the events leading up to the shootings. She told him everything just the way it took place, except that Luke and Sonya had been lovers. She still felt a need to protect her sister any way that she could.

"Margarita followed Luke thinking he was meeting one of his lovers," she had explained quietly. "Except he wasn't. He was meeting me to look for a sick calf who'd strayed from his mother. We'd managed to track him to the north range. It was there that Margarita found us." She swallowed with difficulty. "You know what happened after that."

She remembered how the judge had inquired if there was any reason for Margarita to have thought her husband was carrying on an affair with Abbie.

"Not with me, Your Honor," she answered truthfully. "I'm sorry that they're both dead, sir, but it was a tragic accident on my part."

The judge had listened, debated and finally agreed that Abbie had acted in self-defense. She had managed to protect her mother from hearing about Sonya's affairs, but in doing so, she'd been branded as one of Luke Stone's conquests. Naive, she hadn't realized that Sonya had only been one of many women in Stone's life.

As soon as she was able, Abbie started the search for her sister. She hired a detective who came up with a lead in Santa Fe. Abbie traveled to that city, rented a lovely hacienda, and began to check out the detective's leads. Sonya had been gone exactly seven months. Abbie looked everywhere but to no avail. She turned Santa Fe upside down but not one trace could be found.

She was just about to give up and return home when an old Mexican woman showed up at the hacienda one day. In her arms she held a small baby with carrot-red hair.

"He is from your sister, senorita," the woman told her. "She say he look just like his *papacita*. You take him, raise him, be good *mamacita* to him."

Abbie had looked down at the tiny baby with his sweet little face, and her heart had been lost. He had Luke's red hair, but her sister's blue-green eyes. "This is my sister's child?" she said wonderingly.

"*Si,*" the old woman replied. "She heard you look for her." The gray head shook sadly. "She no come to you ever again, senorita. Where she at now they not allow bambinos. The *patron*, he was going to sell the *niño* so she have me bring him to you."

"Sell him!" Abbie gasped. "To whom!"

"To the Comanche, senorita. They pay good money to the *patron* for babies." The woman patted Abbie's hand with her gnarled one. "She not need you. She with him. He is everything to her. Go home, before your heart get broken more than it is."

"I can't just do that!"

"She tell me to tell you to forget her, to raise the bambino as your own." The woman looked sympathetically at the young girl and the baby. "Forget you ever had a sister," she said softly. "You would not know her any longer, and he will never let her go. She make him *mucho dinaros.*"

That day had marked the beginning of a new life for Abbie. One that she'd never regretted for a moment. The baby boy became everything to her.

Abbie named him Charly Caldwell and took him back to the Bar C and raised him as her own son. She never told a soul who his real mother was, not even Martha. She never wanted him to know that his mother had given him away.

Charly's grandmother found new reason to resume her life. The little boy gave her strength to go on. The delighted grandmother lavished all of her love on her grandson and never once questioned why they'd been blessed with him. He was a precious gift from God who had been sent to make up for their terrible losses.

At first, Martha waited expectantly for Sonya to send some word as to her whereabouts. Abbie never discouraged

145

her, but she felt in her heart it was hopeless. And now, since she had Charly, she wasn't truly certain whether she wanted her sister to return or not. She had protected her mother and Charly at the expense of her own reputation. If Sonya should return, everything just might be exposed.

As the years passed it became apparent that Sonya was not going to come home, and the family resigned themselves to life without her.

San Antonio soon forgot the scandal of Luke Stone's murder. The topic now on everyone's mind was a possible war between the states. It was something they all tried not to think about, but that soon became reality.

Brett Colfax, a young man from a neighboring ranch whom Abbie had been seeing, was one of the first in the area to enlist for the Confederacy. He began to talk to Abbie about marriage.

Martha was delighted, stating how Charly was in need of a father and how well Brett got on with the boy. Abbie gave it serious consideration. She liked Brett very much, but she knew she didn't love him. At nineteen, Abbie knew she was considered an old maid by some, but what people said directly about her never mattered. On that last day before Brett left she had sat with him on the veranda. "I really care for you a lot, Brett," she said softly. "But seeing how this war isn't going to last more than a couple of months, at most, couldn't we wait until you return, and then we can have time for a honeymoon, too."

Brett frowned. "I sure was hoping to get hitched to you before then, honey. I'm getting awful tired of just smooching here on your veranda." His hands had strayed inside her bodice to fondle a breast. "I love you so, Abbie Lee."

Abbie knew she liked Brett, but love? She squirmed beneath his touch. "Just a while longer, Brett, that's all."

Letters were exchanged, plans made, and then one day, Abbie received word that Brett had lost an arm and was a prisoner of war. She had not seen or heard from him since then. A visit to his parent's revealed even more tragic news. Brett's older brother had been killed in action. The Colfax family was devastated by their losses. There appeared no end to this war.

Despite the turbulent times, Abbie had managed to keep the ranch from going under by rounding up wild horses and selling them to the army.

And in the lean months following the war, she began gathering stray longhorns that had roamed the range unmolested for four years, increasing the greater numbers, meandering wild and unclaimed over the vast plains. She saw this as a great opportunity to build up an independent stock business. When the men who had worked for the Bar C began returning from the war, they found a new era beginning. They finally succeeded in accumulating over a thousand head of cattle. But times were still tough. There was no money in the South to buy beef.

Abbie heard that up North, in the rich cities, appetites for beef had developed. But she could find no safe way of getting the cattle to faraway places such as Chicago, Kansas City, and Sedalia. It was across a thousand miles over unfamiliar terrain. Some enterprising ranchers tried; most had failed, or had lost so many men and cattle during the trip that they were now sitting back waiting for the railroad to extend farther west before attempting other extensive drives.

Abbie decided to do the same. After all, she now had contracts with the Union troops in forts throughout Texas. These men had been sent to calm unrest among the Indians and settlers. The Bar C was fast becoming an empire.

"Sonya—Sonya—" Abbie moaned in her sleep, tossing about on the straw-filled mattress. She felt someone shaking her gently.

"Senorita Caldwell, wake up, you are only dreaming."

Abbie fought to the surface of the gray, painful memories. Her eyes flew open to see the padre peering down at her. "I'm awake. I'm fine."

147

He wiped her perspiring face with a damp cloth. "You had us very worried, senorita. I am relieved you have at last regained consciousness."

Abbie touched her bandaged brow with a trembling hand. "I don't know if I have. My head is pounding."

The brown-robed padre smiled understandingly. "You will feel better when my housekeeper brings you some broth."

Abbie studied his face. It was a kind face, with pudgy cheeks and smiling eyes. She found herself breathing easier. "I didn't think I was going to get him here—in time."

Her gaze met his. Padre Felipe did not have to guess for another minute what this woman was to Santiago. He knew by the way she had softly referred to him that there was a bond between them. He was also very aware of the gold ring she wore around her neck. His housekeeper had described it to him. It was the old Don's ring: a family heirloom passed down through the generations. Santiago would not have parted with it unless he cared very much for this woman.

"Where is he? How is he?" she queried anxiously.

The padre began fussing with the pillows behind her head. "Do not worry, senorita. Santiago is being well looked after."

Remembering the dark-eyed girl, Abbie frowned. "By whom?"

"He is in a room above the cantina."

"With the pretty senorita, no doubt," she interjected cuttingly. She tried to sit up and fell back against the pillows. "I want to see him."

"Please, you are not strong enough yet. You need bed rest and nourishment."

"I need to know that Sonny is all right," she whispered stubbornly.

He nodded his head sympathetically. "Very well. I will go see Juana myself as soon as I leave you."

"Who is this Juana?" Abbie questioned, visualizing the

pretty girl running from the cantina and standing possessively between Sonny and Abbie.

"She is the proprietor of the Cantina de Yellow Rose." The padre's face flushed slightly. "Santiago's always stayed there when he came this way."

Abbie's face grew solemn. "That doesn't surprise me."

"They were nothing more than *compadres* in this war we are trying to win," the padre explained quickly.

Abbie nodded. "That may be the case with Sonny, but I don't think Juana thinks of him as her good old *amigo.*"

Padre Felipe smiled knowingly. "You are aware of the Alvarez ring that you are wearing around your neck?"

Abbie immediately grasped it. "I suspected it belonged to his family, but he never said."

"Yes, it does. And it means very much to him. He would not have given it to Juana."

His words made Abbie feel better. "Tell me about him, please padre," she urged.

"You know him as Sonny. His people call him Santiago."

Abbie's eyes widened. "There is so much I do not know. Please go on."

"He is called Santiago by his mother's people and Sonny by those who knew his father. Some people call him a halfbreed. He is not."

"He appears so savage and ruthless at times, padre," Abbie exclaimed, "that it blinds one to some of his aristocratic features, unless you are able to study him without his being aware."

The padre nodded. *"Si,* he does not share anything about himself too easily. He is a very private man." There was a soft knock on the door before the housekeeper entered the room with a steaming bowl of broth for Abbie. "Just set it down on the table, Consuela, and thank you," he told the plump woman. He picked up the earthen bowl and spoon. "Here now, sit up and eat some of this delicious chicken broth, and I will tell you some of what I know."

He debated what he should tell her but knew Santiago would not have brought her here if he did not trust her completely. And it was obvious that she cared a great deal about him just by the look in her eyes each time she said his name. He dipped the spoon into the steaming broth, his eyes watching her expression closely. "Santiago Malone y Alvarez is his Christian name. His father was fond of referring to him as James Sonny."

"James Sonny." Abbie repeated the name tenderly.

The padre continued. "He is from a very old, distinguished Spanish family. His *abuelo,* grandfather, is a *gachupino,* of pure Spanish descent. The family came to Mexico from Madrid after a falling out with a very powerful *marque* over the confiscation of some of the Alvarez lands. It was in Mexico City that his mother met his father. They were married against the old man's wishes. He disowned her for marrying the rough *caballero* who could think of nothing but returning to Texas and starting a ranch."

Abbie refused any more broth, pushing the offered spoon aside. "And that was Sonny's father, Culley Malone?"

The padre smiled. "I see you do know some of it, hmm?"

"Yes, he told me his father was a sheriff in Santa Fe and that he'd disappeared when pursuing the Comanchero, Lucien Rodriquez, into Mexico."

"This is true," the padre said. "Santiago believes Lucien responsible, however his *abuelo* swears since Culley never could make a decent life for his family that he just disappeared out of their lives, knowing that Dona Maria would take her son and go back to Mexico."

Abbie looked surprised. "Could that be true?"

Padre Felipe shrugged. "I do not really know. Santiago swears his father would never have deserted them. It caused a rift between the old man and Santiago. When the war with the French broke out, Santiago joined up with the Juarista rebels."

Abbie frowned. "But then why is he in Texas?"

The padre sighed. "The rest is a long story. Let's just say he is helping his people by making certain they receive the arms that they need to run the French invaders from their lands."

"And how is it you know so much about him?"

"I believe in my country's cause also," Padre Felipe replied, a burning gleam in his eyes. "This village was abandoned when we took it over earlier this year. Every gun that Santiago and his compatriots can manage to get their hands on goes through this village and is transported by wagons to the border."

"And money—what do you do for that?"

"That is something I do not ask, senorita. Santiago provides us with guns. That is all I need to know."

"Padre Felipe?" A deep voice called through the closed door to Abbie's room. "I must talk with you at once. It is important."

The padre recognized the voice of Reeno Sanchez. He smiled reassuringly at Abbie. "I will be back shortly. You rest until I return, and I will tell you of Santiago's condition then."

"Is something wrong?" Abbie asked, sensing his urgency to leave.

"Of course not," he hurriedly replied. "I am always needed for one thing or the other." He pulled the covers up around her neck. "Sleep now, for it is the best medicine."

After the kindly padre closed the door behind him, Abbie heard the two men begin talking in hushed tones. At the words "He's not doing very well," she sat bolt upright, her heart thumping against her rib cage.

"No—it cannot be—not Sonny," she murmured. She listened closer and heard the sound of their footsteps echoing down a long corridor, then a door shutting firmly. She pushed back the covers and slipped from the bed, her knees almost buckling beneath her, she was so weak.

"I must see him," she kept repeating as she pulled on a cotton wrapper that was lying draped over a chair next to the

151

bed. She was powerless against the storm of emotion that overwhelmed her. She had to reach him somehow. She did not realize that she was weeping softly or that she kept whispering the words, "Don't take him from me—please, God. I never even got to tell him—I love him." She brushed the tears aside, a shudder encompassing her slender body as she slipped quietly from the room.

Chapter Seven

The loud, boisterous noise drifting through the opened doors of the dingy Cantina de Yellow Rose did not dissuade Abbie as she swung the door open and stepped over the threshold. It was dim inside the squalid room, the air heavy with the combined odors of spicy *chile macho de puerco* and peppers, intermingling, not unpleasantly, with the pungent scent of burning incense.

Pausing momentarily to look about, Abbie noticed a stairway off to one side that she thought must lead to the upper floor. Without hesitation, she brushed past a saloon girl brightly garbed in a flowing skirt and red peasant blouse who was serving the peones food and drink. She knew that Sonny was here, and she was adamant about seeing him.

The men at the bar stared at the beautiful gringa as she passed by them without notice. A dark-haired girl was singing a haunting melody as a slender, sleepy-eyed musician accompanied her on the guitar. The lovely senorita's eyes widened in shocked disbelief upon recognizing Abbie. Without explanation she stopped singing and hurried toward her.

"Senorita, you should not be out of bed yet," she exclaimed, her eyes sweeping over Abbie's pale, distraught face. She reached for her arm. "Come, I will take you back to your room."

Weak as she was, Abbie remained firm. "You're Juana, aren't you—and you can take me to Sonny?"

The dark eyes flashed back at Abbie almost triumphantly before she covered the expression with down-turned lashes. "*Si,* I am Juana. But I cannot take you to Santiago. He is too sick for visitors." She indicated that Abbie should follow her through a beaded doorway into a storage room which contained shelves of pottery and bottles of liquor. "Do not put yourself through this. If he wanted to see you he would have requested it."

Abbie replied in a strained voice, "I will not be kept from him any longer. He needs me. I need him. Just take me to him. I must know that he is all right."

Juana looked up as a stockily built *caballero,* with coal-black hair, hawklike features, and a sweeping moustache, entered. "Reeno, tell this one she must go back to her sick bed; that Santiago is still too weak for visitors."

"I am not just any visitor," Abbie bristled.

"Senorita Caldwell," Reeno cut in quickly. "I am Santiago's *compadre,* Reeno Sanchez. Won't you please allow me to take you back to the mission?"

Abbie shook her head firmly. "I am not leaving here without seeing Sonny." Her voice did not quaver. "And I don't know why you are keeping me from him."

"Very well," Reeno replied. "I will take you to his room."

"Reeno!" Juana protested frantically. "What do you think you're doing?"

"Circumstances demand it, Juana." He took Abbie by the arm. "Go on ahead and inform Santiago I am bringing the girl."

Juana swept stiffly from the storage room, her lips pursed in angry indignation.

Abbie looked up at Reeno gratefully. "I did not mean to cause trouble. I just need to be with him."

His white teeth flashed beneath the dark moustache. "You

saved my *compadre's* life. It is no trouble, senorita." He sighed. "Do not let Juana upset you. She has always hoped foolishly that Santiago would come to feel toward her the way that she does him. It has never happened."

"And she resents me?"

"She feels this way toward anyone who gets too near him." He led Abbie toward the stairs, smiling warmly. "Come, I will take you to this *mucho hombre* who always manages to capture the most beautiful of senoritas." He observed her intently. "I think that this is one time I would like to steal his *mujer* right out from under his nose."

Grateful for his intervention on her behalf, Abbie found herself smiling widely at this dashing man. It was an innocent gesture, but one that curved her perfectly shaped mouth temptingly, and made Reeno Sanchez doubt whether he'd ever seen anyone quite as beautiful or alluring as Abbie Caldwell. One thing puzzled him. She adamantly claimed she was Santiago's *mujer,* yet when Reeno had told him earlier that Abbie had been insisting on seeing him, Santiago had scowled darkly before curtly nodding his assent. "Ahh, *caramba,"* he muttered to himself. What did his *compadre* intend on doing with this lovely creature now that he was a wanted man and would undoubtedly have to keep a low profile until they could find someway to clear his name?

Reaching a closed door on the second floor, they halted before it. "Wait here. I will see that Juana leaves so that you can be alone with him."

Not long after Reeno entered the room Abbie heard a disgruntled female voice firing off several choice Spanish words that brought a faint blush of crimson to her cheeks. The door was yanked open once again, and before Abbie had a chance to step aside, Juana rushed past her, favoring her with a narrow-eyed glare. "Go in, he is waiting for you."

Abbie entered the room slowly, her heart wrenching when she saw Sonny. He was lying in a double bed, his face looking pale despite the sun-bronzed facade. Yet his silvery-gaze appeared vividly alert as he studied her closely.

"Come over here, Ab." He reached out to her.

It was what she had been waiting to hear. "I was so worried about you," she blurted, relieved to see him, hear his voice. She eagerly sat beside him on the bed, grasping his hand securely within hers. "They told me you didn't want to see me, but I knew they were lying."

"It was my doing, honey," he said quietly, meeting her startled gaze without flinching.

She barely heard Reeno shut the door behind her she was so stunned by Sonny's disclosure. "But—why?"

"I didn't know if I could bear to part with you again if I saw you—and I know I must." His expression was granite hard and unyielding.

Feeling the color drain from her face, Abbie drew back from him. "But—I thought after everything that we'd been through together that we—" The rest of her words stuck in her throat when she saw his jaw set rigidly.

"Live happily ever after," he growled sarcastically. "There isn't a chance in hell of that."

Abbie watched his eyes suddenly close against the pain that engulfed him. He wasn't as well as he had appeared at first glance. She felt a sick sense of foreboding welling up inside her. Her hand still gripped his tightly. Tears threatened but she refused to cry. "You're telling me that you want me—to leave here, without you?"

"Yes, I do," he replied firmly. "Go back home to your family. Forget all about me."

She whimpered once before her pride forced her to keep still, not to beg. He was trying to protect her, she realized that, but she wasn't going to leave him! She would fight him every inch of the way! "I am not going anywhere unless you come with me. You are a foolish man, Malone, if you think I will after I went through hell to save you."

"Oh, Abbie," he sighed. "You have no say in the matter. Can't you see that?" He raised her fingers to his lips and kissed them tenderly before muttering tiredly, "Go on back to the mission and we'll talk more tomorrow." He withdrew his hand from hers.

Abbie was not prepared for his cool dismissal. She stood there feeling a sort of numbness settle over her. He could act so indifferently at times, and right now, she was beginning to have doubts whether he ever truly cared about her at all. Well, she was staying right here in the village until he was well enough to have this out to the finish. Then, if he wanted her to leave, she would.

Abbie called back to him as she walked toward the door. "I'll be back in the morning. And I'm not going anywhere until we've straightened some things out between us. And if you think I am, you're sadly mistaken."

Reeno was waiting for her in the hallway. He glanced up, knowing by the bright, unshed tears in her eyes that things with his stubborn *amigo* had not gone as the pretty senorita had hoped. He was not surprised. "Come, little one," he said with concern. "Perhaps tomorrow it will go better."

Abbie nodded miserably.

The next morning when Abbie awakened, she immediately began to dress for the day. She had it in her mind to go to the cantina this morning just to let Sonny know that she had remained, as she'd vowed, and would not leave until he left with her.

She was surprised to find Reeno waiting for her just inside the entrance to the Cantina de Yellow Rose.

Abbie greeted him cordially, but her manner was stiff. "Good morning. I've come to see Sonny if he's awakened yet." He did not answer. Just by the grieved expression on his face Abbie felt her insides grow cold. Panic welled up within her. She attempted to hurl herself past him only to meet the ironlike resistance of his arms as they encircled her, holding her struggling form so that she was powerless

157

to get away.

"Do not fight me, Abbie," he commanded gently. "You must be strong now, for he would have expected it of you."

"You—you talk as though he—is—" She couldn't bring herself to say the word but stood staring up at Reeno, begging him to deny what was in her mind. He did not. Up to this moment, Abbie had managed to keep rigid control over her outward emotions, but now all of her suppressed pain and fear came bursting to the surface as she cried out her grief. "No! He isn't dead—he isn't!"

She shook her head from side to side, stunned, as his words registered inside her brain. Pitiful, wounded sounds came from within her, and suddenly her knees buckled and she would have crumpled to the earthen floor if Reeno had not been holding her.

He cradled her tenderly, helplessly watching the flow of tears trickle over the slanted cheekbones of her beautiful face. He swallowed over the knot of pain in his throat. "It was all so sudden. One minute he appeared stronger, and the next—" His voice broke when he felt the violent trembling in the slender body in his arms.

"I—want to go to him," she stated softly.

"No—no," Reeno replied immediately. "He would not have wanted it. I'm going to take you back to the mission so that you can lie down." His fingers gently brushed away the teardrops glistening on her long lashes. "We can talk after you've had time to accept this."

Juana stood to the side and observed the two people silently. She had not shed one tear upon hearing Reeno's tragic news. She stepped forward now, her words echoing his. "Yes, go back—and rest. There is nothing here for you anymore."

Abbie viewed both of them, dazed. She heard nothing of what they said to her. Her thoughts were so full of Sonny and the memories that would forever be imprinted on her mind that she did not realize that Reeno had swept her up into his arms and had carried her away from the cantina.

He took her straight to her room and tucked her back in bed, pulling the comforting folds of the light blanket up to her chin.

"I'll be nearby if you should need me," Reeno said, his gaze resting on Abbie's white face.

"Gracias," Abbie returned softly.

The kindly housekeeper hovered nearby, her face revealing her deep sadness. "I bring you something to help you sleep, senorita."

Abbie clung tightly to Reeno's hand as he released the cover, refusing to allow him to leave, making him promise to stay with her. He appeared her only source of strength at the moment and, like a drowning person, she grasped his hand in an effort to draw strength from him.

The housekeeper brought the sleeping powder. Abbie didn't wish to drink it but Reeno insisted.

"Drink it, please. When you awaken, we can talk."

"Very well," she agreed. "But I don't think anything can make me forget, even for a moment." After draining the contents of the glass, she lay back with a tremulous sigh, her very soul feeling as though it were slowly dying inside her. Gradually, sleep overcame her.

He was there waiting for her. Abbie saw him just beyond the gray misty places in one's dreams that harbor every subconscious thought, every buried memory.

Sonny—vitally alive, ash-brown hair falling carelessly over his forehead, silvery-gray eyes mocking, sensuous lips grinning devilishly, unshaven jaw making him look rakish, rugged. She ran to him, reveled in the feel of him against her as he took her into his arms.

"Oh God, baby, I've missed holding you like this," he murmured huskily against her hair. And then his lips were moving along her neck, her eyelids, kissing her lips hungrily, making her weak with wanting as only he could.

I knew he wasn't dead, her mind screamed. I knew. I

159

knew! She broke the kiss to tell him how happy she was that they had all been wrong; that he was alive. And then she found him fading away before her eyes until her arms were completely empty. "Don't leave me, Sonny!" she cried, screams erupting from her throat. She felt someone's hands trying to restrain her, and she clawed wildly at them in her torment.

Abbie welcomed sleep for the next few days. Eagerly she embraced it, for it was there Sonny would come to her. During the day she refused to leave her bed. With all that she'd been through she was just too emotionally drained to face up to reality. At all times someone sat with her. It was either the padre, the housekeeper, or Reeno. Most of the time it was Reeno Sanchez.

Reeno had been like a brother to Santiago, therefore no one thought it unusual that he spent so much time at the grief-stricken senorita's bedside.

On one such occasion when Abbie had awakened terrified from a nightmare, Reeno Sanchez, the man she'd come to know and depend upon, sat next to her on the bed and held her comfortingly.

"I don't know what I'd do without you, right now," she told him honestly, smiling warmly. He laid her back gently on the pillow, her rich chestnut hair spread out gloriously around her, and she found his heart beating furiously in his chest. He knew he must fight these feelings inside him, for she would never be truly his. In her sleep she cried for only one man, the man she had known as Sonny Malone.

"You are strong, little one," he spoke to her in Spanish. "You have been through much these past weeks, and it is only natural that it has taken a toll." Looking down upon her trusting, beautiful face, he thought then of his own inner strength at that moment and wondered seriously how in the world he was going to continue on like this. He was falling more under her spell every day. He'd been warned to watch himself, that she was a temptress that could thaw even the coldest heart. At the time, he'd only grinned tolerantly, listening—but apparently not heeding. He turned from her to walk to the grilled window that overlooked an inner courtyard of the mission. "Are you feeling any better physically?" he asked, his back to her.

"Yes," Abbie replied simply.

"Will you be ready to travel soon, then?"

She sat up. "Back to my ranch?"

"Si," Reeno replied. "I made a promise to Santiago that I would take you there personally."

"Thank you," she whispered softly. "I want to go home."

He closed his eyes to the feeling of despair that washed over him. "He told me to tell you to go on with your life—as if he had never interrupted it." He gripped the edge of the windowsill until his knuckles turned white. "He—said he was sorry for all that he'd put you through—that you should forget you ever met him."

Abbie gasped, tears streaming unashamedly down her face. "Forget him," she sobbed pitifully, tearing Reeno's insides apart. "Having known him yourself, you tell me. How in God's name do you forget a man like him—how?"

Reeno spun around, his face set in grim lines. "You must, for he wanted it that way."

For a few moments the memory of the night Sonny had made sweet love to her came back in such a rush of torment that it caused Abbie to cry out against it. "No!" Then, for the first time since they'd told her of his death, rage consumed her. "All I've heard is what Sonny wanted!" Her turquoise eyes narrowed angrily. "What about what I wanted!" she fumed as healing fury pumped through her. "I wanted him to live, Reeno! I wanted to at least see him one last time before he died, hold him in my arms and tell him I loved him." Casting her eyes away from his sorrowful face, she choked. "We never even got a chance to say good-bye."

"I am sorry," he replied huskily, adding, "and now it is over, behind you. Let him go. Go back to your life and forget. Begin again." He strode, white-faced, toward the door, feeling a need for fresh air to clear his head. "I will check in on you later, *muchacha*. Rest now, for tomorrow we leave."

Abbie waited until the door closed behind him and then swung her legs over the side of the bed. Reeno was right. It was time to begin living again. Sonny was dead, she was alive. And no matter that she'd see his face in every corner of her mind, hear the husky timbre of his voice in the restless wind; she would go on because she had to—and because she knew he would have wanted it that way.

When the old housekeeper came to take her place by the senorita's bedside, she was astounded to find the young woman dressed and heading out the door.

"There's one thing I have to do yet before I can pick up the pieces of my life," Abbie explained to her, a lump catching in her throat. "I want someone to show me where Santiago is buried. I must tell him good-bye."

She stood by Santiago's grave for hours, it seemed to Reeno, who watched her closely from beneath the shade of a cottonwood tree. He had brought her here reluctantly. He knew it was terribly difficult for her, but she bore it all with quiet restraint. Just before she turned to leave, she placed a lock of her hair that she'd clipped before coming beneath the soft earth next to the flat headstone. He saw her whisper something. He knew what it was. Then she stood and quietly walked toward him.

"I'm ready to go home now," she offered simply.

The land goes on forever, grief does not. This was the thought running through Abbie's mind as she stood on the

162

wide veranda of her sprawling hacienda and stared out at the glorious pink sunset.

But how long will it take to lose this awful, aching pain in my heart? And can I get through yet another night dreaming of his arms holding me close? As usual, when she thought of Sonny and their short time together, she became both angry and filled with sorrow.

Restless, lonely, longing for something that was never going to be, she walked across the veranda to take a seat upon a wooden settee and casually survey the solitude around her.

The main house was a gracious adobe structure, long, low, and comfortable with wide verandas and a red tile roof to provide shade from the hot Texas sun. Woven baskets, containing colorful flowers and trailing vines, added a touch of tranquility to the rugged setting.

It was peacefully quiet here, the evening solitude interrupted only by the occasional bawling of a steer, soft laughter drifting from the bunk house, and the howl of a coyote in the distance. Her mother and six-year-old Charly were spending the night with her uncle in San Antonio. It was the first time that she'd been alone in the house since Reeno had seen her safely back home over a month ago.

Abbie had convinced him to stay for awhile. She was reluctant to part with him. He was her last link with her lost love.

"I can't bear for you to leave yet. Won't you consider staying just a few more days?" she'd implored him.

"If it will make you happy," he'd replied, his voice revealing nothing of the turmoil churning inside him.

"Oh, yes, it will!" Abbie had cried.

"Very well, then I will accept your gracious hospitality for a little while longer. But then I must go, Abbie."

Reeno stayed two weeks at the Bar C, taking long walks with her, staying by her side on nights when she prowled the hacienda, unable to sleep, and even helping her get through the time when she, at last, felt able to tell her mother how she and Sonny had met and what had come to pass between them.

It had been almost unbearable for Reeno to hear the emotion and love in Abbie's voice as she'd related different things about their relationship. He doubted, in his own heart, whether she would ever love anyone again the way she had his *compadre*.

And Abbie's mother felt the same way. Martha Caldwell's eyes had watched her daughter closely when she had spoken softly of Sonny, explaining how he had saved her from the Comancheros that night on the prairie, and then again, when she'd been shot. She'd talked of lighter things, too, and smiled as she'd spoken of their squabbling over who was to do up the dirty laundry and dishes.

Martha had noticed that the gallant Reeno had never taken his eyes off of her daughter's face. Once, feeling Martha's eyes upon him, he had glanced over at her. His eyes had mirrored her very own thoughts. Abbie Caldwell and Sonny Malone's chance meeting had grown into something very special. Something Reeno now envied but knew he was powerless to do anything about. She also knew her daughter was only telling them certain things. The rest was hers alone. She did not wish to share it.

The very next day Reeno had left. Abbie had been sad to see him go. She had not tried to talk him into staying longer for she was beginning to suspect what was in his heart. That last day Reeno's dark eyes had observed her intently as he stood beside his mount. Quite unexpectedly, and surprising even himself, he leaned over and kissed her movingly on the lips. She had not pulled away, understanding some of what he was feeling. She had lost her love, Reeno his dear friend. It was a kiss that conveyed feelings too intense to express.

"Vaya con Dios, senorita," Reeno had called softly as he'd ridden towards the sun-washed plains.

"May God ride with you, *compadre,"* she returned. She

had watched until horse and rider were nothing more than a mere speck on the horizon before turning away.

Abbie pulled her thoughts back to the present and went back inside the house. She had made it through another day. It had been easier. Unusually restless tonight she went in search of the housekeeper, Francisca. Charly's birthday was next week and she had promised him a party. Preparations would need to begin tomorrow for she wanted it to be a grand day.

"There you are, Francisca," she said, finding the plump little woman in the large, airy kitchen of the sprawling hacienda.

"Is there something you need, Senorita Caldwell?" Francisca glanced up from the long walnut table where she stood patting a ball of *masa* that would eventually be shaped into the traditional round, flat tortilla between the palms of her hands.

"I wanted to talk with you about the fiesta for Charly's birthday." Abbie went over to the black-iron stove and lifted the lid of a colorful *olla,* savoring the spicy aroma of *frijoles* simmering in chile and tomato sauce.

Francisca smiled. "I have the entire menu completed, senorita. Would you like to go over it now?"

Abbie replaced the lid, turning toward the older woman. "You're busy right now. Morning's soon enough. One of the cowboys from the Broderick spread is dropping off that special gift I'm giving Charly for his birthday. Will you keep it hidden for me?"

"*Si,* I will do this." Wiping her hands on her flowered apron, the housekeeper remembered the note in her pocket. "You were in the study earlier going over the accounts so I did not wish to disturb you." She handed Abbie the missive. "One of the Colfax *vaqueros* brought this for you."

Abbie's face brightened. "Then it really is true! Brett has come back to run the Colfax ranch."

"Their cook tell me it none to soon. His padre is very ill.

165

Senor Brett, he had a rough time in that Yankee prison, but to just disappear like that after he was released—I do not understand," Francisca said. "But now, all will be okay between the two of you again, and I hear that the senor is anxious to see you."

Abbie removed the note, recognizing Brett's shaky handwriting immediately. "I am delighted he is home, but we've both undoubtedly changed since the war." She pressed her lips together thoughtfully. "I wonder where he went after the war? Not one soul heard a word from him. Not even his own family."

Turning her attention back to his message, she finished reading it. "Well, can you believe that. Brett said he'd heard of Charly's birthday fiesta and hoped it included old friends."

Francisca beamed. "See—maybe you should ride over to the *rancho* and invite him personally."

Abbie smiled widely. "Yes. I'm anxious to see him. It's been a long time."

Francisca nodded, delighted to see Abbie taking an interest in his return. She knew the senorita had been unhappy since she'd returned from that awful place, Devil's Bend. But Senor Brett, he would make her forget that desperado who'd kept her with him for so many weeks. Such a man would not have fit into Abbie's lifestyle. Her face sobered then, remembering the *denuncias* she'd read the other day when she'd been in the city. They were wanted posters. Someone was still looking for Sonny, offering one thousand dollars for his capture—dead or alive. The housekeeper shook her graying head, remembering the fierce-looking bounty hunter who had been asking questions that same day all over town. "That one was loco," she mumbled under her breath. "This man they are looking for is dead. Senorita Caldwell told me so herself. And, she of all people, would be the one to know."

*   *   *

166

San Antonio, a large military center, the cradle of Texas liberty, the deathbed of such heroes as Davy Crockett, Jim Bowie, and William Travis, was once again experiencing great change.

The lusty business of the open range and cattle was beginning, and the quiet little river town, soon to become a veritable cattle capital, was undergoing drastic readjustment and turbulent times.

All of this was brought about by longhorn cattle: a tough, rangy breed that had flourished unattended during the war and now roamed in enormous herds across mesquite-covered acres.

No longer were the Texans thinking principally of selling their hides and tallow. Rich appetites were developing for beef in the northern states. These people were willing to pay any sum to satisfy this new, expensive craving.

The big cattle drives were spreading across Texas, and already there was increasing talk of the Kansas Pacific Railroad building a full-grown cattle town at a whistle-stop called Abilene.

San Antonio drew every sort of person, from every walk of life, who was looking for a way to live fast, reckless, and turn an easy dollar. The packed-dirt streets abounded with gamblers, saloon riffraff, enterprising entrepreneurs, and ruthless men who would shoot you down without hesitation if they thought they had a chance of robbing you of a coin or two.

Such was the individual who had just taken up residence on a remote ranch some fifty miles outside of San Antonio.

Lucien Rodriquez stood in the main *sala* of the lovely hacienda, his gaze falling approvingly on everything that he saw. "You ask me if I am pleased by your purchase, Sonya *mia*." He swept her into his arms. "I am very happy with your choice. I think I shall enjoy living here."

Sonya beamed. "We will be ecstatic, I am certain of it."

"It is the perfect cover for me. I shall play the role of a

reclusive Spanish don, and you, *querida,* shall be my connection to the outside world." He kissed her lips briefly, his black eyes gleaming wildly. "And, to your sister."

"But just until we get the ranch, Lucien," Sonya reminded him. "Something that should have been part mine to begin with. My father always did favor Abbie over me. Just because she liked smelly old cows and horses he gave her the controlling interest of the ranch." She smiled evilly. "But now, I'm back for what's mine. And even though I must trade identities with Abbie for a while to achieve success, it will be worth it once we sell the ranch and have all of that money." She raised one perfectly arched brow at Lucien. "After seeing my twin with that gunrunner, it makes me even more determined to seek revenge upon her. To think how she criticized me for my scandalous behavior—the hypocritical slut! Well, her lover isn't around to help her now. And she's going to pay."

Lucien appeared thoughtful for a moment. "I wonder about those stories of Sonny's death, don't you?"

"What do you mean?"

"True, we received word of his death, and your twin did come back to the *rancho* all alone—but still—"

"Lucien, our own men came back from investigating the rumors of his death and told you he had died."

"I'm certain they were correct, for how could one leave such a tempting creature as your twin, otherwise." Abbie's image tantalizingly appeared in his mind. "I am glad her life was spared. It will be so much easier this way for us to have everything." He looked over at his mistress. "And it would have been like killing a bit of yourself, eh?"

Sonya stiffened at the dreamlike expression in his eyes. She didn't like having Lucien in such close proximity with Abbie, for she realized, beyond any doubt, what she represented to him. Her twin meant something to him that she never had. Abbie was beautiful, spirited, wealthy by some standards, and from a respected family. Sonya had hoped she would eventually be all of these things to him, once she took over the Caldwell empire. But she knew deep down in her heart that if she ever truly allowed Lucien to have both Abbie and the ranch in his grasp, he might tell her to *vamos.* Why should he keep her around when he could have the real thing?

Her heart skipped a beat as she viewed him unobtrusively. He was so masculine, so virile. She would not take the chance of losing him to Abbie. There had to be a way of disposing of her twin without Lucien's becoming suspicious?

She reached a tentative hand upward to caress the sharply chisled angles of Lucien's face. He stared down at her but did not make any attempt to kiss her. They had been apart for several weeks, with Lucien trading on the high plains while she had come here to look for a suitable residence for them. He didn't appear too eager to bed her. Well, she wanted him! Eagerly she ran her palms over his thickly muscled chest in hopes of enticing him.

"Lucien?" she queried seductively.

"What?" he replied almost boredly.

"Don't you want to forget about everything for just awhile." She reached up on tiptoe to place moist kisses along his neck, upward to tantalize one ear.

Lucien drew back immediately with a snarl of anger. It was then she realized her foolish error. In seeking to make him forget one thing, she had only succeeded in reminding him of that other, horrendous episode with the Comanches when their chief, Night Walker, had punished Lucien for failing to bring him the firing pins as agreed. She winced, noticing Lucien's eyes darken with remembered pain.

"I am sorry, darling," she hurriedly offered. "Just try and forget—don't remember it—I'll help you."

"I shall never forget what that gunrunner cost me, *bella mia,* and your sister shall pay one day for her lover's mistake. Just you wait and see."

Sonya wanted desperately to turn his thoughts to her,

away from anything that had to do with Abbie. Tonight, she wanted all of him, and she was determined to have him one way or the other. "Am I asking so very much to just forget for one night?" she pretended to pout prettily.

"Yes!" he snarled, his free hand yanking back the long hair from his right ear. "Tell me, could you forget something like this?"

She could not help shuddering at the hideous sight that met her eyes. Jagged, pink scar tissue was all that remained of Lucien's ear. And even though she had been the one to tend him after Night Walker had severed it as punishment, it was still an awful sight. She sighed raggedly. "Oh, Lucien, I didn't want you to return to the Comanches after the gun-runner broke jail. I just knew he would blame you for the loss of those firing pins."

"I had to meet with Night Walker," Lucien replied, his jaw muscles working furiously in an attempt to remain calm. "If I had failed to show up at the appointed time he would have come looking for me anyway. And then the punishment would have been doubly severe." He released his hold on her, and she slowly moved a safe distance away from him.

Sonya shivered inside, trying not to think about how terrible his wrath would be if he ever found out who had really killed the major and was therefore indirectly responsible for his terrible loss. She'd managed to make him believe her explanation of that night.

"Sonny and Abbie were running guns together and they must have murdered the major to eliminate any gun competition," she had told Lucien convincingly. "I'm certain the Civil War has made even my sister scrape for money. Greed, you know, does strange things to some people."

Lucien had looked at her through narrowed, suspicious eyes, but at last, believed her. "*Si,* this is true."

Sonya had breathed a relieved sigh.

Now, as Lucien stared down at Sonya, he wondered once again why she appeared so nervous and upset of late? He assumed it was due to the daring plan that they were about to put into motion. All they needed now was the right moment and a certain individual who was very close to Abbie to play out his part correctly. And Lucien knew just how to apply pressure to this person. Suddenly, he felt a stirring of lust in his loins and looked over slyly at Sonya. He must be careful, he knew, for he did not want Sonya to suspect in any way that he was growing bored with her. Once a whore, always a whore, he mused. Abbie was an entirely different type of female. Such fire, such spirit, and yet, so innocent in many ways.

He fingered a lock of Sonya's lustrous hair which she had allowed to return to its natural chestnut color. "I forgot to mention how becoming your hair is this way. You are an exact replica of your twin," he said, knowing it would please her. "Except for one difference."

"And just what is that?" she inquired, fearing his reply.

Lucien smiled, taking her hand in his, kissing her fingertips. "Why the obvious—of course. She is left-handed and you are right."

"Why of course," she hurriedly agreed, relief evident in her voice.

"You are surprised I had time to notice that, aren't you?"

"Yes, I am."

"Nothing escapes my notice, Sonya *mia,*" he said softly.

She swallowed with difficulty. "Of course it doesn't. And if this gunrunner still walks upon the face of the earth, you intend to find him, don't you?"

"*Si,* I do," he replied solemnly. "I have offered a reward of a thousand dollars for his capture. It will draw every gunslinger and bounty hunter to this area in search of him. If he is still alive, he will be mine."

Sonya wrapped her arms about his neck, burying her face against his shirt front. She knew if that came to pass, everything would be lost to her. Terrified, she clutched Lucien to her. "Enough of this kind of boring talk. How about a personal tour of the rest of the house—the special part I had built on just for you?"

"If it pleases you," he answered with a sly smile.

"It will."

"Then, by all means."

It was just what she had wanted to hear. "Wonderful, darling, I will lead the way." She took his hand and strolled toward the rear of the house where they entered a room in which there was nothing but floor to ceiling glass windows.

Lucien made note of the silvery streamers of moonlight that shone through the sparkling glass, casting a misty glow upon the exotic plants of every scent and color that perfumed the unusual chamber. And in the center of it all sat a gleaming copper tub, just large enough to accommodate two, that was filled with foaming bubbles.

Beside it, thick yellow towels lay draped on matching wicker chairs, and plump, orange pillows were scattered generously before a stone fireplace that would be perfect for lounging before and after they'd finished bathing. Not that they would need a fire tonight. The air was hot and sultry, and Sonya had made certain that an iced bucket of Lucien's favorite champagne sat nearby.

"Is it not magnificent?" she inquired with a wide smile.

Lucien's eyes rested on her sensuous lips, then roamed openly over her lush curves. "Something tells me you plan for us to spend a lot of time in this room."

Sonya entwined her arm in his, moving closer. "But I promise you, darling, you will love every minute of it."

"I will, hmm?" He grinned suddenly.

"I guarantee it."

"Caramba," Lucien growled, "you make my blood boil."

"I want to do more than that," she said throatily, her blue-green eyes heavy-lidded. "I want to make you forget anything else exists, right now, but this night, and us."

He stared transfixed as she began to remove his clothes with agonizing slowness. When he was nude she led him over to the tub.

"Step in, darling," she whispered silkily.

"Will you join me?" he asked, settling down into the scented bubbles, watching her every move.

"In a moment. There is no rush." She pirouetted in graceful splendor amidst the play of moonbeams upon the gleaming, adobe floor, turning this way and that for Lucien's appreciation as she disrobed.

Lucien growled low in his throat. "I think you'd best hurry before I pull you in here, clothes and all."

"Oooh, I just love it when you talk like that," she breathed huskily, slipping out of her underthings and moving to stand beside the tub.

He reached out for her, but she playfully eluded him. *"Malto dios!"* he all but roared. "I grow impatient, *mujer,* powerfully so."

Slowly, she wound her long hair in a careless knot of curls atop her head, her pert, rose-tipped breasts thrust forward impudently as she did so. "Your roar will do you no good tonight, my fierce lion, for this is one evening we are going to savor—slowly." Her eyes heated with desire as she observed him.

Lounging his head back against the tub's rim, Lucien surveyed her slightly flushed face from beneath hooded eyes. She was an irresistible, amoral seductress who had complimented his lifestyle perfectly up to now—until Abbie. He was taunted night and day by the memory of the passionate embrace they'd shared in Devil's Bend. He longed to feel her sleek, tempting body thrashing wildly beneath him as he claimed her for his own.

Abbie Caldwell, and her *rancho* was like an unobtainable prize that he had to capture. It would not be an easy task. Lucien knew she would just as soon shoot him as look at him. The person he would choose had to be someone the little spitfire could trust completely, yet an individual whom Lucien could control. It didn't take long to think of just the right person.

Abbie—lovely lady, he mused, your days of running free are just about over. Soon, you shall become my *mujer,* and only mine. The thought made him grow hard and impatient. With her wealth, he could retire, turn somewhat respectable, and go back to Santa Fe and flaunt his success in his father's self-righteous face.

He hadn't seen his father in many years. Not since that sheriff had forced Lucien to flee the territory just because he'd disciplined one of his *putas* a bit too strongly for with-holding money, and the bitch had died.

All of the other girls had agreed the *puta* had deserved it. But one of them, he never found out which one, had told the town sheriff. He'd come to the cathouse seeking Lucien with a warrant for his arrest. Lucien had managed to slip away out of town, but that damned sheriff had pursued him relent-lessly, until Lucien crossed over into Mexico and joined a band of outlaws. It didn't seem like anything could stop that fool lawman, for he kept right on coming. But finally, Lucien had his *bandidos* lay in ambush for him, and they'd managed to get rid of him most effectively.

Even now, Lucien couldn't help smiling to himself when he recalled just how they'd disposed of Sheriff Culley Malone.

Chapter Eight

Sonya picked up an amber-tinted bottle and held it aloft over Lucien's broad chest. "This will please you very much, Lucien." A teasing smile curved her soft mouth. Tipping the bottle forward, she watched through half-lidded eyes the droplets of spice-scented oil splash down upon his body.

Lucien gasped audibly as the oil made contact with his skin and ran in lazy rivulets down his chest to pool in the indent of his navel.

Sonya poured some lotion into her hands and rubbed them together. She smiled seductively as she leaned forward to place her palms upon either side of his wide shoulders. "And now—we begin," she said softly. Her slender fingers danced lightly upon his tense, sun-browned flesh, enjoying the play of hard muscle that rippled beneath her touch. "How does that feel—mmm?"

"Like I'm in heaven with an angel hovering over me."

"You—heaven?" she laughed throatily. "I don't think so."

He chose that moment to moisten his palm with oil from his chest, then he reached forward and cupped one of her full breasts. He smiled when the nipple immediately stiffened and jutted forward. "I doubt that they have angels in that other place," he teased, rolling the hardened peak between his oiled fingers.

175

Sonya's eyes closed dreamily, and her seeking fingers curved into the softness of his underarms, then over his chest to gently return the exact same touch to his nipples. "That's all right," she said hoarsely, "for I don't think I would fit the mold at any rate."

"I agree, but I prefer immoral creatures, *mi amor*. They are much more exciting."

His thumb was moving circularly over her nipple while his fingers gently squeezed the satiny globe. "Oh, God, Lucien," she gasped.

"You like that, mmm, *bella?*"

"Yes, so very much."

"I also like what you are doing to me."

"I have only just begun," she purred.

"So have I," he replied slowly.

Feather-light fingers moved along his rib cage, teased his taut hairy belly, making the blood surge through his veins in a heated rush. He moved impatiently beneath her fingers like a restless, hungry panther, nostrils flared wide, tongue moistening sensuous lips as though savoring the scent of his prey.

Sonya's heart thudded in her chest when her fingers wrapped around the heart and soul of him. His throbbing staff pulsated demandingly beneath her sliding motion. With the expert touch of a woman of the night, she played him exquisitely, making him her willing slave. The velvet soft tip of him enticed her, beckoning her to savor its texture upon her tongue, yet still she withheld, provoking him into a sense of mindless ecstasy.

Lucien's hands stroked downward to her silken belly, one finger dipping teasingly into her almond-shaped navel. He explored the satiny indentation until she moaned her pleasure.

"Touch me everywhere, Lucien, please *mi amante.*"

His black onyx eyes were heavy-lidded as his hands moved to cup her rounded buttocks, fingers sliding into the warm

176

moistness of her. She writhed her bottom against him, seeking deeper penetration.

"You are a wanton," he chuckled, his white teeth flashing in his dark face.

"Yes—I am—now stand up," she commanded softly between gasps for breath.

He held her bold gaze with his own as he lazily rose to tower over her and lace his fingers through the mass of tangled chestnut hair to press her forward against his quivering belly. His eyelids felt weighted and heavy. They fluttered closed as her warm, wet tongue lapped at the finely textured hair of his abdomen, then moved and swirled headily around his rigid manhood. He jerked upward beneath her nibbling, soul-consuming exploration. His lean haunches pumped against her parted lips as she plied him toward a release so powerful that he shuddered violently in its throes.

She took everything he had to offer and demanded he give her more, finally leaving him weak as a newborn babe. His legs felt as though they would collapse beneath him, and shakily he moved away from her to sink back down into the oil-slick water with a sigh of tremendous relief.

Sonya stepped in before him. "We are not finished yet—not by a long shot." She folded her legs beneath her.

Slowly, inquisitively, he watched her peach-tinted body stretching out full length in the tub, her sleek, shapely legs sliding beneath the frothy bubbles on either side of him, her slender toes seeking, kneading his long, firmly molded legs, moving upward, over his hair-roughened thighs, plying his reawakening member with a boldness that ignited an inferno of desire once again within him. She laid her head back against the tub's rim and observed him with a blissful smile.

"*Perdicion!* Come here, *bruja,*" he half snarled, black eyes glittering.

Before Lucien had time to react, Sonya's dainty feet slid up and around his thickly muscled chest to rest upon his glistening shoulders. "It's your turn, my hungry cat."

177

With a fierce growl of deep-seated need, Lucien moved to gather her hips in his huge hands. He lifted her effortlessly from the water and held her up to delve into the very center of her with his seeking tongue. He took complete control of her mood, her thoughts, her passion, and brought her time and again to the very edge before at last pulling her forward and upon him, setting them both adrift upon the red-hot sea of ecstasy that at last consumed them both.

Abbie rode over to the Colfax ranch, the Triple Star, early in the day before the heat became unbearable. She had paid careful attention to her appearance, having chosen a yellow silk shirt and butter-soft leather riding skirt with matching vest and fancy-stitched boots. She made a striking picture astride her blood-bay stallion, moving fluidly across the rolling Texas landscape.

At mid-morning she crossed over from her land to Colfax property. She was pleased to see a sizable herd of longhorn cattle all marked with the Colfax brand grazing nearby. Brett must have been working hard to gather so many since his return.

She knew it had been especially rough for Brett's family during the war. Every Confederate family in Texas had experienced difficulties of one sort or the other, but the Colfax's had borne more than their share.

As Abbie approached the back of the house by way of the corrals, she almost expected to see Brett's older brother, Pete, breaking wild mustangs in one of the pens. But even as she heard the wild whoops of encouragement coming from the cowboys perched on the high fence, watching a rider breaking a rangy sorrel mustang, she remembered with a sad sigh that Pete had been killed at Gettysburg. Curious as to the identity of the seasoned rider she quickly dismounted and joined some of the men standing along the fence. They all greeted her warmly, having known her most of her life.

"Quite a bronc you have there, Shorty." she said to the lanky foreman standing next to her. "Who's breaking him?"

"The boss." He smiled at her look of amazement.

"But—Brett—with his arm, can he do that?"

"It wasn't easy learning to ride one of them twisters without your balancing arm, but Brett eventually got the hang of it." His face shone with admiration. "He does it with Colfax style, just like his brother used to."

"He certainly does," Abbie agreed as she watched the way Brett rode the snorting bronco. "Pete would be proud of his younger brother."

"Yes'm, I reckon he would at that," Shorty stated thickly.

"How is Brett adjusting otherwise, Shorty?"

"About as good as can be expected, I suppose," Shorty replied.

"This is Abbie, Shorty. Tell me the truth, I want to help."

The foreman never took his eyes off the man and horse as he replied, "Somethin' about him's changed, ma'am. Sometimes you almost think you're imagining it, then others—"

"Others?"

"He seems to have two people inside him at times," Shorty responded in a low voice. "One I love very much, the other, he's unpredictable and spooky."

There was a short, thoughtful silence between them, then Abbie exhaled slowly. "I know he spent a lot of time in that Yankee prison camp. It must have been horrible for him."

"I reckon so," Shorty replied. "And then to lose your arm because of some quack doctor who didn't want to waste the time to try and save it."

Abbie was stunned. "My God. Is that what happened? I didn't know. No one told me."

"It's the truth," Shorty said gruffly. "Brett told me those damned Yankee doctors took off that arm when it first became infected, without waiting to see if it could be saved. And you know somethin' else. I don't think we would have

179

ever seen him again if not for his pa's failing health."

"He must be very bitter."

"With good reason, I suppose. But it ain't doing nothing but eating him up inside. He needs to come to terms with himself."

The foam-lathered mustang suddenly ceased his bone-jarring corkscrews and began sidestepping, hooves pawing up the thick dust. Soon, Brett had him prancing around the corral in total defeat.

"Good ride, boss!" the cowboys called out as they waved their hats in the air in a salute to Brett. Another cow pony would join the Colfax remuda, and a fine one at that, by the looks of him, Abbie thought to herself.

These animals were the heart and life's blood of Texas ranching. Cattle and horses were everything. The Colfax ranch was not as prosperous or near as big as the Caldwell spread, but then the elder Jeb Colfax had not been well for years, and when both of his sons joined the army, the pressures and responsibilities simply overwhelmed him.

Shorty had done his best to keep things running smoothly with every young cowpoke running off to fight the war. It wasn't easy riding range on a thousand acre-section ranch. Abbie had offered the use of her *vaqueros* several times to Jeb, but he had stubbornly declined. It was what she'd expected. Now, seeing Brett coming forward to greet her, Abbie smiled brightly, completely unaware of the breath-taking picture she presented to the young cowboy who had always been head over heels in love with her.

"Abbie Lee!" he called out eagerly. "If you aren't a sight for these eyes."

"So was that ride, cowboy. The way you handled that wild mustang was breathtaking!" Abbie said.

"I'm glad you were in time for the show, ma'am." He grinned, obviously pleased by the compliment.

"So am I. It was impressive."

Brett's face sombered, searched hers. "I'm so relieved

you're back home safe. My wranglers joined your men to search for you when you turned up missing, but they said it was as though you'd dropped off of the face of the earth. They finally had to give up."

"Believe me, I felt at the time as if I did," she heard herself reply faintly. Brett's words recalled that other world, to which even now, if Sonny were still alive, she would gladly return.

Brett surveyed her closely, noticing the faint look of longing in her eyes. "Well, now you're back, and obviously no worse for wear. And it's so good to see you again, Abbie."

She shook herself mentally and smiled. "You too." And remembering his ailing father, she added quickly, "Tell me, how is your father? I understand he's been confined to his bed."

"Yes, he just doesn't have the strength to fight off the illness, I'm afraid," he replied remorsefully. "We know it won't be much longer. We're all just trying to make his last days as pleasant as we can."

Abbie sighed. "I know you've been expecting it, but that doesn't make it any easier to bear. And your mother, how is she holding up?"

Brett shrugged. "Oh, you know Ma. She's a tough one. She'll be fine. We both will."

Abbie prayed that was so. "I know she must be thrilled to have you back home."

"I reckon that's true." Brett chuckled. "She's been fattening me up with her homecooking until I can barely haul myself into the saddle after one of her meals."

Abbie allowed her gaze to flick over him. "You look great to me. I'd say the wide open spaces and fresh air of Texas agrees with you."

"And you," he shot back huskily, surprising Abbie. "I can't remember you ever looking so lovely, so much like a woman." He surveyed her appraisingly, almost making her blush, the soft gleam of his eyes coming to rest on her riding outfit. "All that, and a riding skirt, too. You have changed, Abbie Lee, for the better I'd say."

Again, Abbie's thoughts turned and conjured up Sonny's rugged face. "Much has happened to me also, Brett. You've been away a long time—through many changes. I'm glad you're home. Your family missed you very much."

The sandy-haired young man removed his black hat and swatted the dust from his Levi's. His eyes were cast downward as he asked softly, "Did you miss me too, Abbie?"

For several long minutes Abbie just stood there watching his movements. She knew what he was hinting at. Were they going to pick up where they'd left off before the war? "Brett," she began hesitantly, "I'm not that same carefree girl you once knew."

"And I'm not that same freckled-face kid who used to follow you everywhere. We've both matured, I'd say."

"Let's just take it slowly, get reacquainted before we go jumping into a relationship again, okay?"

"Right," he cut in, his tone hardening. "What you're really trying to say without being blunt is you don't have any desire for a one-armed lover, not when you can have your pick of any man in Texas with two good ones." His jaw set, he turned on his heel to walk away, but Abbie grabbed his elbow and spun him around, taking him by surprise. "Brett, that was an awful thing to say! You know I'm not like that!"

"Then you're an exception from most females," he growled bitterly.

"I already thought you knew that," she shot back hotly.

He was silent for a moment, and then his mood abruptly lightened. He grinned slowly. "Yeah, I guess I should have remembered, huh?"

"I'm disappointed you forgot so easily, Mr. Colfax," she admonished with an easy smile that softened Brett's hardened features immediately.

He reached over to take her hand in his. "Come on," he urged, "let's go up to the house and have Ma pour us two big glasses of her special orangeade. I want to tell you all about my plans for the Triple Star."

She walked along beside him toward the main house. "Good, and I'll tell you mine, and then we'll discuss the fiesta for Charly's birthday. I'd like you to come early so you can help me greet the arriving guests."

Brett met her gaze firmly. "Do you really want that, Abbie Lee?"

"Of course I do, silly," she retorted lightly. "I never do anything I don't want to, Brett Colfax, and that's a fact."

Their gay laughter was music to the ears of Hattie Colfax who stood on the veranda and watched their approach. She had always disapproved of her son's interest in Abbie Lee before. And rightly so, she reasoned. The young woman was a brazen one; she had an illegitimate son to prove it.

Hattie recalled how the scandal of Abbie and her foreman, Luke Stone, had quickly become the talk of the area. All folks talked of for the longest time was how Luke's sweet, little wife had caught him with Abbie and tried to shoot them both. Sadly, she had gotten herself killed along with her no-good husband. And by the very woman he had compromised.

Hattie vividly recalled the trial. Terrible thing for the families involved. She remembered Sonya Marie running away. Poor girl just couldn't stand to hear all the town's folk whispering about her sister. Shortly thereafter Abbie went to Santa Fe. She told everyone it was to find her sister, but they had all known the real reason when she'd returned with little Charly. Lord, Brett had had a fit. But he still insisted he wanted to marry her. Only Hattie knew his feelings for Abbie had changed. He wanted her, more than ever, it seemed, yet he had never mentioned loving her again. Then the war had come between them and they'd parted. And now, it appeared as if they were picking up where they'd left off. Hattie could only wonder if maybe, hopefully, Abbie and Little Charly could save Brett from the devils that seemed to hound him relentlessly since he returned. Praying that it came to pass, Hattie went forward to greet her guest.

As was her usual custom, Hattie laid out a bountiful spread in the bright, cheery kitchen, which had always been the favorite gathering place for friends and family. Abbie helped her with the last minute preparations while Brett went out back to wash up. She was pouring orangeade into the glasses on the table and Hattie was busy heaping fried chicken onto a platter in front of the black-iron stove. They had conversed little since Brett had left the room, each woman uncertain what the other was feeling. Therefore, Hattie's sudden profound statement took Abbie completely by surprise.

"It makes me happy to see you two children back together again. My son needs you more than ever, Abbie Lee," she said softly. "I hope you won't let any differences we might have had between us sway your feelings toward him."

Abbie placed the glass she'd been holding down very slowly. She turned to face Hattie who met her gaze. "Mrs. Colfax, I—I think you're jumping to hasty conclusions. Brett may not feel the same about me as he did before."

"You at least make him 'feel,' Abbie Lee," Hattie stressed, her face sorrowful. "My boy needs to feel good again."

"What can I do, ma'am, that his own family can't?"

Hattie placed the platter in the center of the round table. She wiped her hands on her white, starched apron. "Make him feel like he's a man."

Abbie wasn't certain she wished to continue the conversation, but Hattie didn't leave her any choice.

"It's no secret you and I lost our closeness after your hearing." Hattie paused, a bit flustered. "And—Charly's birth."

Abbie looked down at the pitcher she held in her hands. "I've missed your friendship."

"And I yours," Hattie admitted in a choked voice. "And I want you to forgive me for being so awful to you since then. I know now how terrible it was for you." She placed one hand

184

on Abbie's shoulder. "Please?"

Abbie sat down on a trestle bench next to the table. "I never expected you to ask for my forgiveness," she murmured, surprised. "I always thought you were waiting for me to approach you. And I could never do that, for you see, I really have nothing to feel sorry about. I did what I had to do, and I expect I'd do it all over again if the same situation presented itself."

Hattie sat down beside her. "I don't know what really went on the night your foreman and his wife were killed, Abbie. I don't care anymore. I'm not thinking about yesterdays—only tomorrows—and I'm making certain that the only boy I have left is happy."

Abbie faced Hattie. "You and I cannot make Brett's happiness for him."

"But we can help him, Abbie," Hattie said pleadingly.

"Yes, if he'll let us."

"Oh, he will let you, honey," Hattie enthused. "He's always been taken with you. You've got to try. You're his only hope."

Abbie nodded solemnly. "But I can't promise anything, Hattie. I failed in my last attempt to save a man. I failed miserably as a matter of fact."

Abbie spent a pleasant day with the Colfax family. She hadn't planned on staying as long as she did, but each time she made mention of leaving, Hattie Colfax begged her to stay a little while longer. Finally, after paying her respects to Brett's father, she departed for home. Hattie and Brett had waved good-bye, promising to arrive early at the fiesta.

The sun was descending slowly beyond the hills, a bright red ball of fire hazing the countryside in radiant waves of crimson color. It was a glorious farewell to the day, a lingering promise of a brighter tomorrow.

All things considered, it had been a satisfying visit, Abbie mused, feeling better now that she was once more on the open range. Romeo trotted friskily along beneath her, seeming to sense his mistress's lighter mood. The long, dry grass rustled beneath his hooves as he moved over it, reminding Abbie just how urgently they needed rain. She and Brett had talked of their concern for their spreads if rain didn't fall soon. Brett didn't have a river running through his property like the Bar C. And even though Abbie didn't mind sharing some of her water, she knew she'd have to make certain that the rest of her neighbors understood that they couldn't just drive their herds over and help themselves. She would need her grass and water for her own stock. If there was no rain, there was no graze. And without pasture, the herd would have to go to market before the usual fall round-up. Brett had voiced the same sentiments. It was an explosive situation all the way around.

After serious discussion had been concluded, she and Brett had talked about Charly's birthday celebration. She was glad that Brett was planning on coming. He certainly needed something to take his mind off of his own troubles. She hoped that with time and friendship, Brett would lose some of his bitterness, feel more in control of his life once again. She had promised Hattie that she would do all that she could, and she'd meant it. The rest was up to Brett.

Abbie had been lost so deeply in thought that she hadn't noticed two riders approaching at a fast gallop, until she happened to look up and spot them.

The rider's urgent pace warned her that something was wrong. As they came abreast of her she recognized two of her *vaqueros*. Her breasts heaved against her silk shirt, and her fingers shook upon the reins.

"What's up? Something wrong back at the ranch?"

The two *caballeros* swung their horses in beside hers.

"We had visitors while you were gone, senorita," Pecos, the one man, informed her.

"*Si,*" his companion, Julio echoed.

186

"What kind of visitors?" Abbie queried.

"Some of your neighbors—asking if we've been losing any of our stock," Julio replied.

"Why do they want to know that?" Abbie inquired.

"Seems some of them have lost quite a few in the past few days," Julio informed her. "They think it's rustlers."

"Rustlers!" she breathed sharply. "We haven't, have we?" Abbie shot her men a piercing look.

"None of the men have reported any loss to the herds. But Peco and I were just about to go over to the north range and see how things are there."

The north range lay at the farthest, most obscure point of Caldwell terrain. If cattle were going to be rustled, this would be the likely starting place. "I'm going with you," Abbie stated.

"Red said to tell you he's got everything covered," Julio said, relaying the message from the Bar C foreman. "The cowboys and *vaqueros* are taking turns riding guard. Red's splitting us up into two-man teams, four shifts of six hours each. The ranchers are holding a meeting tomorrow night at Ben Thompson's place to discuss what they're going to do to stop the ones responsible before they wipe some of us out."

"As if we needed something else to worry about, what with the lack of rain," Abbie commented grimly. "We've got a lot of range to cover, plus the mustangs."

Pecos looked over at her. "What do you want us to do, senorita?"

"To start with, pray for rain."

"*Si*, and then what?"

"Guard our property closely," she said with grit in her tone, reining Romeo toward the hacienda. "And make certain no one comes on my land unless they have a real good excuse for being here."

Exhausted as she was from the events of the day, Abbie

187

found sleep elusive as she tossed fretfully upon her bed. Usually, haunting dreams of Sonny interrupted her ability to sleep. Tonight, however, something else was on her mind: the possibility of raiders pilfering her prized stock. She wasn't missing any cattle as near as her men could tell. But the thought that those rustlers could be out there somewhere on her land even now, biding their time, just waiting to slip in and steal her blind, kept her eyes wide open and her mind racing furiously.

She lay in her bed listening to the sounds of the restless night drifting through the opened French doors that led from her bedroom onto the courtyard. It was one of those nights that she desperately needed to sleep, yet she knew by the alertness of her mind that it was useless to try. Sitting up, she chewed pensively on her bottom lip as she stared at her riding clothes draped across a chair. With a smothered oath, she slipped from bed, slipped off her nightclothes and quickly dressed.

"There is no way I can just lie here and not know what's going on." She grabbed up her gun and holster. "I'm riding over to the north range and check on the men."

The guard riding the outer edge of the north range pulled up short on his mount's reins and stared hard at the wavering movement just below him in the valley. The moon lay hidden behind ghostly gray clouds, its wavering silver light appearing to lend every clump of mesquite and jutting cactus a manly form of grotesque proportions.

The herd of cattle were grouped tightly together in the brush-filled flat around the watering hole. The apprehensive guard noticed his mustang's ears twitch nervously a time or two, the subtle quivering of his body, and figured that was enough of a sign for him. He knew someone or something was out there. Cautiously, he withdrew his rifle from the saddle scabbard and urged his mount toward the longhorns.

Shielded by tilting cedars along the hillside, he was able to move within a few feet of the lowing herd without drawing attention to himself.

Just when he caught sight of the darkly clad figures moving through the herd, and then had turned his mount to go sound the alarm, a rope snaked out of the darkness and ensnared him.

Abbie heard the noise of snapping brush before she noticed the dozen riders moving slowly through the trees. A trail of slow-moving cattle was in their midst traveling toward the river that bordered on one side of Caldwell land.

"I'm being stole blind just as sure as I'm sitting here," she murmured to herself in disbelief. "Where are my men?" Frantically she peered around and saw no one. The terrible thought hit her. They'd been ambushed! What in God's name was she to do now? She knew once the rustlers crossed the river they'd take out on a run. Just when she'd decided to go after them herself, she heard someone call her name and turned in the saddle toward the sound.

"Abbie, what in the hell are you doing out here?"

"Watching someone steal my cattle," she grunted, relieved to recognize Brett Colfax riding toward her.

"I was afraid they might have been headed this way," Brett replied. "I saw them moving across the river while I was out night-riding my own stock."

"Where are your men?" she asked hopefully.

He sighed, disgusted. "I never had time to warn any of them, and seeing how I had to act fast, I just came along on my own." At her groan of disappointment, he added, "Pretty dumb of a one-armed man to think he could hold off a band of rustlers, huh?"

"No—no," she quickly assured him. "I flubbed up just as badly by not telling any of mine that I was coming here. I'm glad you're here, believe me. They must have jumped my boys, so for now it's just the two of us."

"Let's follow them without drawing attention to ourselves. Maybe we can get a line on who these men are." He motioned with his hand for her to slip in behind his horse. "Stay close, and if things turn on us, head out of here. I'll be right behind you."

Abbie nodded and followed his lead. She knew he was hoping to reach the cutoff to the river where they'd have an opportunity to pick off some of the rustlers.

They made it with only minutes to spare, hurriedly crouching behind a scattering of strewn boulders with their rifles cocked, ready for action. Abbie's heart hammered so hard in her chest she felt certain it echoed in the stillness.

Brett turned to her. "Don't fire until we have them directly in our sights. We don't want any of them getting away."

"That's right where I want them," Abbie whispered.

The unsuspecting riders moved the cattle right in front of them. Brett and Abbie took careful aim. It was then Brett's arm suddenly slid out from beneath the weight of his rifle propped on a flat boulder, sending a shower of stones skittering downward. The sound reverberated throughout the valley. A bullet whistled by Abbie. She got off one return shot before the cattle broke into a run, the rustlers hiding within the fast-moving herd, all of them plunging into the river and away from their pursuers.

"Damn! Damn!" Brett howled in frustrated rage, his face a mask of anguish.

Abbie didn't waste a second. Jumping to her feet, she raced to Romeo and vaulted onto his back. "Let's go, boy!" The stallion lunged forward.

"Just where do you think you're going, damnit!" Brett shouted after her.

"After those no-goods!" she screamed into the wind. Without waiting to see if he heard her words, Abbie rode off into the night.

Romeo took the plunge into the river without any urging

from his mistress, long legs swimming powerfully against the current.

Up ahead, the bawling sound of cattle drifted back to Abbie. Someone was trying like the devil to steal what was hers, and she wasn't about to let them get away with it. She continued onward, fury pumping through her.

The distance between them lessened. She could just barely make out their moving forms ahead in the shadows as they scrambled up onto the riverbank. The moon came out from beneath its cloud covering, and she saw them perfectly. Indians—brazen enough to come onto her property and run off her stock. A shot whizzed by her head, barely missing her. She returned the fire.

Romeo came out of the water into a stretched-out gallop that closed the distance between the last rider. Abbie lay out flat over his neck, taking careful aim and firing her six-shooter. The Indian she'd gained upon fell with a sharp cry to the ground and lay still. Abbie longed to keep following the rest of them but knew running her horse at breakneck speed in the dark was foolish. He could easily step in a prairie dog hole or stumble on uneven terrain, causing serious injury to himself and his rider. Regretfully she yanked back on the stallion's reins and brought him to a halt. She thought it a distinct possibility that, come daybreak, they could pick up the trail. For now, she would have to give up the chase and return to the ranch to organize her men.

By the time she crossed back to the other side of the river once again, Brett was waiting. He apologized profusely for his clumsiness that had alerted the rustlers.

"Not just your everyday rustlers, Brett," Abbie informed him. "I brought one of them down. He was a Comanche."

"We haven't had a problem with the Comanche in years."

"It's hard for me to believe, too, but I know what I saw. In the morning I'll have one of the boys bring his body back to the ranch."

"Let's head back, Abbie," Brett stated, sounding worn.

"I've had enough of this for one night."

Abbie nodded. "And Brett," she said understandingly as they wheeled the horses around toward home, "don't blame yourself for their getting away. It was unfortunate, but then, it certainly wasn't something you did intentionally.

Brett was silent, his shoulders slumped dejectedly. "You don't have to make excuses. I know what it cost you."

He was right. It had cost her plenty, but it hadn't been his fault. It had been an unfortunate incident that could have happened to a man with two arms.

It wasn't until early morning that they were able to find the Bar C cowboys who'd been ambushed. They had been tied and gagged but left alive. Abbie was grateful for that.

Sadly, none of them could identify their attackers. They had crept up on the guards from behind—everything perfectly planned—right down to their getaway.

"For renegade Indians," Abbie was to tell her foreman later as they sat over iced drinks in the courtyard, "they certainly knew how to use a lariat. That strikes me as peculiar."

Her foreman, Red, was just as perplexed, although he was ready to blame anything bad on the Indians. "That one Injun's body done up and disappeared, ma'am. It appears someone returned for it."

"The Indians are known to collect their dead, but yet— this whole thing doesn't strike me as being right."

"Well, the boys picked up their trail, but not surprisingly it died real quick in a dried-out wash."

"I can hardly believe that the Comanche are responsible for this."

"What other proof do you need, Abbie Lee?"

"More than just a chance sighting in the black of night," she insisted.

Red grumbled, "I just knew things was going to change with the Comanche. I been hearing too many disturbing stories about that one buck, Night Walker."

Abbie sighed. "His father, the old chief, and my pa, got on

well. I wonder if I found a way to talk with Night Walker whether it would help."

"Don't you try any such thing," Red blurted, his face revealing his concern. "He can't be trusted like the old chief. He's one who holds nothing but contempt for the white man. I heard his pa died when he contracted cholera on the reservation, and they put him off somewhere to die by himself. This Night Walker riled up a bunch of the younger braves and they've been raising hell ever since all over the territory."

Abbie had been listening quietly. "I remember my father telling stories about Night Walker as a youngster. I know he loved his father very much, and I can understand his rage over his unfortunate death. He was every bit a Comanche as a boy, and I imagine as a man, he's very much the proud and fearless warrior."

"It's just another excuse for them devils to go on the warpath and kill more white folks," Red declared angrily.

"Perhaps," Abbie replied. "But somehow I don't think that is the case here."

Red could only shake his head. He couldn't remember where he'd first heard the phrase, The only good Indian is a dead Indian. But it was a singular motto that Red believed true. He wished the boss lady shared the same sentiment. It was folks like her who made him nervous when it came to the Indian situation. "I declare, ma'am, if you aren't going to put me in an early grave talking about giving beeves to the redskins like they was just folks, like us."

Abbie gazed over at this man who'd been their foreman on the ranch for as long as she could remember. Red had taught her to ride her first bronc. Now she wondered if she'd ever really known him at all. Or was it she who had changed, become more understanding of the Indians' plight? She knew that if this were true, it was because of the time she'd spent with Sonny and all of the things that he'd told her about the Kahawdi: their customs, beliefs, their deep abiding love for one another.

It became apparent to her then. If the Indian was a great enemy, the white man had made him so. She remembered how Sonny had told her what a Comanche statesman had once stated to him:

"I was born upon the prairie, where the wind blew free— and everything drew a free breath. We wish to wander on the prairie until we die. Is that so very much to ask?"

Later that day, a group of their best men were gathered around the huge oak desk in the Caldwell study. It had been Walter Caldwell's place to sit in the big chair behind the desk and make important decisions regarding his ranch. Since his death, the men had become accustomed to seeing his daughter there. They had accepted it naturally.

Red looked intently at Abbie. "I'm thinking we might want to notify the rangers, Miss Abbie." He glanced away when her turquoise eyes flared hostilely.

"The Caldwells don't need any rangers swarming over their land and stirring up more trouble with the Comanche. And besides, I intend to look closer into all of this before I retaliate against Night Walker. We could be suspecting him unjustly."

"I doubt that," Red replied quickly. "I imagine the rangers will come in on it anyway, what with the other ranchers all fired up over this rash of thieving Comanches on the loose."

"Fine, but let someone else be the one to notify them. I know what needs to be done, and I don't need any outsiders telling me how to do it." She pushed away from the desk and pointed to a hand-drawn map behind her. "I want you men to head teams of lookouts all over our range, from one end to the other. Warn everyone we're shooting anyone seen on Caldwell land who doesn't have reason to be here."

Red's leathery face was somber. "Yes, ma'am, I will surely do that."

"Thank you all for your concern," Abbie added before dismissing them, "and be careful." She watched thoughtfully as the men began filing from the room.

The unexpected sound of a young boy's carefree laugh permeated the tense, solemn atmosphere and made Abbie smile.

She rose from her chair and walked over to stand by the wide windows overlooking her mother's carefully tended gardens of bright red roses. She saw Charly and her mother coming up the stone walkway that led to the hacienda, having just returned from their stay in San Antonio. Lately, everytime she saw his little face, her thoughts were immediately drawn to Sonya. Lord, she thought. How did my sister ever get herself into such a mess? And how could she have given up her own flesh and blood for someone like Lucien Rodriquez? Her poor mother and Charly. They must never know what had really happened in Devil's Bend.

Abbie felt old anger welling up within her. She would never forget how Sonya had been responsible for Sonny's death. And if she didn't have her family to think about she would go back to Devil's Bend and confront her twin, face-to-face. Sonya was a heartless woman—always had been. Abbie had been blind to it before. But not now, not after Devil's Bend. Someday, someone was going to make her pay for everything that she'd done. Abbie only wished she could be around to see it.

"Mama! Mama! Where are you?" Charly's young voice called forth. "Come quickly. See what Grandma and I brung you!"

Abbie was pulled from her brooding thoughts and was just leaving the den when a wiry little body came dashing around the corner and leaped into her arms. She swept him up, hugging him tightly, so grateful for his presence in her life.

"Hey, tiger. I thought you were calling for me to come to you."

"I was. But you was too slow, so I came to you instead." Charly's chubby arms wrapped about Abbie's neck in an enthusiastic hug.

Abbie feigned collapse from his mighty bear hug. "Oh, my! I think one of these days you're just going to crush me in two you're getting so strong, Charly."

Charly chuckled throatily. "Ah, Ma, you know I'd never do that to you."

"Yes, I know," she agreed, meeting Martha Caldwell's soft gaze.

"Did you have a nice visit, Mother?" Abbie asked her.

"Yes, honey, we did," Martha replied, removing her black-lace shawl and handing it to the housekeeper. "And what has been going on here since we've been away? I saw some awfully long faces on the men as they left the house."

"Why don't we go into the living room and get comfortable. I'll have Francisca bring us some hot chocolate." She ruffled Charly's bright red hair. "How's that sound, tiger?"

She held her son's hand as they wandered toward the massive living room that was so large it needed a fireplace on either end of the room just to remove the chill on cool evenings.

Taking a seat on the leather sofa, Abbie allowed Charly to climb into her lap, laughing lightly as he wiggled impatiently.

"Open your present, Mama!"

Abbie glanced down into his eager face and then over at her mother who sat in a chair next to them.

"Charly, why don't you run and tell Francisca about the chocolate."

"First you open your present," he said, a stubborn set to his small jaw that was very much like Abbie's.

She complied and withdrew a lovely hand-carved wooden jewelry box that played a lilting tune when she opened it.

"I will treasure it always. Thank you both," she said sincerely.

Charly immediately sprang from the couch to head

toward the kitchen. "And cookies, too, okay, Mama?"

"If dinner isn't going to be early this evening, then it's fine." When he'd left the room Abbie turned her attention back to her mother. Her face lost its gentle expression. "We lost some of our prime beef to a band of rustlers."

"Oh, my!" Martha's blue-green eyes revealed alarm. "Was anyone hurt?"

"None of our men, thank the good Lord for that."

"Who did this?" Martha inquired anxiously.

"Comanche, by all the signs. But I just don't know for certain."

"All of these years they've left us alone. Strange that they should start acting up now."

"They're starving to death on the reservations, Mother, and since the old chief's death last winter, his son is determined to go back to the old ways." Abbie's winged brows narrowed as she remembered some of the stories Sonny had told her about the Comanche's mistreatment on the reservations. "I suppose I'd turn to stealing, too, if it meant my family's only means of survival."

Martha looked startled at her daughter's soft expression. "I declare, Abbie Lee," she said, shocked. "I've never heard you talk in such a fashion about the Indian's plight until recently. Why is that, I wonder?" She vividly recalled her daughter's mentioning Sonny Malone's affinity with the Comanche.

Abbie shrugged, her face once more placid. "No special reason. I suppose I've just developed a broader perspective, become more understanding of other people and the sacrifices that they sometimes have to make to insure their survival."

"No other reason?"

"None," Abbie replied, looking away.

"Oh, I almost forgot in all of the excitement," Martha exclaimed. "I have that sleeping draught that Doc Webster mixed up for you. I picked it up while I was near his office.

197

Didn't see any reason to have him make a trip all the way out here. I'll tell Francisca to bring it up to you before you turn in."

"Mother," Abbie sighed. "I told you and Doc Webster both to stop fussing over me like two clucking hens. I'm sleeping fine." She met her mother's direct gaze. "Most nights."

"Is that why I hear you pacing around in your room until dawn sometimes?" Martha said gently.

Abbie waved the air with one hand impatiently. "Only sometimes."

"Only every night."

"All right," Abbie relented. "If it will make you and Doc Webster happy to know I'm sleeping sound as a baby, I'll take the draught."

"Good, dear," Martha replied with a smile. Then walking over to take her daughter's hand in hers she said gently, "The pain of losing him will fade in time. It will get easier, Abbie, darling, believe me, I know."

There was silence for a moment as Abbie met her mother's kind eyes. "But how long does it take, Mama—how long?"

Sonny stared down at her and touched her tenderly upon the cheek. The breath caught somewhere in Abbie's throat, yet she reached upward and took his hand in hers to draw him down beside her on the big bed. He felt so solidly strong in her arms, so vitally alive.

Hungrily she took note of his well-defined features which were thrown into sharp view by the moon slanting across his face. It was difficult to remember that this was just a dream—only a dream—for this time, it seemed so real. It was only after she awakened, her arms empty, that overwhelming despair would consume her, and she would cry out to him again and again, yet never receiving an answer. Half of her wanted to stop the dreams, the torture to her soul, while the other half never wanted to let them go.

Abbie called his name softly and cried for joy when his arms immediately went around her, held her tightly against him while his lips eagerly sought her own. His kisses were sweeter than she ever remembered. She held fast to him, so very afraid to loosen her hold or he would cease to exist like so many times before. She kissed his lips, his half-closed eyelids, his smooth jawline, while her fingers explored and caressed every hard-muscled contour of his bare body. She wrapped her arms about his chest and rested her cheek against the silky hair on his belly.

"Love me, Sonny. Love me like there's never going to be a tomorrow." She kissed the soft fur pressed to her lips.

He groaned in ecstasy. "I want you, Abbie. I love you," he whispered fervently, pulling her up to meet his eyes, his hands deftly discarding her gown.

"Oh, yes, my darling—yes," Abbie breathed in delicious anticipation.

His lovemaking was fiercely consuming, yet infinitely caring. She knew, beyond any doubt, that he was loving her with his entire being, his entire soul. His strong, sensuously curved lips mouthed the words she'd waited so long to hear, and her heart sang.

Abbie felt she would never get enough of him. His hands were braced on either side of her, and she could not help but stare up at him in silent wonder. In the pale moonlight, he appeared like some bronze god whom she'd conjured up from the depths of her innermost dreams to possess her completely. She felt she'd never get enough of looking deeply into his silvery eyes. They were so filled with emotion, so alive in intensity. How could something this wonderful be a dream? How?

"Don't ever leave me again, Sonny," she whispered. "I need you so."

"Oh, God, Abbie," he gasped as he thrust deeply within her, his body shuddering from the intensity of their joining.

"My beautiful silken lady, you don't know—but I'm always with you."

And then words were lost in the throes of passion as the world of dreams spun away and Abbie soared together with him to a realm where they as lovers could exist together. She was adrift in his arms, pleasure like she'd never experienced before radiating inside her. She heard him cry out in breathless ecstasy and felt him release his seed deep inside her. Feeling contented, sated, loved, Abbie allowed herself to sigh his name before drifting off—and into slumber.

Chapter Nine

Abbie woke quickly. Someone was calling her name. She struggled to a sitting position, the effects of the sleeping draught still with her. "Yes—yes!" she replied, hearing the doorknob wiggle.

"Darling, you scared me half to death when you didn't answer me right away." It was her mother's voice. "Is everything all right?"

"I'm fine, Mother. You go on to breakfast, I'll join you shortly." That's strange, Abbie thought, I don't remember locking the door last night.

Abbie sat there baffled, listening to the sound of her mother's footsteps receding down the hall. Glancing about the room, she found her eyes resting upon the open French doors leading out to the courtyard, the sun streaming brightly through the entrance. She could have sworn she'd closed them before retiring. A lingering memory crept unbidden to her conscious thought. Her senses reeled when she vividly recalled how the moonlight had filtered through those doors last night, and how strong and virile Sonny had appeared as he'd stood over her bed.

She could still hear his voice whispering her name and the feel of her heart pounding at his nearness.

"Sonny—it is you—I'm not dreaming?"

"Yes. I can't bring myself to stay away from you, beautiful," he'd said, and she'd welcomed him with open arms.

Abbie shook her head dazedly, recalling how different he had appeared—like a dark, menacing savage—his hair in wild disarray, dressed in a long-fringed buckskin shirt decorated with bright beads, breechclout, and long, clinging leggings.

The touch of his hand upon her cheek had been so infinitely caring. And when he'd drawn her close, his own cheek had been smooth next to hers. Even his moustache had been gone! A sob escaped her, and she threw back the covers and slipped from bed.

"It had to have been a dream, only a dream," she heard herself babbling, eyes immediately drawn to the watercolor painting that sat on an easel next to the French doors. She had started it yesterday morning but had abandoned the project when she wasn't able to get the eyes just the way that she'd wanted them.

"Now, I know exactly how they should look," she murmured, walking confidently over to pick up a short-handled brush. Critically, she studied her efforts. "Yes—it's been lacking a certain spark." Recalling how his eyes had appeared last night—so brilliant, so intense—she added a glitter like diamonds to their silvery depths, and the haunting image of Sonny Malone stared back at her.

"Now it's perfect," she whispered. Upon turning away she happened to look downward and saw a tiny red bead winking back at her from the sunlit carpet. It looked similar to the beads that had adorned the fringed-buckskin shirt that Sonny had worn in her dream. But that was impossible! With a startled cry of disbelief she reached down and picked it up. Was she going crazy? Damnit, Sonny was her obsession, one she could no longer seem to control.

Later, eating breakfast with her mother and Charly, she tried vainly to concentrate on the conversation instead of the Indian bead in her pocket. Her mother was chatting about the birthday fiesta the next evening.

"Abbie, dear, I've been giving it considerable thought, and I think it would be nice if we had the musicians begin earlier . . ." Her words trailed off as she watched her daughter pick listlessly at her plate of *huevos rancheros,* at last, pushing it aside.

"No appetite this morning?" Martha queried gently.

Abbie shook her head, reaching for her cup of *cafe con leche.* The rich milk coffee was all she needed this morning to satisfy her until lunch. "I guess the sleeping powder has me still a bit foggy."

Francisca clucked her tongue as she removed the young woman's plate. Charly attempted to follow his mother's lead, pushing his plate toward the housekeeper. "It not work for you, *nino,"* Francisca said sternly, replacing the half-eaten breakfast before him. "You—eat. You a growing *muchacho."*

"Ahhh, Francisca," Charly groaned. He looked up to see his mother fixing her stern, narrow-eyed glare upon him.

"Charly Caldwell," she said in a firm, no-nonsense tone. "You eat every bit of those eggs or you'll not be going riding today."

"Ahhh, Mama."

"And pronto."

"Yes, ma'am," he conceded unhappily, wrinkling his freckled nose at the breakfast on his plate. Taking a deep breath, he swooped his fork dramatically through the air to scoop up a bite of egg.

Abbie bit back a smile before addressing her mother. "Could you go over the last minute preparations with Francisca today, Mother? I have to do some book work this morning."

"Of course, dear."

"And would you make certain she knows to press my white lawn gown?"

"I'll make certain."

"Do you think that gown will look all right, Mother?" Abbie inquired, trusting her mother's judgement more than her own, since she rarely wore dresses.

Martha smiled understandingly. "That should look lovely on you, honey. Everything generally does."

Abbie grinned, glancing down at her pale blue cotton shirt and close-fitting trousers of soft leather. "Hardly," she quipped.

Martha's gaze softened. "You are like a breath of fresh springtime air, Abbie Lee. You truly have no idea how beautiful you really are."

Abbie chuckled. "You're just saying that because I'm your daughter."

"Yep," Charly piped up, between mouthfuls of eggs, "and if you aren't good and eat all of your breakfast next time, Mama, Grandma is gonna have to spank you."

Abbie and Martha exchanged humorous glances and did their best to stifle their laughter. It was obvious that Charly knew who held highest rank in their family.

The Comanche warrior's diamond-hard, gray eyes looked down from the hilltop upon the sprawling hacienda below. He had spent the last few nights camped here amidst concealing boulders, hoping for just a glimpse of the beautiful woman who lived there.

The lovely old casa, surrounded by colorful flower gardens and red-bricked walkways winding gracefully over carefully tended grounds to an enclosed inner courtyard, appeared overflowing with people rushing to-and-fro. He wondered what was going on. A slight movement to his right drew the observant warrior's gaze to a small boy who had just ridden off on his pony and onto the open plains.

The dark-skinned savage's mouth turned up at one corner in a wry smile. His fiercely painted face followed every move the young child made.

The bright red sun cast an eerie glow upon the harsh planes of the warrior's face—that face that Abbie Caldwell saw each night in her dreams.

"I know this young boy cannot belong to her. It cannot be," the warrior Shadow Dancer, murmured solemnly.

"Shadow Dancer?"

The lithe Comanche warrior spun about, relaxing when he recognized his blood brother, Night Walker, riding his way.

"I am surprised to see you, my brother," Shadow Dancer murmured in Comanche.

Night Walker stared hard at the powerfully built man before him. "You left the camp of the Apache dogs we raided so swiftly after seeing the cattle marked with her brand that we did not get time to speak about it. It is not wise for you to keep coming here. This woman with the hair the color of autumn leaves blinds you to all reason."

Shadow Dancer met Night Walker's eyes. He saw compassion there and affection, and it made it more difficult for him to say the words he knew he must. He took a deep breath. "She is too much a part of me to go on any longer this way. I must go to her—ease her grief."

"And you have not done so yet?" Night Walker interceded softly. He noticed his brother's eyes did not quite meet his as he replied.

"As one who walks only in the shadows of her dreams."

"You are concerned because of what the Apache captive told you."

Shadow Dancer's face grew grim. "If Abbie's cattle were in their camp, then that means someone has been rustling them from here. She must be warned."

"And yet, when you came to me and told me you had much to forget, I assumed this woman was part of it."

"I've tried, for her sake, but it is impossible."

"If you still wish to find your father and punish the Comanchero, then you must do so our way. You are considered dead by your people. We are your family."

"I know that, but I believe he is behind all of this. And besides, she is so much a part of me I cannot forget."

"With everything that you seek, the white woman can only hinder you. You must forget her."

"I thought I could, but I know now I was only deluding myself."

"Little Doe will be saddened to hear you do not wish her for your *paraibo*."

Shadow Dancer looked remorseful. "It cannot be helped. Abbie Caldwell is a fire in my blood."

Night Walker nodded understandingly. "We may be great warriors and feared by many, Shadow Dancer, yet we feel empty inside without our chosen ones beside us. I only wish it could have been Little Doe and not this woman who walks in the image of another. If it is as you told me, your life may be in great danger once again."

"I am ready to give up my life for her all over again, if necessary," Shadow Dancer said fiercely.

"She has stolen you away from us," Night Walker whispered. "And I can see that nothing I say will bring you back." He extended his hand toward Shadow Dancer. "May the gods walk with you, my brother. When you are ready to find Culley Malone once again, come to me. I help."

Shadow Dancer nodded as he grasped his chief's hand. "Tell Little Doe I am sorry."

"I will speak to her for you." Night Walker gazed intently at his blood brother. "Once again, I wish to thank you for telling us where to find the firing pins to the repeaters. I give you my word that we will not make war upon the people in this region. It is the same promise my father gave to Walter Caldwell many years ago. It has not been broken."

"There are some who believe that it has."

Night Walker drew himself up regally. His snapping black eyes were bright with anger. "There are those of the *tejano* who are easily influenced. They dress in our clothing, paint

206

their faces like ours, but they are not Comanche. I punished Rodriquez for betraying me once. I can do so again if need be." It was then the chief withdrew a piece of faded paper from inside his buckskin shirt. The paper rustled in the breeze as he looked down at it. In his hand he held a water-stained notice listing a sizable reward for information leading to the whereabouts of a gunrunner known only as Sonny. Dead or alive, the missive stated. He handed it to Shadow Dancer. "Rodriquez, I think, may hold the answer to many things. But beware of him for he is no fool."

"Where did you get this?"

"From a bounty hunter who was looking for you. He strayed too far, too confidently. He lives no more."

"Someone is not convinced of Sonny Malone's demise, it seems."

At the sound of an approaching horse, Night Walker took his cue to leave. He faded into the settling darkness, leaving Shadow Dancer alone to greet Reeno Sanchez.

A bright shower of moonlight shone through the opened French doors in Abbie's bedroom. It was a full moon—a Comanche moon. "A night for making something together," she remembered him saying that first time she'd lain in his arms.

A tear now threatened. The young woman averted her eyes to the mirror in front of her on the dressing table.

Francisca had just departed with her curling irons. The birthday fiesta for Charly will be getting underway very soon, Abbie thought, patting approvingly the cluster of shining curls cascading down her back. "And I think that should just about do it for me."

She found herself staring broodingly into the mirror at the image projected there. The creamy-white dress had deep flounces of gold-edged lace on the hem and a sash, shot through with threads of turquoise and gold, accentuated Abbie's slender waist. A short Spanish-style jacket, trimmed in gold braid, completed the ensemble. Her mother had been right. It had been the right choice. Abbie felt confident of her appearance and her femininity.

With a rueful smile, she found herself staring at the portrait of Sonny now bathed in a fall of silver moonlight. Lord, but she missed him so.

She wished that he could have seen her dressed so. She wondered if he would have found her pretty. Would those magnificent eyes of his have glowed softly when they'd looked at her—like they did only in her dreams?

Her gaze was drawn to his portrait, and her throat constricted. She had forgotten nothing about him. It showed in her work.

Realizing what she was doing, she mentally shook herself. "This has got to stop, Abbie Lee," she ordered firmly. "He's gone, forever. He's only in your mind." Immediately her fingers crept to the ring on the gold chain around her neck. Without hesitation, she unfastened it and dropped it into her jewelry box. Before she could change her mind and retrieve it, she fled out into the hallway and toward the kitchen.

Upon entering the room, one look told her that Francisca had everything under control. Large, decorated *cazuelas* and *ollas* of every size and shape were filled with various foods and placed on long pine tables in the inner courtyard. The rich, spicy scent of *chorizo* in sauce and *chile con queso* drifted on the faint breezes throughout the *hacienda*.

"Everything looks delicious," Abbie told the beaming housekeeper as she surveyed the heaping platters of barbecued beef and chicken.

"*Gracias,* senorita," Francisca said, hurrying past Abbie to deposit another batch of fragrant, hot *bolilos,* excellent rolls, to the already overflowing basket on the serving counter. "The desserts and fruits we will leave for last, *si?*"

208

Abbie smiled, her eyes resting upon the assorted cakes, pies, and fresh fruits in readiness on the sideboard. *"Si,* give us ample time to consume all of this first, Francisca."

Francisca's voice lowered to a whisper. "I have the special cake in the pantry. When do you wish it served?"

"Just as soon as Charly's finished opening his presents," Abbie instructed. "And don't forget my one gift; the one that's been giving you so much trouble of late." Her eyes danced merrily.

"I not likely to forget," Francisca grumbled. "The little *bribon* was quiet for the first time last night, and I thought letting him sleep under my bed had been a good idea." Her eyebrows shot upward. "He quiet all right, for good reason. He chew my one house slipper to little bits."

"Well, I'll see that you get a new pair. Now, I'd best go see if the guest of honor has finished dressing." Abbie left the kitchen and went toward Charly's room where sounds of a battle could distinctly be heard.

"Charly Caldwell, you put on this tie and take off those grubby chaps this instant," his grandmother ordered sternly just as Abbie rounded the corner.

"What seems to be the problem, you two?" Abbie inquired, exchanging knowing looks with Martha.

"Gram wants me to put on—this," Charly said with disdain as he held up a brown narrow string tie. "And to take off my guns and chaps, too."

"Well, cowboy, I bet everyone is going to dress up in their fanciest clothes this evening." Before he had time to protest, Abbie had the tie about his shirt collar and the chaps quickly discarded on the bed. "There," she enthused, "now don't you look handsome." She gave a final pat to an unruly curl at the back of his head.

"So do you, Mama," Charly was quick to reply as he gazed up adoringly at her. He took her hand in his smaller one. "I bet there is nobody in the whole wide world who is as pretty as my mama."

Abbie felt a lump form in her throat, and her eyes bore a faraway expression. "Perhaps," she responded thickly.

The lovely tiled courtyard was alive with the sounds of laughter and excited voices. Flaming torches set in black-iron wall sconces cast a soft golden glow upon the many guests who had gathered for the happy occasion. The sultry air was perfumed by thick clusters of flowering vines that trailed along the outer walkways and climbed the high bricked walls that surrounded the hacienda.

Abbie was pleased that so many of her neighbors had accepted her invitation. She had sent out over fifty invitations to people she knew in and around San Antonio. By the number of guests who were in attendance, it appeared they had all accepted. She glided through the crowd, doing her best to make everyone feel welcome. Once she had looked up to see Brett Colfax smiling appreciatively at her as he conversed with a group of wranglers in a quiet corner of the courtyard. Abbie returned the gesture, and Brett found it hard to believe, considering all of the years they'd been separated, that she was at last going to be his.

"You can't take your eyes off that little gal for a second, can you Brett?" Shorty winked at him knowingly and grinned. "You got stars in your eyes, boy, and I think I can guess why."

Brett glanced from Abbie to Shorty. "Yep, I think you can at that."

He removed a small box from his coat pocket. Glancing down at it, he murmured, "Tonight, sweet Abbie, I'm going to claim you as mine." He watched her covertly, waiting for the right opportunity.

After the guests had sufficiently stuffed themselves with Francisca's delicious fare, Charly started to open his gifts. His gift from Abbie was saved for last. Francisca led the shaggy black and white pup forward with a sigh of relief. Charly had wanted a little dog of his own for a long time. He was thrilled.

"I think you should call him *Bribon,*" Francisca said with a smile.

"I think I should, too." Charly laughed as he attempted to free his pants' leg from the frisky pup's quick jaws.

After Charly blew out the candles on his cake, the younger guests gathered round to break the *pinata* that swung from a tall tree. The children had a gay time trying to break open the brightly painted burro containing the treats. It was Charly, with one well-aimed swing, who befittingly broke open the burro and sent the candies and trinkets showering downward into eager hands.

After the children were ushered indoors, the musicians struck up a festive tune to entice the adults to give in to the spirit and dance. Abbie danced with several *caballeros,* but it wasn't until the pace of the mariachi musicians slowed just a bit that Brett Colfax stepped in and swept her among the dancers to the stirring rhythm of the guitarists.

He gazed down into Abbie's eyes and knew that she was remembering, just as he was, how happy and carefree they'd been years ago, when the world for both of them had held so much promise.

"I've missed holding you like this," Brett whispered, his head bent close to hers, his one arm wrapped about her waist. "It feels right, don't it Abbie?"

"We've grown very close in the past few weeks, Brett," Abbie replied. "And yes, it does feel right."

"You know, Abbie, I been doing a lot of thinking about us, and I can't help believin' that we've wasted enough time." With agility he swept her from the dance floor into the secluded rose garden and before she had time to even catch her breath he had reached into his coat pocket and withdrawn the velvet box. "This is for you. I hope you'll accept it."

211

Tentatively, she watched him open it and saw the diamond ring sparkling up at her. "Oh my—it's—lovely, but don't you think this is all a bit sudden?"

"Sudden? Why we've known each other most of our lives, and if the war wouldn't have separated us, we'd be an old married couple by now." He managed to remove the ring with surprisingly agile fingers and took her hand in his. "Just try it on, Abbie Lee. At least let me see what it looks like on your finger."

Not wishing to offend him, Abbie nodded. "But this does not mean that I've said yes. We'll talk more after things calm down a bit."

Brett nodded, then quickly slipped the ring on her finger. "See, perfect fit."

Abbie was not aware of the tall, dark-haired man who had been observing her closely, his eyes following her every gesture toward Brett. He was someone she would not have expected to see here tonight. Therefore, his presence and his scrutiny went unnoticed by her.

Reeno Sanchez was garbed in a short, Charro jacket and breeches of black velvet, a burgundy shirt with a narrow threading of black on the ruffled front, and shiny black boots. He looked every bit the Spanish gentleman. It was perhaps the reason that Abbie never recognized him—at first—until she happened to glance out into the crowd of faces and saw him grinning widely at her.

"Reeno—oh my God—it is you!" she cried, pulling away from Brett to hurry toward him.

"Senorita, it is good to see you looking so well, and happy," Reeno offered politely.

"And you! It is wonderful to see you again, my friend." Her face glowed softly.

"You are lovelier than ever," he said quietly.

Her gaze swept over his elegant clothes approvingly. "My, this is a side of you I have never seen before. How very dashing you look." She hesitated briefly as Brett walked up beside her and wrapped his arm possessively about her waist. He felt her flinch but did not remove his arm.

Abbie introduced the two men. "Reeno Sanchez, I'd like to introduce my good friend, Brett Colfax." The two men eyed each other speculatively.

Before Abbie could draw a breath Brett interceded. "Sanchez, aren't you the fella who brought Abbie back to us?"

"*Si,* I did," Reeno replied coolly, immediate dislike for this arrogant sandy-haired cowboy making his eyes narrow.

Brett smiled. "Well, it's a pleasure to meet you, Senor Sanchez. I don't know how I'll ever repay you for bringing my little gal home." He grasped Abbie's hand. "You see, Abbie and I are making plans to marry. It seems fittin' that you be here to share in our happiness."

Reeno looked down at the diamond ring on Abbie's finger then shook Brett's extended hand. "Congratulations," he said, as his dark-eyed glance pierced Abbie.

Abbie could not believe Brett's choice of words. She gave him a pointed stare. "Congratulations aren't in order yet, Reeno. I haven't actually said yes."

"Oh, but she will," Brett added with a boyishly charming grin.

Wishing to talk privately with Reeno, she said to Brett, "Would you see that Senor Sanchez gets something to drink."

"Sure honey," he agreed, rushing off.

Abbie felt Reeno's probing stare. "It isn't anything like you're thinking."

"How do you know what I am thinking, Abbie?" Reeno responded evenly.

"I glimpsed a flicker of disappointment in your eyes." She drew her gaze upward to meet Reeno's and suddenly felt a need to defend her inability to control Brett's actions of late. "He's really not a bad sort. We both could be good for each other."

"And what of love?"

213

"Is that any of your concern?"

"I care about your happiness."

"Is that what I had with Sonny?" she responded derisively.

"You are still very bitter, *chica.* Going into a marriage with Brett with your emotions in a turmoil is not good."

Abbie softened, glancing at the diamond on her finger. "I know," she sighed. "And I had no idea he was going to propose marriage so soon. It just happened."

"Does he know you do not love him?" Reeno smiled when he saw a brief glimpse of the old Abbie as she drew herself up haughtily.

"I have done nothing to give him the wrong impression, if that's what you're thinking. He knows I do not wish to rush into anything."

"Bueno." Reeno brightened. "Now, will you allow an old friend a dance?"

"I'd like that," Abbie replied warmly. Reeno took Abbie into his arms. The music had slowed to a gentle, swaying rhythm, allowing them to talk as they danced.

"So, you are trying to put the past behind you, little one, and go on with your life as before."

Abbie stared hard at him. "Before Sonny, you mean?"

"I suppose that is what I was implying," he returned as they glided to the outer edge of the dancers, Reeno twirling her faster about the courtyard.

"There is no longer any reason why I shouldn't." Her eyes held memories.

Reeno saw this and, without replying, twirled her about until she was lost to everything but the exhilarating motion. Her eyes fell closed, and then, abruptly, his arms fell away. She immediately opened her eyes, pausing to catch her breath. When the world once again stopped revolving she found herself standing all alone in the shadows just outside the opened French doors off her room. Strong fingers curled around hers.

"Ab," a deep resonant voice murmured over her shoulder.

She had heard that voice so many nights in her dreams that she knew without a single doubt who it was. She whirled about. In the flickering torchlight bright turquoise eyes locked with glittering, silvery-gray.

"Sonny!" she breathed, her eyes disbelieving even as she saw him standing before her. Overtaken by the shock of seeing him looking so devastatingly handsome and vitally alive, Abbie's knees almost buckled. He held her hand firmly in his, steadying her.

His assessing gaze roamed over her. "You're even more beautiful than I remember," he stated huskily.

For a brief, timeless moment they stared silently at each other, and Abbie found herself wondering if this could be yet another dream. She reached one slim finger upward to caress his clean shaven jaw, trace the smoothness of his upper lip. "My God, you're real," she said in a choked voice.

A crooked smile deepened the grooves on either side of his mouth. "Yes, my silken lady, very much so."

She could only nod numbly, taking in everything about him. He was garbed in superbly tailored clothes. Clothes that cost a great deal of money. A charcoal gray coat and trousers fit his muscular torso to perfection. A black silk shirt with black pearlescent studs made his dark good looks even more formidable.

"I have to hold you, Abbie," he groaned. He pulled her into his arms and held her tightly against his beating heart. His chin rested upon her cloud of rose-scented hair. "I can't believe we're here together like this."

Abbie found her gaze drawn to the portrait of him that was framed in a single shaft of moonlight. She almost felt she had conjured him up from the depths of her soul. But she knew she had not. He was here, in the flesh, very much alive. Everyone's telling her that he was dead had all been a lie!

He felt her abruptly stiffen and tightened his arms around her, sensing what was coming.

"Alive!" she hissed furiously, struggling to free herself

from his embrace. "They told me you were dead!" she choked. "And you're not. You're alive!"

"You almost sound disappointed," he said dryly, never once relinquishing his firm hold. He knew he was in for the fight of his life.

"How could you have let them lie, you despicable, low-down polecat!"

"I've missed you, Abbie," he whispered, lips pressed to her temple.

"Letting me stand by that grave, feeling like my own life had just ended!"

"I did it for you, sweet Abbie."

"You're a cold-hearted monster!"

"I want to make love to you, Abbie."

She started. "What did you say?"

"I want you, Abbie—now—this very minute."

Abbie emitted a strangled cry as his words registered. She stared up at him, torn between anger and resentment and the overwhelming desire to press her lips to his.

"I know how you must feel right at this moment." His eyes caressed her flushed face. "I came here tonight because I can't go on any longer without you. I need you, Ab."

Her turquoise eyes flashing with anger, Abbie wrenched her arm free of his grasp. "You can't go on any longer without me, you say," she burst out explosively. "Well, isn't that a shame! I didn't have a choice when you made me go on without you, Sonny. Do you have any idea what that was like?"

"Painful, for both of us—yet necessary."

"It was like a part of me had died with you," she murmured brokenly, all of the weeks of anguish overwhelming her once again. "I thought when I had lost my father that I had experienced the worst kind of despair there was. Oh, God, was I wrong. Standing by that grave where they told me you were buried was the worst." A strangled sob escaped her as that day came back with stark clarity. Sonny took a step toward her.

"No. Stay away from me. Don't touch me," she spat furiously.

"Abbie, honey, don't do this," he pleaded, his face bleak. "Let me explain."

"No! You lied! They all lied!" She lowered her voice when a laughing couple strolled nearby. "I'll never forgive you for what you've done to me, never."

Sonny's expression didn't change, but Abbie noticed a muscle tighten in one smooth, dark cheek. She stepped backward, watching him warily as he closed the distance between them. She didn't realize she had backed into her bedroom until he moved to shut and lock the French doors, then swiftly did the same with her bedroom door. He turned with purpose toward her.

"I suppose I'll have to prove to you how much you mean to me, Ab," he whispered. Hard passion glittered in his eyes.

"Stay away from me, Sonny." She darted to one side. "You had your chance and you turned me away."

He moved with predatory grace, even before she did, anticipating her action with an animallike cunning that stunned her. "You can't get away from me, little one." His hand shot out, his long fingers burying themselves in her thick hair, exerting a persuasive pressure on the back of her neck. She stood rigid. He pulled forcefully, bringing her soft body up against his hard one. "I intend to make you mine, here, tonight—willingly, or not."

"It will not be willingly."

He laughed huskily. "So you try to tell me each time. But I know better, don't I, dream lover?"

"It was you!" she gasped just before his lips captured hers in a long, languorous kiss that ignited an instant flame of desire within her. She accepted the fullness of his tongue in her mouth with a low moan of desire. His hands slid over her slim form, along her spine, to cup her buttocks and pull her roughly to him.

It felt so right in his arms that she was helpless to protest when his knee slid between her legs, urging them farther apart. Without her being aware he maneuvered her body until her back was pressed to the wall, his hands pressed flat against the wall on either side of her. Escape was impossible. Abbie was stunned by how easily he could make her want him. Her hips moved with erotic grace against his groin, creating a burning need within them both that could not be denied.

He lifted his head slightly. "See, silken beauty, your body does not deny me what is rightfully mine. Why does your heart?"

"I can't control my physical need of you," she retorted thickly. "You've a power over me I cannot fight."

"That power, Ab, is love," he murmured against her mouth. "You're hurt and mad right now, but you know I speak the truth."

"I no more trust you to tell me the truth than I would that Yankee tax assessor who keeps nosing around here!"

"I admit I was pretty underhanded before," he conceded. "But no more, not since I realized how much you mean to me."

She longed to believe his words, yet how could she after everything that he'd put her through? "No, it's too late," she grated hoarsely.

"Ab, Ab," he whispered between light kisses. "I'm going to make love to you, and this time you will know for certain that it is not a dream." His lips moved downward, lightly kissing her chin before tasting the honeyed smoothness of her throat.

Abbie trembled when his hands deftly unfastened the back of her gown and pulled it downward. Her petticoats swiftly followed, leaving her clothed only in her undergarments. She tried to remain rigid, but every nerve in her body reacted traitorously to his caress.

Sonny plied her body with a knowing touch. He remembered every place she loved for him to caress and place his lips, and he did so in a way that had her skin tingling with anticipation.

"I want to feel your bare skin beneath my fingertips," she murmured. She was afire, tearing at his elegant coat and trousers in such an urgent manner that he said gently, "Slowly, *querida,* we have all night."

She shook her head. "No, we do not. I must get back to the party soon."

Sonny's jaw tightened. "To him, you mean, don't you!"

"You have no right to come here and start reordering my life!"

"But I do, Ab," he said convincingly. "When one person saves another's life it creates a bond between them." He ran one long finger lightly over her creamy cheek. "You and I have such a bond."

Abbie could only stare up into his stormy gray eyes in silence. Any sharp reply she might have flung back at him died instantly when she read the depth of emotion within that smoky gaze.

Impatient now, his eyes left hers to openly admire her soft beauty attired in just her lacy camisole and pantalets. "You're the most beautiful woman I've ever seen in my life," he said in that husky timbre that never failed to give her goose bumps.

Abbie felt him tug gently on the ribbons securing her camisole and then felt a sense of coolness as it fell open. Warm, strong fingers reached forward to gently knead her breasts, lightly squeeze her aching nipples, making her knees feel as if they'd give way beneath her. There was no thought of protest when he slipped her pantalets down her slim legs, his lips following the path of his seeking fingers, tantalizing her until she felt like screaming from his sinuous exploration.

"Oh, God. Oh, God," she panted, lacing her fingers in his dark hair to hold him against her alabaster breasts.

His mouth was enticingly erotic, and when his lips skimmed over the smooth flesh of her belly, sliding downward to pull teasingly at the tight curls on her womanly mound, Abbie felt certain she could never get enough of the exquisite sensations he awakened. He kissed her there, tenderly, then tasted the satiny softness of her inner thighs with sensual slowness before moving upward once again, to the hot, velvet center of her.

Abbie innocently undulated her hips, scarcely knowing what it was she wanted him to do. Slowly, his tongue parted the gently curved folds, lightly teased the aroused bud that swelled against it. She thought she'd swoon when he gently took it between his lips to alternately suckle, then nip lightly her yielding charms. She found the room, the world, the very universe spinning away until it was just the two of them and the all-consuming passion that they shared between them. The hot ache of desire that had overtaken her now consumed her, making her twist mindlessly beneath his questing hands and mouth.

Moments later, he was sweeping her up into his arms and carrying her toward the bed. Placing her upon it, he stood silently over her, admiring her perfectly formed body. He undressed beneath her heavy-lidded gaze—slowly—enticingly.

The room was flooded with silvery moonbeams, allowing her eyes to roam freely over the size and width of him. Was it possible for him to be even more handsome than before, she wondered, staring heatedly at his body? She openly admired his shorter hair, his strong, smoothly shaven jaw. But it was the silvery moonlight slanting on his bronzed, muscular form that, at last, compelled her to reach upward and draw him down to her. She found him hard and ready beneath her searching fingers.

His long frame stretched over her. With a small cry of

220

delight she traced her fingers along the corded muscles of his back. She loved the way the sinewy flesh rippled beneath her touch.

Needing to feel him even closer, Abbie opened her legs willingly, her fingers boldly guiding his throbbing manhood deep inside her. His first thrust was powerful, and her body arched upward to meet him with a sob of relief. He moved his hips in a circular motion, slowly at first, then gradually faster. She matched his heated rhythm with a fierceness that equalled his own. They were perfectly fitted: two wild, passionate people who defied all odds to love.

Shudders of ecstasy encompassed their bodies as they increased the tempo to a fevered force. His hand slipped between their bodies to caress her pulsating mound as his rigid flesh drove into her. Abbie's body trembled as the first spasms of exquisite pleasure radiated sweetly throughout her body.

Sensing her release, he quickly joined her, their soft cries of ecstasy intermingling, their hearts soaring together where they could be one.

They lay wrapped in each other's arms, reluctant to break the spell of the moment. Sonny knew they had to talk. There was much that needed explaining.

"Are you awake, honey?" he queried softly.

"Just barely," she answered sleepily.

He kissed the enticing crests of her breasts, laughing huskily when she squirmed beneath him. "You can't sleep, Ab, we need to talk."

"We won't—if you keep doing that," she whispered in between gasps of pleasure.

He raised his head to look down at her. "Don't tempt me." He sighed and pulled her over him, her cheek resting on his chest. "For your sake, I tried hard to stay away from you. I didn't plan on seeing you again. It just happened."

The blunt statement tore at her heart. "I gathered that much." She turned her head away from him.

He knew it hurt her to hear the truth. But he wanted her to know how he felt now. His fingers grasped her chin and forced her to look at him. "I was confused. I didn't plan on your showing up in Devil's Bend that night. And our making love just clouded my reasoning more."

"I know," she replied faintly. "Mine, too."

"And then, I find out you have a twin, and she frames me for murder."

"I still find it hard to believe she would actually murder someone—with her own hand."

"She was desperate," he responded. "I won't go into the details with you, but the major was not in your sister's room for chitchat. There are men who get their kicks out of hurting a woman while they're having sex. The major was taking his anger at Rodriquez out on Sonya. She lost her head and grabbed for a knife lying nearby."

Abbie intervened. "Sonya saw the perfect way to cover her own tracks when you went to help her. She deliberately set you up as the major's murderer. Pretty cold-blooded."

"But she wasn't counting on one thing," Sonny replied, slanting a look at her."

"What's that?"

"You, *cabecilla.*"

"No, I guess she wasn't," she responded softly. "You can't imagine how many times that I've protected her in the past."

"Not this time," he stated in a firm tone. "I'll never forget what she did to either of us."

Abbie took a tremulous breath. "No, not this time. You can't even imagine how many evil things Sonya has done, Sonny. This was just one of the worst. I never thought she'd stoop to murder."

"I aim to clear my name. I plan on exposing her, Ab, right along with Rodriquez."

"I understand," she replied tonelessly. "I want to help you."

"Oh, no you're not," he shot back. "You're staying out of this."

"Why don't you let me be the judge of that?"

He laughed shortly. "Your instincts have not always been the best, sweetheart."

"And yours have?" she snapped, sighing inwardly. Why did they always end up in some sort of battle?

"You know as well as I do the reason I ended up in jail," he replied.

"If you say it was totally to protect me, I swear I'll hit you."

He couldn't help but laugh lightly. "But it was—Abbie honey," he teased. When she sat up and aimed a mocking blow at him, he playfully grabbed her wrist and tickled her small clenched fist with the soft brush of his lips until she was laughing. His voice suddenly became serious. "Let's face it. If things don't go in my favor, at least you'll be in the clear."

Abbie's heart lurched painfully. She snuggled deeper into his arms. "Don't say that, or even think it. At least here, together, there is nothing to fear."

"I'm not so certain of that."

"Why?"

"Have you been losing any cattle?"

"More all of the time."

"That gives me reason to think some of Lucien's men are in the territory."

Abbie sat up with a start. "Tell me how you know this."

He placed a steadying hand on her arm. "After my wound healed, I went to the camp of my blood brother to rest and regain my strength. He told me that Rodriquez had tried to sell him some rifles without firing pins. The Comanche punished him severely. Lucien fled the area, and I thought then that he was gone for good—until we raided an Apache camp in New Mexico and found some of your cattle there."

Abbie's face appeared drawn as she replied. "We missed those cattle about two weeks ago," she groaned. "What are we going to do?"

"I won't let anything happen to you," he said firmly. "I

223

only hope the authorities still believe I'm dead or my coming here could do you more harm than good."

"Why would they have cause to doubt what they've been told? I heard tell the army even gave up searching for you."

"There are wanted posters out on me in San Antonio," he stated tersely. "Someone—wasn't convinced of my demise."

"Who?" Abbie paled.

"I suspect Rodriquez."

"I'm beginning to think it wasn't love that brought you back here."

"This wasn't the first night I've been here, Ab," he reminded her gently.

Her face flamed, recalling the untamed look about him that night she'd awakened to find him standing over her bed. And the Indian bead—it had been his. A startling realization suddenly dawned on her. "What—if I should become pregnant?" It was something she'd wished for when she'd first returned. Now, it would cause many problems. Yet she wanted his child very much. But how did he feel?

"I almost expected, maybe hoped just a little, that you'd already be carrying my child the first time I came to you."

"And were you disappointed?"

He didn't immediately reply but sat up, then shrugged. "It's hard to say. I knew it would complicate a good many things, so I suppose I was relieved."

"Wonderful," she said dejectedly, rising from the bed to draw on a wrapper and tie a sash around her waist. "I guess I'd better hope I'm not then."

He came up behind her, his arms immediately encircling her. "There's already one little fellow in your life, Ab. And I think he's someone we need to discuss."

Abbie froze in his arms. "And just who would that be?"

"The little boy who calls you his mama," he said softly.

"Oh." She gulped.

"Is that all you have to say?" he probed, taken aback by her refusal to confide in him.

224

Abbie's thoughts whirled. If anyone knew that she could not be Charly's natural mother, it was Sonny. Still, she blurted, "He's mine. That's all you need know!"

"Bull!" he roared. "What do you take me for, some kind of a fool?"

"Damn you, Sonny!" she said hotly. "Back off from me! This is all happening too fast."

At once, his temper cooled. They were both getting too worked up over this. He decided to drop it until they had time to become trustful of each other once again. Obviously, Charly Caldwell was someone she did not wish to share with him. He planned to convince her otherwise. And now was as good a time to start as any. "It could be different now, Ab. I've worked it all out so that we can be together. And you can take Charly with us. He'd love it. We can lay low with my blood brother's people until I can clear my name and find Lucien once again." He paused, his hands gently massaging her shoulders. "I want you to pack your things and come with me—now—tonight."

How ironic he should say those things to her at this time, when it was impossible. "Don't, Sonny," she choked. "I can't leave here. There are people who depend on me—my mother, my men."

He turned her in his arms. "Goddamnit, I need you. We need each other."

She met his steely glare with a calmness that made him want to physically shake her. He could handle her explosive outbursts, her taunting words. But he had not been prepared for the cool, levelheaded Abbie he now held in his arms.

"Things are different between us now, Sonny," she said slowly, precisely.

"Why should they be?" he queried angrily.

"Because, I thought you were dead, remember? I went on with my life."

Her quick, calm response sent a chill racing through him. "I'm beginning to think you're hiding out, Ab. You're not

225

going on with life, you're running from it, from me." At that moment Sonny's hand encountered her left one and the ring Brett had placed there. He felt her stiffen. She tried to jerk away from him, but to no avail. Cold, furious wrath gripped him when the sparkling diamond caught his eye. It glinted tauntingly in the moonlight.

"You sure as hell didn't waste any time mourning me, did you! You're actually planning on marrying Colfax aren't you?" he snarled. "Is he your lover now?"

"It isn't anything like you're thinking," she attempted to explain. "It happened this evening. I was taken unawares."

Sonny's face in the dim room expressed fury, and for one intense moment she thought that he might hit her. "Suppose you tell me what it's like then, Abbie?"

"Brett and I were fond of each other before I met you. We were separated by the war, and I've been trying to help him put his life back together since his return." She was totally confused and handling it badly, she knew. "He put it on my finger earlier this evening, and I just couldn't toss it back in his face. He would have been devastated."

"And you just decided you might wear it awhile to spare his poor feelings, is that it?" he growled disgustedly. "Come on, Abbie, you can do better than that." He released her hand and snatched up his clothes. "My, but you've had a busy night! You got yourself engaged by your new love and bedded by your old. And you've managed to do it without either one of us running into each other."

She had never seen him look so harsh, so furious. But damn him! As usual, he was jumping to all the wrong conclusions. And they were wrong, she concluded. "You won't even try to understand, will you? You want to believe the worst of me, so go ahead."

His silver-gray eyes flicked over her appraisingly as he grabbed up his jacket from a chair. "Spare me any more of your logical explanations," he implored tersely. "I'm aware you're not wearing my ring any longer. For all that you claimed to have loved me, it certainly didn't take you long to cast old memories aside, did it?"

The expression in her eyes changed to outraged indignation. "You have no right to say that to me! I went through agony because of you, Malone! And now you come whirling back into my life unaffected by it all and expect me to forget everything and run off with you!"

"And I remember how you vowed to make me pay for putting you through it. Well, you sure as hell have, baby!"

Abbie felt a stinging behind her eyelids and knew she was about to cry. He didn't understand her at all; never did—and never would. "Get out of here," she said flatly, "It's obvious there can never be anything else between us but lust. There could never be love—not with you."

He stalked toward the French doors, his insides twisting at her unfeeling declaration. "With pleasure, ma'am," he said stiffly, his mouth twisting in a laconic smile. "But I'll guarantee you one thing, *gata,* I'm not dancing on the end of your string. When I walk out of here it's *finito.*"

Abbie stood stubbornly proud. He snorted. "Good-bye, Miss Caldwell." He slipped from the room, leaving her mind spinning and her heart breaking—just like he always did.

There was a soft knock on her door. "Abbie," a soft male voice called forth. It was Brett.

"Yes?" she replied, her insides tightening.

"Is there some reason why you left the party, honey? Everyone's been asking for you."

Abbie could not bear to face him. "I developed a splitting headache, Brett, and I decided to lie down for awhile. You go on back and explain for me, will you?" She heard him sigh disappointedly.

"Should I send Francisca with a headache powder?" he inquired.

"No, I'll be fine if I can just stay in bed."

"Well, all right," he agreed with some reluctance. "I hope you're feeling better soon, honey."

She heard his footsteps recede down the hall. Brett had been so attentive and kind. Not once had he lost his temper with her. She glanced down at the diamond ring on her finger. Perhaps she would do well to marry Brett Colfax, and the sooner the better. At least he needed her, cared about her. She shook her head dazedly, glancing over at Sonny's portrait. He had been here, the man she had dreamed of, longed for. He had come to her, made love to her—and left her—without a single regret.

Chapter Ten

Reeno Sanchez cast a speculative eye toward his scowling *paisano* as they sat playing cards and drinking whiskey in a supply shack on a remote section of Caldwell land.

When Santiago had whisked Abbie away from the fiesta last night and she had gone willingly, Reeno had assumed everything would work out fine. *Caramba*. What a mistaken assumption that had been! It seemed the only thing that had gotten settled between them was the fact that they never wanted to see each other again! So much time wasted with this senseless fighting. And over what—stubborn pride—and a man like Brett Colfax.

Reeno had been forced to keep the brash Brett Colfax occupied while Santiago had been with Abbie. It hadn't been too difficult. Reeno had simply asked Brett if he'd fought for the Confederate cause during the war, and the man had rambled on for over an hour about the trials he'd had to endure. Reeno had been relieved to glance up and notice Santiago heading in the direction of their horses. Bidding Colfax an abrupt *adios*, Reeno had followed after his friend.

"Look, *amigo*," he said now, trying to draw Santiago out of his black mood. "It isn't fair to blame Abbie for going on with her life. Isn't that what you wanted?"

They were alone in the room. The Bar C foreman had been

delighted to see Reeno once again, and when they inquired of a secluded place to lie low for a few days, he'd not asked any questions but suggested the supply shack. Reeno filled Sonny's glass once again. He knew why his friend was reluctant to leave. Abbie Caldwell meant everything to him.

"I don't know what I want at this point," Sonny replied irritably.

"You know, you're showing up like that was a helluva jolt for her."

Sonny glared. "Yeah, for both of us." He downed another shot of whiskey. "The two-timing little baggage. I wouldn't have her now, after knowing she's been with Colfax, if she came to me and begged me to take her back."

Reeno frowned. "How is it you're always ready to believe the worst of this woman? And yet you claim to love her."

"I never said that!" Sonny snarled.

"Maybe not in so many words, but by your actions, what else would you call it?"

"A physical attraction," Sonny offered caustically.

"An affair of the heart, Santiago, admit it."

"Damnit Reeno, I don't need you telling me how I feel right now," Sonny growled, slamming his empty glass on the table.

Reeno leaned back, balancing the chair on two legs. "Very well, then we'll change the subject," he said with more patience than he felt. "Since you have now convinced yourself that you and Abbie are *finito,* why are you hanging around here any longer? Let her take care of herself. General Diaz has sent word that they are marching onward to Mexico City. After that, it will all be over. I must see that he receives the arms that he needs for the attack." Reeno arched a dark brow. "Are you coming with me?"

Sonny stared broodingly into the amber liquid in his glass.

"The answer you are seeking is not in that glass, *amigo,*" Reeno stated blandly. "You know very well why you're not going to come back with me. I do too."

Sonny's gaze flicked toward Reeno. "If it weren't for this vendetta with Rodriquez, I'd leave right now and go back to Mexico with you."

Reeno looked sideways at Sonny. "Of course you would. Even though you're not even certain where he is."

"He's been here," Sonny stated with firm conviction. "Some of the steers in an Apache camp I raided with the Comanche were marked with brands from this area. Lucien is the only one who can risk trading with those devils."

"Abbie's foreman, Red, said all's been quiet on the ranches the past few days."

"Lucien probably hasn't returned from the high plains yet, that's why," Sonny replied.

"Ah, how can I leave you when I know this," Reeno grumbled, torn between his loyalty to his friend and his need to return to the real fighting.

Sonny grinned at Reeno's disgruntled expression. "Every man must find his destiny, *amigo*. I am about to meet mine, and your staying or going won't really alter any course I have to follow."

"I thought you might say that. That's why I told Red to drop by later. Abbie told him to hire someone good with a gun to keep watch out here. I already told him I knew just the man." Reeno smiled.

Sonny grinned tiredly. *"Por Dios,* she will have your hide for that."

Reeno grunted. *"La nina* will have to come to Mexico then, for I am going home, *amigo.* And if I thought for one *momento* that Abbie cared for me, I would be trying my best to move heaven and earth to get her away from Colfax."

Sonny finished his drink, a faraway expression in his eyes. "I would give anything if Abbie and I were going with you." He turned to Reeno. "No one here knows who I really am, do they?"

"They only know you as my *compadre,* Santiago, from Mexico."

"Abbie's family and men set great store in you, Reeno. After all, you're the one who brought the boss lady back home all safe and sound."

"Yes, I did, although it is a time I'd like to forget. It is not a happy memory," Reeno commented flatly. "Did anyone tell you the anguish Abbie went through thinking you had—died?" Even now, Reeno still choked on the word.

"No, but I'm sure you're about to," Sonny replied stonily.

Reeno gritted his teeth. "I saw what it did to her. Particularly that last day when she stood by that empty grave, and I watched her place a lock of her hair beneath the loose dirt. A part of her left behind—with you."

Sonny raised his eyes slowly to meet Reeno's, his expression shuttered. "Abbie's a tough one, Reeno. A survivor."

"And yet there's another side of her, isn't there, Santiago? A soft, feminine side. I glimpsed it briefly the other night. She was *magnifico* then, wasn't she?" He watched his friend grow thoughtfully quiet.

"She was at that," Sonny uttered softly, running his long fingers through his ash-brown hair.

Reeno said nothing more but rose from his chair and quietly left the shack. He was bound and determined to make Santiago admit to himself that he loved Abbie and would fight for her. Pride. What good was a man's pride if it lost him the woman of his dreams? And if Santiago didn't make a move soon, it was going to be too late. Brett Colfax would have her.

Reeno swore beneath his breath as he strode toward his horse, *"Que diablos,* sometimes, that Santiago—" He tapped his open palm against his forehead. "He could drive even the sanest of men loco."

Abbie was shocked by the fact that she had lost so many cattle. She stood looking down at the bloated, lifeless forms of the longhorns who had died after drinking from a poisoned watering hole and wondered only briefly who could have done such a terrible thing. And why? She considered the alternatives. There could only be one person who would do such a thing. It was obvious Lucien Rodriquez was out to destroy her. With this water hole gone and no rain in sight, it was beginning to look like she'd be going on that cattle drive sooner than she'd intended.

From Red's accounting, she had lost over forty head last night.

"I can't just sit by and let him do this, Red," she said angrily. "We'll fight him with everything we've got."

"Yes, ma'am," Red agreed. "Them's my thoughts exactly." He glanced sideways at her. "But I have to tell you. Some of the wranglers are taking their families and moving on. They told me to tell you they seen this kind of thing before and they can't take the risk with their wives' and children's lives."

"I can't blame them," Abbie replied. "But that sure leaves us in a heck of a fix." She swung up on Romeo's back. "Hire me someone who can stand up to these men, Red—some tough gun—with no family—and no qualms about killing."

"I already did," he replied, grinning. "A damned good one, too."

"We'll pay him top dollar, Red. Just so long as he can shoot straight and ride herd, I don't care who he is."

"That makes me real happy to hear you say that, ma'am," Red replied.

A warning bell went off in her head. "On second thought, maybe you'd better tell me his name?"

"Santiago Alvarez. He was at the fiesta with Reeno. He says you and him already met." Red grinned and scratched his jaw. "He told me he'd keep a low profile where you was concerned, because you two don't get on too well."

"He's right! It seems crazy, but I have no choice. And he is good with a gun. I have to fight them or they're going to wipe me out." She turned her horse toward the hacienda, her mind immediately recalling Sonny's parting words.

233

"We're *finito*—finished," he had said. Well, as far as she was concerned, they still were. His staying hadn't changed her mind about that.

As Abbie saddled her horse that early Sunday morning, her eyes scanned the far horizon. The weather was proving difficult if not downright defeating. There appeared no end to the dry spell. It hadn't rained in weeks, and it didn't look like it planned on doing so anytime soon. It was just after dawn, but already the sky was a clear sharp blue, promising another scorcher of a day. Abbie fastened her pack filled with her painting supplies onto the saddle horn. She had risen before anyone else so that she could go off alone and indulge in some sketching and painting.

Once mounted, she headed her horse in the direction of the rolling countryside and a section of particularly rough terrain that was isolated and quiet. She'd been working too hard lately. Overseeing the ranch, riding guard herself sometimes, filling in for men who continually came and went. It was a trying time, and her engagement to Brett Colfax made it more so.

As she rode along, Abbie recalled Brett's sudden show of fury yesterday when she'd suggested casually that they wait until after things quieted down with the rustlers to plan their wedding.

He seemed intent on marrying her as quickly as possible, and he even went so far as to state confidently how much better he thought the situation at the Bar C would be once a man was making the decisions again. "What's it going to take, Abbie Lee," he'd fairly shouted, "to make you face the facts. Ranching is a man's work. And as long as those rustlers know a woman is running the Bar C, they'll keep thinking you're easy pickings!" An odd expression had crossed his face. "And let's admit it, you are."

An exchange of heated words had followed, ending with

Brett's turning abruptly apologetic. More often, of late, Abbie was witness to the quicksilver moods of temper that others had warned her about.

It was a two hour ride to her destination. She noticed little as she rode along. Abbie's route took her across a far-reaching section of Caldwell land that she traveled whenever she wished complete solitude. By the time that she had arrived at her destination, the sun was well risen and the day warming.

She unpacked her gear, then led Romeo to a shady spot beside a slow-moving stream. Hoisting her pack of materials over her shoulder, she clambered to the top of the only grassy hillock around. It contained a few pines for shade. A gentle breeze blew steadily. The view was good, and for now Abbie felt at peace. She unpacked her supplies and began to work.

Silhouetted against the bright blue bowl of the Texas sky was a horseman. He bent forward over his painted pony's neck, eyes searching intently the hacienda below. He gave the appearance of a bloodthirsty beast instead of a human being by the manner in which his nostrils flared wide, as if he were sniffing the very air for the scent of a kill. His fathomless dark eyes fixed upon the quiet solitude before him, and he smiled jeeringly. Raising his arm, he signaled with his feathered lance and a frieze of dark-skinned horseman advanced.

Most of the Caldwell wranglers and *vaqueros* were out riding herd on various sections of the range, Sonny included, therefore, only Francisca, Martha, and Charly were at the Caldwell hacienda.

Breakfast was over. Francisca was busy in her kitchen, and Martha Caldwell had gone in search of Charly for their weekly trek to Sunday services.

She had looked just about in every place, and he was no where to be found. Lips pursed in a tight line, she called forth in an exasperated voice, "Charly Caldwell, if you don't come out this instant you're going to go without desserts for the entire week!"

Charly peered down from his perch atop the windmill. It was just too hot today, he thought to himself, to have to get all dressed up in a shirt and tie and endure that long ride to church. He knew he was being a *bribon,* but he just didn't want to leave his pup and sit in some stuffy old church listening to Preacher Miller ramble on about some faraway place that Charly never planned on seeing anyway. He tried to remember the name.

"Hadley—no," he said, shaking his curly red head. "Hades, that was it." Geez, he thought wonderingly, it's hot enough in Texas. Preacher Miller should talk about San Antonio if he wants to go on half the day about a place that can fry a person to a crisp.

"All right, Charly," Martha sighed. "I know you can hear me, young man. You can just stay wherever you're at. I'll go on all by myself." She began walking in the direction of the hacienda.

Charly chewed thoughtfully on his bottom lip, his alert blue eyes gazing out over the terrain. Perhaps he should go on down and go to church with Gram, he finally relented. He felt badly that she wouldn't have anyone to sit with during the service. And he did like those cookies and lemonade they served when church was over. He started to scramble from his hiding place. "Gram!" he yelled. "Wait for me, I'm coming, too!" It was then he saw a brief flutter of feathers off in the distance and stopped dead in his tracks. "Gra—mmm!"

Abbie made broad, sweeping strokes with the piece of

charcoal in her hand, striving for a certain subtle effect. She glanced up several times to study the river, then bent her head once again to add a bit of shading here and there. She wasn't certain when she first noticed the cloud of dust off in the distance, but it didn't take her long to realize what it meant. Riders, coming toward her. With a cry of fear, she threw down her pad and charcoal and began running toward her horse.

Gunshots split the tranquil setting, along with piercing war whoops. Abbie tore her rifle from the saddle scabbard and shot the first screaming Indian who was bearing down upon her. His face was painted in crimson streaks of vermilion. She stared in unbelieving horror at the melange of riders driving stolen cattle and horses before them. Among them was one white man dressed entirely in black with a flat sombrero covering his head.

He rode directly toward her, unafraid, seeming to expect a good fight and looking forward to it. He was not disappointed.

With her rifle out of bullets, Abbie withdrew her six-gun and took aim at him. But before she had time to squeeze the trigger, the *bandido's* gloved hand flicked outward with lightning speed and a black-snake cattle cutting whip coiled tightly about her wrist. She cried out when her gun was ripped from her fingers and sent flying through the air.

"I have heard much about you, *chica*," he drawled insolently. "At last, you meet your match."

Abbie stood without moving a muscle, her eyes defying him. "Go to hell."

The *bandido* reached over and slapped her brutally across the face. Her head reeled from the blow, but she only laughed defiantly. His swarthy face became livid. "You dare to defy me?" he raged.

Abbie sneered. "You are nothing."

Beside himself, the man reached forward and pulled her forcefully into his arms. "We shall see about that."

"Let me go, you filthy animal!" she screeched at the top of her lungs while trying to fight him off with her balled fists.

He was enjoying her struggles immensely. "Go on, *mujer,* fight me all that you want." He chuckled. "You cannot win. There is no one here that will help you."

His words made her think of her mother and Charly. She glared hatefully. "If you've harmed my family I swear you'll live to regret it!"

"Do not concern yourself about them," he ordered gruffly. "I am the only person you should worry yourself with right now."

His brutal mouth came down upon hers so suddenly that Abbie did not have time to react. He crushed her slight weight against him, grasping her chin cruelly, forcing her lips to part and accept his thrusting tongue.

Abbie felt her stomach heave. She gagged, knowing she might vomit at any moment. It was enough to prompt him to break the kiss. She spat in his face.

He grabbed a handful of her flowing hair. "If you ever do that again, I swear I will kill you."

What she could see of his face, she knew he was not Rodriquez. Yet, he certainly rode with the same sort of men and seemed to know who she was. "You will be mine," he vowed menacingly, wiping the saliva from his face.

One of his men, attired as a Comanche warrior, rode up to him. "We got the cattle. Let's *vamos* before her men come looking for her."

The bandit jerked his head around, barking an order to the men. "Let us *vamos, muchachos!*" He held Abbie firmly in his arms. "I have what I've wanted all along."

She felt a sense of panic when he kicked his stallion into a full gallop. He intended to take her with him! Instinct took over. Twisting, kicking, biting, Abbie did everything possible to make him release his hold on her. But his fingers remained like steel talons, biting into the soft flesh of her waist as he gripped her tightly.

"Charly—Mother—oh God, what have they done to you?"

The horrible possibility that they might be lying somewhere at this very moment, hurt, calling for her, prompted Abbie to jab backward viciously with her elbow, dealing her captor a well-placed blow to the stomach.

"Damned bitch!" he yelped, his hands falling from Abbie for a brief second.

They were racing along a ridge when Abbie managed to twist sharply away from him, throwing her weight to one side of his horse. She felt herself falling free, toppling, rolling, landing at the bottom of the rocky incline with a piercing scream of anguish.

On the edge of the ridge, the leader sat astride his snorting steed and cursed the woman staring up at him, her face scratched, bleeding, yet, a mask of triumph.

Behind him, one of the *bandoleros* urged him onward. "Leave the little wildcat! Why anybody would want the likes of that one is beyond me!"

To Abbie's immense relief, he wheeled his horse around and disappeared. She listened as the sound of galloping hooves faded into the distance.

Fearful that her mother and Charly had been killed by the raiding Comancheros, Abbie tried valiantly to climb back up to the top of the ridge. Weak and battered, she lost her footing and plunged to the bottom once again. She could only lie there and pray that someone had been left alive and would find her.

A coyote howled. Abbie sat up, listening. It was almost nightfall, and still no one had come looking for her. Was it possible that they were all dead? The thought was too unbearable, and she renewed her efforts to climb up the steep incline. Suddenly, she stopped, her ears picking up another sound. It was one that chilled her blood.

The soft jingle of spurs on booted feet drew her gaze slowly upward.

Had her attacker come back?

"Go away, leave me alone!" she screamed, staring up at the menacing, shadowy figure on the ledge. Her heart fairly caught in her throat when she heard the distinct sound of a lariat whirring softly overhead. She stumbled backward.

The rope sailed down about her with effortless ease. Abbie fought, but he jerked forcefully, and before she could prevent it, her feet were dangling in the air and she was drawn upward as though she were nothing more than a feather. She swore he would never take her alive and that she would fight him with every ounce of her being! Upon reaching the top of the ledge, Abbie rolled agilely to the side, immediately kicking out with both booted feet. She felt immense satisfaction when she heard his shin bone crack.

"What in thunderation are you trying to do, woman, cripple me for life?"

"Sonny! Is that really you?" She blinked up at his image distorted by the fading rays of the setting sun slanting through the clouds, framing his broad-shouldered form in misty, golden hues.

"What's left of me," he grumbled, astounded when she flashed him a smile.

"I sure am happy to see you." She waited patiently for him to unloosen the hemp lariat that still bound her.

"I never expected to hear those words coming from you," he returned, appearing unconcerned that she was bound tightly and unable to move.

"You can help me out of this," she said, making a shrugging motion with her shoulders.

He laughed mirthlessly. "Can I? I'd say that was a pretty safe way to keep you for the time being. It damn well prevents you from running around all over without someone to look out for you." He helped her to her feet but did not

240

remove the rope. He pulled meaningfully on the end of the lariat before turning abruptly and walking toward his horse.

Abbie was forced to trot along beside him in indignant fury. "Who appointed you my lord and master?"

"Sweetheart, it's about time somebody took you in hand. It may as well be me."

"You," she spat contemptuously, "will never have that pleasure."

They stood next to Viento, both of them silently seething. With relief, Abbie saw that Romeo was nearby. She called to him, and he immediately came to her. She turned haughtily to Sonny. "You've carried this little demonstration of yours far enough, Malone. Now unloosen this knot. I'm anxious to return to the hacienda and see if everyone is safe."

"I've already been there. Everyone's fine. The attack there was staged to divert our attention from the cattle. You lost some prime head and quite a few mustangs." He removed the lariat.

Abbie groaned. "Who in the hell is doing this to me? Rodriquez was not leading this attack."

"That doesn't mean he's not behind it," he returned thoughtfully.

"I'm done for, I'm afraid," she muttered. "Between the lack of graze due to the dry conditions and the rustlers, if I don't get my cattle to market right away, I'm going to be wiped out soon."

"Then, let's take them," Sonny urged.

"You and I, together," she scoffed. "Not a chance." But as she rode away from him, she was considering just that.

"Mother, I really think you should take Charly and stay in San Antonio for awhile with Uncle Willy." Abbie was sitting at the long kitchen table helping Martha snap green beans with Francisca.

Martha stared her straight in the eye. "I am not leaving my

241

home, Abbie Lee. Your pa and I settled this land together. I may not be as young as I once was, but I can still fire a gun if need be."

"*Si*, senorita," Francisca agreed. "Your *madre* was ready to shoot the first *bandido* who set foot near the hacienda. She make Charly stay on top the windmill and come in here to get your *padre's* buffalo gun."

"Mama." Abbie grinned widely. "I always thought you didn't want any part of guns."

"I don't. But I would have given it my best effort."

"Pa would have been downright proud of you, Martha Caldwell," Abbie praised.

"Yes, I think he would have, too," Martha replied wistfully.

"And he'd be very upset with me if I didn't insist that you take Francisca and Charly somewhere safe," Abbie persisted. "If not for your own well-being, then theirs."

Martha knew Abbie was right. After their close brush with those brutal Comancheros, she would do well to take Charly into town. "For my grandson's safekeeping, we'll go to Willy's."

"Thank you, Mother," Abbie replied. "That makes it easier to leave on the drive to Sedalia."

Martha paused to massage her fingers which tended to stiffen at the joints more of late. "I'm downright upset over that, Abbie Lee," she declared bluntly.

"I have no choice," Abbie explained yet another time. "If I don't do something soon, we'll lose everything."

Their conversation turned to Abbie's plans to drive the cattle to Missouri. They became so engrossed in the discussion that they only glanced briefly at Charly when he came tearing into the kitchen with Scamp right behind him.

"I know the drive could prove dangerous, Mother," Abbie declared, "but Red says we can get twenty-five dollars a head in Sedalia for longhorns. And I can't sustain the herd on the grass and water we've got left. They're simply drying up."

Charly came into the kitchen, his eyes studying his mother closely. His brow furrowed in thoughtful concentration. They looked so much alike. But then, hadn't that lady told him his mother and she were twins? He longed to tell his mother about seeing her twin, but he had promised it would be their secret for awhile. As small children will do, he didn't give it another thought but took his place at the table and eagerly awaited his daily snack of milk and cookies.

Martha glanced over at her daughter, one brow arched quizzically. "And that nice-looking young man—will he be going on the cattle drive?"

"We have lots of nice men around here, Mother. Which one were you referring to?" Abbie gave the bean she was holding a particularly forceful snap.

"Santiago, Reeno's friend."

"She mean the *mucho hombre,* the *magnifico* eyes," Francisca offered innocently.

Abbie's head came up with a jerk. *"Mucho hombre* indeed," she snorted.

"Abbie," Martha admonished. "That brave man is the one who saved you from those awful *bandoleros.* How can you possibly not think him dashing?"

Oh, Mother, if you only knew the truth about your knight in shining armor, Abbie thought ruefully, you would not be singing his praises. Aware of the wanted posters that were out on Sonny, Abbie had agreed to call him by his Spanish name, Santiago. They needed each other right now. That was the only reason she had even considered allowing him to stay on here. He was after Rodriquez, and now, so was she. Some of her best men had taken their families and left after the last raid. She couldn't afford to be choosy when she needed all of the help she could get.

"He's an unscrupulous rogue is what he is," Abbie said tersely. "And I wish you'd remember that where the *mucho hombre* is concerned."

"There is just no excuse for bad manners, Abbie Lee, and I

243

think we owe that young man a wealth of gratitude. So I took it upon myself to try and repay him." Martha looked straight at her wary-eyed daughter. "As you should have, immediately."

"What have you done?" Apprehension animated Abbie's voice.

"Why, I've invited him to come to dinner, in his honor, tomorrow evening," Martha exclaimed. "And you won't have to worry about a thing, darling. Francisca and I will take care of everything."

Martha beamed, Francisca nodded assuredly, and Abbie Lee choked.

"You already have, Mother, beyond any doubt."

Chapter Eleven

"Cattle drive! To Sedalia, Missouri! Abbie Lee, you've got to be out of your mind!" Brett ranted, his eyes registering disbelief. He saw by the stubborn tilt of her jaw that she was not. He and Abbie were sitting in the living room at the Caldwell hacienda, tension crackling in the air as they studied each other intently. He had ridden over to the Bar C after learning of the raid, determined to convince Abbie that now more than ever, she should marry and turn the management of the ranch over to him. "You're being just as obstinate as ever, and a woman drover, it's unheard of!"

"I'm not going with strangers," she shot back defensively.

"But they'll all be men!" he said stiffly. "And just how is that going to look, and us engaged." He scowled. "Haven't you had enough whispering about you?"

"I've got more at stake here than just my reputation!" Abbie snapped. "And you're more than welcome to come along."

"No thanks, I'm not risking losing everything."

"Then I guess we have nothing more to say to each other."

"Very well. If I can't talk you out of going on this fool venture, then marry me before you leave. Let a man run this ranch the way your father wanted." He moved closer to her on the sofa.

Her eyes bore into him, and he almost drew away from her. "No one, Brett Colfax, absolutely no one, is going to run this ranch but me. At twenty-three, I think I'm capable of making sensible decisions and running this place the way my father would have wanted."

"Aw, honey," he added quickly. "You know I didn't mean nothing by that remark." He took her hand in his. "I'm just so worried that something might happen to you." He reached over to brush his lips across hers.

Abbie stiffened. Their feelings for each other were not the same anymore. Too much had happened over the years. Sometimes she felt that Brett was a complete stranger. Cold, calculating. He wasn't the same man. "I think you did mean everything you said, Brett, and I'm sorry you feel the way you do. However, if I don't go on this drive, I'll lose everything the Caldwells have worked so long to build. You haven't been hit as hard as I have. The Comancheros have stolen my prime stock. The remaining herd is going to market and that's final!"

Brett stared at her. "You've been avoiding the subject of a wedding date since we became engaged."

"This has nothing to do with the wedding," she hesitated. "And I don't know how my problems are going to just disappear simply by getting married."

"I know that if a man is around to keep his thumb on you a bit, things might quiet down around here considerably," Brett said sullenly, unable to suppress his inner rage any longer.

"Is that what you plan to do after we're married, Brett— keep your thumb on me?" She viewed him through narrowed eyes. "Answer—is it?"

Brett could feel himself quickly losing control. He felt like shaking her until she agreed to his plans. Instead he said through clenched teeth, "You need guidance, that's all. It was simply a bad choice of words on my part."

"You're so right, it was," Abbie shot back.

Brett picked up his hat from a side table. He could feel his temper about to explode. "We can talk more about this later. We're both all fired up right now." He leaned over to kiss her stiff lips. She turned her head aside.

"I don't intend to have a yoke placed around my neck on the day that I marry. That's one thing I'll set straight before we discuss anything further."

He forced himself to grin. "Of course not. Now give me a kiss, Abbie Lee. You owe me that at least."

Abbie could sense the barely controlled rage behind his careful expression. "No. Just go. I can't turn my feelings on and off like you can, Brett."

Brett stood, towering over her, a sudden need to force her to comply with his wishes. He reached for her arm and gripped it forcefully. "I want a kiss from you, Abbie. Now."

Someone cleared their throat behind them. They both flinched at the intrusion, yet Abbie was relieved when she recognized Sonny standing in the doorway.

"Excuse me," Sonny drawled in an exaggeratedly, bored voice. "But Charly let me in and said that you were in here, Ab. He didn't tell me you had another guest." His gaze met Brett's as he entered the room.

Brett saw the black Colts resting so menacingly under the gunslinger's dark dress coat and did a complete change of character. "Ah, Abbie Lee and I were just having a little difference of opinion. Nothing serious." He released her arm.

Abbie stepped between the two men, recognizing the dangerous glitter in Sonny's eyes. "Brett was about to leave," she said, then turned to Brett. "You two have never been introduced. Brett Colfax—Santiago Alvarez."

Neither man made any attempt to extend a hand in greeting. They just nodded curtly.

"You staying for dinner, too?" Sonny queried, his tone mocking.

Brett's eyes were hard. He looked over at Abbie. "I wasn't invited."

247

Abbie glared at Sonny. "I—I've been so busy and all I just never had a chance to do so." She turned to Brett. "I imagine Brett's expected home for supper."

"I think this is one time Ma would excuse me if I don't show up."

Abbie swallowed. "Then, do join us."

"Yeah, Colfax," Sonny agreed blandly. "Why don't you stay. After all, you won't be seeing much of our little gal after Friday."

Abbie seethed. Men! They were driving her crazy! "Don't start," she hissed under her breath at Sonny.

Brett looked from one to the other. He was no fool. There was something between these two. And he didn't like to think about what it might be. He swore that if Abbie was bedding this gunslinger and not allowing him to touch her, he'd find someway to make her pay dearly. She'd cheated him out of her virginity years ago, and he had vowed to make her regret her rash action. The thought that this half-breed could be sleeping with her drove him crazy.

Forcing his voice to sound even, he replied, "Thank you, honey. I always did like Francisca's cooking as much as Ma's."

Abbie glanced from one man to the other, noticing the possessive gleam in Brett's eyes, the dangerously mocking glitter in Sonny's. She sat back down on the sofa, almost groaning when they took a seat on either side of her.

Dinner was a nightmare. Abbie found herself constantly glancing from one man to the other, comparing Sonny to Brett, unable to stop herself.

One was blond, broodingly handsome, and her intended, while the other was ruggedly male, a disconcerting rogue, and her lover. Lord, what kind of a mess have I got myself into this time, she fretted.

Martha made a great to-do over who was to sit where. She took Sonny's arm and led him to the head of the oval table. "Since you are the guest of honor, Santiago, I think it only

248

fitting that you sit here." She fluttered a hand at Abbie. "And you sit right there, in the end chair, next to Santiago, dear. And Brett, in the chair beside Abbie." Beaming, she took an end seat on the opposite side of the table and nodded approvingly. "There, everything is just as it should be, I would say."

Abbie almost gasped when Sonny's hand accidently brushed hers as he placed it casually beside his plate. She grabbed up her wine glass and drank deeply. She was certain it was going to get worse before it got better.

Francisca, who had been busy cooking all day, could be heard singing Spanish love songs in the kitchen.

Sonny smiled crookedly at Abbie's strangled expression. You created this little triangle, honey, his eyes said as they met hers, now squirm awhile, as I've done since I came here.

It was a national pride in Mexico to cling to the eating patterns of Spain. Therefore, *comida* the main meal of the day, was served anytime between two and five-thirty P.M. Out of respect for the guest of honor, the Caldwell hacienda was following Spanish tradition this afternoon. The meal would be a long, drawn-out affair, with many courses. The first course hadn't even been served yet, and already Abbie could feel the strain of having to sit so near Sonny. Her finger's shook each time she picked up her wine glass, and she could have sworn, this last time, that the unscrupulous varmint had chuckled beneath his breath.

"Santiago." Her voice came out shriller than she had intended, and she felt her face flame. "How long do you think you will be staying on with us?"

He favored her with a bored uplifting of dark brows. "As long as you have need of my services."

She nodded over the knot in her throat. "I'll need you on the drive, that's for certain."

Brett spoke up. "Oh, so you're definitely planning on having Senor Alvarez go with you?"

Sonny's intense gaze never left Abbie's face as he replied,

"She wouldn't think of going without me."

Brett watched them intently. "Just what brought you to Texas?" he demanded in a gruff tone.

"I'm here to settle an old debt and to reclaim something that has been stolen from me," Sonny replied calmly.

"Something valuable?" Brett queried.

"I think so," Sonny said softly.

Abbie almost choked on her wine. She had thought this matter between them settled the other night when he stormed from her room in such a fury, refusing to listen to anything that she had to say. Now look at him, she fumed silently. He sits there like His Lordship, in my home, with my own mother smiling, mesmerized by him!

"Mother," Abbie implored. "Will you please see if Francisca is ready to serve? I'm sure our gentlemen guests are getting hungry."

Martha smiled sweetly, appearing not to notice the tension in the room. "Why of course dear, right away."

Abbie would have loved to flee to the kitchen right behind Martha, but she knew she dared not leave the two men alone in the same room. She knew Sonny well enough to realize that the bored, assessing gaze behind that cool glance was deceiving. She watched his every move with her heart fluttering like a cornered vixen.

Sonny directed a point-blank question to Brett. "You had any cattle rustled from your place, Colfax?"

"Some," Brett returned evenly. He faced Sonny squarely. "We've just been lucky, I guess."

"His place isn't as big as the Bar C," Abbie added quickly, uneasy with the steely look in Sonny's eyes. "The cattle graze closer in. Therefore, it wouldn't be that easy for the Comancheros to steal Colfax stock."

"I would think it easier, Abbie," Sonny stated in a colorless voice.

"Why is that?" Brett asked tersely.

"None of your men have been riding herd at night," Sonny

drawled. "Either you've just been downright lucky, or else you know something more about how these Comancheros operate than we do."

Brett's eyes revealed a deadly gleam as they held Sonny's gaze. He didn't try to pretend he didn't understand the ringing accusation. "I know nothing more than anyone else."

Sonny was amazed at how abruptly Brett's manner could change. Couldn't Abbie see the shiftiness in the man's eyes? What was there between them that she felt such a need to protect him? He knew she didn't love Brett, yet, even now, she was quick to defend him. "Your foreman says you haven't had any need to take extra precautions like the other ranchers. You haven't lost a steer, horse—or even a chicken." Sonny's slight smile just barely curled his lips. "I find that downright remarkable, if not a bit puzzling."

"Shorty's mistaken," Brett stated stiffly.

Abbie swallowed constrictively. What could Sonny be implying; that Brett was consorting with thieves? "Oh, Shorty must be mistaken. After all, Brett should know."

"I thought so, too," Sonny replied, his face inscrutable, "but he went on to assure me of the fact. He says it puzzles him as well, but it seems them *hombres* just know not to mess with the Colfax crew."

Abbie was shocked by the insinuating tone of Sonny's voice. There was a fleeting glimmer of something ugly in Brett's eyes before he slowly rose from his chair and addressed Abbie.

"I did not accept your invitation, Abbie Lee, to put up with your hired help's rudeness. Please, give my apologies to your mother and tell her I had to leave." Glaring one last time in Sonny's direction, he spun on his heel and strode briskly from the room.

Abbie turned on Sonny in a fury. "This thing between us has gone far enough! How could you have been so rude to him!"

"Now what do you suppose I said, exactly, that made your

251

beau shoot out of here like his tail was on fire?"

His tone was innocent, but the look in his eye's was anything but.

"Whatever would make you think you said anything wrong!" she cried, longing to smack the satisfied smirk from his face. "Just because you accused a man who was a war hero of consorting with filthy Comancheros; why should he not want to stay here and dine with you!"

"Think over what I said, Ab. It bears considerable thought."

Her back stiffened, and he knew he was in for one of her stinging tongue lashings. "The only thing that bears considerable thought is why I agreed to let you stay on here in the first place. You have gone out of your way to charm everyone on my ranch until they do nothing but sing you praises, and yet, with Brett, you allow your jealousy to blind you to his sensitive nature."

"I am not the one who is blind," he grunted.

Martha came back humming one of Francisca's tunes and noticed Brett's empty chair. "Did Brett have to leave?"

"Unexpectedly, and regrettably," Sonny replied dryly.

"Oh, that's too bad," Martha sighed.

Abbie's eyes darkened to fiery slits of blue as they met Sonny's. If the serving girl had not just placed their consomme before them and her mother not studying them closely, she would have thrown him off the ranch right then and there. Forcing herself to remain calm for her mother's sake, she picked up her spoon and appeared to smile charmingly at their guest. "You're not off the hook that easy, mister," she managed to hiss softly while her mother conversed quietly with the serving girl. "You and I aren't finished—not by a long shot."

"Why, Ab," Sonny whispered infuriatingly, "you don't know how happy that makes me to hear you say that."

Abbie sizzled, her mouth clamping tightly shut.

The meal progressed amicably. Abbie found she consumed entirely too much of the fine white wine that was served with the delicious dinner, and by the time they'd finished their *cafe con leche* and *churros,* long strips of pastry, fried and rolled in sugar, she was seeing everything through a fuzzy, mellowed haze.

His appetite for food appeased, Sonny leaned back in his chair, snifter of brandy in hand. "You must give my compliments to your housekeeper, Senora Caldwell. The meal was superb."

"Why thank you. She'll be happy to know you enjoyed it." Placing her napkin on the table, Martha rose from her chair. Sonny came immediately to his feet. "You must excuse me, Santiago, but I am accustomed to retiring early. I will bid you both good night."

"Thank you for a lovely evening, senora," he told her. *"Buenas noches."*

Abbie sat in numb disbelief as her mother patted his hand almost affectionately. What was the woman thinking of! Couldn't she see he was only being charming in order to corner her daughter alone?

After her mother left the room, Abbie apprehensively saw him rise from his chair, all three of him moving around the table toward her. The sight was most frightening, to say the least. She immediately closed one eye and was relieved when only a single set of gray ones met her own, laughter dancing in their glittering depths.

"Abbie Lee," he drawled amused, "you're soused."

"So what if I am," she shot back angrily. "Being forced to dine with a lowdown polecat for an entire evening and then listen to him accuse one's betrothed of consorting with rustlers is enough to drive anyone to over-imbibe."

He took her hand. "Come on, we'll just go for a walk and see if we can't dry you out some before we put you to bed."

"We—are going to do nothing of the sort," she slurred, attempting to pull away from him, succeeding only in making her head spin sickeningly. Her hands flew upward to

253

grab hold of his solid shoulders.

"I said I'm taking care of you." He swept her up into his arms and strode through a side door out into moon-drenched courtyard.

"Abbie Caldwell's shining knight," she mumbled, laying her wobbly head upon his shoulder.

"Sonny?"

"Yes, Abbie."

"I feel much better now."

"I'm glad, honey," he said tenderly.

They had been walking about the rose garden, the delicate flowers' perfumed scent reminding Sonny of the sweet smell of Abbie's hair. He looked at her now, still a bit tipsy but beautiful as ever. The ice green gown she wore boasted a low neckline trimmed in delicate lace that just barely concealed the curve of her bosom. He could just imagine how soft her flesh would feel if he placed his lips there. Her voice jerked him rudely back to the reality that she would not welcome such advances from him now.

"Why did you insinuate those awful things about Brett tonight?"

"If you must know the truth, I don't like anything about the man," he replied tightly.

"Because he asked me to marry him, that's the real reason, isn't it?"

"From what Reeno told me, he didn't ask—he ordered," Sonny growled. "And you went along with it all meek as a lamb, and that surprises the hell out of me."

"I most certainly did not!" she replied, stung. "I was still mourning you and he was so kind, so understanding, that I thought we could be good for each other."

"I didn't think anyone could manipulate you, but I suppose we all have our weaknesses."

"*My*—only weakness—was memories."

"Are your memories all bad, Ab?"

"No," she choked, "not all."

Wordlessly, Sonny watched her eyes close against the unbidden memories that flooded back. Every nerve in his body cried out to touch her, to kiss her, to tell her that he cared, would always care. For the first time in his life he was frightened by an emotion he couldn't seem to control. What power did this mere slip of a girl have over him to make him tremble inside at the thought of losing her to another? And it wasn't as though he didn't have his choice of women; he did. Even now, if he wanted to, he could return to the camp of the Comanches and take Little Doe for his wife. But no one, absolutely no woman, made him feel like he did when he was making love to Abbie. She was his obsession.

"I never intended to hurt you, Ab," he found himself admitting. "You know that, deep down, don't you?"

"Best intentions have a way of going awry," she sighed heavily. "Even mine—and Brett's."

He withdrew a thin black cheroot from his waistcoat and placed it between his teeth. Lighting it, he took a deep drag before answering. "Tell me all about how the black knight, Brett Colfax, captured your heart, fair maiden."

Smoke curled upward, like spiraling mist around his ash-colored mane. Abbie followed it with her eyes. "You really want to know, don't you?"

"Yes," he replied softly. "I do."

"Can we sit somewhere please? I'm rather weary of circling this garden."

Sonny inclined his head toward a tall, spreading willow in a darkened corner of the garden. "How about over there? I'll play the perfect gentleman and even spread my cloak for milady to sit upon."

"You don't have a cloak," she said dryly.

He shrugged. "Then we'll just have to make do with my jacket now, won't we?"

They settled themselves comfortably, Abbie sitting on

Sonny's dark evening coat which he went to great lengths in laying out just so. He sat easily beside her with his arms resting upon his bent knees, attired in a white linen shirt, black trousers, and expensive black leather boots. A lock of his hair fell rakishly across his forehead. She tried to ignore the overpowering sensuality that emanated from every pore of his body. She breathed deeply to clear her head and began talking.

"It sort of happened the night of the fiesta, when I still thought you were dead. Brett was my beau before the war. And now, we've begun to pick up the pieces where we left off."

"And even though you know I'm alive, you will still marry him?"

"I thought you didn't want me," Abbie replied softly.

"I'd say you never gave me a chance."

"We've nothing in common," she replied. "Brett and I have our families, ranching, and he loves Charly very much."

"That all sounds just like the perfect storybook romance," he said in a velvet tone that didn't take the sharp edge off of his next words. "But does he love you or your ranch?" His voice grew husky. "And most importantly, do you feel the same when he makes love to you as you do when we're together?"

Her heart aching with the need to tell him that no one could ever make her feel the way he did, Abbie reached tentatively upward to brush the lock of wayward hair from his forehead. "Do you need so badly to hear me say the words?" she murmured thickly. "That I have never lain in his arms as I have yours. You've been my only lover."

He tossed the cheroot aside, surprised at how glad his heart felt at her words. He wanted to crush her in his arms and take her there, recklessly and completely, beneath the glittering canopy of stars.

There was no mistaking the look of desire in his eyes, and

Abbie felt her body responding instantly to the unspoken message in their depths. "No, Sonny," she said in a strained whisper, "we have to fight this physical thing between us."

His mouth twisted. "Is that all that you think we have between us—a physical thing?" His hands caught her bare shoulders, and he pulled her roughly against him, his mouth coming down on hers in a demanding kiss.

Abbie was lost in the overwhelming feelings he alone seemed to evoke. She tried to fight the fiery ache that raced sweetly through her veins, making her long for more, so much more, but it was useless. She wanted him with all her heart and soul. When he finally released her lips, she was breathing just as heavily as he was.

"Can he make you respond like this, Ab?" Sonny whispered fiercely, his hand sliding down her smooth shoulder, inside her bodice, to cup her breast. He squeezed the nipple enticingly. "All of you I alone possess, silken lady. And I will not share you—ever."

Abbie stared upward into his passion-glittering eyes. "There is more to a relationship than just loving, Sonny," she said, her voice shaking.

"That may be so," he countered softly. "But tell me. Are you ready to give up the loving with me for a chance at love with him?"

Everything was still around them. For the longest time it seemed they just stayed like that, staring deeply into each other's eyes. She could not answer nor move, nor hardly even breathe, so shaken was she by the silent reply within her. No. She could never give that up. Even now she wanted Sonny more than she had ever thought it possible to desire a man.

"I see the answer in your eyes," he murmured against her lips.

She was suddenly filled with a longing to have him hold her, touch her, love her. But she knew it would be her undoing if he did. She did not wish to be just his plaything, something to casually toss aside when he decided it was time for him to return to Mexico. Instead, she pulled away from him and deliberately turned the conversation to the cattle drive to Sedalia. She heard his exasperated sigh.

"It's against my better judgment to have you stay on here another day," she told him straight out. "However, I need someone who's good with a gun to accompany me to Sedalia. Not only that, I remember your telling me of your affinity with the Indians. It could prove helpful to me on this trip." She glanced sideways at him. "Will you hire on for the drive?"

He was silent for several tense moments. He realized she wasn't going to give him an inch. She was making it clear that she still did not trust him, that he had hurt her badly. It appeared that she really did need him for the drive. Apparently Colfax was not going. This was his chance to win her back. He replied more calmly than he felt. "You've hired yourself a drover, ma'am."

"And Sonny?"

"Yes, Ab."

"I expect you won't try to take unfair advantage while we're away."

"Of course not, beautiful," he replied, the corner of his mouth turning up in a caricature of a smile. "What do you take me for anyway?" Before she had time to make a move, his hand slipped behind her neck to draw her slowly forward.

"What did I just—sa—" Her words were effectively cut off by his hard, demanding lips which savored hers thoroughly. The lingering, warm feel of his mouth moving over hers sent sparks shooting through every nerve Abbie Lee possessed. When he had her absolutely weak-kneed and breathless, he gently broke the kiss.

"I'll remember those words, real well, Abbie, honey— maybe."

She managed to push him away before getting quickly to her feet. "You can be the most despicable of human beings sometimes," she cried, turning away and rushing toward the darkened hacienda.

His voice, softly taunting, called after her. "Good night. Pleasant dreams."

As Abbie reached her room, she could swear she heard voices coming from Charly's room. Hesitating, she listened, head cocked, to the distinct sound of his small voice carrying on what appeared to be a conversation with someone. Puzzled, she crossed the hall to his door.

"Charly," she called softly, opening the door.

Charly rolled over to stare up at her. "Yes, Mama?"

"Did I hear you talking with someone, honey?"

"When?" he replied.

"Just now," Abbie stated briskly, entering his room to stand beside his bed. Her eyes searched the room and observed the closed doors leading onto the courtyard. Everything appeared normal.

"Just my secret pal."

Abbie smiled at the shaggy pup he had hidden beneath the covers. "Well, enough talking for the night, young man." She bent over to kiss his forehead. "Go to sleep. You'll be leaving with Gram tomorrow for Uncle Willy's."

He smiled, then yawned sleepily. "'Cause you're going to drive the cattle to Missouri and don't want Gram and me to get lonely, right?"

She brushed his hair back from his face. "Yes, although I'm going to miss you very much."

"Me too," he whispered, one chubby hand rubbing her cheek affectionately.

Abbie felt tears glistening in her eyes and quickly looked away. She loved him so much. "But you'll have your new little friend to keep you company, and you won't miss me near as much as you think." She ruffled his hair as she pulled the covers up around his chin. "Good night, darling," she murmured, turning toward the door.

"'Night," he returned. But she failed to hear him add, for she had already exited the room. "And maybe, if I tell my new friend where I'm going, she'll come see me there, too."

"Abbie, darling," Brett breathed as she stared down at the diamond ring she'd just enfolded in his hand. "How can you do this to me? How?"

"It just isn't going to work out, Brett," Abbie sighed. "With me gone for over six months it will give us both a chance to think about our relationship and how we feel about each other." She began walking in the direction of the stable, to return a bridle she'd just repaired. It was several days before she was due to leave on the cattle drive. Brett had come over to try and once again talk her out of going. He followed behind her, trying not to think about all that he was losing. Damn her! She was costing him everything! He longed to make her pay for that, oh so very much.

"You can't just call off our engagement like this," he fumed. "Whatever's come over you?"

"Some common sense," she retorted. "I just realized that you and I have different viewpoints on everything, especially where my life is concerned."

Brett clenched his fist, longing to thrash her good. "You don't know yet, but you'll find out soon. I could have helped you out—saved you from a lot of grief and misery."

She entered the stable, somewhat uneasy with the underlying tone of violence in his voice and the expression that had come over his face. "I—really think you should go now, Brett. I don't like the way you're talking to me."

"And I don't care for the way that you've wrecked all of my plans," he whispered silkily. He glanced around and saw that the stable was deserted. Advancing toward Abbie, he backed her into an empty stall, enjoying the look of fear he saw in her eyes.

"Don't come any closer," she warned, sensing his intent. "I'll not let you touch me. I mean that."

Overwhelmed by his pent-up feelings, he reached for her. "I'm through taking orders from you, Miss Caldwell." He grabbed her arm, the strength in his fingers unbelievably powerful.

Abbie swung the bridle she'd been holding with full force, hitting him squarely in the face. He roared with pain and fury yet didn't loosen his hold. Overpowering her, he threw her down onto the hay-covered floor and fell heavily on top of her, knocking the wind from her. His stinging slap to her face brought a cry of terror from her lips. Brett leered over her.

"You need a man to treat you this way. I should have taken you in line right from the start, but I thought you would marry me, and I didn't want to rough you up none and scare you off."

The veneer of the caring young man she had known all of her life was forgotten. It was supplanted by a burning passion to have her body.

Shocked beyond reason, Abbie felt Brett's hand begin pawing her breasts.

She fumbled for her gun, but he twisted it out of her hand, laughing softly as his mouth swooped down upon hers.

Abbie scratched at his face with her free hand, but he was oblivious to anything but his raging lust. His fingers knotted in the fabric of her shirt, and there was a sharp rending sound as he tore it open. His fingers found her bare flesh. "Oh, Jesus," he moaned, "you aren't wearing anything under this shirt, are you?"

"Brett, don't do this. You'll regret it. I know you will." She sobbed frantically.

Brett snickered. "Like hell. I haven't wanted anyone this much in a long while, sweetheart." He ground his hips into Abbie's, and she felt her skin actually crawl from the feel of him pressed intimately against her.

261

He shook her. "Come on, Abbie, loosen up. It isn't like you've never had it before, so quit acting like some damned innocent." He pinned her down with his shoulders while his fingers tore at her trousers.

"I'll kill you for this," she hissed.

Brett was beyond listening. His emotions had carried him past reasoning, and he shut her up by crushing her lips beneath his.

It was all that Abbie could stand. Breaking free of his tight hold, she hit him with her closed fist on the side of the face. He grunted, seeming not to feel any pain, yet his mouth pulled free of hers, and he raised his fist over her chin.

"I hate to have to do this, but I want a piece of you, and Goddamnit, one way or the other I'm going to have it."

Abbie's small fists swung repeatedly out at him, terror prompting her to reach up and bite his cheek. Her twisting beneath him made the impact of his blow less jolting, and before he could inflict another one, someone pulled him off her.

It was Sonny. And she had never been so glad to see him.

Sonny threw the startled Colfax back up against the wall and dealt him several well-aimed blows. Despite having only one arm, Brett was able to defend himself quite well. However, he was no match for the furious Malone. He staggered from the force of Sonny's fists, and his nose was bleeding profusely.

Sickened, Abbie cried out. "You're going to kill him. Stop it, Sonny! Stop!" Still he persisted, until Brett toppled over onto the stable floor, clutching his ribs.

Huge fists clenched at his sides, Sonny loomed threateningly over him. "I could kill you for what you did to her. I could kill you so easy," he growled repeatedly. "But I want you left alive, Colfax. For when I come off of this drive you'll have had plenty of time to have practiced your draw."

Brett groaned in pain. He rolled over. "I—think you broke some of my ribs. I need a doctor."

"You're going to need more than that the next time we meet," Sonny snarled. "You'll be needing an undertaker, for I'm going to kill you, Colfax. I swear by all that's holy that I will."

As if he were nothing more than a sack of meal, Sonny hoisted Brett over his shoulder and strode from the stable to dump him on his horse. Whacking the animal on the rump, he watched with stormy eyes as it galloped away. With quick strides he retraced his steps. Hunkering down beside a softly weeping Abbie, he gathered her close in his arms.

For the longest time, he held her like that, stroking her bruised face, crooning soothingly how he would never let anything like this happen again.

"I'm so sorry, baby, so damned sorry I didn't get here sooner, but I had no idea the bastard was even here with you until Charly told me he saw you two walking toward the stable." He brushed back the tangled hair from her eyes, his lips kissing her gently on the temple. "What in God's name made the man do something like this?"

"I—told him I wasn't going to marry him," Abbie whispered brokenly, "and he went crazy." She clutched Sonny's arm. "He—was going to—"

"I know," he murmured understandingly. "You don't have to say anything more, sweetheart. I'm here, if you want me, from now on."

Abbie hugged him tightly, pressing her face against his broad chest. "Oh, yes, Sonny, don't ever leave me again."

"I promise you, Ab," he whispered just before his lips slanted across hers, "we'll never be parted again."

"Listen up!" Abbie told her men the night before the big drive. They had gathered in the bunk house just after supper to receive last minute instructions from their boss. "We're going to Sedalia, Missouri with two thousand head of cattle. Everything's ready to go: The longhorns are rounded up and branded, our gear's packed, and Shorthand's promised me he'll do his best to feed us proper." Her gaze flicked over the group of wranglers and *vaqueros* gathered around her. She didn't blink an eye. "I know many of you men are working for me because you came back to Texas from the war to find your ranches gone, your cattle scattered, and your lands stolen by carpetbaggers." She saw their terse nods of agreement. "There's not much of a market for beef here in the South, but there is in Missouri. That's why we're going. It's going to be a rough thousand miles, over dry country, with the threat of Indians always over our heads. And when we get to Missouri, they'll be border gangs to try and jump us for the herd."

One bandy-legged cowpoke spoke up. "I hired on, ma'am, 'cause I don't have any other choice. My family's near starving. You've got five hundred head of my cattle mixed in with yours. What am I gettin' for those?"

Abbie faced him squarely. "You'll get three dollars a head for every live steer you get to the railroad. The wages are ten dollars a month, triple if the steers bring thirty dollars at the railroad."

"That sounds right fair, ma'am. Thank you," he replied with a nod.

"Don't thank me yet, cowboy," she retorted bluntly. "You're going to find it real hard to stay alive once we get to that Missouri border. Save your gratitude for when we reach our destination and you have the feel of cold cash in your hand." She turned to Red who was standing beside her. "Red has the list for those of you who are signing on for the drive. But remember this. If you sign on, you agree to finish it."

There was a murmur of voices all talking at once as they moved forward to add their names to the others already there. One name stood out distinctly when Abbie had looked over the list earlier. Santiago Alvarez. She was grateful that he was putting aside his vendetta with Rodriquez, yet again, to help her out. Since Brett's brutal attack, their relationship had taken a new turn. Could they possibly recapture that special feeling they'd shared all of those weeks on the plains? She found herself hoping that they could. She needed Sonny, more than she had ever thought possible.

Glancing up, she saw him making his way in her direction. Even his walk, that smooth, easy stride of his, sent shivers along her spine.

"Reeno sends his regrets, but he must get back to Mexico," he told her. "It appears things are changing in our favor. Soon the war will be over."

"I know," she replied. "He spoke with me before he left. Are you going back there after you find your father?" She noted that he was dressed much like the rest of the men except that he always stood out from those around him. The sight of his dark clothes, the black silk scarf knotted carelessly about his neck, the inevitable mark of his trade, the polished black Colts, took her back to their first encounter, and she smiled.

"I haven't any immediate plans."

"That surprises me."

"Does it? It shouldn't."

"Am I to read something behind all of those carefully phrased words, sir?"

He favored her with a wolfish grin. "Maybe—I was hoping you'd make me another generous offer."

Abbie suddenly felt as though everyone in the room had heard his words. She blushed, then cleared her throat. "My offer to have you hire on this drive could hardly be called generous. In fact, not at all, considering that the last bunch who tried driving a herd to Sedalia was jumped by a Missouri border gang and killed. I hired you for protection, no other reason."

"I'm not interested in your money, beautiful, and you know it."

Damn him, she fumed inwardly. He didn't give a hoot if

265

everyone of her men knew how things were between them. Well, she did! How could she expect them to take orders from her on this trip if he kept being openly suggestive.

"I told you, when I asked you to come with me, that the only desire I'll be sharing with you on this trip is getting the cattle to market in one piece," she reminded him in a hushed voice.

His silver eyes danced merrily. "You don't believe that for even a moment, Ab, and neither do I."

Noticing the men milling around, awaiting their turn to talk with Abbie, Sonny stepped aside. "For now, Ab, I concede. But you and I are going to have many nights ahead of us on that wide-open prairie."

Abbie watched him stride away, wondering how in the world she was going to avoid him for the next one thousand miles. She almost laughed out loud at such a ridiculous thought. Avoid Sonny! Not as long as he had any breath left in his body.

"I know you told me not to tell anyone you was here, Aunty Sonya. But I don't know why we can't tell Gram and Mama," Charly implored the woman sitting beside him in the hayloft. Even at his young age, secrets from those he loved was not something he took lightly.

Sonya stroked his unruly red hair, shaking her head negatively. "No, darling, we can't tell them—not yet. It will ruin the surprise I have planned."

"Me and Gram are going to stay at Uncle Willy's tomorrow. Will you come to San Antonio to see me?"

"I'll try."

"And we'll tell Gram soon?"

"Yes, real soon."

"She'll be glad to see you again."

Sonya smiled. "We're going to spend lots of time together

266

very soon, honey. And the three of us will have a grand time."

Sonny Malone meandered amidst the grazing longhorns, listening to the cowboys and Mexican *vaqueros* croon soothing, low-toned songs to the rangy beasts. Some sang in Spanish, some whatever came to mind. Some men were known to sing a risque line or two about the beautiful "calico cats" in their favorite saloons. No one seemed to take into account a cowpoke's choice of words or melody. All that mattered was keeping the easily spooked cattle contented throughout the long night.

All was peaceful and quiet tonight. The air was warm, the moon was bright, and in spite of all the activity surrounding him, Sonny found himself wishing for a woman's company. But not just any woman's—Abbie's. It had been too long since he'd had any time alone with her. Hell, he'd seen more of her on the ranch than on this trail drive. She appeared to go out of her way to place them at opposite locations. If he was up ahead, she was bringing up the rear, or worse, riding in the chuckwagon with Short Order. Snorting disgustedly, Sonny headed his horse toward the campfire and a steaming cup of Short Order's coffee.

Short Order was waiting, cup in hand as soon as Sonny dismounted. "Figured you'd be coming in soon. Been out there nigh onto six hours now."

Sonny accepted the coffee gratefully. "It took us awhile to get them settled down." He sipped the steaming contents, then faked a grimace. "I swear by all that's holy, Short Order, I have never tasted anything could put hair on a man's chest faster than your coffee."

The cook grinned good-naturedly. "Reckon so. I don't waste much water when I make it. Boil it for nigh onto two hours, and then I throw me a horseshoe into the pot—"

"And if it floats on top, the coffee is done," Abbie finished, smiling widely as she walked into the glow of the campfire.

Short Order grinned. "Heard that one a few times, ain't you, little gal?"

"Yes," she replied fondly, "and by now I've come to believe it, myself." She glanced over at Sonny who was hunkered down next to the fire, legs jackknifed, eyes observing her with hawklike awareness. "Everything going well?"

"So far," Sonny replied evenly. "We've been covering close to ten miles a day, but the longhorns are on familiar rangeland here in Texas. The going will get rougher when we cross over into the foothills. They'll spook easier on unknown terrain. We'll have to watch them real close."

Abbie poured herself a cup of coffee and sat down on a wooden crate filled with food supplies. Short Order meandered over to the chuckwagon to mix up a batter of sourdough for morning. "Stampede is a word none of us likes to think about. I know this drive is tough and going to get a lot worse before it gets any better. No one ever said it was going to be easy."

"You can't trust those fool critters for a minute," Sonny said. "Any little thing can set one of them off and send him charging crazed from the herd. Before you know it, he's scared the rest of them into flight."

Abbie had appointed him her assistant foreman, or *segundo* as the *vaqueros* referred to him, and she was pleased to see he was taking the job seriously. "Have you ever been on a drive this far?"

He grinned. "Huh-uh. Have you?"

"Nope."

He shook his head. "Some team, Caldwell. Do any of your men know this?"

"They trust my judgement. They've never had any reason to doubt my decisions."

He favored her with an admiring glance before looking away into the night shadows. "Viento seemed a might uneasy back there earlier. We were passing through a boulder-strewn section looking for any cattle that might have strayed and he got spooked real bad."

"Did you see anything unusual?"

Sonny shook his head. "Nope, but whatever it was, it had everything else scared, too. There wasn't a sound from any of the wild creatures."

He turned back to Abbie who was staring at him pensively. "Something for you to pass on to the men if they have to go riding that way."

"Yes, I will—for certain." She watched as he filled a plate with beef stew from an iron pot hanging over the campfire. Strange how the only man she could reveal her innermost fears to was him. No matter what else was between them, there was a grudging respect for one another that neither of them could deny. "Do you think we stand a chance of making it in one piece to Missouri?"

He sat back on his heels, the plate balanced in midair. "Now's a heck of a time to be wondering that."

She sighed raggedly. "I have all of the men's lives on my shoulders, and it does weigh heavily on occasion."

"Responsibility generally does." There was a heavy silence. He knew she was seeking reassurance, and that, in her own way, she was asking him to help her stand strong. "I'm with you, Ab, all of the way."

Her turquoise eyes were soft and appeared almost grateful as they gazed over at his. "Thank you. That means a lot to me."

"You're welcome." He smiled before digging in to his food.

Abbie set her empty cup down. Being in such close proximity with him was hard on her nerves. She started to turn away. "Well, I suppose it's my turn to ride night herd. Everyone else has had a go at it except me."

Sonny quelled the urge to jump up and stop her. He knew she would not welcome his concern. "Be careful, silken lady.

Those quiet nights out there are deceiving."

She grinned. "I can carry a pretty good tune, too, you know."

He watched her walk toward the remuda to get her horse. He thought he might just go over and trade places with Hank Johnson who didn't like riding night herd anyway. He'd be far enough away from Abbie so she wouldn't know it was he, yet, near enough to keep a close watch on her.

Abbie hadn't been on the range very long when she spotted one of the men riding toward her. Right away, she knew there must be a problem.

"There's an expectant mama missing from the herd, ma'am," he informed her. "She must have wandered away without my noticing. I turned my head for a minute and that old gal was gone."

"She's looking for a quiet spot to deliver is my guess," Abbie said.

"They always pick the worst times."

Abbie smiled. "I don't expect she had much choice in the matter, Ernie. Mother Nature makes that decision."

Ernie grinned sheepishly. "I'll get some of the boys together and go look for her. Her and the baby would make some cougar a real nice meal."

"No, we'll waste too much time going all the way back to camp. Let's just ride out and see if the two of us can't locate her," Abbie told him. "She couldn't have managed to get very far yet."

They wheeled their horses about and trotted toward the last place Ernie had seen the longhorn. Splitting up, Abbie rode off to search one area, Ernie another.

Abbie rode through an arroyo, the rocks in the dried creek bed making a crunching noise beneath Romeo's hooves. Nothing appeared to move around her.

The moon flitted in and out of dark, eerie, clouds. Abbie

270

had her rifle withdrawn from the scabbard as a precaution-ary measure. As her mount picked his way around several large boulders that littered the dry streambed, she kept her eyes trained on the thickets of pine growing along the banks. Romeo suddenly began acting skittish, prancing nervously beneath her.

Abbie picked up the plaintive sound of a bawling long-horn at the same time she realized where she was. This was the section that Sonny had warned her about earlier. The animal bawled louder this time. Abbie kneed Romeo on-ward, recognizing the plaintive sound as one filled with terror. She was racing through a cluster of large rocks when Romeo abruptly reared straight up, his shrill whinny pierc-ing the night air and echoing off the boulders surrounding them. Abbie was busy fighting for control and trying to hold onto her rifle and did not see the sleek, golden shape that hurtled off of a high boulder toward her.

It was the two hundred pound cougar's vicious snarl that brought Abbie's head up sharply at the last minute. It probably saved her life. She swung the rifle around, intending on firing off a shot but did not get time to do so before the big cat was upon her. The full impact of his body slamming into hers knocked her from Romeo's back to the ground. She landed with a heavy thud, the cougar snarling beside her. Romeo fled in terror. Abbie gritted her teeth to stave off overwhelming fear. She noticed her rifle lying several feet away where it had landed when she'd fallen. As she stared into the cougar's fathomless topaz eyes, she knew she was about to die. The animal lunged, and a shot rang out. In shock, Abbie lay there not moving, the dead cat sprawled on top of her.

"Abbie!" Sonny yelled, rushing to her. He dragged the dead cougar off of her and gathered her in his arms. "Did he hurt you?"

His gray eyes were filled with relief when she shook her head. "No—I don't think so." She moved, then winced.

"Well, maybe bruised."

"Don't try to get up. I'll carry you." Before she could protest he stood with her in his arms and strode toward his horse.

Abbie didn't utter a sound. She liked the reassuring feel of his arms around her. It had been so long since he'd held her like this, and right now, she needed a bit of comforting. She wrapped her arms about his neck and laid her head against his solid shoulder.

"You're fine, sweetheart. It's all over." Placing her on Viento's back, he mounted behind her. "Your horse shot past me on my way here, so I expect he's back at camp by now. We'll head there ourselves."

"Slowly, please," she said shakily. "I need time to gather my wits about me before I face the men."

"You're sure you're not hurt worse than you're letting on?"

"I'm just shook up. I'll be fine—really," she stressed.

When they rode into camp, everyone appeared visibly relieved. Red came rushing forward to greet them.

"Doggone, you had us all plum scared to death, li'l gal!" he said. "Romeo came galloping in here like he'd just looked death straight in the eye and wanted no part of it."

"You're not far from the truth, Red," Sonny stated grimly. "A cougar jumped Abbie when she went looking for a strayed longhorn. It's a good thing I came along when I did."

"And that critter is still back there," she interrupted, "so send a few of the men back for her, Red."

"Will do, ma'am," he replied. "And you take yourself off and bed down."

Sonny helped her dismount. "You'll get no argument there, Red, I assure you," he answered for her.

"I need to clean up a bit first," Abbie said. "I feel as though I have that cougar's scent all over me." She glanced up at Sonny. "Would you mind walking with me to the river? I don't exactly feel like going alone."

Her simply stated request caught Sonny off guard and he stared at her for a moment, surprised.

Abbie misinterpreted his hesitation. "But if you don't want to—"

"No," he hurriedly interjected, "I'd be glad to."

"Let me pick up my toiletries and some clean clothes, and I'll be right back."

"Fine." He stood there watching her walk away, his mind reminding him of things he didn't want to remember.

The dip in the river felt heavenly. Abbie had scrubbed herself clean with a bar of soap and was now swimming leisurely about, enjoying the water's silky coolness on her body. Turning over onto her back, floating, splashing, allowing her long burnished hair to float out around her, she looked every bit like some beautiful water nymph.

It was so peaceful here. Tall cottonwoods and pines graced the river's sloping banks. The cricket's song and the fireflies' golden flash were like a balm upon her rattled nerves. And every now and then she glanced over to the huge flat rock that Sonny casually reclined upon just to assure herself that he was still near. She hadn't mentioned his keeping his eyes trained elsewhere. What was the sense? He knew everything there was to know about her. The way she looked, felt and tasted. He knew all that, and more.

As she swam gracefully about she was aware of his heated gaze upon her. She would turn her head and feel her stomach flutter peculiarly at the sight of him leaning back on one elbow, one knee drawn up, his arm appearing to rest casually upon it. It was a deceiving gesture. No one knew that better than Abbie. She knew he could be as fast and deadly as that cougar she'd faced earlier. But not to her. Never with her.

Always, and yes, even when he was furious with her, she knew he would never hurt her. He was the only person she

273

could really trust. It was like he had told her sometime ago: "When you save another person's life, there is a bond formed." She whispered it, remembering. They had formed that bond. And after tonight, she was certain that he still cared very deeply, and she knew that she did, too. She swam toward him, not one bit afraid.

Chapter Twelve

He watched her swim easily through the water and stop just a few yards away from him. She stood in the waist-high water, her intentions quite clear. His narrowed eyes followed the satiny curves of her body, resting hungrily on the shadowy contours of her naked breasts, the nipples round and hard. The moonlight danced upon the rounded globes, their golden perfection shimmering beckoningly with glistening droplets of desire. He thought he'd never wanted any woman as much as he did Abbie. And no matter how many times he may possess her and long to master her, he knew that he never would. Even now, she was just as elusive and self-possessed as the very first time that he'd met her.

Abbie observed his covert gaze, and her heart skipped a beat. She hesitated briefly, then drawing on years of unfailing confidence, continued onward.

Sonny did not move nor did he hardly breathe as she glided through the moon-kissed river like some pagan water nymph, hair flowing about her like wet silk, eyes telling him she had come to capture his soul. He imagined the sweet taste of her breasts and nipples on his tongue, their softness beneath his seeking fingers, and he groaned with a need so powerful that it took his breath away.

She was the only woman who could make him feel this

way: dazed, confused—and yes—sometimes even fearful of the feelings she evoked within him. And when he held her in his arms, his eyes staring deeply into hers, such an incredible feeling of tenderness consumed him that he knew beyond any doubt he had fallen in love with her.

He was pulling her up against him before he realized, her body melting into his arms, her lips seeking his. Their kiss was hard, demanding, filled with all of the emotions they could not suppress and could not say. A half sob, half whimper escaped her as, demandingly, his tongue sought the softness of her mouth. A shudder rippled through him, and he grasped her taut buttocks and pressed her slim thighs urgently against his.

Neither of them wanted to think about where they were or what tomorrow might bring. They were together now, as lovers, and it was a heady delight.

"You're so beautiful," he whispered, his hands caressing her slim shoulders, the smoothness of her inner arms, moving to cup her full breasts and knead them gently. "And for tonight, you belong only to me." He kissed her with all of the longing within him.

"Make love to me, Sonny," she whispered against his lips. "Make this night last forever."

"I'll do my very best," he murmured.

Abbie felt as though any will she had possessed evaporated at the touch of his hands on her body. She wanted to feel his bare, powerfully muscled form against her, his hardness pressed achingly to her throbbing need. Her hips arched invitingly against him as her fingers undid the buttons on his shirt. She stripped it down his shoulders, her hands immediately clinging to the rippling steel-like muscles along his back.

"You're a delight to the eye, my love," she said, her voice sending shivers along his spine. Desire tore at her in overwhelming waves, and she pressed her lips hungrily against the corded planes of his chest.

276

"And you—are a seductress." His hands wove themselves into her thick hair, grasping the nape of her neck. Snarling softly he reveled in the glorious feeling of her moist lips on his trembling flesh. She played him ever so slowly, enjoying the exquisite feel of his body twisting against her seeking mouth.

"I can stand no more," he gasped raggedly, his hands effortlessly spanning her narrow waist to draw her down beside him upon the cool, moss-covered rock.

"Yes, you can darling—much, much more," she whispered huskily, continuing her maddening exploration, her fingers slipping inside the waistband of his trousers.

He was breathing deeply, nostrils flaring wide, silvery eyes telling her everything she had ever wanted to know and more. She removed the last offending garment, then leaned over to dip her hands in the river. Cupping them, she scooped up a handful of water. Before he had any idea what she was about, she poised between his legs and poured it slowly from his chest to his thighs. He gasped as the cooling liquid came in contact with his heated flesh and saw that she did the same, her eyes following each glistening droplet as it ran in rivulets over the hard-muscled contours of his body. She bent forward, the wispy, silken strands of her tousled mane brushing intimately, teasingly, across his flat, male nipples. When they immediately stiffened, she smiled, then lowered her lips to suckle each in turn.

"Abbie—silken Abbie," he whispered throatily, fingers reaching upward to squeeze her hardened nipples so temptingly near. Erotically, Sonny undulated his hips against hers, his probing manhood hot and velvet textured, pressed to Abbie's inner thighs.

She left him momentarily to fill her hands with water once more. He saw her raise them to her mouth, then watched with heart pounding as her lips brushed whisper soft across his trembling stomach, hesitating at the wiry curls of his groin, teasing the pulsating tip of his throbbing shaft with soft kisses.

He gasped with startled delight, when, without hesitating, she took him fully into her mouth. His buttocks tightened involuntarily at the sensual feel of cool water swirling around his turgid staff. Her action's were bold yet extremely pleasing. There was no doubt that she was the most exciting lover that he'd ever known.

"Yet, surely you are no mere mortal woman," he whispered huskily, "but a sorceress who has ensnared me in your spell." His fingers curled into her tangled mane as she took him even higher, suspending him in timeless ecstasy, triggering an explosion so intense within him that his body shuddered for several long minutes.

Sighing, he asked hoarsely, "Where in God's name did you learn that little trick?"

She smiled enigmatically. "It just came to me, and thinking it might please you, I tried it."

"Just like that?" He appeared amazed.

"Just like that. Now quit talking." She kissed him feverishly, wanting this night to go on forever. She was not to be disappointed.

He pulled her swiftly with him into the knee-high water, his hands cushioning her spine as he pressed her back against the partially submerged boulder. His lips roamed over her breasts and nipples. "I want to kiss your most hidden charms, moon goddess."

A flush of passion came over her, the very thought of what he was about to do exciting her beyond reason. "I want you to—very much," she murmured.

Without hesitation, he rediscovered everything about her, inch by satin inch. He started at the curve of her neck, nipping tenderly the place where it joined her shoulder, moving teasingly over her nipples, knowing all the while that she had bound him to her forever. He kept up the sweet torture until he'd worshiped every place but one.

Abbie wanted him so badly she physically hurt from it.

278

Clutching his mane of thick hair, she whimpered, "Don't make me wait any longer—please."

Before she realized what he was going to do, he grasped her buttocks and lifted her effortlessly up onto the rock, placing his lips at a very advantageous level. "Put your legs on either side of my shoulders, Ab," he commanded softly.

She braced her palms flat behind her, her widened eyes following the movement of his hands as they urged her thighs farther apart, his fingers sliding around her to tightly grip her buttocks. She moaned in expectation as he raised her hips and placed his mouth against the swell of satin skin, tonguing the softness until she thought she'd die.

Driven by a desire so strong that she lost all control, Abbie allowed him to do what he would and enjoyed every minute of it. He wooed her with an infinite skill that made her arch and twist, her panting cries mixing with that of the night creature's throaty song.

When he could stand the exquisite torture no longer himself, he yanked her hips downward and thrust his engorged manhood deeply into her welcoming sheath. She gasped at his fierce entry, wrapping her legs tightly about him.

"You make me crazy—so Goddamned crazy to possess you," he said hoarsely.

"Yes, I know," she whispered.

Their mating was as beautiful and savage as the very setting that surrounded them. And throughout the entire time, he whispered all of the things that he had previously been afraid to tell her. And she did the same.

Abbie knew then, without any doubt, that this was the only man who would ever make her feel this way; like her very heart and soul was melded with his forever. She gave herself up to wave after wave of sensual pleasure until she was certain that she would drown in the depths of ecstasy, so shattering was her release. Head thrown back, he called out her name as the powerful feeling, so intense and so mind numbing, gripped him. Their soft cries mingled with the piercing sound of a nighthawk soaring high over the river, and then all was still.

He kissed her lightly before lying back on top of the water, pulling Abbie over him. Effortlessly, he floated, with her slight form buoyed by his.

"Did you mean all of those things that you said?" he whispered.

"Every word. And you?"

"I've never known another woman like you, Ab. You make me say all kinds of things that I never thought I'd say to any woman."

"Does that bother you?"

"With you—no."

The simple declaration pleased her immensely, and she snuggled her face against his neck. "I wonder where destiny will take us next?" she said softly.

"It's hard to say," he mused. "Up till now, I never was a big believer in love, marriage, and one woman forever." He kicked his feet, sending them gliding smoothly across the dark water. "I still don't know how I feel about a lifetime commitment."

"I'm not so certain either," she said with startling honesty.

Her simple statement took him unawares. Somehow, he had assumed that would be what she would expect. "I'm not so certain I like that kind of talk," he said, halting so suddenly that they both slipped downward, beneath the surface.

In a playful, carefree mood, Abbie quickly pulled free of his grasp and kicked away from him. He grabbed for her foot beneath the dark water, but she eluded him with graceful agility.

An expert swimmer, she broke the surface, treading water as she looked about. She didn't see him anywhere. It was then a hard yank on her ankle brought her down beneath the water into his waiting arms. He held her in an unyielding embrace, kicking upward. Breaking the surface with a yell of triumph, Sonny laughed teasingly.

"Now you are mine forever, water nymph, and I demand you come away with me to my island where you shall remain forever mine." He swam toward the boulder which had become their private paradise.

Abbie could not help laughing in delight. He could be so easygoing at times when it was just the two of them that she found herself wishing that the cattle drive could go on forever.

All too soon, the sun began peeking over the horizon, and they knew their time together, like this, was at an end.

Sonny realized one thing for certain as they rode back to camp: He was falling more in love with her with each passing day.

By the end of two weeks they'd managed to drive the cattle over a hundred and sixty miles. It was hot, dry country, but things were still going well. Today, the wind decided to whip up, and they rode with their bandanas tied across their lower faces.

Abbie reined her horse in beside Sonny's, her eyes squinted against the tempest. She'd eaten enough dirt on this trip to fill her mother's garden three times over. What she wouldn't give for a soak in a hot tub.

"There's rain behind all of this wind," Sonny yelled, drawing her attention. "We'd better watch the cattle real close if it hits."

"Thunder and lightning's the last thing we need!"

"I know that, but we can't buck the elements. We knew that we'd be facing some hard times."

"I was hoping we'd get through this without the threat of a stampede."

"It hasn't happened yet, so don't get panicky." He reached over and patted her hand reassuringly.

She was immediately soothed by the gesture. "I'll go on back and tell the men to keep them close together."

"The closer the better. They can't run easily if they're herded tight."

Abbie wheeled Romeo around and was trotting back toward her foreman when she saw several of her wranglers milling around a prone figure on the ground. She hurried over to them. They looked up when she hurriedly dismounted. "What's going on, fellas?" she inquired, hunkering down beside the injured man.

"He came riding up to us, Miss Caldwell," one of the wranglers explained. "He was slumped over his horse. We thought he was dead for sure, but he weren't. He says they had over two thousand head of cattle, along with Jake Johnson, that they was taking to market in Missouri. They were jumped by a hundred men who stampeded their cattle and killed all their men. Hung the ones they didn't shoot. This cowpoke just happened to have been strung up with a poorly knotted rope. The rope broke, and he kicked his horse into a gallop out of there."

"What kind of person would do such a horrible thing," Abbie gasped when she saw the raw, bleeding rope burn around the man's neck.

He reached up and grabbed the front of her calfskin vest. "That—bunch jumped us as soon as we crossed the big Red—stole every one of—our longhorns," he rasped painfully. "And killed my friends, every one of them."

"Sh, don't try and talk," she said. "We'll get you something to eat and bed you down in back of the chuckwagon. Just take it easy now. You're safe here." She uncurled his trembling fingers from her vest and rose to her feet. "Have Short Order bring the wagon around, Frank. Pronto." She faced the rest of the men. "Nothing like this is going to happen to us, so quit your stewing about it. We're going on, just like we planned."

Not long after, Short Order brought the wagon and they loaded the man into the back. He motioned for Abbie to come closer.

"Don't go—up to Missouri, ma'am," he pleaded. "It ain't worth it. Not when I been hearing tales of a trail all the way to Abilene."

Abbie was stunned. "I didn't know anyone had tried to go there yet. I heard they were building a railroad, but is it finished?"

He shook his head wearily. "Don't know 'bout that, but an Indian trader named Jess Chisum says he blazed his way straight through the nations to Kansas."

"Indians instead of ruffians?"

"Ma'am, there ain't much difference when it comes to brutalness," Short Order spoke up.

"I'll talk with Santiago and see what he thinks," she replied.

"We've got enough supplies to make it if we watch ourselves real careful."

"But if we get there, and there isn't a railroad through yet, we're finished," she reminded her men whose expressions had suddenly brightened. She knew they were weary of this trip already. It was a long, uncertain haul. And after this recent incident, they were even more so. "Let's head them in the direction of the Red for now anyway. By the time we reach it, I'll have made my decision." She walked away, her shoulders suddenly feeling overburdened by the added weight she bore.

They made camp early, fearing rain. It threatened but had yet to begin. Most of the men were riding herd. The others gathered around the campfire playing poker. The enticing aroma of son-of-a-gun stew wafted from the black kettle hanging over the fire. Short Order was busy feeding the wranglers who had just come off shift. Sonny was among them.

Abbie sat off to one side, having just finished tending to the injured cowpoke they'd taken in earlier. He had eaten some food and was now sleeping soundly. She hadn't had time to discuss the possibility of going to Abilene with

Sonny. After he had eaten she would go to him and see what he thought of the idea. The more she considered the possibility, the better it was beginning to sound. Abilene, at one time only a Texan's dream, was becoming a reality to Abbie Caldwell. By the time Sonny had joined her, her mind was just about made up.

Sonny and Abbie stayed up late that evening, watching the gray storm clouds skim across the sky and conversing quietly so as not to wake their sleeping companions. They were stretched out on their bedrolls, their faces close, Abbie doing most of the talking. Normally, she slept under the chuckwagon where she had more privacy. Tonight, she chose to stay close to Sonny. She needed his reassuring presence.

"So, I have to decide before we reach the Red River which way we'll be headed. To Missouri, where we know there's a railroad for certain. Or to Abilene, a shorter trail, with no border ruffians, yet, no one is certain whether the railroad made it through there yet."

"What do you think is best, Abbie?" Sonny questioned her.

She shook her head slowly. "Beats the heck out of me."

"Either way it's a gamble, but then, being a gambling man myself, I'd say let's shoot for the brass ring."

"Take them to Abilene?"

He looked over at her and grinned wickedly. "Why the hell not."

Abbie rolled over to stare at him, her concerned face suddenly breaking into a smile. "Why the hell not, indeed," she repeated excitedly. "We'll just do it, Malone! I'll be the first woman drover in the territory to herd cattle to Abilene."

"I think you're the first woman drover, period, honey," Sonny added, his eyes twinkling.

"Perhaps," she mused. "But I didn't start this journey with that in mind. It was something that had to be done. And now all I want to do is finish this drive and head back home to

284

my family."

"I've been meaning to talk with you about the boy, Abbie," Sonny stated meaningfully. "Until now I haven't asked very much about your personal affairs. I haven't felt you owed me any explanations. I think, at this point, that you do."

"What do you want to know?" she replied, tensing.

"Who the boy really belongs to."

Abbie carefully guarded her expression "You're one of the few who know I'm not Charly's natural mother."

"I don't mean to press you, Abbie, but you know how I feel about you. I just thought you might have a need to tell me, that's all."

"Sonny, I have protected this secret from the beginning. Even my own mother doesn't know the truth. I want it to stay that way for Charly's sake."

His concern revealed itself. "Do you honestly think I would ever do anything to hurt you or the boy?"

She shook her head. "No, of course I don't—it's just—"

"It's Sonya, isn't it?" he answered for her.

She didn't answer for a moment, then replied, "Yes, it's my twin's child. And you're one of the few people who know that."

"I was almost certain anyway, honey. You just confirmed what I've suspected for some time now," he replied, looking over at her. "Is Lucien his father?"

"No. Sonya met Lucien after she was pregnant. Charly's father was a foreman on my ranch. He was killed before his son was born."

"That's a damned shame. How did it happen?" He saw her face at once become grim, yet he wasn't prepared for her answer.

"His wife, Margarita, shot him after she caught him with Sonya in the supply shack on the north range." She released a petulant sigh. "It was a horrible time for my family."

Her honest declaration stirred him, and he leaned over to

kiss her. "My poor, sweet Abbie. I wish I could have been there for you." He saw her lips tremble and knew there was still more she had not told him.

"I killed—Margarita when she turned to shoot Sonya. She had gone a little crazy finding her husband with Sonya. I aimed wide to scare her, but she accidently stepped into the line of fire."

Sonny held her close, his lips brushing her temple. "You don't have to tell me anymore, Abbie. I'm sorry I made you remember this. I didn't have any idea."

"It's all right," she replied. "I've kept this to myself all of these years. You're the only person I've trusted so far with the truth."

"Your secret's safe with me," he whispered.

"Sonya knows, of course," she continued. "She fled after the shooting because she couldn't face the scandal, leaving me to cover up the whole thing as best I knew how."

"It must have been awful for you."

"Yes." Abbie drew in a torn breath and went on to tell him everything that had taken place, right up to the day that she'd returned home with the tiny baby boy whom everyone thought was truly her son. "So, you see, Mother was so ill at the time that she never really knew what had taken place. She accepted Charly as mine, like everyone else, and centered her life around helping me raise him."

"I want you to know," he told her, his anger at the pain she suffered barely held in check, "that I'll never reveal anything you've told me unless you wish it."

She hugged him gratefully. "I know I can trust your word."

"There is something bothering me, though."

A chill raced along Abbie's spine. "What's that?"

"About a week after the attack on the ranch, Charly was hurrying toward the stable and I went over to talk with him," Sonny recalled. "He's an irresistible little fellow, him and that pup always scampering around all over stirring up mischief." He grinned in remembrance. "I asked him where he was going in such a hurry, and he told me to play with his new friend."

"He doesn't have any new friend to my knowledge," Abbie interrupted.

Sonny frowned. "I just assumed he meant the dog, so I didn't think too much about it at first. We parted, and he went on his way. It wasn't until sometime later, when I took my horse on into his stall that I ran into him again."

"Was he with anyone?"

"No, but I have a feeling that he had just left them. I finished rubbing down Viento with the strangest feeling that someone had been watching me the entire time."

"Oh, Sonny," Abbie breathed. "Who?"

"I couldn't find anyone, although I looked everywhere." He was thoughtful. "Perhaps I'm just making something out of nothing."

"That isn't like you."

He ran a finger along her jaw, down her neck. "Honey, Charly's safe at your Uncle Willy's. He's just fine. I'm certain of it."

Abbie's mind raced. "Is anyone ever really safe from Sonya and Lucien?"

"I won't let him harm you or Charly," he vowed, brushing aside her tousled hair to kiss her neck.

"I'm going to hold you to that when we get back to the ranch and you try and go back to your wandering ways." She smiled sweetly. "They're over. You belong to me now."

"Is that so?" he drawled softly, his silver gaze devouring her every feature. "Tell me, how would you like to have to put up with a rough-edged cuss like me for the rest of your days?"

She gave a little shrug, her expression teasing. "Oh—I don't know. It might take some getting used to, but maybe I could learn to like it."

He moved his lips over hers with all of the feelings that

287

were inside him. When he lifted his mouth, she was in an entirely different mood.

"On second thought," she told him huskily. "It won't take much getting used to at all."

He held her in his arms. "I'm in love with you, Abbie," he said unhesitatingly, "and I believe you love me, too. And I don't want any more secrets between us." His gaze held hers, their depths filled with the warring emotions inside of him. "I think it only fair to tell you that I'm not planning on staying in Texas much longer. I've family in Mexico that I have to return to."

His words sliced through her. She knew then that all of her hopes had been false ones. A man like Sonny could never settle down in one place. If his past didn't catch up with him, boredom surely would. She almost laughed jeeringly. And here she had even begun to entertain thoughts of his living with her at the Bar C. The words were out before she could stop them. "And of course, her, Carmelita." She immediately wanted to kick herself.

"Who told you about her?" he demanded gruffly.

"You did, Sonny," she replied, taking him by surprise. "When you were delirious with fever."

"What did I say about her?" he queried cautiously.

She tried to keep her voice light, as if she didn't really care. "You don't actually want me to repeat all that stuff, do you?"

His face went through a series of varied emotions before he at last began to laugh. "Abbie, I've never met a woman who can make me crazy the way that you do."

"Oh, Sonny," Abbie sighed, "how well I know the feeling."

"Do I make you crazy, Ab?" he asked softly, nibbling at her earlobe.

Her mind raced. She did not want to fall any further under this man's spell, for she knew that he would never be entirely hers. There were too many haunts from the past that she was certain would eventually pull him away from her. "You're the most exciting man to come into my life, Sonny. But, tell me the truth. How much longer can I expect to have you? We both know the only reason you've stayed in Texas this long is because of Rodriquez."

Impulsively, he said, "Will you come back with me when I return to Mexico?"

"And leave—my ranch?"

"Would you?" he queried.

"I—don't—honestly know."

He buried his face in her burnished mane. "Think about it. We've still got time."

"Oh, I hope so. I truly do," she stated in a choked voice. She laid her head against his chest, the strong rhythm of his heartbeat lulling her into a sense of security. She liked the feeling very much.

He tilted her chin upward, stared down at her wonderingly. She appeared so serenely beautiful and loving as he gazed into her imploring face that words did not seem enough at a time like this. He stood, drawing Abbie up with him, and together they disappeared into the surrounding shadows where he intended to show her just how very much she meant to him.

Charly Caldwell sat on the back porch of his Uncle Willy's big house in San Antonio, his eyes searching the busy street for one particular person. He placed his chin in his hands and waited.

"Aunty Sonya promised she would come visit me here," he said. "I hope she hasn't forgotten where Uncle Willy lives." He jumped up excitedly when he observed Sonya turning into the garden gate and heading toward the tool house. Glancing over his shoulder to see if anyone was following him and, seeing no one, he ran happily to meet her. He thoughtfully reminded himself not to call her Mama. Sonya looked so much like her that sometimes he just forgot. He remembered how strangely she had looked at him the first time he'd called her that and how quickly she'd corrected him.

"Abbie is your mother, not me, Charly. You may call me Aunty Sonya."

He had been startled by her abrupt change in manner and had looked down sheepishly at his bare toes. "I—didn't mean to say that. It just slipped out 'cause you look so much like her."

"That's because we're twins, Charly. Long, lost sisters. And remember, you must not say anything about my coming to see you, darling," Sonya reminded him, her voice once again sweet. "We want to wait until your mother returns from Missouri and then we'll surprise everyone."

"Gram got a wire from my mother that said she was in some other place. She had decided not to go to Missouri, because there were too many bad men to get past that way."

Sonya did not like this change of events at all. She had promised Lucien she would find out from Charly exactly when Abbie was returning. They had assumed she'd come back on the stage and were planning for Sonya to switch places with her at the last way station before San Antonio. If all went as planned, it would go smoothly and unnoticed by anyone. Sonya prayed she could handle Abbie's role at the ranch. She remembered all too well how much she'd despised ranch life before. But Lucien had assured her it wouldn't be for very long. Just until they could manage to get the ranch out of Abbie's name. "Where was it you said your mother was taking those old cows, darling?"

"I can't remember exactly," he replied, shrugging his small shoulders.

"Think, honey, it's important."

He chewed on the tip of his finger. "It sounded a little like my mother's name is all that I know."

She thought a moment. "Could it have been Abilene?" she queried, holding her breath.

"Yeah—that was it. And she said she'd be glad for my

company since she's coming back all that way on the stage by herself. I wish we could take the stage all the way to the ranch, but Mama said we'll have to ride our horse from here."

Sonya beamed. "My, my, Charly. You are a little fountain of information, aren't you?" She stayed with him a few minutes longer before announcing that she had to leave to tend to some important business. She paused at the door, adding, "But I'll be seeing you again, real soon, honey. And we'll stay together much longer then."

Charly called after her. "At the ranch?"

"Yes, Charly, at the ranch," he heard her reply just before she disappeared from view.

Charly smiled. "Won't Gram and Mama be surprised."

"So she went to Abilene," Lucien Rodriquez said softly, his eyes shining with something Sonya did not wish to define. "It is like her to take on the impossible and win." He walked across the floor in the study of his hacienda and opened the liquor cabinet. Withdrawing a bottle of tequila, he poured himself a drink.

Sonya watched his movements, his entire person with a possessive gleam in her eyes. "How true," she replied stiffly, willing herself with every ounce of strength that she possessed to keep her jealousy under control. They had argued so many times about her twin, and always, he claimed that Sonya was just allowing old resentments toward Abbie to overshadow her business sense. She gazed into his cold, calculating eyes. "Just don't you forget which one of us you are to trade to the Apaches."

Lucien grinned as he walked toward her. He caught her wrists and pulled her up against him, his lips crushing hers in a bruising kiss. Her hands were all over him in an instant. Yet, when he finally lifted his head, it was Sonya who was breathless. He casually took a sip of his drink. "You are the kind of woman that I need, Sonya, for you know to always do as you're told. As long as you do that we will get along just fine."

Sonya's face suddenly bore a wistful expression. "I wish my father wouldn't have left everything in Abbie's name. She was always his favorite. He didn't even leave my mother any of his precious land."

"He left you money." Lucien grinned.

Sonya scowled. "You know very well I never got a penny. The collapse of the Confederacy wiped out my inheritance."

"I suppose your father thought if he left any of the land to you or your mother that you would both sell out," Lucien said. "And you would have." He shrugged. "He gave it to the one person he knew would nurture it."

"I don't like it when you talk like that, Lucien." Sonya pouted. "You make me sound like some empty-headed chit."

He kissed her lightly. "At the time, *nina,* would you have felt better if he would have left Abbie the money and you the ranch?"

Sonya smirked. "What do you think?"

"I think you would not have liked that." He smiled knowingly. "I know you and your twin very well. You are nothing alike, except in appearance." He smiled blandly. "But then, two women exactly alike would be very boring, *si?"*

It made her uncomfortable when he talked that way. Sometimes she almost believed he would prefer her to be more like Abbie. She tilted her head to look up at him. "Do not forget which one of us is your *mujer,* Lucien. As you say, we may look alike, but the difference is there to tell."

Lucien could only think how much he was looking forward to discovering firsthand all of those subtle little differences that made Abbie what Sonya would never be. But to Sonya he merely said, "I'll only be gone a few weeks. Just long enough to convince her to sign that deed over in your name. Then, I will see to it that you are never bothered with her again."

"And don't forget your promise to me, Lucien."

His fingers tenderly touched her pouting lips. "That we will sell everything, leave the Comancheros and become rich down in Mexico. I remember."

"As soon as possible," she urged.

"Sometimes, *bella*," he said casually, his fingers moving downward to stroke lightly over her rounded breasts, "I think that you are the one who is running from something, but from what I do not know."

Sonya gave him a half smile, her features frozen. "That is ridiculous, Lucien. Whatever would I have to fear?"

Lucien turned away from her when a step came and a shadow fell across the room. He gestured for the man standing in the doorway to come forth. "So, we were able to convince you to come see old friends." His smile was cold.

Brett Colfax gazed at the two people: Lucien, hard and mean. Sonya, softly beautiful, yet just as deadly. They made a perfect match. He took a seat on the horsehair sofa. "You didn't leave me much choice. That breed, Rico, showed up at my ranch threatening to tell my family about some things if I didn't come here with him."

"One *momento*, please." Lucien shot Sonya a dark glance. "That will be all, *mujer*, and close the door behind you."

She nodded obediently and left the room in a flurry of starched petticoats. Pulling the door shut, she paused, then leaned one ear against the thick portal.

Lucien faced Brett. "I want you to take a little trip for me."

"I'm through, Rodriquez!" Brett blurted. "I've had enough." He had ridden with the Comancheros after the war. At the time, he'd been desperate for money and bloodlust. Now, all he wanted was to put it behind him before his family discovered what he'd been. He knew he couldn't let that happen.

Lucien's eyes darkened. "If you would have gotten her to marry you like you were supposed to then this wouldn't be necessary."

"I tried beating some sense into the little bitch, let her know who was boss," Brett ranted. "But that gunslinger came in on us and nearly killed me. I need help, there, Lucien. He's out to get me."

"I think, *amigo,* that you brought all of that upon yourself," Lucien shot back. "I should have known from past experience not to have entrusted you with something so important. But knowing how she felt about you from all of the things that you told me, I thought your marrying her would definitely work in my favor. I was even going to offer you a price for the bride—as an added bonus."

Brett had never met anyone as ruthless or unfeeling as Lucien Rodriquez. But he saw something besides determination in his black gaze. "So, that's it. You want Abbie, just as much, or more, than you do her land." He snorted. "Well now, what do you know. Our invincible leader has a weakness."

Lucien suddenly appeared uneasy, even nervous. "Look, Colfax, let's get down to why I had Rico bring you here."

"You want her so bad it hurts, don't you?"

Lucien twirled the clear liquid around in the glass. "Every man has just one thing he longs to possess. This woman, Abbie Caldwell, represents many things to me. She will not come to me willingly. But there are other ways." He poured Brett a drink and walked over and handed him the glass. "If you do this last thing for me, I will forget that you ever existed after I have what I want."

Brett's hand visibly trembled. "I don't know. What about that gunslinger?"

"I will give you a place to lay low until I can have someone take care of him for you."

"You make it sound mighty tempting."

"Then you will do it?"

"How long will I have to be away?" Brett asked. "And just what is it you want me to do?"

"Kidnap Abbie Caldwell and bring her to the Comanchero

village." Lucien could have laughed at the stricken expression on Brett's face except that he despised his sort intensely. "Consider the alternatives, senor."

"It sounds like I don't have much choice in the matter."

"You have a choice, senor. Either the gunslinger will come looking for you when he returns to settle his vendetta, or your parents are to learn the truth about their hero son." He arched a dark brow. "That his favorite pastime after the war was raiding ranches. That he enjoyed scalping the poor settlers even after he'd plundered their ranches and raped their women."

Brett's head jerked up. "You sonofabitch. You know I'll do anything to keep them from finding out about that."

"Can I trust you to carry this through until I have everything that I am after?"

"Yes—yes, I'll do what you ask," Brett said tiredly. "Although sometimes I wonder why I just don't put a gun to my head and end it all."

Lucien stared at Brett over the rim of his glass. "I want you to abduct Abbie when she comes in on the stage from Abilene and see that Sonya takes her place. And, without anyone seeing you."

Brett slung him a fierce look, his voice hoarse. "You're taking Abbie back to the canyon, aren't you?"

"Yes, I will place her in Ortega's personal care. He'll watch over her until I get there."

"Abbie will never give an inch, Rodriquez. She'll die first."

"Of course she will. She likes living just as much as the rest of us."

Brett flinched. "Abbie—with you."

"Is there something wrong with that?" Lucien growled.

"It's not exactly a match made in heaven."

"The best kind never are."

"I'll agree," Brett said. "Because I want that gunslinger off of my back. You know the men who can do it."

"I will see what I can do, *amigo,*" Lucien said.

Brett paused at the door, adding meaningfully, "We're even after this, Rodriquez."

"*Si,* after this." Lucien nodded.

Sonya hurried away from the door just as the knob turned, and Brett stepped out of the room. Was what she'd overheard true? Tears stung her eyes as she ran toward her bedroom, wishing more than anything that she had never been born a twin, and least of all, Abbie's.

The closer the stagecoach got to home the more impatient Abbie became. She was anxious for an end to this journey that had kept her away from her family and ranch far too long. She pressed her tired back against the leather cushion and closed her eyes. She could feel the salesman across the aisle watching her closely. He sold pots and pans, he'd said, and had gone on endlessly about the need for his product out here in the primitive West.

Surprisingly, they were nice pans, and Abbie had purchased some. She studied him through barely slitted eyes, trying not to smile. He was some dandy, with slicked-back hair and a drooping moustache that he continually twirled between his fingers as he talked. She watched him shift his hawklike gaze upon two young women sitting next to her who had boarded at the last stop. Abbie groaned when she heard him take a deep breath.

"How do, ladies. Name's, Anthony, but you can call me Mr. A." He tipped his derby hat, his diamond rings glinting in the warm sun that shone through the windows. "And I have a deal for you on some waterless-wonder pans that's just gonna have you on the edge of your seats."

The two women scooted as close to Abbie as they could get, while viewing the salesman through wide, disbelieving eyes.

"He's harmless if you just let him roll on," Abbie leaned over to whisper in the one girl's ear.

"Oh," the girl whispered back, "I was beginning to wonder."

Abbie suppressed a smile and turned toward the window, pulled the shade up and settled back to daydream about the time she'd spent with Sonny while they were in Abilene.

The trail drive had been successful. They had driven the herd right down the center street of Abilene to the gaping stares of the townsfolk. A relief to everyone who'd made the treacherous journey was the sight of the rails that lay completed next to the stock pens.

Abbie had managed all on her own to strike a satisfying bargain with the Smithfield Trading Company who agreed to pay her thirty dollars a head for the entire herd. She was happy with that. Everyone else was, too. She had paid off the wranglers, left out enough for expenses and a bit of celebrating and, not one to trust banks since the fall of the Confederacy, packed the rest away in her money belt. Things were definitely looking up.

The only thing she hadn't accounted for was the fact that someone in charge would have to oversee the loading of the longhorns into the train cars that were to carry them up north. More delays, she had thought dejectedly. She was never going to get home to her family.

Sensing her dismay, Sonny had volunteered to stay and wrap matters up for her. She had protested at first, but he'd only insisted, promising to take the next stage out as soon as the cattle were safely off.

"Go on, sweetheart," he'd said as they did their own style of celebrating later that night in her hotel room. "I won't be but a week behind you at most, and I know how you're wanting to get to your uncle's."

Abbie lay back on the bed with a sigh, her thoughts solely concentrated on her son. "I wouldn't feel so uneasy if mother hadn't had to rush off to San Marco to tend her sick aunt. I can't stop thinking about that day you saw Charly going off to meet some new friend."

She supposed she must have looked so distressed over the incident that Sonny had at last placed his glass of champagne on a table beside him and took her into his arms.

"Go, honey. I'll only be a few days behind you at most. And then we'll all be back at the ranch together."

"You've convinced me. I'll go."

Sonny had looked pleased by her decision but did not fail to remind her to make certain that someone was with her at all times until he returned.

"Because of Brett, you mean?"

"I still don't trust him, and I intend on making him pay dearly for what he did to you."

"I wish you'd just let it alone. Your forcing him into a draw can only mean certain death for him."

"He only needs one hand, same as me. It'll be fair and square." He'd stared hard at her for several seconds. "I can't let him get away with what he did."

She'd pulled free of his arms. "I don't like senseless killing. And besides, his family needs him."

"Are you certain that's the real reason?" he'd queried gruffly.

"Of course, what other reason could I have?" Bothered by his gruff expression, she'd moved close to him once again. Long, slender arms curled around his neck as she'd pressed her hips against his. "Enough of this talk about Brett. Now that we've had the appetizer, how about the main course?"

As he'd rolled his body over onto hers and took her swiftly and fiercely, he'd whispered softly, "I never want to take the chance of losing you again, silken lady, for you mean everything to me."

Abbie gave herself up to the beauty of their passionate lovemaking, yet deep within her, she still remained somewhat unsure of Sonny. She knew he loved her, but yet there was a side of him that she did not know, was even a bit frightened of. He was not like any man she had ever met. There was something dangerous and untamed about his look, that even she did not know.

Now, jostling along in the stage toward home, Abbie found herself wondering what had truly happened in Mexico to have made him leave everything he believed in and come to Texas. She knew bits and pieces about him from Padre Felipe. But Sonny would tell her nothing. Whatever kind of life he had led before she'd known him was still a mystery to her.

Brett Colfax sat nervously in the saddle and craned his neck once again to look down the hillside at the way station. He glanced over at Sonya. "I see something coming up ahead. You ready?"

"She'll do fine, Colfax," the darkly sinister Rico replied before Sonya could open her mouth. He grinned jeeringly. "Probably better'n you. You drool at the mouth anytime you get within two feet of that sweet meat."

"Yeah," Brett sneered. "I heard about the time you tried to carry her off after raiding her land." He laughed, smacking his palm against his knee. "She showed you who was the boss that day, eh?"

"I wasn't trying to run off with her," Rico quickly replied, flushing scarlet in spite of himself. "I just wanted to shake her up a bit."

"Well, you found out that's not so easy to do, eh, Rico? She marked you up good with those sharp claws of hers, didn't she?" Brett goaded the red-faced man.

Rico growled and made like he was going to lunge from his saddle toward Brett, when Sonya reined her horse between them.

"Will you two stop this!" she yelled over their threats. "I can't believe you're ready to fight each other over her."

Rico and Brett glared at her, the sound of rumbling wheels finally drawing their attention. As soon as the stage rounded the bend and pulled up to the way station, the threesome rode silently forward.

The fast-talking salesman was the first to step down from the stage, his jaws still moving at an amazing speed. He turned to help the women. "Yes sirree, everyone's entitled to instant credit with the big Mr. A." He smiled brilliantly at a lovely redhead. "And for you, sweet girl, it is purely a pleasure."

Good lord, Abbie thought with inner amusement, the man actually got every one of us to buy something from him. Remembering the money belt around her waist, she quickly unfastened it and, opening up the crate of pans she'd purchased, she placed the money belt inside one of the pans and replaced the lid. Then she pushed the crate under her seat, knowing full well no bandit would think to look for money in a crate of pots and pans. Humming to herself, she stepped down from the coach and went to join the others.

"There be plenty of vittles waiting for you inside with Aunt Susie while I see to a fresh team of horses," the driver informed her. "And eat up, 'cause this is our last stop before San Antone."

Abbie looked around at the bright sunshine and took several, invigorating deep breaths. "Texas, ah, how wonderful it is to be back."

She noticed the comfortable log house with smoke curling invitingly from the chimney and felt her stomach growl hungrily.

A huge woman with gray hair and a jovial, kind face, stepped outside to wave her onward. "Hurry up there, young woman, before they eat everything up on you." Abbie quickened her step. "I'm Aunt Sue, and I been looking forward all day to having some women folk to talk with." With the toe of her man-sized boots, she nudged a couple of sleeping hound dogs stretched out in front of the door. "These old boys make fine watchdogs, but they're either out roaming all night or passed out before the hearth all day."

"Sounds like some husbands I've heard about," Abbie

300

replied with an easy smile, and both women grinned widely.

The two women hit it off immediately, and all through the hearty meal, they laughed and talked, until before Abbie realized it was time to depart.

Abbie and the driver walked on outside ahead of Mr. Anthony, who had just sold a set of pans to Aunt Susie.

After a few minutes of waiting patiently, the driver excused himself and went back inside to retrieve the salesman. "That city slicker's gonna make me run behind on my schedule with his doggone prattle about them miracle pans."

Abbie had only strayed about twenty yards away from the house to stretch her legs some, when she was suddenly alerted to another's presence and, glancing over her shoulder, she gave a small gasp.

"Don't move, don't even breathe, missy," one of them growled.

Abbie froze, aware of her vulnerable position. She glared up at them. They were vicious looking, their faces covered by masks and wearing long ponchos and wide sombreros. She happened to notice one of their guns: a big Texas pistol, one that looked very familiar.

Her eyes narrowed. "I should have let Santiago gun you down that day you attacked me, you bastard."

"Keep your voice down!" Brett warned, glancing around him.

The other bandit came forward and reached out to grab her.

Abbie jumped backward. "Don't you put your mangy hands on me!"

The bandit grinned. "Me and you's been close before, little wildcat. You just don't remember."

To both men's amazement, her left hand made a lightning play for her six-shooter, and she would have shot the man before he could have blinked an eye if not for Brett's foot coming forward to kick the gun from her hand. She cried out

301

in anguished pain and fury as her gun flew from her fingers to land upon the ground. Her eyes met those of the man towering above her, and she cursed him with every vile name she could think of. She held her throbbing wrist, her eyes wide and disbelieving as she saw her twin sister step out from behind some towering boulders.

Abbie knew then, beyond any doubt, what fate lay in store for her. The bandit's mention of his *patron;* the fact that Sonya was here with Brett. Lucien Rodriquez was behind this, and the sudden realization that all of this time Brett had been affiliated with Rodriquez left her devastated. She struggled for self-control, the need to run from them almost overpowering reasoning. They closed in on her.

"Get her, Rico," Brett ordered. "From the looks of that salesman, he'll keep them busy awhile so's we can make the change. I'll keep guard. Rico, take the women over behind those boulders and have them exchange clothes."

Rico flung Abbie ahead of him. "Get moving, honey."

Abbie turned on Sonya. "You're going to regret all of your awful deeds one day very soon, I promise you that."

Once behind the boulder, Sonya slipped out of her split riding skirt and handed it to Abbie. "Listen to me. I know what you're thinking, and at first, I wanted this just as much as Lucien. He promised me we'd sell everything and go to Mexico where we'd begin a new life."

"By everything, I take it you mean *my* ranch."

"It should have been part mine, Abbie Lee," Sonya hissed, "and you know it."

"Thank God, Pa had more sense."

Sonya tossed her head defiantly. "If you had more sense and not got mixed up with that gunrunner and come to Devil's Bend, Lucien would have never got himself heated up over you."

"I don't have time to argue with you. Get to the point."

"I overheard Lucien talking to Brett, and I know he's dead

set on having you and getting rid of me," Sonya whispered, glancing around the sheltering boulder every few seconds to see if Rico was listening. He wasn't. "We've got to try and help each other the way that I see it."

"How?" Abbie shot back.

"I can't go into everything now, but if you keep your mouth shut and don't tell Lucien who really killed the major, I'll get you out of this somehow."

"I don't really have any choice in the matter, now, do I?"

"No, you don't, and what difference does it make anyway? Sonny's dead. Let him take the blame for it."

"I can't forget what you did back in Devil's Bend, Sonya," Abbie replied.

"Do as I say, Abbie, and I'll take care of Charly and get to you as soon as I can. And whatever you do, don't weaken and give into Lucien's demands—any of them."

Abbie slipped into her twin's skirt and blouse, regarding her closely. Suddenly she knew what she must do if she were to save her own life and that of her son's. Her aquamarine eyes narrowed when they fell upon her twin. Her spine stiffened in determination. "I don't trust you, Sonya, but I'll remember your words."

"Time's up," Rico stated. Grabbing Abbie's wrists he quickly bound them with a blue scarf. "The *patron* does not want your pretty skin all marred with rope burns." He laughed, then swept her up in his arms and tossed her onto the back of a horse.

Brett took hold of her reins, and she felt her horse surge forward. She grabbed hold of the pommel. She knew she had little chance of getting away with her life, but she was going to give it her very best effort. Tangled strands of chestnut hair whipped about her face in the cooling breeze, giving her the appearance of a cornered she-wolf as she glared accusingly at him.

"I'll see that you hang for this, Brett, if I don't find some way to kill you first myself." She felt a bitter-sweet sense of satisfaction when she saw him flinch as though she'd struck him.

He gave her a keen, hard look. "Rodriquez has already slipped the noose around my neck. You may as well be the one to tighten it."

"Oh, please spare me the self-pity, Brett," she snapped, her eyes scornful. "Santiago tried repeatedly to warn me about you, and I was fool enough to defend you."

The other *bandido* waved his arm impatiently. "Enough! Are we going to have to listen to the *mujer* whip you with her sharp tongue the entire trip back?" He inclined his head toward Abbie. "If she doesn't shut up, I'll give her something to think about—*comprende?*"

Brett simply scowled darkly at him. Abbie rode proudly beautiful, refusing to show fear, her long skirt blowing unhindered around her bare legs, her hat caught by the wind, whipping about her shoulders, held fast by the cord around her neck. She did not look at Brett again, but she did glance back over her shoulder to see her twin watching her with a look of regret on her face.

For now, she knew she was at their mercy. She had no way of escaping, yet she would, somehow. She would find a way to get away from them. She knew she had to. For at the end of this nightmare journey she knew what awaited her: Lucien Rodriquez.

Chapter Thirteen

Abbie wasn't certain where they were taking her. The journey was almost dreamlike so silent were her two companions and the bleak, unending prairie they traveled across. For days on end they rode through shallow valleys over sod that was springy beneath their horses' hooves and land that she had never seen before, until at last she began to realize where they were taking her.

"The lost canyon, the Comanchero hideout. That's where we're going, isn't it?" she asked Brett.

He turned to give her a strange, probing look. "Don't ask too many questions. You just might not like the answers."

"I have a right to know!" she snapped, furious. "It's my life you're handing over to that monster, Brett."

"It wasn't supposed to happen like this, Abbie Lee. It was that goddamned willful nature of yours that messed up our plans." He stared almost longingly at her. Her long hair was tousled about her shoulders, her eyes blue points of fire as she held his gaze. He thought she'd never looked as magnificent as she did right at that moment. "But then, knowing you, I should have expected you to get fiesty just as soon as I tried to wear the pants in the family. It's gonna be different with him, Abbie."

She frowned. "Don't go placing any bets on it, Colfax."

As they rode onward, he found himself almost wishing that things could have been different with them. He had tried to protect her from this, but she wouldn't let him. Everything always had to be Abbie Lee's way, or no way at all. Well, this time, she was going to dance to someone else's tune. "Oh, honey, are you in for the surprise of your life."

"Maybe Rodriquez is, too," Abbie remarked. "Did you ever stop to think of that?"

"That gunslinger of yours isn't going to find you where I'm taking you." He scowled at her. "You know that sonofabitch left me with three cracked ribs. He darned near killed me, and you stood by and let him, too."

Abbie glared. "Am I supposed to feel sorry for you after you tried to rape me?" She laughed shortly. "Of course I am. Just like always. Well, save your breath. I just hope he gets the chance to finish what he started."

"Shut up, Abbie," he said stonily. "I didn't want anything from you that you hadn't already put out to him before. You were used goods, baby. What could it have mattered. Just one more."

"You're crazy, Brett," she breathed. "I don't know why none of us hasn't seen that before. You're dangerous."

"Don't ever call me that!" he screamed, his face becoming contorted and ugly. "You don't know. You have no idea what I went through in the war, what I've been going through ever since!"

Abbie was stunned into silence. This man, this other Brett, was the one who had attacked her. Her mind whirled dazedly. Was something like that possible? Did he indeed have two people inside him? The possibility terrified her.

"*Perdicion!*" Rico shouted as he rode up beside them. "Must I listen to the two of you bicker back and forth this entire journey!" He yanked her horse's reins away from Brett. "It is your turn to scout up ahead," he told him. "And use the time to cool off, eh, *amigo.*"

* * *

They reached the formidable Staked Plains by climbing an escarpment that was treacherous and heart-stopping in its rugged beauty. Abbie found herself fascinated riding along the edge of the mysterious, unknown territory. She had heard so many stories about the land that the Spaniard, Coronado, had invaded in 1541 with one thousand men all told. Using stunted cottonwood and willows found near streams, they had marked a visible route of their passing, where some still remained today. But never had she expected to see it with her own eyes.

Here the earth stretched straight across, an unending plane of brown, rustling buffalo grass perfectly level, sharply contrasting with the cornflower-colored sky. A gentle wind blew dancing mirages across the forbidding emptiness, lending a host of eerie phantoms to the wavering grass.

Abbie thought that Rico must instinctively know his way, so determinedly did he follow the invisible route. When she heard some of the bandits mention their Comanchero encampment, she knew her worst fears had been well founded. Her heart sank. She could never escape from a place rumored to be so impregnable.

Later that day, just before sundown, they came upon trails marked in the earth by the scars of many travois poles. Yet, as Abbie strained her vision to peer into the gloom settling around them, she saw no evidence of grazing pony herds, tepee villages in the distance, or any moving object that even so much as resembled a savage. It was chilling to behold.

Brett gave an order to stop and rest the horses. Abbie sank wearily to the ground to rest her head upon her bound hands. She looked up, hearing footsteps halting beside her. It was Brett. He handed her a canteen and inquired if she was hungry. He appeared to have forgotten his earlier anger and seemed to want to talk. When she complained that her hands were numb from her bonds, he untied her.

"Just don't try anything foolish," he warned. "Rico has a thing about killing. He likes it."

"That doesn't make him any different than the rest of you

now, does it."

Brett sat down next to her. He chewed on a strip of dried beef and began talking about the Comancheros and how he'd first met Rodriquez. Abbie listened silently.

"To shorten a long story, I met him in Mexico where I'd gone to prove something to myself, I guess. I had all of that hate twisted up inside of me, and seeing as how I couldn't get back at the Yankees, I chose to join up with a band of counterguerillas who fought for Maximilian. My having one arm didn't make any difference to them. They were willing to take anyone; force in numbers I suppose, and I was eager to kill."

If he was looking for pity, he did not receive any. She felt nothing but the lowest contempt for the spineless stranger he had become. "You would have been better off never coming back, Brett. I don't know what your family will do if they ever find out the truth."

"I never intended for it to go as far as it did, I swear," Brett explained pleadingly. "I met Rodriquez in the silver mines near Orizaba. Both of us had just turned in a couple Juarista sympathizers to the military garrison."

"I remember hearing of that awful place," Abbie murmured, shivering. "Men imprisoned underground, forced to mine the silver ore to finance Maximilian's armies."

Brett shrugged indifferently. "It wasn't much worse than that hellhole the Yankees kept me in."

"Oh, forgive me," Abbie said acidly. "I keep forgetting that no one has ever suffered more hardship than you."

He hadn't even heard but was staring broodingly into the campfire. "I wish I had walked the other way that day in Orizaba." Glancing over at Abbie, he continued. "Lucien and I got to talking while we were filling out the necessary paperwork and discovered that we were both fed up with fighting somebody else's war. The French promised us big money. We'd seen very little. Lucien said he'd been on the run when he'd come to Mexico, but now he was ready to head back to Santa Fe and round up his men. He told me he could use a man of my experience and that the money would definitely be good. That's the day I became one of them."

"The Comancheros."

"Yes."

"Never would I have figured you to ride with such cold-blooded killers."

"Sometimes a man loses sight of what really matters in life," Brett replied. "And when he finally finds it again, it's too late."

Abbie felt a faint glimmer of hope. Perhaps if she forced herself not to antagonize the darker side of Brett, she could rationalize with him, use him to stay alive. She took a deep breath. "And what would you do, Brett, if he told you to kill me; that he couldn't take the risk of my escaping and exposing his plans?"

His expression was dark and unreadable, yet his words were unhesitating. "I'd sure feel badly about that Abbie Lee, but then, I guess I'd have to comply."

She had trembled violently, her voice shaky and nervous. "Then you'd better kill me now, for I plan on running for my life whenever I can."

The other man, Rico, ambled over to them, his voice registering his amusement. "I would hate to have to do that here and now, senorita, but if you force my hand—" He tossed his serape over one shoulder, revealing a wicked-looking knife strapped to his belt.

Brett had been furious. "You'll do nothing to her, Rico! She's my responsibility and you're not to touch her!"

"Don't start giving me orders, Colfax," Rico snarled. "That mournful tale of yours don't buy nothing with me." He placed his hand on the butt of his gun. "And I've got my orders, too."

Abbie had taken both men by surprise when she screamed angrily, "You can both go straight to hell! I will not be discussed like some meaningless piece of horse flesh you've just

309

stolen!" She stormed over to mount her horse and shouted. "Make haste, my fierce *bandidos* or this captive may just leave you eating her dust."

Brett had hurriedly vaulted into his saddle while Rico hastily grabbed their gear and followed, both of them riding like the wind to catch up to the *magnifica gringa* who was turning out to be more trouble than they were beginning to think any one woman was worth.

Brett caught her after a short chase yet made no move to retie her hands. Night fell swiftly. Abbie felt as if she just blinked, and darkness suddenly cloaked the land. After another few miles of riding, Brett, who had taken control of her reins again after her flight, halted before her.

"Rico said when we came upon this sheer drop-off we was to wait until he could lead the rest of the way."

"What drop-off?" Abbie queried, discerning only blackness ahead.

Brett swiveled in the saddle. "It's there. I can feel the stiff wind blowing upward onto my face."

At that, Abbie experienced such a chilling blast of cool air that she huddled down into the woolen poncho that Brett had given her. Her mind invisioned all manner of horrors within the yawning chasm of hell. For surely that was what it was. And the ruler of all that was evil would be waiting, and it was there that her journey would end.

They descended the mighty crevice within the earth which gashed across the plains for unending miles, hundreds of feet in depth and enclosed by sheer declivity on every side. Abbie's horse sent rocks spewing downward into that formidable black hole. She shuddered upon hearing them bounce echoingly off the plunging walls before the sound came once more, and the stillness.

"I didn't even hear it hit the bottom," she mumbled in numb disbelief.

Abbie thought only mountain goats could have made it down these uneven, twisting trails, but the horses showed no fear, and on the last leg of their descent, they broke into a sure-footed trot that had her reciting every prayer that would come to mind. When it seemed like they were going to gallop forever through this maze of ink-black paths, Rico called out a password in Spanish, and Abbie heard shouting from below.

"Avanza! Adelante!"

Tiny pinpoints of light could be seen in the distance. They were there.

Abbie knew the quietness of the night could not last. She stretched her aching body, abruptly awakening to the sun's shining through a crack in the wall of the tiny shack where she'd passed the remainder of the night. The door opened and an old crone stepped inside.

"I bring you something to eat," she told Abbie who had sat up and cautiously observed her movements.

"Who are you?" Abbie asked.

"I am called Bonita." She unbound Abbie's wrists and handed her a bowl of corn mush. "Here, you eat."

Starving, Abbie accepted it and hurriedly began eating. Bonita did not seem in any rush to leave but stood silently watching her. Abbie gave pause for a moment and glanced upward. "Why—why are you looking at me like that?"

"My *mirado* tell me you are the twin sister of *el patron's mujer*. He say you and she are pictures of each other." She considered her own words. "It is so."

"There are differences."

"I do not see them."

"Look closer, senora," Abbie said. "It is as plain as the nose on your face."

Bonita studied her keenly. Abbie held her hand that contained the spoon.

"Ah!" Bonita exclaimed, her eyes rolling heavenward. "It is there before a person's eyes, is it not? *Zurdo,* left-handed!"

311

she exclaimed.

"And Sonya only uses her right hand," Abbie said, trapped between an inexplicable desire to laugh and a sudden impulse to jump up and run screaming madly through the compound for someone to help her. "I wonder how well she'll make out having to do everything left-handed." She became silent, hearing Brett's voice coming through the opened doorway. Oh, how she hated him, now!

"Good morning, Abbie," he said. "Were you able to get any rest?"

She favored him with a scowl, noticing his rumpled clothes and stubbled chin. "You don't look like you did," she said nastily. "But why should you give a damn anyway?"

He jerked his chin at Bonita, dismissing her, and walked over to Abbie. "My, but we're bitchy this morning. And here I came to tell you I've secured you nicer quarters." He reached over to pick strands of straw from her hair. "I thought you would be grateful."

She saw the rapacious gleam in his eyes and wondered what had brought about the abrupt change. Today, he was that other, terrifying stranger. She smacked his hand away, managing to upset the bowl of mush and splattering it over his boots.

His eyes were drawn to it. "Abbie—Abbie," he sighed, shaking his blond head. "You are such a damned hellcat. Perhaps if you had been a tad more predictable like your sister, you would never have gotten yourself into this mess." He stomped his boots clean.

"You—are the one who got me into this!" she snapped.

"I tried to spare you."

She laughed hollowly. "By marrying me and turning everything over to Rodriquez."

He pulled her to her feet and nudged her toward the entrance. "I wanted to be free of him, Abbie. It was the only way. And besides, we would have had my place. We could have been happy there if you would have given me a chance."

312

"I'll never let anyone have my land. I'll fight him every inch of the way."

"He isn't any fool, Abbie Lee," he warned her. "He has ways of making people do all kinds of things they don't think they ever will."

"Not me, Brett," she said assuredly as they stepped out into the bright sunshine and crisp fresh air. Abbie blinked, staring up in awe at the towering granite walls of the canyon which held her prisoner. It was virtually impregnable and hopelessly inescapable.

Brett took her hand in his. "Look around you real good, honey. This is home for awhile. What do you think of it?"

They began walking. She could not help the shiver of apprehension that coursed through her. He noticed.

"You ruined it all, not me. You've got no one to blame but yourself for this. I can't help you now—damned, stubborn woman. Here—he is king."

She stared at him, and for the first time since her capture, she began to feel real fear. It was intensified when, all at once, slicing through the hushed stillness, a terrible scream swept through the canyon, so edged with agony that the hackles on the back of her neck stood on end.

"What was that?" she asked Brett as they walked toward a thick cluster of white tepees. The shriek of pain came once more. Seconds passed. Abbie held her breath, her heart racing, but it came no more.

Brett laughed. "You'll get used to that sound, sweet. It's just the Kiowas having themselves a bit of fun with some captives they brought back from a raid, I expect."

Abbie trembled, wondering if she, too, might end up suffering the same fate as the poor wretch who'd been tortured. Torture, she thought; it was something she had not considered, nor wanted to.

"Where—are we going?" she queried haltingly.

"Up there." He pointed to a house high on the pointed edge of a lofty cliffside. "Rodriquez's home away from home."

"What is Lucien planning on doing with me?" she asked him, almost afraid to hear his answer.

"Taking real good care of you, honey, I reckon—until he gets tired of you like he already has your twin," he replied coldly. "And then, who knows?" He allowed his eyes to stray toward the Kiowa camp. "Perhaps—"

"No," she gasped. "Even he is not that cruel—is he?"

His solemn face told her everything. "Don't you ever think that. He'll turn you over to those savages without even blinking an eye, Abbie. He's the most ruthless man I've ever met."

"Oh, God," Abbie moaned.

"Sorry, honey, but that's the way it'll probably end up. But you've got time. He's plenty interested in you. I imagine your sister will end up there before you, anyhow. I know Lucien's just been using her. He needs her right now to stay at the ranch—but after he has everything tied up the way he wants it . . ."

She stared up at him, feeling as though this could not actually be happening. Even when they walked past clusters of adobe huts, pitifully primitive structures with half-naked children, chickens, and dogs all romping about in the dust, she found herself too dazed to even notice. Numbly, she said, "How did you know I was coming in on the stage and that Santiago stayed over in Abilene?"

"Charly just happened to tell Sonya when she snuck around to visit him at your uncle's."

Abbie moaned pitifully. "So, she was the one in the barn that day, and she must have found out Charly was at Uncle Willy's and went there, too."

"She won't let any harm come to your boy, Abbie. He is her nephew, her own flesh and blood."

"Is that supposed to mean something to Sonya? I'm her twin, and the only thing she's ever done for me is try and destroy me."

"That's 'cause she was always jealous of you, Abbie Lee," he replied. "You were your daddy's pride and joy. And his leaving the ranch to you and her a bunch of bonds that ended up as worthless as you know what on a bull was just too much for her to accept."

They walked past the deplorable shanties, and Abbie got her first good look at the men who made up the Comancheros. Her heart chilled. They were fierce-looking breeds: Mexicans, half-breed Indians, white hombres, all with the same hard, killing look about them. She hoped and prayed that she could survive this nightmare.

Her steps faltered on the pathway leading to the lofty casa where her journey would end. She hated herself for begging, yet the words came anyway. "Don't do this. Charly needs his real mother, not the likes of Sonya. Please, please, help me." She clutched his arm.

He shrugged it off, replying unfeelingly, "Sonya can play mommy for you. She's been looking forward to a reunion with her mother and Charly."

Tears formed beneath Abbie's eyelids as they continued their climb to the rough cedar house overlooking the scurvy village. "May you rot in hell for what you've done, Brett Colfax," she said with more fire than she felt.

He didn't even blink as he replied, "We're already there, Abbie. Don't you know?" Pointing to the house, he said, "Take a good look, 'cause that's your new home, Abbie Lee."

They were greeted at the door by a stern-faced man whom Brett introduced as Ortega, Lucien's personal *mozo,* servant. He was a thin man, with a drooping moustache and black, pitiless eyes.

He inclined his head politely to Abbie. "The senorita shall find we were expecting her. Everything has been provided for your comfort. *El patron,* he is a generous man." His lips moved in a thin smile. "You are an exact image of your sister." He looked her over thoroughly. "Except I detect a willfulness that the *patron* will have to tame. He'll like that. It presents a challenge."

Brett chuckled. "I see Ortega here knows his senoritas,"

he said, grinning at Abbie. He saw her gaze fasten upon the curved steel blade at the *mozo's* side. "You'd better be a good girl, for he knows how to use that machete better'n anyone I've ever seen."

Abbie blanched at the deadly looking weapon hanging from Ortega's belt yet kept her voice even. "If you will show me which room is mine, Ortega, I should like to go there." She thought he favored her with a gloating smirk just before he crossed the floor to a bedroom.

"You will find everything that you need in here," he informed her. "If you do not, I will see that you get it."

Abbie brushed past him to enter a surprisingly large room furnished with heavy furnishings of cedar and rawhide. There was a stone fireplace between two windows and fur rugs scattered about the floor, yet it was the huge bed, covered by a thick, buffalo robe that caught her eye immediately. She spun around. "Is—is this the only bedroom?"

"*Si,*" he replied before adding, "*El patron* wishes to respect your privacy. When he returns he will occupy the loft upstairs until you and he have had a chance to become better acquainted."

"So, he is not here yet," she murmured, more as an after-thought than a question.

Ortega was quick to point out that *el patron* would arrive shortly.

Abbie looked about speculatively, turning back at last to face the men with a haughty toss of her head. "If the senors are through waiting for me to collapse into a quivering mass of tears, I would like for you both to get the hell out of my room!"

"As you wish it, senorita," Ortega said blandly. He inclinded his head toward Brett, who followed behind him.

"Have a pleasant stay, Abbie. See you around," Brett returned jeeringly.

She sighed with relief when the door finally closed behind

them. The first thing that Abbie did was to run to a window and peer outside. There was nothing but a sheer drop-off below. With a groan of despair, she realized there was no escape from this room. She stumbled over to the bed and fell back upon it to stare morosely at the beamed ceiling. She was beginning to think that her only glimmer of hope was the slim possibility that Sonya would help her like she'd said. She wasn't going to hold her breath, but it sure didn't hurt to pray.

Sonya had risen early that morning and was just putting the finishing touches on her toilette, when Charly's voice sounded out in the hallway.

"Red's back, Mama, come quick!"

The ivory-backed brush she was holding froze in midair. "Damn," she swore beneath her breath. "I manage to convince my mother that we'll be fine while she tends her sick aunt in San Marco, and now the wranglers are starting to drift back from Abilene. If Lucien truly meant what he said, about my just having misunderstood his words to Brett, then he should be sending for me soon." She threw down the brush on the dressing table when she thought of yet another problem. Money. She was running low and did not know the combination to the safe in the office. "I hope they haven't spent all of their pay on whiskey and women, because I have no idea what Abbie did with the money she got from the sale of cows." She stomped her foot. "You've got to remember, Sonya, not to call those beasts cows anymore." Lord, she still hated this life just as much as she always did. She tied her hair back with a red ribbon, turning at the soft knock on the door. Thinking it was Charly, she called, "Come in, honey, it's not locked." She watched in stunned fascination the tall man entering her room. "By all that's holy—" is all that she could say.

Sonny grinned, his eyes lighting when they fell upon her.

317

"You look surprised, baby. I told you I wouldn't be far behind you." He came toward her.

Sonya was more than surprised; she was mesmerized by the sight of him. She could well understand her sister's interest in this man. He was so rugged looking, so intense, that he took command of a room simply by walking into it. She started to glide toward him, meet him halfway. She observed the confident way he moved, his face covered by a dark shadow of a beard, lending him a rough, almost barbaric sensuality that made her pulse quicken. When his silver-gray eyes swept over her, locked with her gaze, she felt her heart plummet, knowing beyond any doubt that her worse fears had materialized. "Sonny—"

"Hey!" he growled teasingly. "What kind of welcome do you call that?" He closed the distance between them in two easy strides and took her into his arms.

"Charly—Francisca," she sputtered. "What will they think if they find you in my bedroom—like this?"

He frowned. "Yeah, I should have thought, I guess, but I was just so damned eager to see you."

His chin rested atop her head, his warm fingers caressing her spine. Sonya could feel his aroused length pressed against her and almost wished she could let him make love to her. She remembered their encounter in Devil's Bend, and she found her breathing quickening. Pushing away from him she said, "Please, darling, I'm not completely dressed yet. Will you wait for me in the kitchen? I'm afraid we're both not in any position at the moment to give each other the sort of welcome we'd enjoy."

"Later, after I've had a chance to clean up a bit, I'll be back." He kissed her hungrily. "And then, you and I are going someplace private." He took her hand in his and noticed the bandage around her left wrist. He frowned. "What happened, Abbie? Nothing serious I hope."

"No, just a minor sprain," she explained. "With most of the wranglers still not back, I was helping out stacking feed

318

bags and just overdid it."

"Well, make certain you don't use that hand until it's better." He touched the injured limb to his lips.

"Oh, I won't. I can hardly move it as it is."

She closed her lips tightly in concentration as soon as he'd left the room. God help her if this man ever discovered that she was Sonya, and the one responsible for everything that had befallen him in Devil's Bend.

"Oh, Lucien," she wailed. "Whatever have you gotten me into!"

She decided right after sundown to sneak away from the ranch and go to the hacienda and confront Lucien with this news. Surely, he would not expect her to stay here now, not when her very life was in danger.

But Sonya found out later, when she stood confronting Lucien in the living room of the hacienda, that he did indeed wish for her to remain at the Bar C. She was beside herself.

"I got by all of them, even my own mother, but this man will know, I tell you! He'll kill me!"

"How?" Lucien argued. "With your hair the same shade as Abbie's, the only real difference is your eye color, and he'll be so busy looking at your other attributes he won't even notice."

"And you do not think that he and I are going to get that close?" she snorted. "You do not know this man the way that I do. He was her lover, Lucien!"

Lucien turned away from her, the declaration disturbing him more than he'd ever thought possible. "Shut your filthy mouth, whore! She is nothing like you—nothing!"

Sonya's eyes were clouded and confused, looking upon this man that she adored. "Lucien," she gasped. "Why are you more concerned for her than me? Did I truly hear correctly that day you were discussing all of this with Brett—are you planning on getting rid of me—for Abbie? And what of the revenge you swore on this man and Abbie?"

He spun around to stare hard at her. "All in good time. I wish to savor every moment now that we have them right where we want them." He placed a hand beneath her chin and raised it to meet his intense gaze. "Sonya, *mia,* how can you ever think that I would double-cross you after all that we've been through together—all that we've meant to each other." He kissed her, brushing aside two large tears which had trickled down her cheeks. "It won't be for much longer, and then we'll be together always."

Compliantly, Sonya nodded, wondering, even as she did so, why he alone had the ability to make her risk anything—even her own life.

The bright golden rays of the March sun cascaded in the windows and played upon the sleeping woman's features. Lucien Rodriquez stared longingly at her from the open doorway. He moved silently to stand beside the bed. Hand slightly trembling, he reached one finger forward to trace a feather-light pattern over her peach-tinted cheek. She stirred, turning over onto her back, her slender arm thrown back over her head. He pulled his hand away and sat down carefully on the bed to openly admire her fresh beauty.

Abbie's eyes flew open. "You! What are you doing in my room!" She pulled the buffalo cover up around her neck.

"Buenos dias." Lucien grinned. "And for now, it is your room. But that will all change in good time."

She looked away, unprepared for his presence or his boldness so early in the morning, and completely shaken by the admiration she'd glimpsed within those night-black eyes. "I want something settled between us right now. I do not intend to let you touch me or share this bed." She met his gaze head-on. *"Comprende?"*

"Are you ordering me around in my own casa?" He had to smile at her straightforwardness, even if he was somewhat taken aback by the intense hatred emanating from every fiber of her being. *Dios,* she looked so much like Sonya, except for those incredibly stormy eyes. Sonya had never looked at him like that in their entire time together. Submissive, whining; that was Sonya. This twin was an entirely different story.

Abbie debated whether to answer him, then sat bolt upright in bed clutching the cover about her. "You take it anyway you want to, it doesn't matter a damn to me. But know that I would rather kill myself than let you touch me."

"You would not get the opportunity," he replied coolly.

"Don't place any bets on it, *carnicero.*"

"Do not push me too far, *mujer,*" Lucien growled, "or I will see to it that you are tied to that bed whenever I am not with you."

"You'd enjoy every minute of that, wouldn't you *basura!*"

Lucien quirked one thick brow. "I would enjoy having breakfast is what I would enjoy. Now get out of that bed. I've decided you shall prepare it for me."

Abbie's mouth tightened to a thin line. "Where's the *mozo?* He is your servant, not I."

With a move so fast that Abbie did not have time to retaliate, Lucien grasped her wrist and jerked her from the bed. She stood, breasts heaving beneath the silken gown, shouting obscenities that made even his ears ring.

When she was out of breath, he said calmly, "Now, if you are quite through throwing your little tantrum, I am still hungry."

Abbie stormed behind the dressing screen that had thoughtfully been placed in the room and yanked on a peasant skirt and white blouse. She was so angry she felt like screaming. So she did. Leaving Lucien to begin wondering just what he had gotten himself into.

Abbie could feel Lucien's eyes upon her back as she sat on

the front porch steps, trying to think of some way to escape. He was sitting at the table eating the breakfast she'd reluctantly prepared for him.

"Do not think such thoughts," he called to her, automatically sensing what she was considering. He tried smiling at her when she jumped to her feet and frowned in his direction, then she turned her back. He was growing weary of her foul temper. "Your cooking is not half bad. I am pleased." He saw her back stiffen and found himself automatically tensing. It seemed no matter what a person said to this one, she screamed. And loudly.

"Why, because *el patron* commands it," she said cuttingly, facing him.

"It is my right."

Abbie pressed her nails into her palms until the pain took her mind off of the arrogant man behind her. "I only made breakfast because *I* was hungry."

"I think that is what you would like me to believe."

"I don't give a damn what you believe."

"Will you keep your voice down, *gata,*" he demanded. "You're going to wear the old man's legs off running back and forth up that trail to see which one of us is killing the other."

She leaned against the railing, glancing back over her shoulder. "You can always take me back and forget this whole thing if you're growing weary of putting up with me."

His mouth turned up in a knowing smile. "You would love for me to do just that. But it is too late. You are my ticket to everything that I've ever wanted."

Abbie knew then, with chilling clarity, that Sonya's declaration had been correct. She watched him rise from his chair and stretch his thick arms over his head. His movements were deceptively lazy. She knew better. She remembered how quickly she'd come flying off of that bed. "Stay away from me," she said, her voice unwavering. "I need time to breathe without having you constantly standing over me."

322

"Most of my women enjoy it."

He swaggered toward her. Abbie watched him, thinking how confident he was that he would eventually woo her to his bed. He leaned against the frame of the open doorway, his swarthy face so gloating, so leering, that she spat at his feet.

"Did that give you pleasure, doing something so disgusting?" he asked in a tightly controlled voice. He was totally enthralled with everything about her.

She stood, chestnut hair cascading around her shoulders, long legs braced stiffly. "If you must know—yes—and it made me feel a helluva lot better!"

"*Bueno,* and since you have no wish then to act like a lady, or for me to treat you as such, then we shall get down to the hard facts."

"Such as?" she posed.

"You, your ranch, and your son's life."

She stared at him, her eyes stormy blue with rage. "Leave Charly out of this!"

"That depends totally on you."

"You bastard!"

"You must realize by now that I will stop at nothing to get whatever I desire." He spoke in low, even tones, but his fathomless eyes burned with an unspoken message that she clearly understood. Before she could move, he'd grabbed her arm. "And I think it's about time that I gave you a lesson in manners." He dragged her along behind him into the house and threw her into a chair.

Fighting for breath, she raged back at him. "Santiago will kill you for this!"

His laugh was mirthless, his eyes gleaming with lust that her nearness aroused. "He is the least of my worries. I know, Abbie, that your lover, Sonny, and your hired gun, are one and the same."

Abbie tried not to blink an eyelash as she stared mutely up at him. "You—you are out of your mind."

323

He appraised her mockingly. "Your own twin told me this news before I came here. She was frightened to death of him, I suppose because she'd seen him murder the major right before her eyes. She begged me to help her—" He paused.

Abbie closed her eyes to the overwhelming feeling of hopelessness and anguish that encompassed her. "And did you?"

"Of course," he crowed triumphantly. "I imagine he met his fate at the hands of a certain bounty hunter that I know. Matt Kiley. Ever heard of him?"

Abbie nodded miserably. Half of Texas knew the infamous gunslinger. He made all other fast guns look pale by comparison.

He drew her up into his arms and tilted her chin to kiss her lips. "Now, do we understand each other a little bit better, *chica?* Do you realize that you have met your match, your master?"

She faced him with her head held proudly, her eyes damning him the entire time he explained how she was completely at his mercy.

Chapter Fourteen

Sonny was madder than hell. He passed back and forth in the solitary supply shack, mumbling beneath his breath and tossing down shots of whiskey. The more he drank the madder he got. "The lady is sorely trying my patience," he grumbled. "I've tried repeatedly to see her, and all I get is the cold shoulder." He realized he hadn't seen her but twice since he'd returned over a week ago.

He knew she was deliberately avoiding him. "But why—what have I done to her that she seems to have forgotten everything there was between us?" A sudden thought left him cold and filled with a sense of dread. Was there some reason why she was sneaking around by herself, riding alone, hardly paying attention to her own child?

His mind began conjuring up all sorts of images. He was so confused and hurt by her abrupt change that he felt he could only attribute it to one person: Colfax! She must have started seeing him again. Although Brett hadn't been around since he'd tangled with him, Sonny realized the soft spot Abbie still held for the man. Was it possible she had realized she still cared for the man? The thought of them together, maybe intimately, drove him beyond reason.

"I don't know how she could have forgiven Colfax after what he did to her, but then, who can account for a woman's feelings toward some men." He could just hear her comforting him. "Poor, dear, Brett, I know you didn't mean it." He sneered. "What a fool I've been."

Then again, he mused, maybe it was better he found out about her now. He just couldn't believe that she'd whisper velvet lies and promise him love like he'd never known, and then cast him aside without one regret.

"I don't even know why I'm hanging around here any longer," he said tersely. It was becoming obvious the closeness that they'd shared on the cattle drive had only been a convenient act on her part. "Talk about fools; she only used you to make certain her precious cattle got to market. She vowed to get you, you fool, and you helped her do it. How long are you going to hang around? She has done everything but tell you to get lost." Yet, he knew there was one thing that kept him here for certain.

"What if a child is born of our union?" He thought on that and knew, if she had become pregnant, there wasn't any way in hell he was letting Colfax raise his child! Furious, feeling like his own worst enemy, he threw the empty bottle against the wall and watched it shatter into tiny pieces. An idea suddenly came to him. One he should have thought of a long time ago. "I think this time—I'm going to have the last say, silken Abbie." He strode out the door and toward his stallion. "We'll just see if you see any more of Colfax. We'll just damn see!"

"Lucien, you lied—you lied!" Sonya screamed to the empty rooms and listened to the words echo back in her face. She'd come back to his hacienda several times the past week, refusing at first to believe that he wasn't coming back.

"You promised me you wouldn't run out on me, and you did!" She turned on her heel and ran from the house. "I won't let you do this to me. You don't intend to have Abbie sign any papers turning the ranch over to you. You knew all along—you wanted her over me! With her you'll have what you've always wanted. Wealth, an empire, and a wife you can flaunt in your father's face!" But she knew as she galloped her horse back to the Bar C that she would never let that happen. She would stop him. The only way that she knew how.

Francisca had left a light burning for her in the entrance hall. Sonya quietly entered the hacienda and shrugged out of her jacket. She listened for sounds of anyone who was up and, upon hearing only the constant ticking of the mantel clock, sighed with relief. She wasn't up to Charly's chattering, or Francisca's puzzling glances.

"I'll leave first thing in the morning," Sonya murmured to herself. "I know the way to the canyon. I can be what he wants. I know I can if he'll just give me a chance." She stiffened her sagging shoulders, thinking how she would go to the canyon hideout and exchange places with Abbie once again. She knew she couldn't keep up the charade forever but long enough to prove to Lucien how much like Abbie she could be if that was what he really wanted.

Assuming that she was alone, she walked into the living room and stood before the fireplace to stare into the glowing embers. She began to plan.

"Good evening, Abbie. I've been waiting a long time for a moment alone with you."

She gasped, recognizing that voice, and spun around to see Sonny sitting across the room, staring at her with the strangest expression in his eyes.

"What are—you doing here this late at night?" she asked, her heart pounding wildly.

He was on his feet within seconds, his booted feet soundless on the polished wood floor. "Searching for answers."

"Can't they wait until morning?" She quickly looked away

when he drew closer. "I'm really very tired and not much in the mood for talking."

"You're never in the mood for much of anything where any of us are concerned," he said sarcastically. "You've been ignoring Charly, letting this place go all to hell because you're too tight-fisted to part with any money. The men are running low on supplies again, Abbie, and you haven't paid up your last bill at Ralston's store. What is it with you?" He could barely contain his temper. "Or should I rephrase that. Who is it that demands so much of your time, and even now, has you brooding like your heart is breaking?" The distinct possibility that it was Colfax made him go a little crazy inside. He wanted to touch her, had to touch her. She was his; that was how he'd always think of her.

He brushed his hand across the tumbling masses of her hair, crushing it between his fingers, drawing her around slowly to face him. "I can't wait any longer, Abbie. You owe me that much, silken lady."

Caution overcame her, forcing her not to flinch when her body came up against his. She knew by the feel of his powerful form that his want of her raged even now within him. She sighed shakily. "All right," she replied. "We'll talk if that's what you want."

"I had hoped it's what you would want, too."

"I've had a lot on my mind lately."

"Obviously—not our relationship," he stated tersely.

"Why do you keep pressing me about some relationship you imagined we had?" she said edgily. "It's over. I never intended it to go as far as it did."

He stared down at her with a dangerously narrowed gaze. "Do you remember all of the things you said to me, Abbie? The times that we shared? Do you honestly expect me to believe that was all playacting?"

She favored him with a look that fairly chilled his soul and one that she hoped would cool his ardor. "Such a romantic you are, Sonny," she said. "We had us some good times, but

328

now it's over. You wouldn't be happy with me, any more than I would be with you. Now please, let's put an end to this kind of talk once and for all."

Sonny was totally unprepared for her cutting words. He grasped her face between his hands, his fingers biting into her soft flesh. "You little bitch," he snarled. "You were using me all along for your own gains, weren't you? Well, you played your part beautifully, my darling, but if you think I'm going to just walk away and let Colfax have what's rightfully mine, you're crazy." He pinned her arms behind her back, a bitter-sweet pleasure racing through his veins as he felt the rigid points of her breasts pressing into his chest.

"What—do you mean?" Sonya gasped.

He quirked a brow at her. "You don't even have the decency to act like you know what I'm talking about, do you?"

Before Sonya had time to think, he moved one hand beneath her blouse to cup her breast, to massage the nipple until it rose to his touch. "You're still a hot little number, aren't you. Well, I'll tell you what I'm going to do and you're going to abide by it. I'm hanging around until I find out for certain whether you're pregnant or not. For there's one thing I will not have, and that's scum like Colfax raising my child. Is that clear?"

Sonya became fidgety beneath his questing fingers, a slow burning ache centering in her loins. His eyes bore into her. His hands felt so sure as they plied her soft flesh that he set her blood on fire and made all thoughts of escaping him fly right out of her head. "You can't force me to love you, Sonny," she whispered huskily, but even to her own ears her words were slurred with desire.

"I don't want your love, *gata*," he murmured, "but I do want your body." His arms banded around her, rendering her helpless against his strength. Slowly, his lips descended toward hers, ignoring the fear in her wide blue eyes. She followed his body to the floor and moaned lightly as he rolled lightly atop her.

The weeks of wanting her and the bottle of whiskey he'd consumed made his passion flare out of control. It isn't for love, he kept reminding himself, not for love.

Sonya had never seen such burning intent in anyone's eyes. She struggled wildly, terrified of his overpowering closeness and of what he would do if he discovered who it was he held in his arms. She twisted her head from side to side. "Let me, go! You're crazy drunk!"

He laughed coldly. "Not near drunk enough, baby, to make me forget. I'll never forget." He bruised her lips with a punishing kiss, but his hands were gentle between her legs.

She was weakening, she knew it, and when he impatiently tore off her blouse to bestow light kisses along her neck, she threw all reason to the winds and dug her nails into his back. "Oh yes—yes." She moaned, writhing beneath him, raking long fingers along his spine. Lost in the throes of passion, Sonya was not aware that he suddenly lay motionless atop her.

His mind was reeling, something about this scene bringing back memories of another time, another woman. For a fleeting moment, he was swept back in time, and the scene with Sonya in her hotel room came vividly to mind. Her nails relentlessly digging into the flesh of his back made it crystal clear. He knew of only one thing that would prove it to him beyond any doubt. He laced his fingers into her tangled hair and wrenched her head back roughly. Those wide, fathomless eyes stared back at him in turquoise splendor. But in their sultry depths he caught slight of flecks of green. And he knew beyond any doubt who it was he held in his arms. It all fit together perfectly now. But my God, where was Abbie? Still confused, he sought further proof. He raised his hand as if to strike her, and immediately her right hand came up to protect her face. It was Sonya! Lucien must have gotten to Abbie. He knew Sonya was the only one who could tell him where Abbie was. But he doubted whether she'd do that for fear of Lucien's wrath. He would just have to force her hand

and hope she would eventually lead him to Rodriquez's hide-out.

"Please, don't hit me," he heard her whimper.

Recovering his composure, Sonny drew her into his arms. "No, I'd never do that. I'm sorry. I was just angry."

"I don't like it when you get like that. You frighten me."

"You're mine, Abbie. And I intend to see that you remain mine, always."

"What—what are you saying, exactly?" she queried anxiously.

Francisca's voice, calling from the back bedroom, brought an end to their confrontation.

"Is everything okay, senorita?"

"Answer her, Abbie," Sonny said softly, standing and pulling her to her feet.

Sonya swallowed over the lump in her throat to call out to the housekeeper. "Everything is fine, Francisca. Go back to sleep."

There was a moment of tense silence before Sonny reached down and retrieved her torn blouse from the floor, placing it about her shoulders. "I don't know what came over me. I apologize."

Sonya watched him through slitted eyelids, recovering her composure gradually. "Well, now that you've managed to awaken the household, will you kindly take your leave?"

"Yes, but not before I tell you why I came here in the first place."

"Make it quick," she urged.

"And very clear, I hope," he said, eyes raking her. "You'll not be going anywhere after tomorrow without my permission. I don't want you even leaving the house, at least until I can manage to get a reverend out here." He smiled coldly. "I'm going to tame your wild ways, love. Every last one of them."

Before she even had time for his words to register, he was

walking out of the room. By the time that she managed to reply, he was gone, the front door shutting firmly behind him.

"No, no, that can never happen," she gasped, blue eyes rounding. "I must leave here. Come daybreak, I'm going to the canyon, and Lucien be damned."

Abbie stared at Lucien's back as he sat at the hearth before the fire. She continued to refuse his demands, his advances, and she knew that his patience was wearing thin. She knew he wanted her more with each passing day. Only his extreme pride kept him from taking her against her will.

After that first time, when he'd threatened the lives of her family if she did not comply with his wishes, he'd thought she would bend to his will. But when he came into her room later that night, his black eyes burning with his inflamed passion, she stared coldly into those eyes and he at last turned away.

"I do not intend to make love to a woman who looks at me as if she'd like to stick a knife into my back," he roared.

"I cannot come freely to a man I know is holding the lives of my loved ones by a mere thread. I am not like that, Lucien. I have to feel something for you if I am to come to you willingly."

Lucien bristled. "But I adore everything about you. I don't want just your ranch. I want you, heart and soul."

"Why me?" she cried. "Why not let me go, spare my family, and I will let you have the ranch? You and Sonya can have it all."

He laughed sharply. "*You*, turn over the Bar C to *me*, and just forget it all." He grasped her wrist in his in a lightning swift move that surprised and stunned her. "I am blind to many things when it comes to you, *mujer*, but I am no fool."

She attempted to twist out of his grasp. "If you lay one hand on me against my will I will curse you until your dying day."

He grasped her arms hurtfully, his eyes a bit wary. "You win round one, *la princesca*," he growled. "But there will be more rounds to come."

Abbie closed her eyes to the overwhelming feeling of anguish that gripped her. She had never felt bested in her life by anyone, but at that moment, Lucien Rodriquez had come close to doing so. "You may take my body, Rodriquez, but you'll never have my soul."

"Ah, but I will, sooner or later," he said confidently. "It is only a matter of time and persuasion, and I will have all of you."

She faced him with her head held proudly, her eyes damning him as he told her bluntly and in graphic detail how she was eventually going to succumb to him.

"But not tonight. You need time to think more on what I expect from you when I do make love to you. But I will return." He paused in the doorway to add silkily, "We will go slowly, at first, savoring each new delight that we discover. I think I shall dismiss Ortega for this evening. I should like you to cook my dinner and bathe me."

"I will do nothing of the sort."

"It only takes one word from me and my *bandidos* will head for the Bar C—and the boy."

Her expression sullen and resentful, Abbie watched him leave. She knew it was only a matter of time before he tired of the chase and demanded her surrender. And under the circumstances, there was nothing that she could do but comply.

Charly Caldwell made no sound as he followed the woman posing as his mother to the stable. With a perceptiveness beyond his years, he rationalized the events of the past few days. As he watched her pass by Romeo's stall and chose a quiet, unassuming mare, he knew for certain that this was his Aunt Sonya, not his mother. He wondered if his mother was playing some sort of game with him. But he was tired of games. And maybe if he told Aunt Sonya how much he missed his mother she'd take him with her to see her. "Aunt Sonya," he called softly.

Sonya looked up, startled. "Charly!" she gasped. "What are you doing out of bed, and why are you following me?"

"Are you going to see my mother?" He ignored her question, his chin thrust forward stubbornly.

"Uh, yes," Sonya replied quickly. "I am. And none too soon I would say, seeing as how my portrayal is wearing a bit thin around the edges."

"I think I'm the only one who knows," he said. "And even I didn't know for certain until just now, when I saw you pass up Romeo for the mare. I know my mother only rides her stallion."

Sonya could not help feeling even more inadequate as she tugged herself up into the saddle. "Go on back to the house, Charly, and keep still about what you know. I'll send your mother back, I'm certain she's more weary of all of this than I am."

"I want you to tell me where my Mama is," he persisted. "I know I cause her a lot of trouble sometimes, but if she'll come back—I'll be real good."

"Is that why you think she and I traded places?"

He looked down sheepishly at the toes of his boots before replying, "I thought it might be."

Sonya sighed. "Well, it wasn't." She kicked the docile mare forward. "Now I want you to promise me, Charly, that you won't try and follow. I know for certain that your mother would be very mad about that."

"I promise," Charly said, his fingers crossed behind his back.

"Good boy. Now go on back to the house and act like you haven't seen me."

He watched her ride away. For several long minutes, he just stood there, thinking. Then, mind made up, he put a bridle on his pony and followed in the direction she had gone. "I think I'd better come along, Aunt Sonya, just to watch out for you." He kept a close eye on the horse and rider in the far distance. "'Cause you sure don't set a horse too well, and you just might fall off and hurt yourself. Then I might never see my mother again."

His saddle packs tied firmly on Viento, Sonny led the pinto from the last stall where they'd kept out of sight and swung up into the saddle. He picked up his field glasses and trained them on the two riders hurrying into the rising sun. "Charly, Charly," he sighed, "if you aren't just like Abbie. Always taking everything into your own hands and making my job twice as difficult."

He had been waiting for Sonya to make her move, and she had. But damn! He sure as hell hadn't counted on the boy. A cold wind blew across his back. He'd have to hurry and catch up with Charly without Sonya's seeing either one of them. Replacing the field glasses in his saddlebags, he urged the stallion into a brisk trot into the cold, biting wind.

The rider on the pinto horse rode into the observant man's line of vision, as he, too, watched the little entourage heading west across the prairie. He saw three riders, but only one held any interest for him. He observed his dress; he looked like any other cowhand: a thick, sheepskin jacket, dark pants, and a silk scarf wrapped about his throat.

If the man had been an ordinary sort, he probably would have let Sonny ride on without so much as a backward glance. But the stranger was far from ordinary. He was a bounty hunter. And at the moment his gaze was riveted on the twin black Colts on Sonny's hips. The sun glinted off the black and silver handles, reflecting in the bounty hunter's eyes. His upper lip, which was pulled down on one side from

335

a knife scar, lifted at one corner in a snarl.

"You're a dead man, mister. You just don't know it yet."

It took some doing, but Sonny at last caught up with Charly without drawing attention to himself. Before the boy could protest, he grabbed the reins from his hands.

"I don't want any argument from you, Charly. Turn that pony around and get back home."

"What about Aunt Sonya?" Charly exclaimed, then, realizing his outburst, covered his mouth with his hand.

"It's all right," Sonny said solemnly. "I know who she is. Sonya couldn't have filled your mother's place in our lives no matter how hard she tried." He released his hold on the pony's reins. "And she sure did try, didn't she?"

"Yes, and I feel kind of sorry for her," Charly said. "She never seems very happy, does she?"

"That's because she's given up so much, for so little, and she has failed to realize that yet." He smacked the pony on his rump. "Now get going, Charly, and don't look back."

Sonny watched for a moment to make certain that he continued onward, and then he hurried forward to keep Sonya within range.

Charly saw the stranger dressed in a long coat and flat sombrero riding toward him. He didn't like the man's looks at all and tried to avoid him, but the stranger kept his horse directed in a straight line, until they were finally abreast of each other.

The man's eyes were dark and cold, and Charly found himself staring at the parchmentlike skin beneath them in order to avoid their black, fathomless pupils.

"Howdy, boy," he said. "Like for you to tell me who that fella is on the pinto?" He paused to turn up the collar on his coat when a strong wind blew across his thick neck.

"Santiago Alverez," Charly breathed softly.

There was a distinct twitch in the parchment skin. "Well

ain't that just lucky for me. I reckon he's the one I'm after."

"Why?" Charly barely whispered.

"Gonna collect me some money and a bonus if I bring him back alive."

"You a sheriff?"

The stranger laughed brittlely. "Just as good, I reckon." He reined his horse around Charly's pony. "Keep heading in the same direction you was, kid, and you won't end up getting yourself hurt."

Charly saw the distinct bulge of a gun beneath the coat on the man's hip. He knew he had to warn Santiago. He didn't know why this man was after him, but he had the look of death in his eyes. He cupped his hands over his mouth and yelled as loud as he could. *"Santiago!"*

The sound carried across the low hills and reached Sonny. He turned in the saddle, saw the man and the way he rode confidently in the saddle, and knew why he had come. His copper-skinned countenance showed no sign of fear as he wheeled Viento around and stood his ground.

When the bounty hunter was within a few yards of him, the man said, "Been hunting you down for quite some time, and I would never have found you if someone hadn't tipped me off to your whereabouts."

"You talking to me, mister?" Sonny drawled, hands appearing calm, relaxed at his sides.

"Reckon so. Name's, Kiley, Matt Kiley, and I rode out from San Antonio looking for a gunslinger wanted for a murder up in Devil's Bend." He draped one side of his long cloth coat behind his walnut-handled pistol. "You look like you're that man."

Sonny shook his head slowly, laughing softly. "Well, I figured sooner or later one of you would find me. All I can say is you'd better be mighty fast on the draw."

Kiley didn't flinch. "I am."

"Then make your move. I don't have all day to hang around here."

The seasoned bounty hunter stared hard at the gunslinger. He saw the look of self-assurance in the thrust of his jaw, the coolness of nerve in his eyes, and for the first time in his life, Matt Kiley had doubts about walking away from this show-down. He wished he hadn't been so greedy for that bonus Rodriquez had mentioned if he brought the man back to him alive.

"I'd prefer to take you in standing up, but it don't make no never mind to me. You can either go back straight up or flat out," Kiley stated gruffly.

"You aren't taking me anywhere," Sonny stated, his tone silky and deceiving. He continually watched Kiley's eyes, the slight quiver of his hand. The bounty hunter went for his gun and made his move, lightning fast, yet his gun never cleared his holster before two bullets tore into his chest. He toppled from his horse like a felled tree and was dead before he hit the ground.

Chapter Fifteen

Throughout the next two days Sonya traveled steadily, crossing over into Comanche territory, familiar country to Sonny. He wondered if they were watching. Of course they were, he thought. Nothing moved upon the Llano Estacado, that they weren't aware of, but Sonya progressed onward, oblivious to the fact that her pursuer had insured her safe passing through this land.

Throughout the journey, Sonny acquired a begrudging respect for Abbie's twin. She was not as inadequate as she appeared at first glance. Maybe she couldn't ride a horse as well as Abbie, but Lucien had taught her quite well how to survive off the land.

When she stopped to camp, she picked a location against the wind. She knew which plants and roots were edible and used them all to supplement her diet of dried beef. And at night, she slept without a fire next to sheltering boulders or in some shadowy ravine. Sonny felt it was her determination to reach Rodriquez that gave her the courage to attempt such a trek to the lost canyon.

The entire time it was like a game of hide and seek. Sonny kept deliberately out of range and downwind of her horse. Even though Sonya could not detect his presence, he was concerned that his stallion would give him away if he caught the scent of the mare.

The following morning, Viento woke Sonny before dawn with a tug of his rope on the saddle horn. Sonny raised his head and peered around. It was gray and damp, the possibility of light rain bringing him quickly to his feet.

"I can only hope it holds off," he murmured, patting the pinto on the neck. "I'm glad one of us is keeping an eye on things." Just when he had the saddle on the horse, the first raindrops started. He mounted, realizing with a sickening sense of dread the possibility that he might lose Sonya in the drizzle. He had assumed correctly. He saw the perfectly flat land before him, yet there was no sign of her anywhere. The cold rain continued, and he turned up the thick collar of his jacket before quickly yanking a slicker from his pack. Even as he continued to look for her trail, he knew it was hopeless. She had disappeared in the enveloping mist, apparently taking a route not familiar to him. He had lost her and, God forbid, possibly Abbie, too.

"For Christ's sake," he growled in disgust, "how am I going to find her now?" Looking around the grayness that stretched for miles, he felt an overwhelming sense of hopelessness. It was then his keen sense of hearing picked up the faint sound of rustling movement passing over the crusty ground. Comanches were the quietest raiders in the world, but to one of their own, their sound was distinct. Sonny waited, daring to hope. He was not disappointed.

Progressively amidst pointed rocks, the hunting party of the Kwahadi Comanche rode directly toward him. Sonny saw his brother, Night Walker, superbly mounted on his prancing black stallion, riding ahead of his braves.

Sonny raised his hand in greeting yet did not speak, waiting respectfully for Night Walker to address him first.

"Greetings, my brother," Night Walker said. "My scouts rode back to our camp while the moon still shone to tell me that they'd seen a white woman, trailed by Shadow Dancer, upon the plains. I think on this, and then we come. You have

340

need of your people?"

"My heart is glad to see you."

"It is good we come then?"

"Yes. Rodriquez is as elusive and dangerous as any foe I've encountered," Sonny said grimly. "He has stolen my woman, and now his *herbi* seeks revenge on him for betraying her. I had her sighted and before my very eyes she just seemed to melt into the cliffs."

"My scouts have told me of this place you seek. It is the Comanchero stronghold, within those cliffs. It lies on the other side of that sheer wall of rock. But there are many who guard it."

"Do they know how to find the way in?" Sonny's voice contained a note of desperation he could not hide.

Night Walker's dark eyes were expressionless as they met Sonny's. "It is possible, but it could mean Rodriquez will kill your woman before he will let you take her from him."

"Yes, but I must take that chance."

Night Walker did not hesitate. "I owe you much, Shadow Dancer. My braves and I will gladly ride with you. We will wait until the moon rises, and then we shall swoop down upon the village without their being aware."

For the first time since the nightmare had begun, some of the tenseness in Sonny disappeared. He stared into the brightness of the fire. "It is as you warned me. Rodriquez is a deadly foe. He is cunning and ruthless, but he made one big mistake. He took something from me that means more to me than my own life." His eyes narrowed. "And he shall pay for that—the Comanche way."

The sudden drop in temperature had continued throughout the day, and Sonya shivered beneath the buckskin jacket, yet she gave no thought to turning back. Dusk was falling. Below her perch on a high cliff she could see pinpoints of yellow light dotting the hills and valleys, appearing like fallen stars burning on the ground. She knew the trail, the password for entry, yet if her plan was to succeed, she would have to ride past the guards when they grew drowsy from the cold and their long vigil. She was certain most of the village would be sleeping.

She twisted her hair into a knot atop her head and covered it with a dark sombrero. She sat back to wait until the moon rose high in the sky to light her way along the narrow trails.

Several hours later, Sonya mounted her horse, gazing down into the inky blackness where the sheer granite walls dropped away to nothingness. Confidently, she reined the mare toward the hidden path and began her descent. She smiled to herself. "I am coming to you, *mi amante*. We will be together again and this time, forever."

Upon reaching the bottom of the canyon, Sonya ducked low when a ricocheting bullet screamed past her.

"*Alto!* or you are dead!"

Quickly, she called forth the password. "*Camisa de Hierro,* Iron Shirt." She held her breath. At last she heard the voice yell back.

"*Avanza!*"

Breathing a sigh of relief, she nudged her horse onward in the direction of the house on the far cliffside.

When the raiding party of Comanche rode out across the land that night, beneath the full moon, Shadow Dancer led their way. He was dressed as one of them, his face painted in crimson vermilion, his eyes appearing even more deadly behind the painted face. War shields and feathered lances were held in readiness, all of them riding toward the inevitable showdown. When they reached the place where Sonya had disappeared, Shadow Dancer indicated that they should halt.

"This is the place," he said to Night Walker. "I do not know which way to go from here."

342

"There is a passage that leads along the bluffs you see off in the distance. It is a place of death if one does not know the way—and sometimes—even if they do."

"Do you?" Sonny queried.

"Yes. I have been there," Night Walker replied solemnly. "Long time before. It is the place where I sought my vision. I remember it well."

"It must have been where Rodriquez's woman went, and during the storm, I did not see which way she entered."

Night Walker kneed his pony onward toward a narrow crack in the vast canyon wall that appeared to Sonny to lead nowhere. "Come, we go now to get your *herbi* and seek revenge for the wrong that has been done you."

"I want Rodriquez taken alive," Sonny said, his jaw set hard with suppressed fury.

Night Walker did not reply. He did not think it necessary. His blood brother knew he would not interfere in his long-awaited vendetta with the Comanchero. He had his own way of avenging the wrongs that had been directed at his people because of Rodriquez.

Abbie sat alone on the big bed in the room she thought of as her prison cell. It was late at night, and she was awaiting Lucien's return from the village. She had not seen him since early morning. She had heard him talking with Ortega earlier about an argument he'd had with Brett. She couldn't help but wonder if it had been about her. She hadn't seen Brett since he'd brought her to the house that first day. It was just as well. They didn't really have anything left to say to each other, anyway.

A knock on the door signified Ortega's wish to enter. She knew it was he. Lucien never bothered to knock. He just walked in. "Enter," she called.

Ortega came into the room. *"El Patron,* he told me to inform you that he will be home shortly. He intends to spend the evening with you."

Inwardly, Abbie seethed, but not a flicker of emotion crossed her face. "Are we to spend another night matching words with each other?"

"I do not think, all night, no," Ortega replied, his meaning not lost on her.

Abbie met his stare, sensing that Lucien was not intending to sleep alone tonight. She forced herself not to show fear. "Am I permitted to draw water from the stream for my bath?" she asked.

"You may. There is no escape from this canyon, as you well know."

She stared at him without speaking, remembering how she'd tried to escape Lucien that first night, after he'd turned his back on her for only a moment.

"You recall what happened the last time you bolted, eh, senorita?"

She looked away, grateful when she heard the door close behind him. How could she ever forget that night. She'd been truly terrified and had let it show, tearing from the house and toward the winding path leading down into the village. Lucien had caught her easily in his arms. She was ashamed that she'd allowed her fear to show in front of him. She'd seen him smile when he'd caught her.

"Your heart is beating like some cornered wild thing," he'd breathed softly against her ear.

"Let me go," she'd rasped. "I hate you! I'm sick of being with you!"

"Oh, I think maybe you are beginning to like my being near you, but your pride will not let you give in." He'd nuzzled her neck with his moist lips and she'd struck out at him. With a shout of laughter, he'd thrown her over his shoulder and taken her back to the house.

"I am accustomed to having a woman around me all of the time to see to my every need. Now, since meeting you, I want only one. And I shall have you."

"Never!" she'd screamed.

"Yes," he'd whispered. "And soon."

He took her into the big bedroom and threw her onto the bed. "Any woman in this village would love to be where you are right now, including your sister. Why do you persist in playing these games? You are so innocently lovely. You make me think of many ways in which I would like to show you the joys of love."

"You don't know the meaning of the word!" she'd said heatedly, staring up at him with blazing eyes.

He'd looked longingly down at her for a moment, then spun about and stormed from the house. His face had actually expressed regret.

Now, upon hearing Ortega moving about in the other room, Abbie opened the bedroom door to see him dragging the heavy wooden tub before the blazing hearth. He glanced at her. *"El Patron* say to take your bath early, then draw water for his." He brushed off his palms. "I'm going down to the cantina where I will remain for the night. *Buenos noches."*

Abbie frowned. If Ortega was leaving who would see to Lucien's needs? "Wait a minute, you aren't going anywhere! I'm not scrubbing his back for him!"

"He told me he no longer requires my help with his bath." He cast Abbie a pointed stare. "He is tiring of the game, senorita. He is not accustomed to having to chase after his women."

"I don't care what he's accustomed to. I'll never scrub that man's back!"

Ortega laughed coldly. "You think you are so strong, don't you, with this game of hard to get that you have been playing, but I know."

He turned to leave, adding just before he closed the door, "All you have done is prolong the inevitable. He has been like a stallion chasing the spirited mare along the narrow cliffside. He knows deep down what she is doing, the fruitlessness of her flight, yet he enjoys it himself for a time, knowing that soon, he will catch her." He sneered. "Be careful, senorita, that tonight, you do not stumble."

Abbie stared at the closed door. Was Lucien growing weary of waiting for her consent? The disturbing thought nagged at her as she went through the array of colorful clothes that Lucien had provided for her. Would he seek revenge on her family like he'd threatened if she didn't show some sign of relenting to his demands? Could she take that chance? For days, she'd remained strong and had kept him at a distance, but now, it was as the *mozo* had said. He was getting tired of the game. Well, she would just have to plan a few new moves to keep him interested in the chase.

After a quick bath, she dressed in a loose-fitting *camisa,* much too low but modest compared to the rest of the wardrobe, and a red-patterned, ankle-length skirt. After securing her long hair in a tight knot on top of her head, she glanced in the mirror, then quickly pulled the *camisa* out of the skirt's waistband, allowing it to hang loose. That would just have to do. She didn't want to lure him too close. With firm resolve she went into the other room to begin dinner.

Lucien sat down at the table. "I am surprised that you are still here. I thought when Ortega told you he would be leaving for the night, you would surely find some way to sprout wings and fly right out of this canyon." She didn't reply but just watched him silently as he held up his empty coffee cup. "Your *cafe* is very good. It surprises me to learn what a good cook you are."

No doubt, she thought, he'd heard differently from her twin. "I can cook—if I've a mind to."

"I imagine you do many things well—when you have a mind to." Used to Sonya's placid spirit, he was finding in this woman a stubbornness and spirit equal to his own. She was strong and accustomed to bending everyone to her whim, regardless of the strength of her opponent's will. She would find out his strength tonight.

"Something you shall never truly know, Lucien," she taunted.

He laughed. "But, I shall, *chica*. Just you wait and see."

"I don't think so," she replied calmly, pouring herself a cup of coffee.

"This kind of talk does not please me, Abbie. I want it to stop."

Abbie forced herself to remain unmoved by his words. She was praying that she'd not misjudged his manly pride. Her only hope was the fact that he would want her to come willingly into his arms. And she vowed that would never happen.

"I'd like my bath now." He pushed back his chair and smiled at her. "And someone to scrub my back."

"You can scrub your own damn back."

He shook his head slowly. "That does not please me, either."

Abbie left the table, her hands shaking. Was Ortega right? Would she stumble tonight? No, never, she swore. She could be just as tough as Lucien. Without hesitation she carried water from where it had been heating on the hearth to the large, wooden tub. She poured it slowly, taking a deep breath upon hearing the sound of his boots, one, then the other, hitting the floor behind her. With supreme effort she forced herself to remain calm, even though she'd felt like tearing from the room and the sight of his brown, muscular body boldly stepping into the tub.

"I am ready, whenever you are," he said, their eyes meeting.

"I'm afraid you'll be soaking forever if you wait for that," she couldn't help responding bitterly.

He shook his head and motioned with his hand for her to come closer. "Tonight I want something from you. Come. There is nothing like a woman's touch to ease away the cares of the day."

She knew she would have to comply. She moved hesitantly beside him. Picking up a cloth she began scrubbing his shoulders. Kneeling behind him, she closed her eyes, vowing to never let him know how humiliated she felt forced to serve him in such a way.

"See," he said softly. "It is not so difficult for you to touch me, is it? I have a body that pleases women, Abbie. It could be so with you."

She had been washing his back with brisk strokes, but upon hearing his suggestive tone, she could stand no more and tossed the cloth at him. "You requested your back scrubbed. The rest is your territory."

"Come back here," he demanded.

She ignored him, clearing away the dirty coffee cups. "I just hate to have dishes sitting around until morning, don't you?"

"Are your nerves getting the better of you, *nina?*" he taunted, knowing, too, some of the ways to evoke a response from her. "You know I will make you my woman before the night is over, don't you, *querida?* Your mind fights me, but your body is ready to surrender. You are the type of woman who never gives in to anything easily, not even loving a man."

"This has nothing to do with love. This is rape. Do not confuse the two."

Stepping from the tub, he wrapped a towel around his waist. "We shall see how you feel when it's all over."

Abbie immediately averted her eyes upon glimpsing what her touch had done to him. He was the most conceited man she'd ever met! She watched him swagger toward her bedroom. "I am going to leave you now. You may attend to the dirty dishes if the sight of them bothers you so, but I will expect you to come to bed when you are finished."

Her mind raced furiously. She had to get some fresh air or she swore she might pass out. Perhaps it would help to sort out her thoughts. "Lucien, I need to get some clean water for the dishes. I'll be right back."

He called back. "Very well. But do not stray too far or you may make the guards nervous."

As she filled the bucket at the stream, an occasional hoot and holler drifted across the canyon from the cantina where most of the men chose to gather in the evening. Just when she felt like she did not stand a chance in hell of evading Lucien yet another time, she looked up to see Sonya coming out of the shadows toward her.

"Well now, aren't we just the picture of domesticity," Sonya said, observing closely her twin's attire. "Something Lucien picked out for you, no doubt?"

Abbie dropped the bucket with a startled cry. "I don't believe my eyes. I never thought you'd truly come."

Sonya glared. "It wasn't easy. You failed to mention that Sonny was very much alive. I might never had gotten here if he'd discovered who I was."

Abbie quickly asked, "A bounty hunter—did he show up?"

Sonya shook her head. "Not that I know of. Last I saw of Sonny he was madder than hell because he thought you'd been less than nice to him lately."

"And, of course, you didn't want him to know who you were and where Lucien had taken me," Abbie snapped, eyes damning her. "Then you might be exposed as the major's murderer."

"And I don't intend to swing by the neck just so Lucien can have you and the ranch all to himself," Sonya retorted. "The only reason I'm even here now is to get you away from him before he double-crosses me and forces you to marry him."

"I'd never do that!"

"Oh, yes you would. If he threatened you with Charly's life you'd do anything. And he just might make good on that threat, Abbie. So don't think because he desires you that the boy is safe. He'll hold him over your head for the rest of your days—just like he did to me."

"I don't doubt that that's true." She held Sonya's gaze. "Is Charly safe?"

"He's fine," Sonya replied, a slight catch in her voice. "A nice kid. You've done a good job. And Abbie, the boy only knows me as his aunt."

"Thank you for that, anyway." Abbie suddenly looked off toward the guarded entrance, a plan forming in her head. "Sonya, just how did you manage to get by the guards?"

"If you know the password, this place is not invincible."

Abbie caught her meaning. "Does that same method apply for getting out of here?"

Sonya nodded slowly. Comprehension brightened Abbie's intense features. For the first time in years, their thoughts were exactly the same.

"Come here, Abbie. Sit beside me." Lucien could not still the beating of his heart when she entered the room. She wore nothing but the flowing white *camisa* that fell just past her thighs. Her hair had been loosened from on top her head and tumbled like a silken waterfall down her back. She walked slowly, purposely toward the bed.

"I have waited forever for this moment, it seems," he said huskily. He lay partially covered by the thick buffalo cover. He was almost breathless with anticipation as he patted a place beside him on the bed.

She did as he asked, trying to calm her racing nerves when she saw him reach upward, feeling his fingers bury themselves in her long hair, working their way along the graceful curve of her neck to touch her cheek. "You will not regret coming to me, for I intend to love you well. After this night, you will know I am *muey macho,* and you will be back every night for more of the same."

"I do not want this, Lucien, yet you have left me little choice." She turned her face away from him.

Ah, he mused, pleased. She is so refreshing, so compliant once you force her hand. He smiled to himself, thinking how carefully he'd played her emotions. He knew her mind might still fight him, but her body was more than ready.

Confidently, his hand slipped the *camisa* down her shoulders. His eyes feasted upon her full breasts, the jutting nipples, and he whispered huskily, "I think it is I who have become your captive, *mi amour.*" He lowered his mouth to cover one rosy crest with his lips.

She came into his arms with a sigh of pent-up desire, and he knew beyond any doubt that he had been right about her. But he was beginning to wonder about himself. When he'd first captured her it had been to make her his and seek his revenge swiftly and unmercifully. But now he wondered if perhaps she had somehow planned it just this way. His feelings toward her had changed. He did not hate her as much as he desired her, wanted her as his, always. He longed for her to feel the same way about him, and the knowledge that she viewed him with contempt had begun to bother him immensely.

"I think I shall never let you go," he whispered.

Just when he thought she would let down her last restraint, he felt the fingers upon his back curl into claws and rake white-hot streaks of fire down his flesh. He flinched with pain, knowing she had drawn blood, feeling it trickling down his spine. *Madre Dios,* his mind screamed, not this one, too. He had enough scars already from her sister. He pinned her arms back over her head.

All pretense of softness left her. She became the raging, spitting virago he had come to know so well. Rolling out from under him, she doubled up her knees and kicked him hard in the chest with her feet.

He gave a soft grunt, his hands grasping his chest. "Such fire, it never ceases to amaze me," he breathed hoarsely, his eyes hard as jet. He grabbed for her ankle just as she was scrambling to get off the bed. "Oh, no, my little tease, you are not about to leave me yet." He yanked her roughly back beneath him, his breathing heavy, his manhood rubbing back and forth against the softness of her belly.

"You like to tussle before a tumble—that is good." He grinned. "So do I." When she tried to twist away, he caught

351

her about the waist and flipped her over onto her stomach. He grasped the perfect round swells of her buttocks with his large hands and buried his fingers in their splendor, eyes glazing at the hint of reddish curls barely visible between her thighs. It was that place that he sought—that he had to possess.

He stretched her out full length upon her stomach and moved to lie on top of her, carefully, so as not to crush her with the full weight of him. She struggled, but in this position she could no nothing.

One leg forced her thighs apart, his fingers slipping downward across her upswelling curves to touch her trembling mound and part the curving folds.

She froze when he moved his fingers inside her, and he covered her protests with soft words of reassurance. His hand lay flat against her, his finger sliding slowly in and out of her, then moving faster, bringing sobs of pleasure from her throat. He continued until she was writhing wildly beneath him. Then, with a cry of choked passion, he swiftly thrust his hard shaft within her, fusing their bodies in fiery unison. Her back arched upward, her nails, harmless now, clutching at the bed. The heat was increasing, driving him wild with incredible pleasure. He moved his lips across the nape of her neck, biting softly, feeling her satiny sheath tighten around his engorged manhood each time that he nipped her just so.

She was exquisite in her passion. Never had a woman excited him so. "You are *magnifico, mi* little *gata*," he murmured against her tangled mass of hair. Moaning, twisting, they sought their release, and it came, fiercely, powerfully, and completely.

He lay still on top of her, stunned and completely satisfied. His mouth was near her ear. He kissed it gently. She made a contented sound—then froze when he whispered, "And just what did you do with Abbie, Sonya?"

Chapter Sixteen

Sonya didn't move. Lucien grasped her by the upper arms and pulled her against his chest.

"Por Dios if you harmed her in any way, Sonya," he threatened, his fingers biting into her flesh.

She thought he looked mad enough to kill her. "I didn't hurt her!" she screeched.

"Then, where is she?"

Sonya sneered at him. "Where you can't touch her."

"You jealous bitch," he snarled. "You've cost us everything." He threw her to one side of the bed. Leaping up, he yanked clothes from a bureau and pulled them on, then started for the door.

"You'll never catch her. She's gone, Lucien!" Sonya screamed harshly. "She's probably riding free with the wind—away from you."

He spun around, his face livid. "You will pay for this, you *loca* woman. You've thrown everything away! Do not leave this room. After I find your sister I will come back, and then you shall answer for what you've done."

He hurried away, leaving Sonya sobbing softly. Seconds later, shots rang out over the canyon. Sonya tore from the bed and rummaged through Abbie's clothing in search of something suitable to wear. She dressed hurriedly in a split riding skirt and blouse, praying the entire time that her twin would get away.

The moon was out, murky and yellow in a bleak cloud haze. A night bird swooped by Abbie. She ducked over the pommel, the mare carrying her past the buffalo-dung fires where the Kiowas sat choking down rot-gut whiskey and playing dice. As she followed the stream that would lead her to the trail she sought, there came the distinct sounds of drunken laughter, nickering horses, and the ever constant wind that blew through the canyon.

She rode safely past the dangerous savages toward the natural platform of rock where the guards stood and watched. One called out, "Who goes there!"

My God, it was Brett. She lowered her voice and yelled out the Spanish password.

"*Advanza!*" he replied.

Abbie urged her mare onward and began the treacherous climb to the top of the canyon when the first warning shots rang out behind her.

There was a shout from the darkness. "*Alto!* you were seen just going in the canyon. State your business here!"

"Like hell," Abbie said through gritted teeth. She drew her gun just in case and jammed her heels in the lumbering mare's sides.

Without further warning, bullets began spewing orange fire all around her, bouncing off the canyon walls, sending chips of granite flying everywhere. She didn't know if she could make it, but she was not about to give up now. She heard a horse thundering up the rocky path behind her and screamed when a cattle cutting whip whirred through the air and snaked about her middle. Her gun was jarred out of her hand. All she could do was clutch the pommel and hope that he didn't pull her from the mare to tumble over the cliff.

Lucien held fast to the handle of the black whip,

determined to drag his quarry from the saddle. "You aren't going anywhere, *chica,*" he growled. He snarled to Brett to close off the trail ahead of them. Brett ran along the rocky edge until he was ahead of Abbie.

"Don't worry," Brett called confidently. "She won't get by me." He jumped down, blocking the exit, his rifle resting in the crook of his arm. His attention was fixed on Abbie, and therefore he did not notice the first Comanches moving stealthily along the shadowed boulders, until, across the moonlit canyon, the first Comanche war cry echoed.

Lucien looked up to see the whole upper canyon filled with dancing horses, painted savages, and flashing steel.

"*Madre di Dios!*" he gasped.

Abbie sat frozen, one of Lucien's arms reaching out for her just as the main thrust of the Comanche war party thundered down the treacherous trail; a whole calvacade of brilliant plumed warriors. And at their head rode one man, his silver-gray eyes glittering with blood-lust and focused on his target.

Brett heard the chilling cry of death and spun about as the pinto stallion bore down upon him, forcing his back up against the granite wall. His rifle flew from his grasp to plunge over the edge of the yawning chasm. "No! No!" he screamed. "Rodriquez is the one you want! He's the one behind it all!"

Sonny's horse pressed closer. "I should have known you were connected with the Comancheros," he growled. He looped a rawhide thong around his neck and flipped the end to another brave. "Hang on to this one. I have plans for him later." Brett struggled to get away, but the jeering brave jerked roughly, dragging him along the trail into the thick of the battle.

Sonny saw Abbie ahead, thrashing wildly in Lucien's arms. He was trying in vain to drag her over onto his horse. Behind them, farther down the trail, a whooping party of Kiowas were converging on the scene.

The Comanche, lithely graceful upon their charging steeds, hung low over their ponies' sides and charged into the Kiowa's midst. Long knives slashed a bloody trail down the winding mountain of rock. Two of the enemy were knocked from the trail to plummet over the side, their far-off frenzied shrieks echoing chillingly through the night. Abbie screamed Sonny's name just as her frightened mare whinnied in terror and reared back on her haunches. Yells of the Comanche, the cry of the Kiowa, and the crack of gunfire was everywhere.

Lucien dropped the whip, fighting to keep his stallion from going over the side as Abbie's mare threw her full weight against them. "Goddamnit! You stupid woman! You're going to kill us both!" His face was a mask of terror, his fingers still clawing at the reins as he toppled backward off his horse, one foot catching in the stirrup. The wild-eyed stallion regained his footing and careened madly through the melee up the narrow trail. Abbie cringed, watching Lucien's body bouncing off every rock and flashing hoof like a broken rag doll.

Sonny weaved his stallion through the masses of flailing limbs and clashing battle-axes, and in one catlike move, he sprang up onto the pinto's back and leaped from his horse to Abbie's. Expertly, he brought the frightened animal under control, maneuvering the terrified beast away from the edge of the cliff. "I'm with you, baby, just hang tight," he said to Abbie. He kicked the mare forward, following behind Lucien's stallion.

"Stop his horse, Sonny!" Abbie wailed,. "Oh, do something! He's being trampled to death!"

Sonny whistled for Viento. All around them the battle raged. A Kiowa emitted an ear-splitting cry before springing from a rock above them. Sonny hurled his knife with lightning speed, the blade embedding in the savage's chest and sending him hurling over the yawning chasm, his scream of death mingling with those of the wounded and dying.

Someway, and Abbie would never remember later how, she found that they had made it to the top of the canyon, Lucien's horse racing madly ahead of them. Viento galloped easily beside the mare, and Sonny quickly vaulted from Abbie's mount to the pinto.

"Stay behind me. I'm going to try and stop his horse!" His fiercely painted face was set determinedly.

"Go on, I'll be all right now."

He removed a pistol from the waistband of his buckskin breeches. "Here, you might need this." He tossed it across the space that separated them.

She caught it easily, feeling once more secure with the hard steel pressed against her palm. She watched him tear across the mesquite-covered plains to save Lucien, knowing full well it would be to take him prisoner, to kill him the Comanche way.

Sonya had run from the house and down into the wide gorge, her heart pounding with fear. Everywhere came the screams of the dying. Frantically, she tried to evade a charging Indian pony that was headed directly for her.

"Ah! Lucien, where are you! Help me, help me!" she cried, running for her life. She scrambled down a rocky incline. Seeing Ortega wielding his deadly machete overhead, attempting to stave off two Comanches, she screamed to him. "Ortega—oh, help me!" She watched horrified when a brave jumped the *mozo* from behind and plunged his blade into Ortega's back.

He fell, and the brave leaped from his horse to claim the coup, scalping his victim and waving the bloody trophy overhead.

Sonya felt her arm wrenched from the socket when one of her attackers charged by on his pony and caught her by the wrist. He snatched her up and flung her across the front of his pony, her head dangling dangerously close to his mount's

galloping hooves. She screamed until blackness overwhelmed her.

The fierce leader of the Comancheros did not die, but
many others had. His sworn enemy had managed to save his
life. Battered and bruised, but miraculously with no broken
bones, he was taken back to the winter camp of the Kwahadi
along with a handful of other prisoners. The Comanchero
village, the jaws of the gorge littered with lifeless bodies, was
no more. Smoke from the burning buildings could be seen
for miles. It had been virtually destroyed.

Abbie watched it all from the top of the canyon with a sort
of numbness. She thought it must be what hell looked like.
She had never seen anything more grisly in her life. She felt a
tear trickle down her face when she thought of her twin. Was
she one of the victims? She turned toward Sonny who was
beside her, feeling bile rise in her throat upon viewing
Lucien's battered form lying across his horse, his arms and
legs tied together by a rope slung under the animal's belly.

"Is—is he alive?"

"Yes."

"Must you treat him so cruelly?" She swallowed. "He's
injured."

"Am I supposed to feel badly?"

She found herself staring into his cold, aloof eyes, appearing even more merciless by the black paint streaking his face.
"I don't know you when you're like this," she whispered
breathlessly, making note of the fringed-buckskin shirt, the
knee leggings hugging his muscular calves, and the colorful
headband holding back his thick hair. "I am frightened by
this side of you, Sonny."

He suddenly winced, glancing down at a deep gash that
bled profusely on his forearm. "You have nothing to be
afraid of. You're my life, my love, Abbie. Don't you know
that by now?"

She bowed her head, forcing herself to remain calm. She knew he spoke the truth. "It's just disturbing to hear you talk so callously about another's life," she murmured. "I fear for my twin. I don't want anything to happen to her."

"I swore that I would make them both pay for all that they did to us. The Comanche do not take their enemies lightly, not even your sister, Abbie."

Her head shot up. She saw in his eyes that he meant to destroy them. She didn't know whether she could allow that without trying to do something to stop him. "I don't think I could ever forgive you if you did that."

Later, after they'd ridden through the entire village, searching for but not finding Sonya, Sonny grabbed Abbie's reins.

"Enough! I'm taking you back to the Comanche village," he told her firmly. "Both of us need to rest before we start back to the ranch."

Solemnly, she undid her neckerchief and leaned over to tie it around Sonny's forearm where his wound continued to bleed. "I think you'd better let me tend to you when we get there. You've got some bad knife wounds."

He shrugged, as if it were of no importance. "I'm fine." He reached forward to caress her cheek, his expression softening. "And you'll be, too, Ab, trust me."

"I don't honestly know if I can," she breathed softly. "Not where my sister's life is concerned."

They rode to join the rest of the tribe. It was Abbie's first glimpse of the prisoners they'd taken. When she saw Sonya's limp form slung across the jeering brave's pony, she had to fight to keep from screaming out her rage. Sonny swung around in the saddle, his eyes warning her not to open her mouth.

"What will happen to them?" she managed to whisper to him later when they were riding alone.

"Their fate will be decided when we reach the village."

"Oh, God," she moaned. "Don't let them torture her,

Sonny—please."

"Be quiet, Abbie!" he hissed in a steel-edged voice. "My people risked their own lives to save yours. Do not shame me before them."

For the first time since Sonny had known her, Abbie followed quietly behind his horse, eyes downcast. He knew he had sounded completely without mercy. But at the moment, after all that they'd been through, that's exactly how he felt.

A blue norther—a freezing wind from the north—swept through the winter camp of the Kwahadi, followed by snow.

Abbie clutched the furry buffalo robe around her as she stepped out of the warm tepee that she shared with Night Walker and his family. She studied the glistening landscape, the rows upon rows of tepees. The secluded village, high in the Palo Duro on the Staked Plain, lay beautiful and serene beneath a blanket of light snow for as far as she could see. Yet, tonight, the tranquility would be broken. The prisoners' fate was to be decided.

Abbie ducked her head against the biting wind, the soles of her fringed leather moccasins making a soft crunching sound as she covered the distance between the ornately painted lodge of Night Walker to the smaller dwelling which housed several Comanchero prisoners. She was dressed in clothes that had been provided for her by the Comanche: a two-piece dress made of smooth, honey-brown doeskin, with heavy fringe along the slitted sides which brushed her bare thighs each time she moved. Her chestnut hair streamed down around her shoulders, a beaded headband holding it in place. Passing by the guest lodge where she knew Sonny was staying, she felt a stabbing sense of jealousy when she saw a lovely, sloe-eyed Indian maid just entering the dwelling, carrying a steaming copper kettle.

Abbie knew how the unmarried maidens of the village felt

toward this warrior they called Shadow Dancer. She hesitated momentarily. She had wanted to speak with him. He had not approached her since their grim ride back to the village the day before. She knew it was due to the many gift-bearing visitors who filed continually in and out of his lodge.

He had counted many coups on this raid. There was even a special celebration tonight in his honor.

"Is that when my sister and the captives will meet their fate?" she wondered aloud, then shuddered. She knew she had to find a way to speak with Sonny, for she could never just stand by and allow that to happen.

Two Comanche braves guarded the entrance to the prisoners' lodge.

"Your chief gave me permission to see my sister," she said, having been told that one of them spoke English. "May I enter?"

Their faces remained impassive, but one of the braves pulled aside the tepee flap for her to enter.

Sonya almost didn't recognize her sister at first. She watched her warily from where she sat wiping Lucien's brow with a cloth. Her mouth fell open in astonishment when she recognized Abbie. "You almost look like one of them." She gave her a pleading cry. "You've got to do something to stop them. You can't let them torture your own flesh and blood!"

Abbie held one finger to her lips. "Keep your voice down. One of the guards understands English. If they hear us talking like this they'll send me away."

"Abbie, you can't just let them kill us. You won't—will you?"

"It's beyond me why you should expect me to feel sorry for you." Abbie sighed. "But I intend to talk with Sonny and do my best." She glanced down at Lucien's still form lying beneath a covering of buffalo robes. "How is he?"

"How do you think he is?" Sonya sobbed. "He's half dead from what that savage of yours did to him!"

"Lucien's done worse, Sonya. Here, I brought you some

herbs, one they call Medicine Woman gave me." She handed Sonya a buffalo skin bag. "It will help to prevent against any infection."

They stood looking at each other. Slowly Sonya extended her hand and took the bag. "If they allowed you to bring this to me, then do you think he plans to kill him?"

"I—can't say, because I don't really know," Abbie murmured. "I know he's been looking for Lucien since he came to Texas. He believes him responsible for his father's disappearance some years back."

"I know nothing of that," Sonya hurriedly replied.

"No, but you do remember how the major met his death, don't you?"

"It was an accident, I swear," Sonya hurriedly explained. "He knows that, and you tell him—if he lets me go—I'll confess. Yes—I will!"

"I'll want that in writing," Abbie told her. "Then, I'll see what I can do to help you."

"If you can find anything to write on around here," Sonya replied.

"There's a Bible in Night Walker's lodge, left to him by one of the black robes. I'll tear a page from that and I can get a feather quill and some red dye to use as ink."

"Write a murder confession on the page of a Bible," Sonya said dryly. "My, my, how quaint."

"Maybe it will do your soul some good," Abbie said.

As she was leaving, Sonya grabbed Abbie's hand. "Can you get me something to eat? I'm near starved to death."

"I'll bring you some food tonight if I can possibly find a way." She turned without another word and left the tepee. Outside, she made certain her face revealed none of the tumultuous emotions she was feeling within. Her back was straight, her steps sure as she strode back to Night Walker's lodge.

Entering the dwelling, she saw Night Walker's wife, Singing Bird, stirring a blackened pot on the tripod over the fire.

She was a pretty woman, with large, doelike eyes and long, shining black braids decorated with sleek crow's feathers. She smiled when she saw Abbie. It was a warm smile, one that Abbie returned. The aroma of savory stew and rich coffee tantalized her nostrils.

Singing Bird motioned for Abbie to sit down on a pile of thick furs next to the fire. She had no sooner done so when she heard men's voices approaching the tepee. They were speaking in Comanche, but she recognized Sonny's deep voice. Her heart beat fiercely.

Singing Bird nodded her head silently at each man as they entered the lodge. It appeared that Sonny had been invited for dinner, and Abbie could not help but watch every move that he made. He wore a long tan shirt and fringed buckskin leggings with bright beadwork. His ash-brown hair lay curled softly about the nape of his neck. She had always thought before that he was too ruggedly handsome for his own good. Yet, tonight, she found him truly magnificent silhouetted against the golden flames of the fire, his copper-hued face alive in its intensity. He fairly took her breath away when he addressed her in that smoky, husky timbre.

"My brother tells me that you have been very helpful to his wife, and that you are brave and strong—a prize worthy of any warrior here." His white teeth flashed. "I am very pleased and have to agree."

"Your presence here, as well as your words, surprises me," she replied, bringing her gaze around to meet his.

Sonny searched that gaze. The clear ice-blue of her eyes revealed none of the feelings in her heart. Always before they were so open and expressive, allowing him to read every thought and emotion. But not tonight, he thought. Tonight, I see nothing.

"And why is that?" he inquired.

"I thought you already had had your dinner."

Immediately he surmised she must have witnessed Little Doe entering his lodge earlier. He felt Night Walker suppressing his laughter. Singing Bird quickly began serving up the meal. "You thought wrong," he returned.

Night Walker hid his laughter. "My brother is considered an eligible bachelor here among his people," he explained proudly. "Many young maidens would gladly share his blankets if he would but have them. I told him it is time. He needs a good woman to look after him."

Abbie fixed her stony-eyed gaze upon Sonny. "Yes, he does have a certain animal magnetism about him that some women tend to find irresistible."

Night Walker grunted. "Why you not wish to be his *paraibo*, chief wife?"

Abbie almost choked on her stew. Was this the custom among the Comanche? Was it the custom for their chiefs to choose wives for the warriors? Well, not for me, she thought obstinately.

"Well, aren't you going to answer the chief's question, Ab?" Sonny asked, his eyes wickedly amused.

"It just isn't as simple as you make it sound," she replied to the great war chief. "The white man's way is different from the Comanche."

"*Tejanos* way take too much time," Night Walker grumbled. "You do not need the black robes. I give you my blessing."

"With all due respect, chief, I don't wish to talk about this right now." She set down her bowl of food. "I have other matters I wish to discuss." She ignored the warning look in Sonny's eyes.

Night Walker studied her closely. "You are good worker, make Singing Bird very happy. You welcome to become Night Walker's wife, share chores with my *paraibo*."

Abbie felt her face freeze into a smile. Good God, this man seemed determined to marry her off, one way or the other. "You honor me by asking, great chief of the Kwahadi, but my place is in the white man's world. I have a family and a son whom I must return to."

"I will return you to them as soon as the weather clears," Sonny told her.

"I—I cannot think about this with gladness in my heart until I know what you intend to do with my sister and the other prisoners."

"That not your concern," Night Walker replied sternly. "They are prisoners of the Kwahadi."

Her frightened eyes flew to Sonny's. "Sonny, you cannot do this—I beg of you."

There was a tense silence. Sonny spoke at length. "You will not offend Night Walker's hospitality with talk of this, Abbie."

"She is my sister," she shot back in a dangerously soft tone. "What do you expect me to do? Just sit back and let you give her to that brave who captured her?"

"Silence, *herbi!*" Night Walker roared. "You must learn patience and the ways of the People if you are to live here among us." He scowled at her. "You worry about this woman who shares your image, and yet, I have heard that she was the one who helped these people capture you. You should be seeking revenge for what they did, not mercy."

"We are both of the same blood! I cannot."

"You go help Singing Bird with evening chores," Night Walker said, thereby dismissing her. "I will think on this before the council meets to decide their fate."

Abbie rose to help Singing Bird clear away the dishes. The men settled back to talk and smoke while the women worked silently about the lodge.

Abbie strained her ears to see if there was any further mention of the fate of the prisoners. There was none. Obviously, they would not discuss it in front of her. As soon as she finished her chores, she took her leave of the tepee and walked out into the crystal-clear night. Beneath her robe she had managed to hide some pemmican for her sister. She walked toward the prisoners' lodge.

After seeing that Sonya had eaten undisturbed, she told

her sister quietly that she was doing everything she could to see to her release.

"Tonight, before the victory celebration, the chief and his council will meet. It is then all of the prisoners' fates will be decided."

"Oh, sweet Jesus," Sonya sobbed brokenly, her hands covering her face. "I knew Malone was trouble the first time I'd laid eyes on him."

"It's too bad you didn't have that same premonition about him," Abbie stated tiredly, pointing at Lucien. "He's caused you nothing but grief from the first day you met him. And now, he just might cost you your life, too."

The great chief of the Kwahadi crossed his thick, muscular legs and sat down before the fire in the council lodge. His warriors did also. He wore his colorful headdress, the other members of the council also dressed in their finery. A council meeting was viewed upon with great respect by the People. Sonny sat next to his brother. A pipe was lit, then passed around to each brave. There was silence for a time while the members meditated and thought about their reasons for being here tonight. At last, Night Walker spoke.

"My brother, Shadow Dancer, has helped us many times in our fight against the blue soldiers and their government. He shares our wish to remain free. Many times he has brought us rifles to help us in this fight, hunted buffalo by our side, and counted coup as bravely as any among us. You all were witness to the many coups he had in the canyon of the Comancheros." He paused to fix his hooded gaze upon each man.

There were murmurs of agreement. It was obvious there were none among them who disagreed.

"These men we allowed to walk among us as traders. We bought their goods and welcomed them to our camp many times," Night Walker continued evenly. "But they have raided through Texas claiming to be one of us, and they took Shadow Dancer's woman to live as their leader's slave. Their chief, Lucien Rodriquez, captured the woman of our brother's heart to seek revenge against him. But he did not realize the cunning of his foe or the bravery of the woman. Now, they are our captives. Their fate must be decided."

One brave called Spotted Horse, spoke. "It should be Shadow Dancer's decision as to their fate. His was the woman who the Comanchero tried to steal."

"Yes," another called Eagle Feather, agreed. "It should be his choice as to their punishment."

Night Walker turned to Sonny after his braves had finished speaking. "You have heard your brothers. It is agreed. The prisoners, Lucien Rodriquez, Brett Colfax, and the woman, are yours to do with as you wish."

Sonny knew his brothers would expect him to choose a harsh punishment, one that was slow and painful. His mind raced as he slowly, and in a voice devoid of all emotion, said, "Since you all have stated that you will honor my decision, then this is what I decide. The one they call Colfax has only one arm. He is weak and will not last long under torture. I have chosen to fight him—one arm tied behind my back. If he fights bravely, and survives, he will be sent from our village on foot. If he lives, it will be because the Great White Father was willing."

Night Walker and the other warriors all nodded their approval. Sonny continued. "Rodriquez's life I will trade him for that of my father's. If Culley Malone no longer lives, then neither will Rodriquez."

"And what of your *herbi's* sister?" Eagle Feather asked.

Sonny replied without hesitation. "I shall trade her."

Chapter Seventeen

"Trade her, to whom?" Abbie gasped later, when they were alone.

"To the highest bidder," Sonny replied, his voice lacking any compassion.

Abbie walked across the chief's lodge to confront him. Her eyes were a chilling blue. "I—won't allow it. You are talking about my twin sister. She may not be the most worthy of human beings, but she did help me to escape Rodriquez. Isn't that worth something?"

"She also framed me for murder and almost killed us both back in Devil's Bend," he lashed back. "Not to mention her part in Lucien's scheme to take over your ranch. Have you forgotten all of that?"

"No," she choked softly, turning away to stand silently watching the smoke waft upward through the center opening in the lodge poles. "And I know I told you that I wouldn't try and protect her again. But I never thought it would ever come to this—my sister with a bunch of—" She stopped herself when she realized what she was about to say.

"Finish it. Savages—just like me, baby—like all of us when you get right down to it."

"She gave me a signed confession," she told him quickly, pointedly. "It says she killed the major. I promised her I'd

369

help her, in return for your life."

His gray eyes glittered. "I would like to see this confession."

"Oh, no. Not until I have your word about Sonya."

"I cannot go back on my decision with the council. She's to be traded."

Sonny did not try and touch her, yet he longed to. He knew he must remain strong in his plan if he was ever to have Abbie's love again. He would give her Sonya, but he wanted something in return. He wanted Abbie. But she would have to come to him. He was a respected warrior. He would not beg for her affections. It was not the Comanche way. To save his honor, he must appease his Comanche brothers and his little wildcat, and without either side suspecting his true motives. She was afraid of him, of everything here. He knew that it was because she did not understand the Comanche way. It was not unusual; few of the *tejanos* ever did. But he knew them well, understood their beliefs, their customs, their fight to hold onto their very culture. Soon, if the white-eyes had their way, the Comanche would be destroyed.

He was determined that she would understand and remember a way of life that was slowly vanishing forever. His eyes happened to fall upon several completed charcoal sketches that vividly depicted the everyday life of the Comanche. He understood now her look of joy the day that he'd brought her several items he'd picked up from a ragtag caravan of traders who were seeking new territory for their goods.

Sonny had bartered for many lovely things, and as an afterthought he'd had the trader toss in the pad of paper the old man had been doodling on.

Using wood ash from the fire, Abbie had managed to capture with startling depth and accuracy many aspects of the Comanche's way of life. He was stunned.

"Abbie," he said softly. "I told you that I would trade Sonya. I did not say that you could not bargain for her."

370

Abbie stared back at him with a twisted smile. "Your braves have many ponies, fine furs. Just what have I got to trade that you might want?"

"I don't really think that I have to answer that," he replied huskily.

"You're very clever. I should have remembered. My sister, for my body." Her blue eyes held his steady gaze. Slowly she began to unlace the doeskin tunic. "I accept."

"No, Abbie," he murmured silkily. "Not just your body. I want all of you. I want you to become my wife."

"Here!" she said, stunned.

"Well I didn't figure you'd be jumping for joy. But I half expected you to take me up on my offer." He was getting more than a bit aggravated now, grumbling in that familiar caustic tone of his that Abbie could relate to. It eased her fears.

"I suppose next you'll be telling me how you expect me to become the obedient Comanche wife and obey your every command without question."

"While we're here—out of respect for their customs—yes."

"And what becomes of Sonya and the others if I say yes?"

Sonny could not help but grin. "I said nothing of the others, Ab." He moved to take her hand in his. "You set a high price upon yourself."

"I want you to promise me that you will not kill them. Punish them. They deserve that. Make them think that they are going to die so that they never forget or come back again."

"Does this mean you agree to my terms?"

"If you agree to mine."

He enfolded her in his arms, laughing softly. "You never change, Ab. You are still the most stubborn female I've ever met."

"Sonny?"

"Yes, Abbie?"

371

"Even more so than Little Doe. I've seen how she persists in trying to win your affections. Remember, I am to be your only wife."

He kissed the tip of her nose. "She is a very good worker and most obedient, I am told."

She wrapped her arms about his neck and pulled his lips down to hers. "But can she make you feel like this?"

"Never in a thousand years," he murmured against her yielding mouth.

The council was pleased with Shadow Dancer's decision concerning his three prisoners. The fate of the remaining Comancheros was also decided. They'd be punished but given a chance to live.

They would have to survive the strenuous test of endurance and strength in a special ceremony which the entire tribe would attend.

When Brett Colfax was told that Sonny would meet him on equal terms, in a fierce clash of knives, he had paled but finally agreed.

The Comanches and Abbie gathered in a circle to watch the forthcoming battle between the two men.

Sonny faced Brett, their faces devoid of emotion. Night Walker raised his hand. "Let the battle begin."

The two opponents began moving in opposite directions, circling warily, knife blades glinting in the sun. With a growl, Brett suddenly lunged forward, swiping viciously at Sonny with his knife. Sonny sprinted to one side, slicing Brett's wrist as he did so. He gasped painfully. Brett was a worthy opponent but no match for the skill of a Comanche warrior. Sonny escaped his deadly advances again and again. Abbie would never forget the moment when Sonny had moved with the litheness of a stalking wolf to slash Brett's knife arm several times before dancing back out of reach. Brett had dropped the weapon with a howl of pain. It was then Sonny

372

brought him down without one shred of mercy and moved in for the kill. She'd never known how she'd stood silently without crying out as he'd straddled Brett's chest and placed the razor-edged knife at his throat. Her heart gladdened when she heard Sonny's words.

"I should take your miserable life for everything that you put Abbie through." He pressed the blade against Brett's throat. "But I have given my word. You shall have a chance to live." He jumped up and yanked a trembling Brett to his feet. "I want your boots and your clothes. Then you're free to go."

"Go! Out there?" Brett yelled incredulously. "I'll die out there."

Sonny reclined his head toward the plains. "That is the only chance I'm giving you, Colfax. If you stay here, you have none."

Brett stood shakily observing the silent Comanches who had gathered all around him. His gaze met Abbie's. It was filled with contempt. "I'll go," he growled, and began removing his boots. "You've left me no choice."

It was agreed that Sonya would become Abbie's handmaiden. She was to live like the rest of the slaves until it was time to return to the Bar C. Abbie kept the written confession in a safe place. She had promised Sonya that they would do everything that they could when it came time for her to stand trial.

Lucien, hearing of Sonya's written confession, had cursed her unendingly. He would never forgive her, he'd said, and never wanted to see her again.

Sonya was devastated and hated her position in the camp. She complained continually to Abbie about the backbreaking work that her sister made her do.

Lucien Rodriquez was Sonny's alone. On a day when the March weather unexpectedly turned springlike and the sun shone brightly in the cloudless sky, he was staked out wearing just a breechclout and left to bake in the searing rays. Sonya cried the entire time, objecting to everything she was required to do in helping Abbie prepare a lodge for use after her marriage.

"Whatever were you thinking of when you agreed to marry that savage!" she spat at Abbie after she entered the dwelling bearing yet another bundle of twigs. "Did you see what he's done to Lucien? He's going to let him die after he let that awful Brett Colfax go."

Abbie barely glanced up from where she was busily repairing a tear in one of Sonny's shirts. "Hang the wood in bundles over the fire, like I've shown you."

Sonya sighed, disgruntled. "I know—I know—the smoke seasons the wood and kills all of those horrible crawly things that seem to be everywhere."

"Just plain old bugs, sister, nothing you haven't put up with before, I'm certain, considering some of the places you've lived with Lucien."

At mention of his name, Sonya began crying once again, and Abbie found herself thinking how happy she would be when her wedding day finally came and she would no longer have to share a tepee with her twin. Never had she been around any one woman who had such an endless flow of tears.

"I talked with Sonny earlier, and he said that if Lucien agrees to tell him what has become of his father, that he will allow him to live."

"As a Comanche slave!"

"Would you rather see him dead?"

"I believe that Lucien would rather die," Sonya replied brokenly.

"And how many lives has your precious Lucien destroyed by trading them off to the Indians like they were animals?" Abbie queried sharply. "In my opinion he is getting no more than he deserves."

"Are you going to that awful ceremony those heathens are having tonight?" she asked Abbie.

Abbie realized her sister was referring to the victory celebration over the Comancheros. "It is expected of me."

"I declare, Abbie Lee," Sonya stated angrily. "Never, have I seen you behave so. Why you act as though you'll do anything at all that half-breed tells you."

Sick to death of listening to Sonya, Abbie replied evenly, "I gave my word, and it's the only thing that has kept you from befalling the same fate as the others." She watched silently, feeling little satisfaction, as her sister turned on her heel and fled white-faced from the lodge.

The weather was warming more each day. Today was a lovely, clear morning, perfect for a wedding. The sun shone brilliantly upon the two people who stood before their chief and repeated the words that would unite them as man and wife.

Abbie, dressed in a white elk dress heavy with fringe and adorned with glistening elk's teeth, her hair plaited in two shining braids, stood beside the tall, handsome form of her chosen warrior, Shadow Dancer.

Sonny held her hand firmly. He was attired in a brushed antelope tunic and breeches, with long fringed moccasins that reached to his knees. His voice was strong and sure as he repeated his vows before the Great Spirits and the People, and few doubted the love they saw in his eyes for his woman.

Abbie repeated his words in a hushed, throaty whisper, her eyes never leaving his face. And when he drew his knife to slash first his hand, and then hers, not one whimper escaped her lips.

Their hands moved across the space that separated them, palms pressed together, their lives now joined as one.

Sonny drew her close to his side, whispering softly, "You are forever mine, Abbie. Nothing shall ever come between us again."

Night Walker gave them the tribe's blessing for a long and

happy life. "You are now one of the People," he told Abbie. "I proclaim your name as Chikoba, daughter of the Kwahadi and *paraibo* of our brother, Shadow Dancer. May the gods walk with you."

Her hand entwined securely in her husband's, they walked the distance to their private honeymoon lodge.

"My husband," she said, just as he swept her up into his arms and carried her inside the tepee that was scented by fresh pine boughs that cushioned their bed of soft furs. "Tell me what this name means that your brother bestowed upon me?"

Sonny kissed her, then lifted his head to smile devilishly. "The walls of our lodges are very thin, *paraibo*. It seems that your penchant for throwing about the pottery in your fits of temper amuses my brother. He has decided to call you She-Who-Breaks-Something."

A full moon appeared like an orange ball of fire in the velvet-black sky. Throughout the entire Kwahadi village the chanting and the music reverberated. Abbie sat with the rest of the People in the circle clearing that had been designated for the evening events. Her eyes strayed to the tall pole in the center of the clearing from which hung many scalps. She sat transfixed by the sight of one in particular. It blew freely about in the gentle night breeze: long, flowing black hair that prompted her to wonder whether the victim had been white, Indian or, one of the captives. Forcing her eyes away from the grisly sight, she viewed the many warriors who were beginning to converge upon the scene.

The drums beat out their throbbing message, as one by one the young lords of the camp began dancing, acting out their daring raid upon the Comanchero village.

Overhead, the flames of the huge fires leaped higher and higher, seeming to reach upward for the midnight sky abounding with twinkling stars. The dancers grew wilder, bodies glistening with sweat, painted faces of red and black, the Comanche colors of death, appearing macabre in the flickering light.

Abbie saw him then, dancing in the light of the fire, naked except for his moccasins and breechclout. Even though the ritualistic dance depicting Shadow Dancer's coups was not something she had looked forward to seeing, she now found herself quite breathless watching the flaming, moon-kissed shadows play across the rippling, copper muscles beneath his skin. He gave the appearance of some sleek, powerful wolf, with his gleaming silver eyes and strongly muscled legs.

When the tale of his bravery in battle was complete, he waited for witnesses to deny or verify his reported coups. None could deny what they had seen with their eyes the day of the raid. With a triumphant cry of victory, his powerful voice rang throughout the night.

Abbie's eyes followed as he melted into the shadows, her heart beating queerly and her breath rasping in her throat. It was then the women's turn, and they rose to sway their graceful bodies to the slow drumbeat. Abbie followed as one of them, arms raised to embrace the streamers of moonlight that fell upon her upturned face. She hummed along with the women, chanting the Comanche lovesong, her heart yearning for only one man.

Eyes closed, hands outspread, she did not realize that Sonny had joined her until she felt the touch of his fingers lightly encircling her slim waist. Their bodies swayed together. She opened her eyes to see his staring heatedly into her own, and Abbie wished that the night could go on forever. Until she recalled what was to take place next.

It was only when the women once again stood away from their men to form two long lines on either side of the fires that Abbie shrank back from the huge fires. She looked around her for Sonny, but he had fallen back, leaving her alone.

Silhouetted against the burnt-orange tongues of fire, the

People chanted and danced, their drums now beating out a different message. It was intense, blood-chilling, as were the expressions on the People's faces. It was the women who seemed to be the center of attention now. Abbie was swept along in their midst, her eyes round with dawning awareness. The remaining prisoners were to be turned loose in the midst of the frenzied group of women.

"I cannot be a part of this," she murmured, and slowly backed out of the lighted circle. Under the cover of darkness, she ran white-faced to her lodge, daring not to look back when she heard the excited *yee-yeeing* of the women rising to a fevered peak.

Sonny observed her departure from beneath hooded eyes. He understood, yet he was bound by honor to remain. Later, he would go to her and comfort her the only way that he knew how.

It was very early in the new day when Sonny left the glowing embers of the victory fires to walk over to where Lucien Rodriquez lay staked out. He stood between Lucien's bare legs, his face appearing carved out of stone. "Are you ready now to tell me what you did with Culley Malone?"

Lucien had witnessed the grueling ordeal of his comrades. It was a sight that he would never forget. Many had not been able to withstand the torture. Some had been strong. But how many had escaped into the darkness he did not know. He tried to focus his eyes on the figure looming over him, but his eyelids were swollen shut by the sun. Nightmare visions danced beneath them, anguished screams echoing in his brain. Last night's ceremony would remain with him always. He began to tremble. Completely broken, he rasped, "Y— es—I—am ready."

"Good. Afterwards, I will turn you over to my brother, Night Walker, to do with you as he wishes," Sonny stated, "Now, about Culley Malone?"

The many blisters on Lucien's lips made talking extremely painful, but he was more than ready to do anything to escape the burning death he knew awaited him with the rising sun. "He is in a mine—in Orizaba—as a Juarista prisoner."

"Perdicion!" Sonny raged. "You would do such a thing to him for all of these years! Better that you would have killed him!" He pulled a knife from a rawhide sheath at his side and held the gleaming blade inches from Lucien's ear.

"I should take the other one from you, Comanchero, just so you'll remember me for the rest of your days."

Lucien felt the cool, sharp steel placed behind the curve of his ear, and a hoarse cry of fear burst from him. "No! *Dios* have mercy!"

"Mercy," Sonny growled, his face contorted in fury beneath the grisly paint. "You're a fine one to talk about mercy!"

Lucien began screaming hoarsely. It was then the knife slashed downward and severed the bonds on his wrists and ankles. "It is not what you deserve, but it was what we agreed upon."

The Comanchero leader was sobbing raggedly. He was so weak that Sonny was forced to sling him over his shoulder and carry him back to the prisoners' lodge. Once there, he dumped him on a pile of buffalo rugs and left without another word. Neither Sonny nor the two guards saw the slender female shadow pressed flat against the outside of the lodge wall.

Sonya had dressed in her sister's buckskin clothes and managed to steal extra clothing and supplies. The entire village was sleeping now. They could manage to slip away on two ponies if they were careful.

In Texas, spring came early. Although it was only late March, the air was heavy and warm. She was certain they could now survive the long trek to Mexico. She knew where they would go. To the place where Lucien had told her it had all begun. The hill country of Orizaba, where he'd said one could hide out and never be found.

Sonya peered around her with a keen eye. She had taken a knife from Abbie's cooking utensils and made her way to where Lucien had been staked out. Finding him not there, she had thought at first that Sonny had lied and he had been killed. She knew by listening to another woman that had been taken from the Comanchero village that they were the only two prisoners left. The others had either fled onto the plains or had not survived the earlier trial.

"I will not let you become one of those savage's slaves, Lucien," she'd vowed under her breath. "You are still the *patron,* my *patron.*" She slowly cut a long slit in the back of the tepee. When she thought it large enough, she crawled inside and crept silently to Lucien's curled form.

The faint glow of daylight shone through the walls of their lodge. Sonny stood in the entry, staring down at Abbie's sleeping form on the tumbled robes. He was a bit surprised to find that she was alone. He had expected Sonya to have come and awakened her sister for their morning bath in the river. Shaking off his uneasiness, he watched his beautiful wife. She meant everything to him.

Abbie whimpered softly, one bare arm drawing protectively to her chest. His heart ached for her. He knew she found it difficult to accept the severe punishments the People had inflicted upon their captives. He wished there was some way of making her understand how the Comanche ways were slowly dying, and that nights like the one that just passed were necessary. He knew all too well how the white man's soldiers and rangers had hounded the Comanche until many had simply relinquished their heritage and now lived without pride or will on reservations.

"Silken Abbie," he whispered, "how I wish you could understand, and forgive, for it is their very existence that is being threatened."

The soles of his moccasins barely whispered as he walked over to sit beside her. He knew, if the People were to survive, that it was vital they feel strong and invincible in the face of their enemies. But right now, with Abbie, he wished to forget all of that. He reached out a hand to lightly brush away a tear that had squeezed from beneath her eyelid to linger on feathery lashes.

"You're awake?"

She nodded slowly, then opened her eyes to look at him. She saw the sorrow in the silvery gaze and cried out to him. "I need you, Sonny. Hold me."

He lay down beside her and took her into his arms. The cover that lay over her fell away as his lips claimed hers, and his hands moved over her naked body. Her arms encircled his neck. His body was slick with sweat, the knotted muscles beneath his broad shoulders smooth against her fingertips. She held fast to them, needing, wanting him so she was beyond reason.

"I love you so," she whispered.

"Oh, Abbie, I never thought to hear you say that again."

Her hands quickly removed his few clothes, all the while savoring the feel of him beneath her searching touch. His hands gently tangled themselves in Abbie's chestnut hair. Lowering his mouth to her breasts, his tongue flicked teasingly across her engorged nipples as he rolled swiftly on top of her.

Wrapping her long, slender legs across his back she sighed with ecstasy when she felt his fullness thrust inside her. Their coupling was as furious and wild as the storm within them. They wanted to become one in every way: in thought, in word, in body. Abbie clung to him, sobbing softly against the protectiveness of his chest. He understood her tears, and continually murmured words of love as they moved together in a fiery passion that soon claimed them both. They soared the heights together, and when with his last powerful thrust they reached the peak, Abbie cried out her love to him in a voice so intense that it shook him right down to his soul.

They lay together quietly, passion spent, their heads close together.

"Did you threaten Sonya with her life to get her to not come here this morning?" Abbie asked.

He raised up on one elbow to peer down at her. "No, I assumed she'd gotten used to sleeping with Morning Star and was content to do without your company for one morning." He frowned. "Maybe I should check around for her."

"No, she never leaves her warm bed until I'm up and about and have a fire going so she can warm herself when we return from our bath. She's still sleeping, I'm sure of it."

Sonny frowned. "I'm not so certain, and I don't like what I'm thinking."

Abbie's eyes flew to his. "What—tell me!"

He leapt to his feet in one smooth motion, quickly dressing. "Rodriquez," he growled. "She went to him."

Abbie rolled over and grabbed her skirt and tunic. "She couldn't get past the guards."

"I don't put anything past your sister, honey."

She saw him grab up the knife he'd tossed down earlier. "Sonny! Please!" she screamed in terror, her fingers flying over the laces of her tunic. "Wait!"

"Damnit," he swore as he yanked aside the door covering. "If she tries to free him, I'll make her pay dearly." His mind was fixed in single-minded determination, completely oblivious to the woman running behind him, her heart feeling as though it had been torn asunder.

Reaching the prisoners' lodge, Sonny swept past the bewildered guards and entered the tepee. He found it empty.

Abbie heard his enraged shout and stopped dead in her tracks, her hand covering her mouth. "They're gone. Oh, God." She watched Sonny storm back out of the lodge, his face a mask of fury. And even though she felt guilty, a part of her was glad Sonya had escaped.

"Gather our warriors. Tell them the Comanchero and his woman have escaped," he told the guards in Comanche.

Abbie did not understand his words, but she fully comprehended the look on his face. "Leave them, Sonny," she pleaded. "You punished them enough."

He turned on her. "You don't understand, woman," he snarled. "Lucien broke completely after witnessing the torture last night. He told me where to find my father."

"Then you have what you've wanted!" she screamed back. "Culley's alive! Haven't you made them suffer enough!"

He caught her to him, his hand grasping her arm so roughly that she gasped. "It is not enough! He put my father in a stinking hellhole to rot underground, shut away from life itself! For that, I took his pride from him, broke him completely. And now, he'll take my father from me."

"You—mean he'll kill him. How—when he is half dead himself."

His eyes narrowed to mere slits. "Your sister—if there's anyway possible she'll help him get there."

"Sonny," she started, "I think if Sonya and Lucien have managed to escape death this once that they'll not risk it."

He spun away from her. "You're wrong! And I'm going after them. And nothing you can say will change my mind."

Abbie faced him, shocked by the gleaming look of death she glimpsed in his eyes. "I won't be a party to any more of this," she choked out. "I'm going back to my ranch." She turned and ran from him. Suddenly, she heard him calling her.

"Don't let us part like this, *paraibo*. We vowed we'd never leave each other again."

She halted, head down, tears glistening in her eyes. "And you swore that you wouldn't have my sister killed. You're going to go back on that vow, Sonny, and it will be like killing a part of me."

383

"What in God's name do you want from me, Abbie?" Sonny hurled back at her. "I have my own flesh and blood to think about. Culley Malone is my father."

"And Sonya Caldwell, for all that she is evil, is my sister."

"And I am your husband," he said, before she heard him walk away.

Chapter Eighteen

"My son has cholera," Night Walker said solemnly. "I have seen it before, in other villages." He had come to his brother's lodge to tell them the awful news, his heart heavy with his burden.

"I will help," Abbie said quickly. "Take me to your son. I know something of the disease."

"I do not think you can," Night Walker replied, remembering how the sickness had ravaged other villages in a way that no mortal enemy ever could.

"I've got to try," Abbie insisted, rushing from the tepee.

Sonny put his hand on his brother's arm. "I will stay, you need me."

Night Walker was grateful. "I am sorry. I know how important it is for you to find your father."

"My people are also important," Sonny assured him as they left the lodge. "It can wait a while longer."

Entering the chief's lodge, they found Abbie working feverishly over the boy. Her mother had helped nurse several families in the next county who were found to have cholera. She knew it was important to keep plenty of fluids in the victims and to ease their cramps and nausea with a tonic of boiled mint. She knelt down next to the child. He was coughing pitifully, his face contorted in pain from the cramps that gripped him.

"I must have wild mint and plenty of water." She glanced up. "Quickly."

"Tell your *paraibo* that I drive bad spirits from *Tuinerp*. She no touch," the medicine man said, hovering over Abbie's shoulder. He held up a medicine pouch. "This—make Wolf Cub strong again." He stared indignantly at Abbie where she was already stripping the boy's soiled clothing from him.

"Quit wasting time arguing," she snapped. "Night Walker, fill this cup with water. He needs fluids immediately."

Although it was unheard of for anyone to make demands of a great war chief, Night Walker didn't hesitate to do as she requested. He sat stoically beside Abbie and followed her precise instructions.

When the medicine man protested further, Sonny took him aside and said, "I am sorry, healer of our people. But Chikoba knows of this sickness of the white-eyes. She is our only hope."

When the child vomited the liquid she'd just given him, the old medicine man pointed an accusing finger at Abbie. "She is going to kill the child."

Night Walker, who sat watching Abbie work over his son, held up his hand for silence. "My brother's wife will not let her nephew die." His sad dark eyes met Abbie's. "She has a healing touch."

"I will do my very best to save him," Abbie said.

"That is all that I ask," Night Walker replied, handing her another cup of water.

Furious, the medicine man strode from the tepee without another word.

Sonny wrapped a comforting arm about Singing Bird. "Come, we shall go together to get wild mint. Your little one is in good hands."

Abbie diligently gave of her time and energy to nurse the

386

ailing families of the Kwahadi. And there were many. Wolf Cub survived, but others did not. The grateful chief told Abbie that she could have whatever was in his power to give.

"I wish for an end to the People's suffering," she said and, realizing that she truly meant it, she turned to gaze up into her husband's eyes, a look of wonder on her face.

"It makes my heart glad to see how you have grown to love and respect our people," Sonny said proudly.

"Yes, it does mine, too," she replied. "And I do love them, very much."

That night he took her back to their lodge and laid her tenderly upon their blankets. She was so tired from her nightly vigils with the sick that she did not have the strength to undress herself. He removed her garments, bathed her, and rubbed down her stiffened muscles until she sighed with contentment. They sought solace in each other's arms until they both drifted off to sleep.

As soon as they were able, the People made ready to leave their winter home in the high canyon and travel to the wilds of the plains. The cholera had left them weakened and fewer in numbers, but still they gave thanks to the Great Spirit for those who had survived.

It was a sad day for Abbie when Sonny informed her that they would be leaving the People. She knew where it was that he intended to go. Abbie fought the impulse to beg him to go back to her ranch. She knew he would not. She longed to see her family, but Sonny was her husband, and she would not go back without him.

Never would she have dreamed that parting from the Comanche would cause her so much heartache. The many sketches that she'd made while she lived as one of them were carefully rolled in buckskin. They were to travel light, her husband informed her, but the sketches, he agreed, were not to be left behind. She studied him carefully. His thoughts were once again brooding. She knew without even asking what it was he was thinking about.

"I'd like to send a message to my mother. If she is in need of funds, I want her to know where I hid the cattle money. I cannot be certain your trader friend managed to give her my letter." She realized he was watching her closely. She smiled. "I hid my money belt in a crate full of pots and pans that I bought. I'm certain they were unloaded with my gear, but knowing Sonya, I'm sure she just stored them away somewhere."

"You never cease to amaze me, Abbie," he chuckled softly. "And I have to admit that was an ingenious hiding place. Not many *bandidos* go around stealing pots and pans."

"My thoughts exactly when I purchased them," she replied laughingly.

"Would you wait until we get to the border town of Eagle Pass to send your wire? I don't want any lawman getting any notions to come after us."

"All right." She thought of the Bar C, and her mother and Charly. And even though she loved the ranch and her family very much, for the first time in her life she found that she loved someone else more. "Sonny?" she said softly.

"Hmm?" he replied, looking up from his packing.

"I know you're worried about your father, but I think everything's going to work out fine."

"Does that mean you're not against my plans to go to Mexico?" he asked.

"I was never against your going," she said. "I was against your vendetta that won't let you rest until you've destroyed Rodriquez and my sister."

He did not reply. He knew she had been watching him closely, reading his thoughts as she'd learned to do so well. He strapped the polished Colts about his hips, knowing it was answer enough.

*   *   *

During the next few weeks they traveled at a constant pace toward the border of Mexico. They made love each night beneath the twinkling canopy of stars and shared the joy of doing even the simplest of tasks together. It was an idyllic time for them, far away from civilization and the cares of the world.

"How different our relationship is now from that first time, when you took me away with you, and we fought like snarling cats the entire time," she said. "I think I even loved you then."

"I'm not likely to ever forget, silken Abbie," he murmured, his lips playing softly against the throbbing hollow of her throat.

"Nor will I ever let you," she sighed, responding with fiery abandon to his body moving over hers.

His lips brushed across her skin to her breasts, teeth gently nibbling at the rigid little buds until they were stiff and delightful to suckle. Long fingers slipped downward to part chestnut curls and slip into the silky wetness of her quivering womanhood. "I love you so damned much it scares me," he said huskily, bringing her legs up to encircle his shoulders.

She thought that she would surely die from the heat his long fingers ignited within her. His lips hungrily closed over hers, his hands lifting her hips to meet his first piercing thrust. He moved harder, faster, his surging body taking hers to heights of pleasure she'd never thought possible to obtain.

With fiery, all-consuming passion, their bodies melded as one. For a brief timeless moment, they clung together, adrift in a sweeping storm of ecstasy. When it was over, and the waves of pleasure began to subside, they pledged their love once more with words, then slept.

True to his word, they stopped at Eagle Pass on the Rio Grande to send a wire to her mother. He figured he was close enough to the border that he didn't have to worry about any lawmen coming after him. But not wishing to take the chance of running into any more bounty hunters, he waited

389

on the outskirts of the town while Abbie went to send her message and pick up supplies.

Remembering his telling her about the incident with the bounty hunter, she hadn't protested and promised to hurry. Sonny had watched her leave and settled back beneath a mesquite tree to wait. He began thinking about where he would take her when they reached Mexico. He could only think of one place. His own *estancia* left to him by his *abuela*. Hidden in the lush hill country surrounding Orizaba, it was the perfect place for them to go. She hadn't been feeling well of late. He assumed that it was due to days spent riding beneath the hot sun. He closed his eyes and allowed his thoughts to wander. Thinking of Mexico brought Carmelita to mind. And the child. He could only hope that Reeno had convinced her to leave. If she was still there when he arrived with Abbie he'd have a lot of explaining to do.

Several hours later, he heard the sound of a horse approaching. Springing to his feet, he caught sight of Abbie cantering toward him. Her face appeared flushed with excitement. He rushed to meet her.

"How'd everything go?" he asked after she reined in her foam-lathered mare and dismounted.

She fairly flew into his arms, her face alive with excitment. "Sonny—the revolution in Mexico is over! The last of the French troops pulled out in March."

He swung her around, his spirits soaring. "That's the best news I've heard in a long time."

"That means we can go to Mexico City to see your family."

"No—not just yet."

Her astonished expression met his. "But don't you want to see how well they have fared?"

"Of course," he said, his hands cupping her face. "But the fighting will still be going on. Our armies will have to rout out the last of the die-hard Imperialists before the country is safe once again. We'll go on to Orizaba."

She knew he was thinking of his father. "But if the French have left, surely the Juaristas will reclaim the mines in President Juarez's name and set the prisoners free."

"I'm certain they will," Sonny agreed. "And my father has no way of knowing that Rodriquez is out there somewhere, waiting."

"Neither do you, for certain," she replied.

"I know, Abbie," he said intensely. "This thing between Lucien and myself will never be finished until one of us is dead."

Her heart heavy in her breast, she remounted her horse. "Don't make me a widow, Sonny. Not now of all times, please." He heard the catch in her voice.

"What are you talking about?" His pulse began beating rapidly.

She sat proudly beautiful. "I'm carrying your child."

"My—child." He said the words softly.

"Yes, I saw the doctor while I was in town just to make certain. He confirmed my suspicions. Our baby should be born in late fall." She was stunned by his next words.

"This changes everything," he said. "I'm sending you back into town so that you can take a stage back to the Bar C."

"No!" she retorted stubbornly.

He walked over to stand next to her horse. "A Comanche's woman does what she's told without question."

"A part of me is a Comanche's woman, Sonny," she said evenly. "But the other part will always be Abbie Caldwell. And *she* is not going anywhere but with her husband." When she had the nerve to look at him, she saw a softness in his face that eased his harsh features.

"Damn, Abbie, but marrying you hasn't changed you one bit," he grumbled, displaying a crooked smile.

"Oh, but never give up trying, my darling," she said lightly, "for one of these days you just may succeed."

"Possibly, when we're both old and gray, and even that's a big maybe."

She looked him in the eye. "Will we grow old together, Sonny?"

He reached up to draw her body into his arms. "Of course we will, beautiful."

"I want that so very much," she whispered against the curve of his shoulder.

He lifted her chin with one finger, his eyes hot as they beheld hers. "If we're going to get across the border today, Ab, I'd suggest we get a move on it, for I'm very tempted to just stay here and satisfy this impetuous passion you seem to evoke within me each time you're near."

Her spirits soared. "We're leaving—now. Before we both change our minds."

It was twilight when they rode into Mexico. They took all of the out-of-the-way trails toward their destination. After days of unbearable heat and mornings when Abbie thought she'd surely die from the nausea that gripped her, they arrived at his hacienda.

Although Sonny had described his *estancia* to her, Abbie found she was quite stunned by the first glimpse of her new home. It was truly lovely, sitting amidst towering old trees, heavy with flowering wisteria that delighted her senses immensely. They rode up to the two story stucco house, dismounting before a large circular fountain that stood before a wide veranda.

"The people who have been taking care of the place for me will certainly be surprised," Sonny told her. He led her across the veranda and opened the heavy carved door. The first thing that Abbie saw when she stepped over the threshold was a lush-figured woman coming down the center stairway into the entrance hall. Her almond-shaped, dark eyes registered shock upon seeing Sonny, and then something else, something that made Abbie's heart sink. Her gaze turned to Abbie. There was a brief, uncomfortable silence and then she recovered her composure and hurried toward them.

"Santiago, you should have let us know you were coming." She smiled stiffly at Abbie. "And that you were bringing a guest."

Abbie glanced over at Sonny. He appeared tense. That was impossible; he was always so self-assured. She heard him laugh lightly.

"Abbie is no guest, Carmelita. She is my wife."

"Oh—I see," Carmelita stammered, clearly shaken. "I had no idea."

Abbie stood between her husband and the striking beauty, feeling like a total fool. Why in the world hadn't he warned her? How could he have been so thoughtless of her feelings, and Carmelita's. She flashed him a look of pure fire before addressing Carmelita. "I hope we won't be putting you to too much trouble."

Sonny grasped her elbow and propelled her over the cool green tiles into a large, comfortable *sala*. "This is your house, Abbie. You won't be putting anyone to any trouble." He glanced back over his shoulder. "Will she, Carmelita?"

"Of course not."

But Abbie heard the hollow ring to her words. "Sonny—it's been a long journey and I'm really very tired. Could I please be shown to our rooms?"

"Certainly, sweetheart." He noticed how pale she was and thought she looked like she might faint at any moment. Abbie, faint? "Carmelita! Go up and turn back the covers in my rooms—*pronto!*"

As soon as the woman left the room, Abbie said, "Good God, Sonny, why didn't you tell me she would be here?"

Over her adamant protests, he swept her up into his arms and began carrying her toward the stairway. "I was hoping that she would have moved out by now. I only let her come live here because she had no family. They were killed by the French. What else could I do? I felt sorry for her."

"Do you expect me to believe you feel only compassion for this woman?" she stated in a carefully controlled voice.

393

"It's the truth!" Sonny growled.

"I saw the way she looked at you—the way you returned that look."

"And assumed—the wrong thing."

"You've been lovers."

"Were—were lovers—all right," he snapped testily.

They reached the top of the stairs, and Abbie fought back tears. "If I would have known she was here I'd have gone back to the ranch."

"I've never known you to run from anything, Abbie Lee," he said.

His implication that she was ready to turn tail and run got her dander up. "Put me down, Malone. I can walk the rest of the way on my own." And she did, with Sonny following behind her.

When they walked into the lovely suite of rooms with its wine velvet hangings and dark, rich furniture, Carmelita had just finished putting fresh linens on the bed. She plumped up the pillows.

"I opened the windows. It shouldn't take long to air out. I'm afraid no one has used this suite since Santiago stayed here last."

Abbie wondered who had shared it with him. "Thank you, it's fine."

"Would you see if Gina can fix us something to eat and have her bring it up here?" Sonny asked Carmelita.

"Gina is visiting in Orizaba with her sister this evening."

"Then you rustle us up something."

Carmelita stiffened. "If you wish it?"

"I do," Sonny stated evenly.

She quickly left the room, leaving the door open behind her.

"She didn't like your asking her to wait on me," Abbie said quietly, sinking down onto the luxurious feather mattress.

"She'll do what she's told," he said offhandedly.

"Like always?"

Sonny crossed the room to sit beside her, his face breaking into a grin. "Not all women are firebrands like you, my darling."

"What is Carmelita like, Sonny?" she asked, her expression serious.

He enfolded her in his arms, his lips brushing hers. "Nothing like you, silken lady."

"You are evading my questions just like you always do."

"I answered it."

"But not in the way that I wanted," she said breathlessly.

He stroked her hair, threading his long fingers through its silky mass spread out around her. "I don't want to talk about the past tonight. Only the future—yours, mine, and our child's."

"That's such a lovely sound," she murmured, eyes closing dreamily.

He kissed her lips, then lifted his head. "How long do you think it will take Carmelita to fix us something to eat?" His voice held a message she could not ignore.

She opened her eyes slowly. "I don't think by the mood that she was in when she left that we can expect dinner anytime before midnight."

"My thoughts exactly," he said huskily.

"Oh, Sonny," she said and laughed. "Don't you ever get tired of making love to me?"

"You were born for loving, Ab, my loving."

She sighed and snuggled deeper into his arms. It came to her then, although of little surprise, just how very much she loved him, and would fight for him—and win.

Abbie woke early the next morning to find that she was alone. She was confused for a moment. Where was she? Sitting up, she suddenly remembered. Swinging her legs over the side of the bed, she went to the window and pulled back the draperies. It was a beautiful morning, warm and bright with sunshine. In the distance lay the snowcapped peak of Orizaba, and at the base, the charming village where the emperor had once his summer home. She felt good this morning and so loved, cherished.

A movement below the window suddenly caught her eye. Sonny was astride Viento, smiling down at Carmelita and a little girl of about three who were standing beside the pinto. Her insides twisted as a searing pain tore through her. The child was dark-haired and beautiful. Sonny held out his arms to her, and she eagerly went to him. Abbie tried to still the pounding of her heart and the unbidden thoughts whirling around in her head.

"It cannot be." Yet, realistically, she knew it was very probable. "Oh, no, dear God, not that." She turned away from the window, feeling as though her world had just ended.

The conversation that she'd had last night with Sonny while they were eating the dinner came back to her. They had been sitting cross-legged on the big bed, drinking wine, munching on the tortillas Carmelita had prepared, happily making plans for their future. Suddenly, Abbie felt a need to know more about the woman who lived in her husband's home. And a child—a child? She blurted, "Sonny, I have to ask about Carmelita. How you feel about her now?"

He had known she wouldn't be able to leave it alone. But he knew he could not tell her everything without talking with Carmelita first. "I want you to know that no matter what happened before I met you, it is only you that I truly love, wish to spend my life with."

"Is this your subtle way of telling me that you no longer consider her a part of your life?"

The soft candlelight flickering on his face revealed his intense expression. "We're friends, will always be friends. Her brother rode with Reeno and me for Diaz. We were all *compadres* before the revolution. Carmelita was there, too—young, beautiful, and lonely."

"You had more than just an affair with her, didn't you?" She hated herself for asking, but she had to know.

"We were very close, yes."

"Did you love her?"

"No—I've only had one true love in my life, and that's you, Ab."

Abbie sighed. "She loves you, Sonny."

Sonny gave a short laugh. "Carmelita does not love any man, sweetheart. She's had too rough of a time with men. She is grateful to me, I realize that."

"Grateful—why?"

There was a moment of silence before he replied. "For being there when she badly needed someone." He took a sip of wine. "Her brother was killed raiding a village. He died in my arms. With her family all dead, Carmelita was all alone. By the time I got back to her village again, she'd become a *soldaras* to three men in the Mexican army."

"The same people who murdered her brother?" Abbie gasped.

His reply was harsh. "She had no choice. They forced her." His face turned to hers, grim, filled with hatred. "Do you have any idea what that must have been like for a young girl? What they must have put her through?"

Abbie swallowed, remembering, shaking at the visions that danced in her mind's eye. "Yes," she breathed shakily.

"We all have some nightmare to forget, I suppose." He shrugged. "At any rate, I finally found her and managed to buy her back. I brought her here to live, and when I left, she stayed on to look after things."

Those last words echoed over and over in Abbie's mind as she sat on the bed for awhile and thought about the scene that she'd just witnessed. Was the child his flesh and blood? And would he feel honor bound to remain with her when the only vows they'd ever exchanged were those in an Indian ceremony?

She didn't know how long she sat there, thinking,

brooding, not knowing what to believe, when a knock sounded on the door. Abbie glanced up, startled by the intrusion.

"Yes?" she called out.

"It is Carmelita, senora, I have brought you a tray."

"Come in." Abbie smoothed back her tousled hair and forced herself to appear calm.

The door swung inward and Carmelita entered. "I saw that you had opened the draperies and assumed you must be up and around." She set the tray on a table next to the wide windows, then began straightening up the room. "Please, go ahead and eat. Don't let me interfere. I'll just pick up a bit for you."

Abbie moved to take a seat before the table and poured a cup of coffee. She couldn't help but notice over the rim of her cup that Carmelita had picked up Sonny's dusty traveling clothes from a chair. It was a natural gesture, something she'd probably done countless times before, but at the moment, it was all that Abbie could stand.

"Leave my husband's things. I'll see to them myself," she said crisply.

Carmelita halted her actions, her expression one of complete innocence. "I am sorry. I was only trying to help. Santiago told me you are expecting a child and that you haven't been too well. He wants you to take it easy. I am to see to that."

"He—he told you about the baby?" Abbie questioned, wondering how the woman could face her so calmly.

"*Si*, he is very proud. He wished to share his good news with someone who cares very much about his happiness."

Abbie set down her cup, fighting to keep her voice carefully controlled. "And you do care, don't you, Carmelita?"

"I owe Santiago my life, senora. I want only what makes him happy."

"And do you think I will make him happy?" Abbie

398

watched the dark eyes closely for any sign of malice, but there was none.

"I do not honestly know," Carmelita replied. "I know you love him very much—and that he loves you."

"And does that bother you?"

"Why are you asking me all of these questions?"

"Because I know that you shared my husband's life before. That you were—lovers." There, Abbie thought, it's out in the open now. Let her deny it. She was stunned when Carmelita answered coolly.

"Your husband is a man—a virile man. We may have been lovers, lived here together, but we have never been in love. I will miss him in my bed, yet I do not think he will miss me." She frowned. "But why am I telling you all of this. Can you not see this for yourself? Do you not trust in the deep feelings he has for you?"

Abbie's face flamed. There was one other question she wanted an answer to. It was then a child's inquisitive voice could be heard outside in the hallway.

"*Madre?* Where are you?"

"In here, angel," Carmelita replied. "Come in, I want you to meet someone."

Abbie sat very still, watching the door open slowly and a darling little girl enter the room.

She was beautiful, almost as lovely as her mother. She had long dark hair, night-black eyes that twinkled merrily, and a tiny rosebud mouth that was turned up at the corners in a shy smile. She hurried to stand behind her mother's skirts.

"Doretea, this is Santiago's wife, Dona Abbie Malone y Alvarez. You must greet her properly."

Doretea curtsied before Abbie.

"She is a lovely girl, Carmelita."

"*Gracias,* you are very kind," Carmelita replied. She took the child's hand. "Come, Doretea, we will leave the senora to eat her breakfast."

Abbie watched them leave, her mind in a turmoil. She had lost her nerve, or maybe she just didn't want to know who the father of this child was.

Do I believe what my own eyes tell me and confront him? And what do I do if he says yes? Abbie buried her face in her hands, suddenly feeling very tired and uncertain about her life.

Chapter Nineteen

Sonny wasted little time in getting to the village. He knew if the mines here were being reclaimed for *el presidente,* that Reeno would undoubtedly be in charge of the procedure. He was one of Diaz's most trusted officers, and for an assignment of this importance, they would need their best men.

Riding through the winding streets that were once more filled with the faces of happy people, Sonny found himself contemplating the turn of events in his own life: the war, the men who'd died by his own hand, and the assassination of the butcher who had ironically brought Abbie into his life. And now, a child of their union. Would it change things between them? Would a child form an even stronger bond between them? "Beautiful, silken Abbie," he murmured. *"Mi vida,* my only love, I cannot honestly say that I am ready to be tied down yet. There is still a part of me that is so damned restless, so unsure as to where my life is going."

By the time Sonny reached the small military garrison that served the men fighting for *el presidente,* Don Benito Juarez, he'd convinced himself that as long as he had Abbie, everything would eventually work itself out. After all, wasn't this the happiest he'd been in a long while?

Seeing Reeno's big roan tied to a hitching post beside an old adobe building, he tied up Viento and entered the

401

anteroom. A bored looking clerk told him that Major Sanchez was in the back office but in conference.

"With General Diaz, senor. However, since your credentials check out, I shall have one of the guards show you the way."

"*Gracias,*" Sonny replied. He followed the guard to a small office where he saw Reeno studying a map that was spread out on a table before him. He wore the familiar uniform of his country.

"I almost didn't recognize you with all that braid you're wearing."

Reeno glanced up. "Santiago!" he shouted. "How good it is to see you." He smiled widely. "I sent word to the Bar C when the war ended. Did you get my message?"

"No, I haven't been at the Bar C for months," Sonny replied, shaking his friend's hand. "I heard about the victory when I hit the border."

Reeno appeared concerned. "Did you and Abbie have another falling-out?"

Sonny grinned. "Abbie and I are married, Reeno. She came with me, against my better judgement, of course, but then you know that gal."

"*Si* I do," Reeno exclaimed. "I think you have found yourself a woman who is equal to you in every way."

"Night Walker heartily agrees with you. He became so taken with her I had to marry her myself before he did."

"So, that's where you were. With your blood brother."

Sonny leaned one hip against the edge of the table. "It's a long story. Let's just suffice to say that we've made it through some pretty bad times together, and now I'm looking forward to finding my father so he can be around to see his first grandchild."

Reeno patted Sonny on the back. "You are going to be a *papacita?*"

"So I'm told."

"That is good news."

"I think I'm gonna like the idea myself, once I get used to it."

Reeno grinned in amusement at his friend's expected remark. He would make a fine father. Santiago with a wife and a child. He supposed miracles really did happen. "So, tell me, are you and Abbie staying at the hacienda?"

"Yeah."

"You don't sound too enthused."

"I thought by now you'd have spirited Carmelita away to your place."

"She wouldn't leave without making certain that you were in good hands. I expect she'll accept my offer of marriage now that you're being well looked after." It came to him then why Santiago sounded somewhat disgruntled. "Things are not working out too well having two women under the same roof, eh?"

"Hell no," Sonny grumbled. "I bring my new bride home expecting to have the place to ourselves, so I purposely avoid saying anything about Carmelita, and what happens: Carmelita is there to greet us just as soon as we walk in the door."

"Mierda!" Reeno swore. "It's a wonder Abbie did not shoot the both of you."

"She thought about it. I could see it in her eyes. But she was very gracious in front of Carmelita." He sighed tiredly. "I managed to soothe things over for now, but I didn't tell her about the child. She's going to suspect all kinds of things as soon as she gets a look at Doretea. I think the only one who can possibly make her understand now is Carmelita."

Reeno picked up a bottle of tequila and a wedge of lime from the table and handed it to Sonny. "You look like you need this, *compadre.*"

Sonny took a long pull on the bottle and then sucked down hard on the lime. "I don't feel it's my place to reveal the circumstances surrounding Doretea's birth. Yet, I know the truth is going to have to come out if I'm going to stay married."

"I think now that Carmelita knows that you no longer need her to take care of you and the *estancia,* that she will now accept my offer of marriage," Reeno said.

Sonny snorted. "You're certainly getting yourself a loyal woman." He stared hard at Reeno. "We were never more than good friends, Reeno. The other—well, it happened before you began showing any interest in her. You understand?"

"Si," Reeno replied. "There are no hard feelings. I love her for what she is now." His white teeth flashed in his coppery face. "Everyone is entitled to make a mistake, eh?"

"I'm not quite sure if I know how to take that," Sonny replied with a mock frown.

"Yes you do," Reeno snorted.

Sonny leaned back and stretched his arms above his head. "Yeah, I guess I do at that." He opened a silver-inlaid cigar box and removed a cigarillo. "Listen, I've got a favor to ask of you." He struck the match against his thumb nail.

"It's about Culley, isn't it?"

"Yes. I found out for certain that he is alive. That's why I'm here."

"Dios! That is wonderful news," Reeno said warmly.

Sonny set his glass down and took a drag on the cigar, his eyes straying to the map on the table. "You've been reclaiming the mines for *el presidente,* I see."

"Slowly but efficiently," Reeno said. "We only have a few areas left. There are several spread out in the hill country around here. All have been deserted by the French armies of course, leaving the mines and prisoners tended by the guards and a few scragglers who will undoubtedly swear their undying loyalty to Juarez when given the opportunity."

"Rodriquez told me that he'd turned my father over to the mine here in Orizaba as a Juarista sympathizer," Sonny informed Reeno. "I'm going with you and get him out. He's been working in that stinking hellhole long enough."

Remembering his friend's hot temper and fast gun, Reeno was quick to say, "This is not a personal vendetta that I am undertaking, Santiago. Our orders are most specific. I am an officer in *el presidente's* army and must act accordingly."

Sonny saw the worried look that Reeno favored him and decided he'd curb his tongue. "I want to find Culley before Rodriquez does. Can I count on your help?"

"Can I expect yours?" Reeno shot back.

"Damnit, whatever you want—just name it."

"Corporal!" Reeno yelled to a young man standing out in the hall. "Take my good friend here and have him fitted for a uniform. He has decided to become a regular soldier and help us finish this war." Even as he spoke he could hear Sonny's soft snarl.

"Why you, crafty—"

"Major to you, Captain."

Sonny scowled when the corporal returned with a tunic and trousers. He accepted it as if it were a noose being placed around his neck.

Reeno flashed him a devil-may-care smile as he took his leave. "There's a dinner tomorrow night for the officers and their wives at the Casa del Norte. Bring Abbie, and wear your uniform."

Sonny swore profusely under his breath. What had he gotten himself into this time? Damn Reeno to hell for leading him into it. He stormed out of the building and mounted the pinto to head out of town.

Reeno left the window where he had watched his friend's departure to stare transfixed at the area circled in red on the map. He had been warned that this was a particularly dangerous mission and must be undertaken with extreme caution. It was a known fact that the mines were laced with sticks of dynamite. All it would take to blow the mine and the enemy into oblivion was one match and one glory monger.

"And God knows the asinine Frenchmen left enough of

those around."

"It's hot as hell tonight and I've got to wear this damned tunic buttoned up to my neck," Sonny snarled, long fingers pulling on the high collar. "I don't know how I ever let Reeno talk me into this."

"Because everything must run its proper course now, Sonny," Abbie replied, checking her appearance in the floor-length mirror and feeling satisfied. All afternoon she and Carmelita had been working to alter one of the gowns they'd found quite by luck in a quaint shop in Orizaba. When Sonny had returned yesterday to throw the uniform distastefully on the bed and announce his commission in *el presidente's* army, Abbie had been speechless. He had not commented further, except to tell her that they were expected at a dinner the following evening for officers and their wives.

"Tomorrow evening!" she'd exclaimed.

"Yes, at six o'clock."

Knowing she had absolutely nothing to wear, she had been grateful when Carmelita had volunteered to go shopping with her. The gown had taken quite a bit of altering to fit Abbie's slender form, but Carmelita had proved a genius with needle and thread. The gown now fit her to perfection.

"Wasn't it nice of Carmelita to spend so much time with me preparing for tonight. She even did my hair. Do you like it?" It had been parted down the middle and secured off her neck by a silken net.

"You look beautiful, honey," Sonny said, coming up behind her.

"Well, I had my doubts when we first bought this gown, but Carmelita assured me it was the right choice." She twirled around in the off-shoulder voluminous gown of silver-shaded satin.

"I'm glad to see that you two are trying hard to become friends."

Abbie paused, one feathered brow arching upward. "She's been most kind to me. I can't fault her for falling under your spell, for you see, I know very well what that is like."

Sonny surveyed her with that half-mocking, lazy smile that she had come to know so well. "You really are something special, beautiful." He pulled her close. "And I can see right now I'm going to have to watch you very closely tonight so none of those hot-blooded Spaniards get the idea to steal you away."

She was pleased by the compliment, but surprisingly, uncomfortable by his closeness. She could understand Carmelita's attraction to him, and even their love affair. After all, it had been before she'd met Sonny. But for him to have a child, in whose future he did not appear in the least concerned, cut Abbie to the quick. And kept her from responding to his touch.

"Don't you think we ought to go now, darling?" she said, twisting out of his arms. "It's fashionable to arrive a little late, but not after everyone has sat down to dinner."

How cool she was, Sonny reflected, studying her from behind narrowed eyes. "I don't know what is bothering you, Ab. And for some reason you refuse to discuss it with me. But don't carry this too far. I've told you before, I won't dance on your string."

"Nor I, on yours," Abbie coolly announced before draping a matching shawl about her shoulders and walking out of the room.

The hacienda of Gen. Porifio Diaz was lovely, set amidst a tropical paradise of sweet-scented flowers and vine-hung trees. By the time Sonny and Abbie arrived, the large *sala* was overflowing with uniformed officers and their ladies. Upon seeing Abbie, Reeno came rushing forward to take her hand.

"Senora, how wonderful you look." He gallantly kissed her hand.

Abbie was delighted to see him. "And you, Major. We must find time to talk about old times, *si?*"

Placing her arm in his, Reeno flashed Sonny a grin before spiriting Abbie away. "Most certainly. You and I are old friends, are we not? You must allow me to escort you to dinner. But first, there is someone I would like you to meet."

She saw General Diaz smiling at her from across the *sala,* and she gripped Reeno's arm tightly.

Reeno chuckled. "He does not eat pretty ladies for dinner, Abbie."

"I know that," she whispered, "but I've heard so much about The Tiger, Diaz, that I find I am just a bit nervous."

"Well, don't be," Reeno assured her. "I told him all about Santiago's beautiful wife, and he's been most anxious to meet you. He appreciates beauty, as you can see by everything surrounding us."

"What have you told him about me, Reeno?" Abbie asked pensively.

"Only how you saved our young friend, Santiago's life, and how you steal every man's heart that you meet."

Abbie gasped. "You didn't!"

"Why not? It is the truth."

"But you make me sound as if I do nothing more than sweep men off of their feet."

Reeno knew she had no idea how truly lovely she was, nor was she aware of the envious looks she was receiving from the other women in the room. She appeared like a glittering diamond in the soft silver gown. He held onto her arm as he performed the introductions, for he felt her trembling beneath Diaz's appraising eyes.

"Senora, I have been looking forward to meeting you. Major Sanchez tells me that your country has its own tigers as well." He smiled, his severe features softening. "And tigresses, from what I have heard."

Abbie found her misgivings lessening and smiled back. "You have heard correctly, General."

His smile widened. "Would you possibly consent to leave that handsome husband of yours long enough to sit beside me at dinner? I am most anxious to hear about this *rancho* that you alone have built into an *impirio*."

Abbie glanced back at Sonny who was conversing with a group of other officers, seemingly unconcerned about her whereabouts, and she replied, "I'd like that, General, *gracias*."

As it turned out, the general was one of the most gracious and charming men that Abbie had ever met. A true gallant man, Abbie thought later, as she sat between Diaz and Reeno during the meal. He was younger than she had expected, in his early thirties, and ruggedly handsome. They spent the entire meal talking of her ranch and the importance of their two countries remaining united against their enemies. It was a conversation that Abbie would never forget. Nor would the general.

Once, she'd happened to look up to see Sonny looking bored to death, listening with little show of interest to a pretty young woman on his right. The woman kept fluttering her lace handkerchief each time she talked and rarely paused in her verbal torrent to draw an even breath. Abbie could not help but smile. Reeno caught the gesture, and their eyes shared a moment of amusement.

Later, the ladies moved out into the cool, tree-shaded courtyard where they were served refreshing glasses of *naranjada,* orangeade.

The hand-picked group of officers had all gathered in the general's large office where they were to discuss the impending sortie. The ladies were polite to Abbie, but she sensed a coolness about them that she could only attribute to the general's having asked her to be his dinner companion. Shrugging it off as best she could, she chatted with some of the officers' wives, and even though they were an odd mixture of classes and personalities, they conversed easily. Quite without her expecting it, the young woman who'd been seated next to Sonny at dinner inquired how long she had been married.

"Just a few months," Abbie replied, sipping from her glass.

"Ah, so your wedding was recent then?" another asked.

"Yes," Abbie replied.

"I'm certain you made a lovely bride, dear," the handkerchief lady enthused. "Where did you say you and your handsome husband were married?"

Abbie smiled sweetly, some little imp within her making her reply amusedly, "I didn't, but if you would really like to know, it was on the Staked Plains, madam, with several hundred Comanche." She watched the white handkerchief flutter rapidly before the woman's pale face.

"Oh, my dear young woman, how awful for you. Not to be married in the eyes of the church. Although I don't know why I should be shocked with some of the things I've heard my own husband tell me about that devil, Santiago," she rattled on. She leaned closer. "Why he was even forced to leave Mexico." And seeing that she had Abbie's undivided attention, she hurriedly added, "He was the general's own assassin—don't you know?"

Abbie found herself staring blankly at the woman, silence all around her. Her first reaction was one of shock and total disbelief. "No—you are mistaken. My husband was in Texas to secure weapons for the armies."

The women all favored her with sympathetic, if not somewhat gloating, looks.

"It is quite true, my dear. And if you don't believe us, ask that woman he keeps at his hacienda. She knows."

Abbie recovered her composure, murmuring softly, "If I should like to know, ladies, I will ask my husband, not our housekeeper." She tossed her head proudly. "Well, I must say, ladies, you've certainly gone out of your way to make me feel welcome. And now, if you will excuse me, I'll leave you to sharpen your claws on another unsuspecting victim."

The women exchanged stunned looks, their mouths pursed indignantly. Only the sudden appearance of the men disrupted the strained atmosphere. Sonny immediately noticed the determined set to Abbie's jaw and moved to join her. His dark head bent over hers, he inquired solicitously, "Honey, are you feeling all right? You look upset about something."

"Get me out of here," she whispered. "Please."

"What is it, Abbie?" he inquired anxiously.

Her eyes blazed when they met his. "I don't think you wish to discuss it here, so we'd better leave, but by God, Sonny, this is one explanation I'm going to have from you."

All the way back to the hacienda she sat stiffly across the carriage from him, her mind reeling. The woman's words kept ringing in her ears. An assassin, a cold-blooded killer. She had accepted everything else about him, but this was too much to bear. And she found herself beginning to believe it, recalling the side of him that had always frightened her, the cold side, the killing side. Even now, he had come to Mexico with one burning thought in mind: to save his father, he had told her. No doubt, also, to inform his general of Rodriquez's threat to their takeover of the silver mines. She was certain he would kill him this time if he found him. Had he already received orders tonight to go on the mission and eliminate any risks that got in the way? Did that include her twin?

Sonny stared at her. "Abbie," he queried urgently, "will

411

you please tell me what is bothering you? I can't imagine what I could have done this evening to make you so coldly furious."

"It's nothing you did at the dinner," she answered.

"Well, that's nice to know. I thought perhaps that you were angry with me for putting up with that foolish Gonzales woman at dinner," he replied. "She does manage to go on." He stretched out his long legs. "I hated leaving you with those vipers, but I had really had little choice in the matter."

She smiled coldly. "Duty calls, correct?"

"Yes, and sometimes I wonder why in the hell I got myself involved in all of this again."

"Because you've got what you were seeking when we came to Orizaba," she returned.

"What are you talking about?" he snapped. "I could care less about this damn uniform or the prestige behind it." As if to prove his point, his fingers ripped impatiently at the buttons on his tunic until he'd opened it halfway down his chest. "Now, I can breathe."

Abbie did have to admit he looked every bit the devil-may-care rake with the gilt epaulettes glittering beneath the coach lamps and the sword hanging from the gold and satin belt around his waist. "You said you rode with the general before, didn't you?" she asked.

"I told you that already."

"But you never told me exactly just what your function was."

He frowned. "As a guerilla, it wasn't exactly the kind of thing one discusses around a lady."

"Did you kill many people for your country, Sonny?"

He looked at her. She appeared in total control. "I don't like the turn of this conversation. So let's drop it."

"I want one answer from you first."

"What?" he said gruffly.

"Did you ever assassinate anyone?"

He saw her shiver and moved to sit beside her. She drew

412

away. He yanked her next to him. "Don't move," he ordered, "and don't open that lovely mouth of yours until I'm done talking."

By the caustic inflection in his tone, she knew better than to argue. She nodded stiffly.

"I can see those biddies ran off at the mouth again tonight." He ran his fingers through his neatly trimmed hair. "I'm afraid their tales far outshine anything I've ever done." His eyes took on a faraway expression. "There was one incident, a very personal and painful one, that I never told you about. I didn't, because I couldn't bear to remember."

Abbie felt his pain and knew he was speaking the truth. She took hold of his hand. "Will you tell me now?"

He swallowed and began reliving the constant nightmare that lurked in his innermost thoughts even today. The day he'd ridden into Chihuahua ahead of everyone else and found his brother's family lying dead in the village plaza.

When he was finished, Abbie was weeping softly in his arms, and he was holding her, clinging to her, letting her share his emotions in a way he'd never believed possible with anyone.

"I feel like such a complete fool, Sonny," she said. "I wish you would have confided in me before this."

"Abbie, you haven't wanted to believe a thing I've told you since you've gotten it into that stubborn but beautiful head of yours that I'm out to gun down your sister." His dark brows drew together as he fixed that silvery gaze upon her. "You know that's true."

She knew that was probably correct and that now was the time to ask him about Carmelita's child, but she was so afraid he might tell her the truth, and tonight, she didn't want to face any more truths. She only wanted to love him.

"Sonny," she whispered throatily.

"What, pretty lady?" he said, his lips already nibbling her earlobe.

"Have you ever made love in a carriage?"

"More truths, Ab?" he said dryly.

"Well—have you?"

"No."

"Would you like to?"

"Right now."

"Mmm," she purred.

She felt the whisper of long fingers along her thighs. "Silken Abbie, we've already begun."

Chapter Twenty

It appeared to Sonny, as the days slipped quietly past, that he was finally able to assuage many of Abbie's doubts. She gave her love to him freely and passionately. And slowly, he was beginning to lose some of the awful bitterness that had always seemed so much a part of him. Sitting in the courtyard with her now, on such a lovely morning, he felt so filled with bliss and total contentment that he was almost sorry he would have to leave her this one last time. But he had to see this vendetta through to the finish and pray that he'd be coming back with his father. His life would then be complete and at peace.

Sonny watched as Abbie opened a letter which had just arrived from her mother. She began reading it to him.

Dear Abbie and Santiago,
Everyone sends their love and congratulations. We are all fine, although we miss you very much and will be glad when you are back home. Don't worry about the ranch. Red is doing a fine job. And I found the money, dear. Francisca had put the crate under your bed. Imagine our astonishment to find all of that money in a set of pots. Such attractive pots— and they even cook nicely. At any rate, all is prospering here.

Daughter, I don't know why you two decided to run away and get married so suddenly, but I can only assume it has something to do with your breaking your engagement to Brett Colfax. I suppose you wished to keep things quiet. And I must say, I approve of your new husband very much. He's just the sort of man a strong-willed girl like you needs.

And speaking of Brett, he returned from a lengthy cattle buying trip and abruptly sold his ranch. His father had passed on right after his return, and he and Hattie just packed up and were gone before anyone knew. Too many painful memories, I suppose.

Abbie, Charly told me something about Sonya visiting now and again at the ranch while I was away. I understand she left to join you. I am so sorry I missed her. Daughter, I would like for your sister to come home with you. Tell her how much we all miss her, please.

Charly sends his love and told me to inform you how good he is behaving. And he is. We look forward to seeing all of you very soon.

Must close now. A nice gentleman that I met in San Marco is coming to call. He is in railroads. Says they are the mode of travel for the future. Can you imagine that!
Love to you both.

Mother

Abbie finished reading and folded the letter neatly away in the envelope. She glanced at Sonny.

"I know you don't share my sentiments, but I'm glad that Brett survived."

"Smart move, that boy moving on like that," he stated without emotion.

"And I don't think we have to worry about him ever coming back."

Thinking about her twin, Abbie's eyes suddenly glistened with tears. "Will we bring Sonya back with us?"

416

Taking her hands in his, Sonny said, "Abbie, I'll do everything in my power to persuade her to turn herself in. You know she'll be charged with murder."

"Sonya is a grown woman, and for once she'll have to pay for her own mistakes."

"This time, you can't protect her, Ab," Sonny said.

"But you will testify for her, tell them how the major treated her?"

"Of course. When the jury hears the entire story they'll go easier on her."

"I hate to think of her locked behind bars," Abbie said. "But she's been in a prison of sorts with Rodriquez, and at least this way, she'll be free of him."

Sonny's eyes held hers. "I'll be leaving in the morning, Ab. We've received confirmation from some American Legionnaires helping us round up what's left of the Imperialists that the mine on the other side of Orizaba is still in their possession. I know my father is there. I have to believe that."

Abbie swallowed over the lump in her throat. "Don't forget who else is out there. And he's more dangerous than ever."

"I'm not likely to forget, honey. But I'm not going to have to look hard, for he'll come to me. And this time, we'll finish it—once and for all."

"Please be careful, Sonny," Abbie whispered, wrapping her arms about his neck, fear overwhelming her.

"Yes, silken lady," he replied, kissing her parted lips, "for I have someone very special to come home to. And together, we're going to have the best life ever, I promise you."

"I know we will," she said, before pressing her lips firmly to his.

Passion flared between them. His hard eyes glinted into hers and, not wasting another precious second, he carried her from the courtyard, right past the gaping servants up the stairs to their bedroom, where he promptly kicked the door soundly closed.

Carefully, as if she were the most precious possession in the world, he laid her on the bed and stretched out beside her. There, in every way possible for a man to show a woman how much he loved her, Sonny did so for the next several hours.

It was as though nothing else existed for them but this moment in time and this love that they shared. With infinite slowness he undressed her, his eyes admiring every luminous, satiny part of her, his lips thrilling her with their heady exploration. No part of her body was left unworshiped. His hands and lips bespoke his message, making her gasp with delight, so wonderful were the sensations that he aroused. And when his body at last covered hers, she was ready, wrapping long legs about his shoulders to experience his first thrust to the fullest.

His strong hands slipped beneath her buttocks, and even though she gasped upon realizing his intention, it felt simply too wonderful to protest anything that he had in mind. She clung to him as he raised up and took her with him. He then eased back slowly onto his knees, bringing her body off the bed and against him.

"Place your legs about my waist, Ab," he encouraged softly.

She complied, her mouth closing hard over his. Slowly, teasingly, he began to rotate his hips against hers, his hands cupping her bottom to hold her to him. "You're my lady, Abbie, and I love you."

Her body moved against his, writhing, taking all that he had to give. "Sonny, oh, God, I love you so."

"You're so warm," he breathed huskily. "Is it good for you, baby?"

"Yes, oh yes, just like every nerve that I possess in my body is on fire."

Silvery eyes squinted at her lazily, belying the tremors of excitement coursing through his veins. He closed his eyes to the exquisite sensations churning inside him. His hands massaged and squeezed her buttocks as Abbie gasped and bucked against him, feeling the fire raging out of control.

When he felt her release, he let himself go, and together they experienced love's ultimate pleasure. Long, shuddering tremors shook them both with his last powerful thrust, then gradually diminished, and they quieted. Together, they fell back onto the bed, sated, completely content just to lie in each other's arms.

Morning found Sonny busy in his office winding up last minute business, when Carmelita walked in and closed the door behind her. He gave her a puzzled look.

"Is there some reason you wish to speak with me in private?" he asked. He was seated behind his desk, booted feet propped up on the glassed top.

"*Si*, we must talk."

"Do we have something to say that we haven't already discussed?"

"I think that we do." She sat on one corner of the desk, her gaze commanding his.

"Carmelita, whatever we had between us was great, but—"

She smiled, shaking her head. "That is not what I wished to talk to you about."

He looked at once sheepish. "Oh, I—I just assumed."

"Men always assume, *querido,* that is their problem."

Sonny grinned. "Especially some more than others, right?"

"Well—" She shrugged. "One can't blame you for thinking that way about me. After all, we were lovers for several years. But that is over. You have a lovely wife, and a child on the way, and I can accept that. You've done so much for me and the child. Now, I do this for you. I move on, take Doretea and begin a new life."

His expression grew concerned. "Are you sure? You don't have to leave here unless you really want to."

"Your wife, she is not the kind to have another woman

hanging around her man. This house is just not big enough for two women and a man such as you." Her eyes beheld him admirably. "I am still a young woman, with the same appetites, the same desires. And there is someone who I think will be relieved to hear of my decision."

Sonny sat up straight, his hands reaching for hers, but she drew away. "All I've ever wanted was for you to be happy, you deserve that."

She glanced down at her lap. "Now that I know that you are in good hands I can. You know I would never have left you as long as I felt you needed me."

"And here all of these years I thought you were the one who needed me."

She smiled, veiling her emotions with thick lashes.

"Will you at least stay until I get back?"

"If you wish it."

"I'd feel better if you were here with her while I'm gone."

"She is nice, but nothing I do is for her, Santiago," Carmelita replied quietly.

"I know," Sonny murmured. "You always were the best friend I'll ever have." He knew this entire situation was difficult for her, yet he didn't want to leave Abbie in the house alone. "I've explained to you about Rodriquez and Abbie's twin. Abbie will defend Sonya to the bitter end. She doesn't seem to realize the danger she places herself in each time that she is near that woman. And I don't want them near her again."

Carmelita took a deep breath and exhaled slowly. "All right, I'll stay. And I will watch her closely for you."

"She probably will resent it."

"Perhaps it's time for the two of us to talk. I think there is something more bothering her that only another woman could understand."

Sonny nodded, his eyes viewing Carmelita admirably. She was a wonderful woman. He would miss her in his life. She had always been there when he needed her. But of course, now, he had Abbie. And that was all the woman he needed. "Talk—about what?" he thought to ask.

"Woman talk. Nothing a *muy macho* man like yourself would understand."

"Oh, I think he would," a strained voice stated behind them. Abbie stood with a tray of refreshments in her hands, her face pale and drawn. She had only heard Carmelita's last statement and now viewed her husband's admiring gaze beholding the other woman.

Sonny jumped up to go to her. "We didn't hear you come in, honey."

He rushed to assist her with the heavy tray. "Let me help you with that."

Abbie was suddenly filled with bitter contempt for both of them. "Oh, but I wouldn't dream of interrupting your cozy, little scene with your ex-mistress. It is *ex*, isn't it, Sonny? I was waiting any moment for you to ask her to become your *paraibo*, too." She shoved the tray at him, suddenly all of the doubts she had been feeling raging to the surface. "After all, we were married in a Comanche ceremony, and that allows you to take as many wives as you want." Her voice continued to rise. "And heaven knows, she has borne you your first child. That's the least you can do!"

Carmelita's soft cry made Abbie feel suddenly very spiteful and mean. She saw that Sonny was angry enough to strangle her. She had only heard the end of the conversation. Had she assumed the wrong thing? No, she thought stubbornly. I know what I heard and saw. They still love each other. They're bound together by their child.

"That was the most rotten thing you've ever said," Sonny snarled, setting the tray down forcefully on the desk. He lifted an eyebrow at her. "And you've said some pretty mean things. I think you owe Carmelita and me an apology."

"Like hell," Abbie hissed. "I think you owe *me* something. An explanation. I want to know now what you intend to do about her and the child."

Carmelita began walking toward the door, her head bowed. Sonny called after her. "Don't go, Carma, please wait. I understand now what you were trying to tell me. This lady of mine does need a good talking to." He grabbed Abbie's arm and pulled her toward a chair. "I swear, Abbie Lee, if you weren't pregnant I'd turn you over my knee." He towered above her. "As it is, I'm going to give you your explanation, although you sure as hell don't deserve one."

Carmelita stood stilently staring out of the window, her back to them.

Sonny knew there was only so much he could tell Abbie. He had promised Carmelita a long time ago that they would never discuss the secret she carried with her. He began pacing back and forth as he talked.

"While I can understand how you might think that Doretea is my child, I would have thought you'd know me well enough by now to realize I would never allow any child of mine not to carry my name. If that little girl was mine, I would have married Carmelita."

Abbie stared at him. Had she been reading more into their feelings for each other? Were they innocent? "Why didn't you talk to me about this before now?"

"Would you have believed me? And besides, I made a promise to Carmelita that we'd never discuss the past until she felt she was ready to." He sighed raggedly. "Oh, Ab, don't you see? I believed in our love. I thought by showing you how much I loved you and this child that you are carrying, you'd realize I could never have fathered Doretea without openly declaring her as mine." He halted before Abbie, his features hard, unyielding. "But you always wanted to believe the worst about Carmelita and me, didn't you? And you think you finally found something today that proved you were right about us all along."

"Stop this!" Carmelita cried, spinning around. "You are both going to say things that you do not mean and will regret! I will tell you, senora, what it is you wish to hear." She

422

came over to stand beside Sonny. "Your man belongs to no one but you. His love, his life, his fidelity, are yours alone. My little one is not Santiago's child. I wish with all of my heart that she was, for then I would have him, and you would never be tearing him apart like you are now."

"You don't owe me any explanations," Abbie murmured. "It's certainly clear enough. I misunderstood. I am sorry."

Carmelita shook her head sadly. "You have wanted this, and now you are going to listen to it all." Slowly, but with determination, she told her story. "I have known Santiago for many years. He and my brother rode together for the revolution. We have always cared for each other, but love—I do not know if I have that to give a man. You see, I spent two years as a captive of the French army. A *soldadera*—a whore to whichever soldier wanted me for the night. Santiago bought me, brought me here to live, and gave me a reason to go on living when I discovered I was to bear a child. But not a love child, Abbie." Her voice broke. "A child I hated the entire time I carried her. For you see, my beautiful baby— my angel—is the result of my sins. Santiago gave her all of the love she needed until I could bring myself to forget. I can assure you he is not her father, but I cannot tell you who her father is—because I don't even know myself."

For several long moments the room was deathly still, except for Carmelita's soft sobs. Sonny gently enfolded her in his arms, one hand caressing the back of her head.

"It's okay, honey," he said tenderly. "You'll feel better having talked about it now."

Abbie sat totally stunned by what she'd just discovered. She watched her husband comforting the other woman with a strange sense of detachment. What she had made Carmelita remember was so cruel, so heartless. But she hadn't known. She hadn't meant to hurt her. Forcing her legs to move, she rose from the chair and walked toward the door. "I didn't know. I just didn't know," she said to them, then quietly left the room.

Sonny felt no sympathy for Abbie at that moment. He watched her walk away, and for a brief second, he almost wished she'd never come into his life.

It was Carmelita who finally came to Abbie, later, after Sonny had left without even saying good-bye.

Abbie had spent the rest of the morning closeted in their room, feeling as though her world had shattered. When she'd heard the sharp slam of the front door and had run to the window to see Sonny riding away, she knew he never wanted to see her again.

"I've lost you. I severed the fragile thread of trust that was between us," she said regretfully.

She heard Carmelita calling from outside the bedroom door. "Abbie, please open the door. I want to tell you something."

Abbie was crying softly now, tears of anguish streaming down pale cheeks. "Go away. We've nothing more to say to each other."

"Stop acting like a child," Carmelita said sternly. "He's coming back to you. He's just angry and hurt right now."

As if in a trance, Abbie unlocked the door and stood back so that Carmelita could enter.

"Here." Carmelita handed her a glass of warm milk. "I thought you might need something to soothe your nerves." She watched Abbie closely, her face revealing her concern. "This is not good for the child, *nina*. You must get hold of yourself."

Abbie accepted the glass. "Thank you." She wiped at her eyes with a handkerchief before sipping the milk. "You did not deserve the tongue-lashing I gave you earlier. I am so sorry." She gave the woman an imploring look. "I know I read too much into my husband's concerns for you and Doretea. I was jealous. That's all I can say."

"That is why I am here." Carmelita smiled faintly. "I think

we need to have this thing out between us. On friendly terms," she hastily added.

Abbie smiled. "I am willing."

"And no more tears—from either of us."

They sat down to talk.

Sonya carried the bucket from the stream that ran down the mountainside into the clear pool at its base and hurried back up the steep footpath to the crude cabin deep amidst thickly leafed trees and profuse vines that obscured the small hut from view.

"Lucien, get up," she said urgently, setting the bucket down and staring at his prone figure on the rumpled bed. "I heard the sound of many horses on the goat path. The soldiers are coming!"

Lucien rolled over and opened one eye to peer up at her. "You'd better be right this time, *mujer*. You told me you thought you heard them last week, too. And it was nothing but a goat herder driving his herd to market."

"It is them this time," Sonya said. "I heard the rumor only this morning in the village. They're on their way to the mines to take them over for *el presidente.*" She picked up a pair of wrinkled trousers and threw them at him. "Get some clothes on and go out on the ledge and see. If it is the soldiers, it is time to send the message to my sister."

Lucien pulled on his trousers, his movements unsure. He had waited for this moment, even as he feared it. He was not afraid of dying, for he no longer feared death. He had been forced to endure something far worse than dying: torture. Having one's manhood broken down until you were a mass of sobbing, quivering flesh begging for mercy had destroyed much of the confidence he once possessed. He had allowed Sonya to think she was making many of the decisions now, simply because it was easier and suited his purpose.

"I can't wait to see the look on that filthy half-breed's face when he discovers I got his woman after all." He leered at Sonya. "I'm going to use Abbie as my hostage and walk right into that strong room and help myself to all of that silver."

"You won't be doing anything if you don't get moving," she said simply. "They'll have released all of the prisoners and hauled off all of the silver and you'll still be in bed."

"Shut up!" he roared, raising a clenched fist in a threatening manner. "You dare to talk to me like that after all that I've been through because of you."

She knew he was referring to the major's murder, yet she raised her chin defiantly. "I paid you back. I'm the one who saved you from those savages. Without me you'd have been a dead man."

He lowered his hand slowly, his eyes narrowing. "Without you, *bella,* I would have never have found myself there in the first place."

"Don't try to blame me for the little trick you tried to pull with my twin," she sneered.

"You have become very hard, Sonya *mia,*" he growled. "But perhaps we've both been too greedy, eh?" He snatched up a pair of field glasses from a cluttered table. "Together, we shall make that half-breed and the woman regret all of the pain and humiliation that we suffered at the hands of the Comanches." He smiled at her. "It begins."

"That is how I like to hear you talk," Sonya said. "Now hurry, for I have to go to the village and find the boy who is to deliver the message to Abbie."

"I hope you are right and she will come. If she doesn't we will have to think of another plan."

"If Abbie thinks her precious lover has been injured and dying, she'll come," Sonya said assuredly. "I know my sister." She eyed Lucien. "You know, every time my twin's name is mentioned you get a certain gleam in your eye. Do you know even yet what it is you want, Lucien?"

"*Si,*" he replied confidently. "I do." But for the briefest

426

moment the naked truth in his eyes was visible—and noticed.

"For your own sake, you'd best be telling me the truth."

"I'll be back in ten minutes," he said and left.

Sonya hurriedly began to change her clothing. When she was dressed in a shirt and trousers, she sat down to compose her thoughts and contemplate their next move.

Sonny wiped the sweat from his brow with the back of his hand as the calvary regiment slowly penetrated the thick, misty jungle that would lead them to the silver mine. The horses were in single file now, the ascent up the narrow goat path tedious and nerve-wracking. His foul mood was not helped by the stifling heat and the endless trailing vines that seemed to reach out like that of a woman's soft caress on his cheek. Like his woman, he thought, his wild, passionate *gata* with her caress of silk and her body like soft velvet. And in spite of everything, he wanted her more now than he ever had. He would tell her that, too, just as soon as he had Culley out of that hellhole and could return to her. He and his father would go back together, and Abbie would be there waiting. She would be—she just had to.

They came out of the damp ravine, and he looked over at Reeno who had reined his horse in beside him.

"You ready? We're almost there."

"Yeah, I've been ready for a long time. Forever it seems," Sonny replied.

"Do not worry, all will go well," Reeno said. "We have taken over several mines in other areas, and we've always managed to have the element of surprise on our side. A few shots fired and they run like rabbits. And always, they surrender without a fuss."

"It all sounds so simple."

"When presented with almost certain death, or swearing

their allegiance to the true government of the people, what do you think their choice is?"

Sonny could only hope Reeno was right and that there would be no battle for the takeover. Every man in the detail had been forewarned of the dynamite reportedly laced throughout the shafts. No one wished to enter a mine with the possibility of its being blown sky high around him. No, he thought. It is all going to go smoothly. And soon he'd be reunited with his father and Abbie.

Abbie and Carmelita were fixing supper in the big kitchen, the servants all having the night off. They were enjoying this time together, just the two of them. It gave them time to talk, to get to know each other better. Whatever doubts and differences that had been between them they had managed to lay to rest. Carmelita had just confided to Abbie that she was considering Reeno Sanchez's offer of marriage.

"Why, that's wonderful," Abbie replied warmly. "And you couldn't find a better father for Doretea."

Carmelita looked up from the work table where she was peeling potatoes. "I didn't have time to tell Santiago. He's going to be happy, *si?*"

"Very, and I hope you'll let us give you a reception here after the wedding."

"That would be nice. If you are certain it won't be too much trouble."

"I want to do this, Carmelita," Abbie said. "Please, it will give me a chance to do something for you for a change."

"If it makes you happy, then it is fine with me," Carmelita replied.

Both women paused when a scratching sound at the back door interrupted their conversation.

"Who could that be?" Carmelita stated to Abbie. She picked up a rifle from where it sat propped against the wall and opened the door. A young peasant boy was standing on

428

the stairs.

"What do you want?" she asked.

He stared apprehensively at the rifle in her hands. "I—I have message for Senora Alvarez. It is important," he said nervously, his eyes never wavering from the long steel barrel.

"Let him in, Carmelita," Abbie urged, coming up behind her. She felt a sense of inexplicable fear as she faced the boy. "I am the senora. What is the message?"

The boy swallowed. "Your husband, senora, he has been badly wounded. You must come at once—before—"

Abbie felt a bubble of hysteria form in her throat. "Where?" she asked. "Where is my husband?"

"On the mountain pass just the other side of the village."

"Yes, I know where you mean."

Carmelita turned toward Abbie, concern clearly visible on her face. She did not want Abbie to go alone, yet she could not leave Doretea unattended. "Senora, you should not go by yourself." She placed a hand on Abbie's arm. "I do not like this."

The boy quietly slipped away as the two women stood talking. They didn't even notice that he was gone until Abbie pulled away to shrug out of her apron and take the rifle in hand.

"He certainly left in a hurry," Carmelita commented pointedly. "Please, Abbie, wait until I can get someone from the village to stay with Doretea so that I can come with you."

"That will take too long. I must get to him. You heard that boy!"

"*Si,* and I don't like any of this. Abbie wait!" she yelled.

But Abbie was already down the stairs and running for the stables.

The mare was winded by the time they reached the dark barranca that she had to descend to get to the mountain trail. Abbie had only one thing on her mind: finding her husband, getting there before it might be too late. Her heart was pounding from fear. But not fear for herself, fear at what she would find. The horse shied at a rabbit darting across their trail, her iron-clad hooves echoing sharply against the shale-covered ravine. As they came up onto the narrow trail, a hand snaked out of the darkness to grab her mount's reins. Abbie's fingers clutched the rifle, but it was too late. Someone yanked her from her horse and then everything suddenly went black.

Chapter Twenty-One

Abbie awoke to the sound of Spanish-speaking voices. Familiar voices that made her heart pound and her mouth go dry. She barely opened her eyes. A dull pain throbbing in her head made her grit her teeth. She was lying on a bed, her hands tied to the iron bedpost. Her eyes flew open when she saw Lucien Rodriquez standing beside the bed, favoring her with that wolfish smile she'd learned to despise. It was his black eyes shining with something Abbie understood only too well that made her begin screaming as though she were demented.

"No! Stay away! Don't touch me!"

He was amused. "Such a greeting for old friends. But it was good of you to come just as soon as you were summoned."

"I should have known you'd be behind something this horrible!" she spat at Sonya who had just entered the cabin. "You're never going to change! You're still his puppet and always will be." She glanced around her, frightened. "Sonny—what have you done to him? Where is he?"

"At the mine, I imagine," Sonya replied with a shrug.

Abbie was inwardly relieved. "It was all just a ruse to get me here."

"*Si,*" Lucien replied. "And soon we'll all join your husband."

"You two never learn, do you?" Abbie snapped. "You can't get by an army of men. They'll kill you both."

"Oh shut up Abbie!" Sonya shrieked back at her. "Haven't you realized by now that I'm not as stupid as you think I am?" She strode across the room to confront her twin. "I didn't have any help when I took Lucien away from those savages, and it's me who's going to see that this plan works."

"And it's you who shall feel my husband's wrath when he hears what you've done," Abbie interceded. "I will not save you this time—either of you!"

"You won't need to," Sonya sneered.

Using all of her strength to keep panic from overwhelming her, Abbie flung back, "Remember how much Comanches value their honor and their families? If you harm me, or the child that I'm carrying, they'll hunt you down like the jackals you are and kill you—the Comanche way."

A fearful shiver raced down Sonya's spine. She had seen what the savages had done to the others and to Lucien. She didn't think it would matter that she was a woman. They would make certain she died slowly and painfully. Frantically, she brushed the thought aside. It didn't matter anyway, for they weren't going to get caught. They had planned too carefully for that. Hadn't they?

Lucien pulled Sonya to one side. "Do you think she means any of what she's saying? I don't want to feel that knife against my flesh ever again."

Sonya's mouth twisted into an ugly smile. "My fierce desperado, look at what the mere mention of the savages does to you. We will go ahead with the rest of our plans. We won't need that ranch if we can get enough silver out of that mine."

"I just can't forget the look in Sonny's eyes that night, or the feel of that cold blade pricking my skin," Lucien murmured. "He'd better not catch us or even you shall feel his full wrath this time."

"Abbie being his wife and carrying his child only makes it

that much easier for us," Sonya said. "Why, we'll walk right into that mine with her as our hostage, and Sonny won't dare let anyone get in the way. He'll fill our saddlebags with silver and watch helplessly as we blow the mine up with all of them in it. Your revenge will be complete, *querido*. You'll have won."

"But just to make certain, I think we should keep Abbie with us until we are safely out of Orizaba."

"What are you planning on doing? Keeping her all for yourself?" she queried, eyes narrowed. "Maybe going on without me—leaving me buried in that mine?"

"That's ridiculous!" he replied quickly, appearing shocked at the suggestion.

"For your sake, Lucien, I certainly hope so," Sonya said slowly, watching his face with shrewd eyes.

"Sonya *mia*," Lucien crooned, "how can you accuse me of such a thing when you know it is you I depend on, you who matters to me more than anyone."

"Don't listen to him Sonya. He's been using you all along!" Abbie interceded, seeing all too well what was going on. "You'd better listen to me. He does intend to get rid of you. Look at him!"

"This is not true," Lucien growled. "She's crazy."

Abbie kept up relentlessly. "He isn't going to just take all of that silver and go away with you. He wants more than that." She cast Lucien a knowing glare. "Tell her—tell her about wanting to have the ranch—and me—so that you can flaunt your success in your father's face. It's what you always wanted!"

Sonya reeled backward, her eyes turning flinty as they fell upon Lucien's features. He leaped toward Abbie threateningly, his hand raised.

"Tell her to shut up, Lucien. I do not like that kind of talk," Sonya pleaded. But Abbie kept on, desperate to drive a wedge between them, buy herself more time. "He wants me more than he ever has you, Sonya. Ask him how he wooed me while I was his captive. And about the night of love that he had planned—the one that you interrupted?"

"Do not talk too much, pretty lady," Lucien warned Abbie. He grabbed her around the throat.

"You—you did make love to me that night, knowing all along it was me, didn't you, Lucien?" Sonya queried pitifully. "Tell me you did."

Lucien released his hold on Abbie to go to Sonya and push her roughly back against the wall, pinning her there with his big body. "She is just jealous because I didn't make love to her." He pressed his hips to hers. "You are the only woman for me, you know that."

"I know that when I came into your bedroom that night, you appeared as though you had been waiting for someone." Her eyes flew to his. "And you made love so passionately, with such emotion. Tell me you knew all along that it was me!"

Flashing her a smile that could always melt her heart, he breathed huskily. "I knew—*bella*—of course I knew."

She thought hard about that, searching his face for reassurance, needing to believe in her heart that it was true. He had known it was her—he had! "I knew it, I really did," she breathed in relief.

He kissed her into submission, chuckling down deep in his throat. Raising his mouth inches from hers, he murmured, "There isn't a woman alive who can love like you, *mi amante.*"

"Oh, Lucien," Sonya sighed, "if you would just say those words to me more often, I would never have cause to doubt you."

Abbie watched their blatant display of lust with a sense of panic. Was there no end to her sister's gullibility where this man was concerned? How could she make her see, before it was too late, what Lucien had been planning all along. He was going to leave Sonya in that mine and take her and the silver. Abbie knew it. She could just see it in his eyes.

434

Sonya, oh Sonya, she wanted to cry out. Please see—before it is too late!

"If you do this thing, Sonya," Abbie said, trying one last time to reach her, "you'll be signing your own death warrant."

Sonya pulled free of Lucien and walked over to confront Abbie. "You have always resented the fact that men preferred me over you, Abbie," she ranted. "I know. Don't try and deny it. Brett told me many things about you. He said you had ice water in your veins and didn't know how to take care of a real man." She tossed her head flippantly. "It's too bad we don't have time to show you just how much fun it can be."

"You are disgusting!" Abbie hissed, her skin crawling.

Sonya only laughed. "I was only teasing, sister dear." She yanked a lock of Abbie's hair, pleased with her sister's soft cry of pain. "Just teasing."

"Quit acting like two spitting she-cats!" Lucien demanded. "If we intend on getting to the mine before sunrise tomorrow, we're going to start out now." He began gathering food-stuffs from a shelf on the wall. "Sonya, go fill the buffalo skins with water."

Sonya glanced from Abbie to Lucien, uncertainty in her gaze. "You're not sending me away just so you can be alone with her, are you?"

"Oh, for Christ's sake!" he exploded. "I thought we had all of that settled between us."

She hung her head. "We do, but she has always stolen everything from me, even my son. I will not let her get the chance to take you, too."

Lucien grabbed up the water skins and tossed them at her. "The quicker you get there and back, the less chance there is of that happening."

When she hurried out of the door, leaving Abbie alone with Lucien, he swaggered over to sit on the bed next to her. Gone was any trace of the contempt he showed toward

Sonya. Desire now shone in his gaze. He ran one finger along Abbie's cheek, downward inside the low neckline of the blouse she wore.

"Don't Lucien," she said through clenched teeth, "or I'll tell her. I swear I will."

He grinned, shaking his head slowly from side to side. "No you won't, my fiery *muchacha,* for you know what will happen if you do. I would make you regret it, very painfully. And you must think of the child inside you . . . hmm?"

"I was right all along. You have been playing a part. You're using Sonya to do your dirty work for you and making her believe that you intend to take her with you. You don't, do you?"

He laughed jeeringly. "You, the silver, and revenge are all that I want, if that answers your question. Just as soon as I have the silver and have set the dynamite off in the mine shaft, it'll be just you and me—for as long as I decree."

"You—intend on killing them all, don't you?" she asked, horrified.

"All—save you."

"I won't let you. I'll find a way to stop you!"

His hand rested on her heaving breast. She cringed when he exerted pressure. "If you try anything, say anything, I swear I'll make certain you regret it."

"Either way, I shall regret it," she returned fearlessly. "But know this: before this is through, you will, too."

With a splintering force that jarred every bone in her body, he smacked her across the mouth with his open hand. Abbie screamed from the pain that ripped through her.

Sonya came running into the cabin. "What is going on? You can hear her shriek all the way down the mountainside."

Lucien was standing next to the bed, his black, pitiless eyes staring into Abbie's. "She tried to lure me into leaving you behind and taking her with me instead." He dared Abbie with that look to deny it. "You were right about her, *chica.*

436

She is so jealous of my interest in you she can't stand it. But I showed her what I thought about her offer. She won't try anything like that again."

Sonya slung the filled water skins on the rickety table and turned to glare at her sister. "All of my life you have stolen what's mine. But no more. I have something, at last, that you can't take away from me."

Abbie had learned many things from living with the Comanche. One of them was patience and the ability to conceal her innermost emotions. She would study her quarry carefully. For she knew it was possible, if one was very clever, to turn the hunter into the hunted, without their being aware.

The captain of the few remaining Imperialists of the small garrison protecting the silver mine was not quite certain what he should do when he suddenly looked up to see a darkly clad man leaping stealthily through his office window. He hardly had time to rise from his desk chair before he felt the sharp edge of a knife pressed to his throat.

"*Dios mios!* do not kill me, I beg of you!" he squealed in terror, his eyes bulging from their sockets.

The fierce brigand's deep voice was edged with steel, brooking no denial. "I will spare your miserable life, Captain, if you agree to do everything that I tell you."

"*Si,* whatever it is—I agree!"

"Very good. You're a smart man," the intruder whispered silkily. He increased the pressure of the blade, persuading the captain to walk before him. "Nice and easy. We're going outside now and order your men front and center. Then after I'm certain I have all of their weapons, you and I are going to open the gates and allow my friends to pass through."

"*Si—si*—that is fine with me."

Mocking laughter rang in the captain's ears. "I kinda thought it might be."

"Who are you, senor? Why are you doing this?" the captain asked haltingly.

The man replied proudly, "My name is Santiago Malone y Alvarez. My regiment is taking over this mine in the name of the true government of Mexico. You may swear your allegiance to *el presidente* or meet your death. The choice is yours."

The captain swallowed with difficulty. "I am no fool, senor. I assure you my men and I will do nothing to stand in your way."

Sonny smiled to himself. Reeno had been right. The takeover had gone smoothly.

"This one was the easiest yet," Reeno told Sonny later as they fanned out from the rest of the men, combing the long dimly lit tunnels beneath the ground in search of any Imperialist stragglers. "And I know why." He grinned at his friend. "Damn, Santiago, but I have to admire your nerve. You scaled that stockade wall just like one of them Comanche brothers of yours."

Sonny shot him a sideways glance. "Don't sing me too many praises, *hermano,* I only volunteered to get out of wearing that damned uniform for awhile."

Reeno observed the familiar dark clothes and the crisscrossed cartridge belts slung across his friend's chest. This is what he did best; what he thrived on. He looked completely unaffected by his surroundings. "You enjoy living constantly on the edge, don't you? I don't think you intend to ever change your wild ways—or even if you can."

Sonny raised one dark brow. "Can we save this conversation for another time and place? Right now the only thing concerning me is finding Culley." He grabbed a flickering torch from a wall sconce. "The captain said if Culley was here that we'd find him down at the end of the main tunnel in one of the prisoner's cells. We've gotta be coming to them soon."

Reeno brushed frantically at a bat that swooped blindly

out of the darkness toward him. "Ah, *caramba,* this is an awful place." He covered his nose with his handkerchief. "The stench alone is enough to suffocate a man."

"Decay mostly," Sonny said. "I imagine they don't waste anytime burying the prisoners who don't survive. Most likely toss the bodies down any accessible mine shaft."

Reeno shuddered. *"Dios,* to think they just dump them like unwanted rubbish turns my blood cold."

"Yeah," Sonny said. "But that's the way it is, I'm afraid." He ducked his head to pass beneath a low-hanging shelf of rock into a narrow, damp passage. "This is it, the end of the line." He wasn't surprised to find that a silent prayer was on his lips. He held the torch up as high as he could. What he saw made him want to gasp.

Reeno crossed himself. "We are surely in hell itself," he breathed hoarsely.

The sounds of groans and cries for water could be heard coming from the cells that ran the entire length of the tunnel. The rattle of chains, the hoarse cries, the stench of rotting human flesh, all of this brought Reeno to his knees to retch chokingly. Sonny understood. He swallowed painfully and continued onward alone.

With one single purpose in mind, he went from cell to cell, eyes peering through the darkness for the familiar face of his father. Some of the men were so dirty and covered with filth that he had to ask their name to make certain he hadn't accidently passed by his father. Not one, so far, was Culley Malone. Sonny didn't let up until he'd searched every last cell and then went back and talked to every man. His face was bleak when he returned to where he'd left Reeno.

"He's not there. He's not anywhere with those poor devils. One of them said he saw him two days ago, but not since that time."

"We—we can't be too late. Don't even think it," Reeno hurriedly replied. Sonny sighed. "To tell you the truth, I don't know what to think right about now." He spun

439

around. "Let's get out of here."

They began walking back the way that they had come with Sonny setting the pace. "I just can't accept that he's dead. I'd know it. I'd feel it in my gut," he said through clenched teeth.

"I'll have our men get those poor devils out of there just as soon as we have some place else to put them," Reeno told him.

"Damn, Reeno!" Sonny suddenly swore. "I couldn't have come all of this way for nothing! He's here somewhere."

"Perhaps there has been some kind of mistake. We'll talk with some of the guards."

"Yeah, they probably know what goes on around here more than their captain." Sonny quickened his pace.

They strode out into the refreshing night air and made their way toward the center stockade.

Sonny hesitated, his sharp eyes peering around him. It was something he felt immediately. It was in the air, thick and heavy, like a shroud of death hanging over him.

"Lay back, Reeno," he warned. "I feel—" The first bullet ripped over his head, drowning out his words and sending him sprawling on his belly in the dirt.

"What the hell—" Reeno yelled, diving for cover behind a water barrel.

"Where are the men?" Sonny snarled.

There came a chilling laugh. "I don't think they wish to shoot," Lucien Rodriquez announced. "Not with this pretty senora sitting before me."

Sonny rolled over beneath a wagon, his gaze narrowing upon recognizing the woman sitting before Lucien on the horse. He drew his pistols, but there wasn't any way he could fire without hitting his wife. "You're a dead man, Lucien, if you harm her in anyway!" he roared, his fingers itching to pull the triggers.

Lucien rode brazenly forward, Abbie tense in front of him, her face ashen, her fingers entwined in the stallion's mane. "I have something here to trade to you. Come out.

Let's talk about it."

The soldiers were all watching, rifles poised, waiting for a signal to open fire. Reeno barked a crisp order for them to hold back.

As Lucien came closer, Sonny saw the barrel of the pistol Lucien had pressed to Abbie's side. "Let Abbie go, Rodriquez. This has nothing to do with her."

"It has everything to do with her," Lucien said meaningfully, and Sonya, who had been waiting on her horse by the stockade gates, urged her horse slowly forward to join Lucien. Rifle resting in the crook of her arm, she rode slowly past the tense soldiers, her eyes never straying from Lucien and Abbie.

Lucien heard her horse draw up behind his. "Point that rifle straight on Malone, and if he makes a wrong move, shoot him," he ordered tersely. "Now, Major, have everyone here place their rifles in the center of the yard."

Reeno gave the order, and the men promptly obeyed.

"*Bueno,*" Lucien said. "Now, it is time for the big reunion." He inclined his head toward Sonny. "You, Abbie, and I are going inside the mine to pay our respects to your father." He ordered Sonya to wait outside. "And if anyone gets any foolish notions, fire your rifle, and I shall be forced to shoot these lovely people on the spot."

Cursing beneath his breath, Sonny could only stand helpless while Lucien advanced ever closer. He knew once they were in that mine that they would never come out alive.

"The knife, too, Malone," Rodriquez added. "I know how good you are with it. I don't wish a repeat performance."

Sonny watched him through narrowed, assessing eyes, finally slipping the knife from the sheath on his belt. He knew it was now or never. Hesitating only briefly when he heard Lucien click back the hammer on the gun, he heaved the knife swiftly forward. It landed point down in the soft dirt between Lucien's mount's hooves. The animal reared back on his hind legs, flinging Lucien's gun hand up into the air.

With a swiftness that amazed everyone, Abbie brought her elbow back sharply and jammed it into Lucien's Adam's apple. He screamed in agony, bringing the butt of the gun down on the side of her head. Pain exploded white-hot inside Abbie's skull, and through an enveloping mist of red, she saw Sonny lunge across the space separating them to grab Rodriquez, all of them tumbling to the ground. Abbie rolled clear of the men and lay still.

Chaos erupted. Sonya, never an accurate shot, trained the rifle on the two men, hoping to get off a clear shot at Sonny. Springing into action, Reeno swiftly drew his revolver and expertly shot the weapon from her hands. She shrieked in horror at the blood streaming from her shattered fingers.

The next few moments were like some unbelievable nightmare that Reeno was certain he would never forget. The soldiers had converged upon the scene, panic prompting them to open fire, their shots going wild, sending Reeno sprawling over Abbie's prone form protectively. Sonny and Lucien wrestled in the dust, their snarls of rage muffled only by the sound of Sonya's anguished sobs and Reeno's crisp orders to his men.

"Cease firing, you fools!" he yelled, his body still shielding Abbie's.

Moving fast, Sonny kicked out forcefully with one booted foot and caught Rodriquez beneath his chin. The big man was thrown backward, landing inside the mine entrance. He rolled to his feet, quickly observed the armed soldiers racing toward him, and turned to flee into the depths of the mine.

"You'll never take me alive—never!" he roared, his words echoing off the granite walls.

"Lucien, don't leave me, don't leave me!" Sonya cried pitifully, her eyes disbelieving, her mind in shock.

"Follow that man!" Reeno shouted, and the soldiers hurried to obey his command.

Sonny rushed to Reeno's side where he now cradled Abbie

against him. "Is she hurt badly?" her queried urgently, his eyes revealing his fear.

"I hope not—she is so still," Reeno breathed shakily.

"Oh, but he shall pay for this," Sonny swore intensely. He touched his lips softly to hers. "Abbie, sweet, open your eyes—please."

Her eyelids fluttered briefly, her hand reaching out for his. Her face revealed her relief at seeing him. "I thought—he—would kill you for certain," she whispered shakily.

"I'm fine," he soothed, brushing the dirt from her face.

Reeno shifted her in his arms. "Stay here with her. I'll go in after Rodriquez."

Sonny's eyes met Reeno's. "No—this is something that I have to do."

"You know the chance you're taking?" Reeno searched that silvery gaze for some sign of uncertainty or fear, but the only thing he saw was the cold, hard glitter of death that bespoke the turmoil raging inside of his friend. He grasped Sonny's hand. "Be careful, *compadre*. He will not let you bring him out alive."

He nodded curtly. His face might have been carved out of granite. "Take care of Abbie, promise me that, Reeno."

"Si, you know that, hermano."

Abbie made a strangled sound in her throat even as she struggled to break free of Reeno's strong arms "Please, Sonny, let Rodriquez go. This isn't worth it! Sonny!" she screamed frantically when he unclenched her fingers from his. She watched through eyes blurred with tears as he rose to his feet.

"Mi vida, mi amor, I'll come back to you," he murmured huskily before turning away.

In the confusion that had followed, no one had noticed that Sonya had picked up her rifle and quietly disappeared.

The soldiers were ordered to quickly evacuate the prisoners from the main tunnel. Sonny paid careful attention to each bedraggled human being that emerged from the mine, but Culley Malone was definitely not one of them.

"Are you certain you have every man?" he questioned the sergeant.

"*Si,* all of the cells are empty, *Capitan.* Only the man you are seeking remains. And how we will find him in that maze of twisted tunnels I do not know."

"I'm the only one going in, Sergeant," Sonny informed him. "I want everyone else to stay out of here and back from the entrance. You know of the dynamite strung out through these tunnels?"

"*Si,* it was put there in case of an enemy takeover."

"If Rodriquez knows about it—well just stay clear."

The sergeant readily understood. "I wish you God's speed," he said, his feet already carrying him swiftly toward the entrance.

Comanche raiders are the quietest hunters there are. He'll come, silently, with eyes that can slice right through the darkness and seek out his prey. The thought kept Lucien hurrying blindly through the winding passageways, his only light, a torch he had grabbed from the wall. It flickered threateningly if he ran too fast, so he was forced to walk at a clipped pace, afraid to even look over his shoulder, afraid at what he might see.

The secret cavern where they keep the silver ore; I must reach it, I have to reach it, he thought frantically. He remembered it was off the main tunnel, deep in the bowels of the mine. He recalled how years ago, when he'd first discovered the secret strong room by mistake, he'd just taken a new prisoner to his cell and somehow had made a wrong turn that led him to the deepest, darkest area of the mine. He'd stumbled into the cavern by accident and upon more silver than any man could imagine. Immediately, he was surrounded by heavily armed guards. After he'd identified himself, one of the guards had personally escorted him from the stronghold. But not before his observant gaze had noticed the narrow shaft by which they were hoisting the silver ore up and to the outside. There was an iron trapdoor with a bolt on the inside securing the shaft when it wasn't in use. Lucien knew this. He'd come back later to the spot on top of the high mountain in hopes of gaining entry. The door was bolted tight from the inside.

"There is nothing and no one to stop me now," he babbled excitedly.

His fingers clawed their way along the damp tunnel. He turned a sharp corner and found himself abruptly standing in a large open chamber, the sparkle of silver in the soft torch light, like diamond-encrusted stars glittering beckoningly just for him.

Lucien could not contain his ecstatic cry of joy. In haste, he began weighting down his pockets with the precious silver. He was so intent on gathering as much as he could that he paid scant attention to the shadow creeping up behind him until he heard his name called. He spun around astounded.

"You! Go away!"

Sonya stood there with disbelief in her eyes. Even when faced with the truth she refused to believe it until she had heard him actually say it. "You never did mean to take me with you did you? You were—only using me."

Lucien froze when he saw the rifle pointed straight at him. "*Mi amante*—it is not the way that it looks. Come—help me." He held out one hand, the silver sifting through his fingers. "Come here, *mujer*—your *patron* commands it."

Sonya calmly pulled back the hammer on the rifle and aimed it at the sticks of dynamite lying nearby.

Sonny heard the click of the rifle. He had been following Lucien through the torch-lit tunnels, only his keen sense of hearing and the faint light from the torches lighting his way. Tension quivered through his body as he stealthily moved forward. He knew when another person emerged from an adjoining shaft and fell in step behind Lucien. He hadn't known who it was until he saw Sonya's form silhouetted against the shadowy walls. She didn't see him until it was too late.

"Drop it, sweetheart, nice and easy like." He trained his pistol on her.

Sonya didn't move but just stared straight ahead at the man she'd given up everything for. "No—I think not. I am finished taking orders from all of you."

Lucien stood unmoving, arms outstretched, eyes imploring as he begged Sonya not to pull the trigger. "It was all for you—please believe that."

"Sonya," Sonny called gently, "don't. He's not worth it." He began walking slowly toward her. "Give it to me. I want to help you."

She watched him with sad eyes, eyes that were so much like Abbie's that it prompted him to keep moving toward her in an effort to save her.

"He lied to me. It was all a lie."

"Don't give him your life, too," Sonny pleaded.

"You are the only one!" Lucien screamed. "You've always been—always will be!"

"Now—you shall be forever mine," she murmured, her finger curling around the trigger.

Sonny saw the expression in her eyes change, glimpsed briefly the raw, aching pain in her soul, and knew just before she pulled the trigger that she intended to blow them all to hell.

The force from the blast was centered in the strong room and blew the top of the deep cavern completely away. The tunnels leading off of the cavern began crumbling in all around Sonny as he lay dazed behind a huge boulder where the explosion had flung him. That fact had saved his life, but he knew if he didn't move fast he would certainly be buried beneath the rocks and beams that were falling everywhere. He thought of Abbie and how much he loved her. He wanted to live to see the child their love had created. It gave him strength. He pulled himself to his feet and forced himself to move, to run, to escape death.

"Sonny!" Abbie cried out, managing to break free of Reeno's arms. She ran toward the mine before anyone could move to stop her. She felt overwhelming agony rip through her as the mine shafts crumbled in before her eyes.

Suddenly—he was there. His arms were around her, strong and secure, and Abbie felt like her life had just been handed back to her.

"It's over, baby, at last it's over." He kissed her tear-stained cheeks, her softly parted lips, and smoothed the damp, tangled strands of hair away from her face. "It was you who gave me the will to make it out of there. You're my strength, my only love." His arms were strong around her. She knew she never wanted to be anywhere else. She clung to him, pulling his head down to kiss him with all of the love inside her.

Oblivious to anything else but the joy of being in each other's arms, they did not realize the sorrow they had yet to face until the soldiers began hurrying around them. Reeno placed his hand on Sonny's shoulder.

"I'm sorry. I'm afraid whoever was in the mine—didn't make it." He viewed them compassionately then, hearing the sergeant calling for him, he rejoined his men.

Abbie's eyes were shadowed with pain. "Sonya," she gasped.

"She didn't want to come back, Abbie," Sonny hurriedly explained. "She realized, at last, that Lucien had only been using her. She deliberately set off the dynamite with a rifle shot."

"Poor Sonya," Abbie wept. "She could have had so much, and she chose him instead." She stared at the ruins of the silver mine. "Your father, Sonny, what of him?"

"I wish I knew, Abbie. Even after all of these years there still seems to be no answer."

Reeno came rushing up to them, his face wreathed in smiles. "He's alive!" he shouted. "Your *padre* is alive. I just received word from one of the guards that there was a man sent to the sweatbox yesterday for attempting an escape. It seems this particular man is in that box so much because of his refusal to conform that nobody thought to inform the captain when he was put there."

"Where is he?" Sonny questioned anxiously.

"I sent some men to get him," Reeno replied. "The guards said they've never met a more stubborn man in their lives."

"That's Culley." Sonny grinned. "There isn't a man alive who can break his spirit."

"Sounds very much like his son," Abbie said, her eyes shining brightly as she gazed upon her husband. When she caught sight of the tall, broad-shouldered man being supported between two guards, she had no doubt who it was. "Culley Malone," she breathed.

"Yes," Sonny replied softly. "It damn sure is." He strode quickly toward him.

The man angrily pushed the guards away. He swayed uncertainly, but at last, stood proudly on his own. He was ragged looking and weak. His hair was long, and a matted beard covered his face, but there was no mistaking the shining look in his silver-gray eyes when they caught sight of his son. "James Sonny—can that really be you?"

Sonny was beside his father immediately. Snarling at the guards who hovered nearby to get the hell away, he gave Culley his own shoulder for support. "I never gave up on you. I always knew I'd find you someday." Carefully, he guided his father's steps toward the captain's quarters where he intended for him to rest. With each movement, he willed strength from his body to his father's. "Don't try and talk now. We've got plenty of time for that later."

Abbie joined them, and together the threesome entered the building. Reeno watched them, knowing that, at last, his friend's long search was over. He had found what he'd been seeking and more. He was a very lucky man.

Sonny did indeed feel that he was the luckiest of men. After they'd all had a chance to bathe and change into clean clothes, Abbie joined her husband and father-in-law for a quiet dinner in Culley's room. They spent the remainder of the day in quiet seclusion where they eagerly shared their plans for the future and talked, at last, about the past.

It was painful to hear about the years Culley spent digging in the mines, living worse than an animal, determined to survive, to see his family once again. "I never gave up," Culley said fiercely, staring into Sonny's eyes. "I knew I'd make it, and that somehow, I'd find my way back to you and your mother."

"The man who put you here is dead," Sonny announced flatly.

Culley fell silent and searched his son's face. "Did—you kill him?"

Sonny shook his head. "Not that I didn't try. He was killed by the explosion in the strong room."

"As was my twin sister," Abbie added softly.

"I'm sorry about your sister," Culley told Abbie. "But not about him. He was no good, a cold-blooded killer."

"Thank you," Abbie said. "And no matter what he was, I know she wouldn't have wanted to go on without him. To Sonya, Lucien Rodriquez was everything."

Sonny pulled her close, kissed her tenderly, before releasing her again.

Culley saw the look exchanged between his son and beautiful wife. He knew he had many days ahead in which to reminisce. He thought they should be alone. He understood. He'd want that, too, when he was reunited with his beloved wife. The realization brought a feeling of tremendous peace within him. It was over—all over. He wasn't even aware of the fact that he had closed his eyes, or that Abbie and Sonny had slipped quietly from the room.

It was a very happy Carmelita who greeted them upon their arrival back at the Alvarez hacienda. When Abbie hadn't returned that night, she'd gone to the military garrison the next morning to plead with them to send someone to the mine for Sonny. A recruit had been dispatched immediately and had returned with a message from Reeno to the general. It was the general himself who had explained to her what had taken place, and that Abbie and Sonny were alive and well.

If Sonny was surprised to see the warm welcome that Carmelita bestowed upon Reeno when they all rode up to the casa, he didn't show it. He watched the two of them embrace and, catching Reeno's sheepish grin, he winked at him.

Later that day, after he'd made certain his father was settled in and resting comfortably, Sonny went downstairs to join his wife and friends who were waiting for him in the sala. Abbie made room for him on the sofa and eagerly settled into the curve of his arm. Reeno and Carmelita sat across from them on a settee. Reeno spoke first.

"Well, it all turned out for the best, I suppose. And there is nothing left of this war now but formalities and a few papers to be signed."

"And it's a good feeling," Sonny replied. "I'll be leaving here soon. For a long overdue reunion with my family in Mexico City. I can't wait to see the look on my mother's face."

"I am happy for you," Reeno said warmly. "It appears you have found what you were seeking, and more." His gaze moved admirably to Abbie. She was looking up at Sonny, her eyes shining with a love so powerful it brought a lump to his throat. They were made for each other, he thought. He could only hope that one day, he and Carmelita could know such devotion.

"She's my lady." Sonny murmured huskily, pressing a light kiss to her lips, "my beautiful silken lady."

"You must not go before our wedding," Carmelita said quickly. "We've been trying to tell you, Santiago, but you were so busy you weren't ready to listen."

Sonny glanced over at his two friends. "I was somewhat preoccupied of late, but no more." He caught Abbie's eye. "Do you want to go to a wedding, Ab?"

"I wouldn't dream of missing it," she replied smiling. "And we're having the reception right here just like we planned, Carmelita."

"It sounds like everyone knew about this wedding but me," Sonny commented wryly. "I have a feeling this is what you were trying to tell me the day that I left, isn't it?"

Carmelita nodded. "Will you consent to giving away the bride, Santiago?"

"I would like that, Carma, very much."

The men grinned as both women promptly launched into a discussion about clothes, food, and what a little doll Doretea would look like in a dress patterned after her mother's. And on and on, until finally, Sonny took Abbie by the arm and began slowly maneuvering her from the room, sweeping her up into his arms with a soft growl. "The hell with weddings for now, ladies. Right now, the only thing I feel like discussing with this lady are honeymoon nights."

Abbie caught her breath even as she smiled. Silvery eyes held hers, and she nestled into his arms, her heart nearly overflowing with her love for him.

"And that's what they'll always be, won't they Sonny?" she whispered, her turquoise eyes lifting to his. "Every night we shall repeat our vow of love and find it only grows sweeter as the years pass." She kissed him with all the love inside of her.

Sonny climbed the stairs with his lady in his arms, knowing that she was right. Each time that he held her, kissed her, made love to her, was like the very first time. Yet, always better, and always with him loving her more than he ever thought possible. "Yes, my silken lady, always," he murmured. Entering their room, he laid her upon the bed and stretched out beside her. He began kissing her, gently at first, then harder, hungrier. "Enough talk," he whispered hoarsely, "love me, Abbie, love me just like that very first time."

Epilogue

Abbie sat at her dressing table in the master suite of the Bar C hacienda, listening to the laughter drifting through the opened French doors off the courtyard. Everyone sounded as though they were having a wonderful time. She was almost ready to go join her husband and friends who had gathered together on this day marking their first wedding anniversary to hear Sonny and her repeat their marriage vows. Both sides of the families had been invited, and all were present.

Abbie knew that Sonny was glad to see his family again after so many months of being away.

His parents had chosen to remain in Mexico City and help his grandfather manage their vast holdings, ironically one of which was a very prosperous silver mine.

Culley had announced that if anyone knew anything about mining for silver, he was the one. He had vowed to help restore the once grand hacienda of the Alvarez family to its former splendor and to ensure that the mines were run efficiently and humanely. It was the least he could do, he'd said, for the father of the woman he'd loved and dreamed of for so many years. Sonny's mother would have gone anywhere with him, she was just so happy to have him back in her arms once again. But inwardly, she was pleased that they would be residing in Mexico, although she'd never thought her husband would want to settle down anywhere but in his beloved Texas. The old don himself put aside old resentments and had at last welcomed Culley into his family.

Abbie had been astounded upon hearing from Sonny's grandfather the actual size of the lands and investments all bearing the Alvarez name. She had suspected, long ago, that Sonny had come from a wealthy background. It seemed that assumption had been correct. Santiago Malone y Alvarez was rich in his own right, with many vast holdings. The Alvarez name was as well known in Mexico as the Caldwell name in Texas. Her husband, the fierce brigand who had stolen her heart, was fast on his way to becoming a millionaire.

"Yes," she murmured, feeling at peace, "even though we'll bear the scars forever of Sonya's tragic death, everything has its purpose—everyone their destiny. And I have found mine."

Abbie's mother had taken the news of her daughter's death very hard. They hadn't told her what had actually taken place; just that Sonya had been killed in a mine explosion trying to rescue a man whom she'd loved more than life itself. In a sense, it was the truth. The written confession that she had given Abbie was accepted by the government, and Sonny's name was cleared of all murder charges. There had been no way of sparing Martha from that, but she didn't have to know all of the sordid details. Martha had always known Sonya was a confused and unhappy child. It grieved her to know that her daughter had never found happiness. Martha had accepted it all with quiet dignity. There was nothing else that she could do. Time would have to take care of the pain and help her to forget her tragic loss.

Of course, there was the new man in Martha's life to help her through this loss. Abbie was certain it wouldn't be too much longer before he convinced Martha to marry him. And until then, she had her loving family. They would be staying in Texas for six months before returning to their hacienda in

Orizaba. Sonny and Abbie, being equal partners in every way, had agreed to divide their time between her ranch and his.

She had been so lost in her daydreams that she did not hear him come up behind her, until his husky voice called her name and sent shivers along her spine. She turned around.

"Silken lady, it's time. Everyone's waiting." He held out his hand and she accepted it. His eyes appraised her, the pale blue dress that clung softly to her perfect form, the lace mantilla adorning her hair. "You're even more beautiful than the first time I married you." A lazy smile touched his eyes as he reached inside the pocket of his tailored black coat and withdrew a velvet box. "Here, I want you to wear these today."

She opened the lid to gaze in wide-eyed wonder at the necklace and earrings of brilliant aquamarine stones and diamonds glittering on the bed of velvet. "Why—they're absolutely beautiful," she breathed.

"They're no match for your stunning beauty, Ab, but then, nothing is." He took the box from her fingers and removed the necklace. "Here, let me put this on for you."

She held up her long hair from her neck. He put his head toward hers, seemingly intent on fussing with the delicate clasp, his fingers brushing across the nape of her neck. He smiled when he felt a quiver of desire race through her. Even after a year, and parenthood, they still desired each other just as much as they always did. "There, done." He pressed his lips just behind her ear. She gasped. He laughed deeply, watching her attach the dainty aquamarine studs to her ears. He spun her around to face him, the message in his eyes quickening her breath. "Shall we go milady? I am anxious for this wedding to be done and over with, for tonight, you will belong only to me."

The ceremony could not have been any more meaningful than the one that they'd had that long-ago day in the camp of the Kwahadi. But it was lovely, and they vowed, before their friends and family, to love and cherish each other for the rest of their days. Sonny placed a beautiful antique gold ring on Abbie's finger, and she surprised him by placing his family ring that he'd given her onto his. Padre Felipe pronounced them man and wife beneath the arbor of soft pink roses and the glorious Texas sun. Sonny kissed his bride, both of them knowing that their love was far better and stronger than it had ever been before.

Amidst all of the well wishes and festive laughter, Abbie heard the childish gurgling of her children, and looked up to see Francisca coming toward them, a toddler held in both arms.

"I bring the twins, senora. I know you would want to see your babies before I put them down for the night."

Abbie looked upon her two precious children, her heart overflowing with love for them. They were beautiful, healthy babies. A boy, Rafael, with dark hair and gray eyes, who was beginning to show every sign of having his father's daredevil personality, and a tiny daughter, Danielle, with chestnut ringlets and soft blue eyes, further enhanced by an enticing smile that already had her father wrapped around her little finger.

Sonny held out his arms to his daughter, and she eagerly went to him. He hugged her close. Feeling a slight tug on his coattails, he turned to see Charly looking up at him. He reached down to ruffle the boy's hair.

"What do you think, son, is this a party, or not?"

Charly's face was shining with excitement. "It's great, Dad. But I wanted to tell you that your Indian brother, Night Walker, he's waiting for you on the other side of the corrals. He says he has that certain something you've been looking for."

Sonny motioned to Reeno, who was in attendance with his new bride, Carmelita, to come over to him.

"What is it, *hermano?*" Reeno asked, stealing Danielle from her father's arms. "Help Abbie attend to the guests until I return, will you?"

"Don't be gone too long, darling," Abbie said. "And tell Night Walker he is welcome to join us."

"I will, but I'm certain he will not." He kissed her cheek, whispering in her ear. "I shouldn't be too long. Go on and have a good time."

"I'll see you later," she murmured, their eyes meeting in perfect understanding.

Something woke her, a strange sound, a sixth sense. Fresh brewed coffee wafted to her nostrils. She lay there upon the bedroll, unmoving, eyes still closed, her only clothing the long-tailed shirt which fell in soft folds around her slender thighs.

She slowly opened her eyes, and although it was dark and she was alone, she was not afraid. She stretched sensuously, reveling in the freedom of the wide-open plains, the canopy of stars overhead, and the sound of the night creatures stirring around her. This was her land. She had missed these quiet times. There weren't too many anymore.

Abbie stirred, knowing he was there watching even before she heard his husky voice address her from the shadows across the campfire.

"I see sleeping beauty has awakened."

It was a voice that sent gooseflesh scurrying along her spine. She rose, unafraid to face him.

"I think you'd better come up with a real good reason for being here," she said throatily. "This is Caldwell land—and this—is a private party." She knew she stood perfectly silhouetted against the dancing flames.

"You want some coffee, ma'am? I've got some brewing here for you."

"You bring me some—over here."

She heard his throaty chuckle. "Remember what happened the last time you said something like that, beautiful?"

She remembered. She smiled. "I'm counting to three, and then you know what comes next?"

"I think I'll remember until my dying day," she heard him say just before she had a brief glimpse of a darkly tan, wonderfully familiar face coming at her from out of the darkness.

She was crushed in Sonny's arms, his lips slanting demandingly over hers as together they tumbled back onto the bedroll. He kissed her as if this was the very first time, filled with all of the pent-up emotions that she alone seemed to evoke. His passion was relentless, hers just as fiery and wild. She was once again that half savage, half temptress, who had bound him to her that very first night when he'd ridden boldly across Caldwell land and had taken her as his prize.

They were, as always, perfectly matched. Slowly, he pressed her arms back over her head and raised his lips from hers. "Your shining knight is back, milady. Your wish is his command."

Her eyes were wide on his, so blue and intense that he thought he might lose himself forever in their shimmering depths. "I want you to make love to me, slowly and completely, every night, for the rest of our lives."

"Nothing will give me greater pleasure, love." He lowered his lips to the vee of her shirt and kissed the valley between her breasts. He threaded his fingers back through her hair and held her still beneath him while his lips and tongue sought out that sensitive area between her breasts that set her senses on fire.

Beneath a full Comanche moon he loved her, the dancing silver moonbeams and the orange-red glow from the fire reflecting off their naked bodies in an aura of rapturous splendor.

Her hands sought the feel of his magnificent body, touching, arousing, savoring each corded muscle and hollow plane that she discovered. She pressed her half open mouth against his neck as his lips nibbled the tip of her earlobe. The desire within her became a raging inferno and she bit him impatiently, urging him to give her all that she sought, not make her wait any longer.

He laughed huskily, taking her mouth savagely with his. He caressed her tongue with slow, languorous strokes that nearly drove her out of her mind. His hand kneaded her breasts, fingers brushing intimately across her swollen nipples. Aching with his need of her, he held back, savoring each moment, wanting her to remember this night forever. One hand slid down her stomach, kneaded the softness of her belly, to gently cup the mound of her womanhood and caress it tenderly.

Abbie writhed and arched beneath him, completely lost to the magic of his touch and the fire raging through her veins. Her own fingers sought out the hot, hard length of him, feeling his manhood throb beneath her touch. With a low moan he slipped one finger inside her sweet, swollen sheath and reveled in the sleek, moist softness that met his touch.

Raising up, he peered down at her, his face glistening with sweat and passion. "I love you, silken lady," he whispered, entering her swiftly, taking her very breath away by the intensity of his first thrust.

"And I you, my fierce brigand," she murmured, wrapping her legs tightly around him, "and I always will."

Abbie heard the soft whinny and woke immediately. Sonny was lying beside her, watching her with that lazy-lidded stare that brought a smile to her lips.

"We don't have visitors, do we?" she queried, snuggling down deeper into the folds of the bedroll.

"They've come and gone. Night Walker sends his respects."

"Why didn't you wake me, darling? I would have liked to have seen him."

"He did not wish to intrude on our privacy. He just delivered something for me."

"Did you tell him we will bring the children to visit him and the People soon?" Abbie asked.

"Yes, he was glad to hear that," Sonny replied. "It may not

459

last too much longer, you know."

"What is that?"

"Their freedom," he answered. "The government is determined to get every one of them onto reservations. Night Walker told me the rangers and the soldiers have been hounding the Kwahadi relentlessly. They want them to go peacefully to Fort Sill before more bloodshed is spilled."

Abbie placed her hand on his arm. "I know how badly you feel, darling, and I share your feelings. But there is nothing we can do. There is nothing anyone can do. It has been coming for a long time. Night Walker and his people know this and eventually will have to accept it if they are to survive."

"Yes, I know." They were silent for a moment, both of them thinking, and then his mood suddenly changed and he pulled her swiftly to her feet. "Come with me. There is something I have for you, something only a Comanche warrior's *paraibo* would understand." She followed him down to the river where tethered there with Romeo and Viento was a sleek black mare just like the one that she had been chasing on the night that they'd met.

"Is that why Night Walker was here? He brought the mare, didn't he?"

"Yes," Sonny replied, his eyes meeting hers. "It's normally a custom with our People for the husband to gift the bride's father with many fine horses. Since that isn't possible, I told Night Walker to search for the very best one he could find, and I think he came up with the right choice."

"She's mine?" Abbie gasped.

"Yes, a wedding gift from a very happy and grateful husband."

She went eagerly into his arms, her face pressed into his neck. "It will always be this way with us, won't it, Sonny?"

He touched his cheek to hers, his heart full of love. "Yes, silken lady, always."

And Abbie knew that somehow, it would be.

CAPTIVATING ROMANCE
by Penelope Neri

CRIMSON ANGEL (1783, $3.95)

No man had any right to fluster lovely Heather simply because he was so impossibly handsome! But before she could slap the arrogant captain for his impudence, she was a captive of his powerful embrace, his one and only *Crimson Angel*.

PASSION'S BETRAYAL (1568, $3.95)

Sensuous Promise O'Rourke had two choices: to spend her life behind bars—or endure one night in the prison of her captor's embrace. She soon found herself fettered by the chains of love, forever a victim of *Passion's Betrayal*.

HEARTS ENCHANTED (1432, $3.75)

Lord Brian Fitzwarren vowed that somehow he would claim the irresistible beauty as his own. Maegan instinctively knew that from that moment their paths would forever be entwined, their lives entangled, their *Hearts Enchanted*.

BELOVED SCOUNDREL (1799, $3.95)

Instead of a street urchin, the enraged captain found curvaceous Christianne in his arms. The golden-haired beauty fought off her captor with all her strength—until her blows become caresses, her struggles an embrace, and her muttered oaths moans of pleasure.

JASMINE PARADISE (1170, $3.75)

In the tropical Hawaiian isles, Sarah first sees handsome Dr. Heath Ryan—and suddenly, she no longer wants to be a lady. When Heath's gaze rakes Sarah's lush, soft body, he no longer wants to play the gentleman. Together they delight in their fragrant *Jasmine Paradise*.

Available wherever paperbacks are sold, or order direct from the Publisher. Send cover price plus 50¢ per copy for mailing and handling to Zebra Books, Dept. 1842, 475 Park Avenue South, New York, N.Y. 10016. DO NOT SEND CASH.

If you enjoyed this book we have a special offer for you. Become a charter member of the ZEBRA HISTORICAL ROMANCE HOME SUBSCRIPTION SERVICE and...

Get a
FREE
Zebra Historical Romance
(A $3.95 value) No Obligation

Now that you have read a Zebra Historical Romance we're sure you'll want more of the passion and sensuality, the desire and dreams and fascinating historical settings that make these novels the favorites of so many women. So we have made arrangements for you to receive a *FREE* book ($3.95 value) and preview 4 brand new Zebra Historical Romances each month.

Join the Zebra
Home Subscription Service—
Free Home Delivery

By joining our Home Subscription Service you'll never have to worry about missing a title. You'll automatically get the romance, the allure, the attraction, that make Zebra Historical Romances so special.

Each month you'll receive 4 brand new Zebra Historical Romance novels as soon as they are published. Look them over *Free* for 10 days. If you're not delighted simply return them and owe nothing. But if you enjoy them as much as we think you will, you'll pay *only* $3.50 each and save 45¢ over the cover price. (You save a total of $1.80 each month.) *There is no shipping and handling charge or other hidden charges.*

—————Fill Out the Coupon—————

Start your subscription now and start saving. Fill out the coupon and mail it *today*. You'll get your FREE book along with your first month's books to preview.